By C. W. Gortner

The Vatican Princess
Mademoiselle Chanel
The Queen's Vow
The Confessions of Catherine de Medici
The Last Queen
The Tudor Vendetta
The Tudor Conspiracy
The Tudor Secret

The Vatican Princess

The Vatican Princess

A NOVEL OF LUCREZIA BORGIA

C. W. Gortner

BALLANTINE BOOKS
NEW YORK

Copyright © 2016 by C. W. Gortner

Published in the United States by Ballantine Books, an imprint of Random House, a division of Penguin Random House LLC, New York.

BALLANTINE and the HOUSE colophon are registered trademarks of Penguin Random House LLC.

LIBRARY OF CONGRESS CATALOGING-IN-PUBLICATION DATA
Names: Gortner, C. W., author.
Title: The Vatican princess: a novel of Lucrezia Borgia/C. W. Gortner.
Description: First edition. | New York: Ballantine Books, [2016]
Identifiers: LCCN 2015037198 | ISBN 9780345533975 (hardcover: acid-free paper) |
ISBN 9780345533982 (ebook)
Subjects: LCSH: Borgia, Lucrezia, 1480–1519—Fiction. | Nobility—Papal States—Fiction. |
Borgia family—Fiction. | Rome (Italy)—History—1420–1798—Fiction. | Italy—History—
1492–1559—Fiction. | BISAC: FICTION/Historical. | FICTION/Biographical. |
FICTION/Literary. | GSAFD: Biographical fiction. | Historical fiction.
Classification: LCC PS3607.O78 V38 2016 | DDC 813/.6—dc23 LC record available at
https://lccn.loc.gov/2015037198

Printed in the United States of America on acid-free paper

www.ballantinebooks.com

2 4 6 8 9 7 5 3 1

First Edition

Map by C. W. Gortner

Book design by Victoria Wong

In memory of Paris

Desidero vobis omnem diem

Se gli uomini sapessino le ragioni della paura mia,
capir potrebbero il mio dolor.

(If people knew the reasons for my fears,
they would be able to understand my pain.)

—LUCREZIA BORGIA

SAVOY

Milan

DUCHY OF
MILAN

MARQUISATE
OF
MANTUA

REPUBLIC OF
VENICE

Venice

DUCHY OF
FERRARA

REPUBLIC
OF
GENOA

DUCHY OF
MODENA

ROMAGNA

Imola

Ravenna

Forli

REPUBLIC
OF
LUCCA

Florence

REPUBLIC OF
FLORENCE

Pesaro

Urbino

Adriatic Sea

DALMATIA

CORSICA
(Genoa)

REPUBLIC OF
SIENA

Perugia

Orvieto

Spoleto

PAPAL
STATES

Nepi

Tiber

Subiaco

Rome

Tyrrhenian
Sea

KINGDOM OF
NAPLES

Naples

SARDINIA
(Naples)

The City States
of Italy

Map not to scale
Design: C.W. Gortner

Infamy is merely an accident of fate.

That is what my father used to say. He would pronounce this laughingly, in that careless way of his, waving his fleshy hand adorned with the papal ring of the Fisherman, as if with the mere flick of his fingers he could dispel the noxious cloud of accusations that hovered over us, the spiny whispers about vice, bloody corruption, and unholy abuse.

I used to believe him. I used to believe he knew everything.

Now I know better.

How else to explain the chaos strewn in our wake, the ravaged lives, the sacrificed innocence and spilled blood? How else to justify the unexpected trajectory of my own life, forever wandering the labyrinth of my family's ruthless design?

There can be no other reason. Infamy is no accident. It is a poison in our blood.

It is the price of being a Borgia.

PART I

1492–1493

The Keys of
the Kingdom

*God desires not the death of the sinner
but that he should pay and live.*

—RODRIGO BORGIA

CHAPTER ONE

"Lucrezia, *basta*. Stop indulging that filthy beast!"

My mother's hand swept out, each fat finger squeezed by a ring. I avoided her slap, instinctually bending over my beloved cat, Arancino, who hissed and flattened his ears, his slitted eyes displaying the contempt I felt. I knew why Vannozza was here. Since Pope Innocent's recent death and the gathering of the conclave to elect a new Holy Father, I'd been expecting my mother to arrive in the Orsini Palazzo on Monte Giordano where I lived, swathed in her veil and black skirts despite the summer heat, ensconcing herself in our *camera* like a harbinger of doom.

Now that she was here, all I wanted was to see her gone.

"Out!" She stamped her foot, spurring Arancino to action. Leaping from my embrace, he dashed through the open doors into the dim corridor.

I didn't feel the scratch on my hand until a bright bead of blood welled. Sucking at the nick, I scowled at my mother as she gestured peremptorily. "Honestly, Adriana," she said, "how can you let her keep such a creature in the house? It's unhealthy. Cats are the devil's spawn; everyone knows they can steal a baby's breath."

"Fortunately, we have no babies here," replied Adriana from her chair, her voice as smooth as the light-gray silk of her dress. "And the cat comes in handy on occasion"—she shuddered—"especially in the summer, with all the rats."

"Bah. Who needs a cat to get rid of vermin? A bit of poison in the corners is all you require. I do it myself every June. No rats in my house."

Even as I trembled at the thought of poison left all over the house for my cat to wander upon, Adriana drawled, "Perhaps not that you can see, my dear Vannozza, but in Rome, as we both know, rats can come in all shapes and sizes." Though Adriana didn't return my grateful gaze, I was assured that she would never countenance the careless strewing of white death. My Arancino, whom I had rescued as a kitten from drowning by the stable hands, was safe.

My mother's attention returned to me, keen as a blade. When I left her care, I was only seven years old. She had just married for the second time, and my father summoned me from her palazzo near San Pietro in Vincoli to reside here with Adriana de Mila, the widowed daughter of his eldest brother. Adriana had overseen my upbringing, which included lessons at the Convent of San Sisto. She was more of a mother to me than this plump, sweating woman had ever been. As Vannozza now scrutinized me like a customer debating a purchase, not for the first time I wondered how she'd managed to retain Papa's affection for so many years.

I could see little of her once-fabled beauty. Now in her fiftieth year, my mother's figure had been coarsened by repeated childbirth and pleasures of the table, so that she resembled a common matron; her gray-blue eyes—which I'd inherited, though mine were of a paler hue— surrounded by pockets of seamed shadow, her red-veined cheeks and hawkish nose accentuating a permanent frown. Though she wore costly black velvet, the cut of her gown was no longer in style, especially when coupled with her antiquated heavy veiled coif, under which the stippled gray of her once-golden tresses could be glimpsed.

"Is she eating?" Vannozza asked, as if she sensed my own critical assessment of her. "She's still thin as a street cur. And so white: You'd think she'd never seen the sun. I suppose she hasn't shed her first blood yet, either?"

"Lucrezia's natural pallor is quite in fashion these days," replied Adriana. "And she's not yet thirteen. Some girls need extra time to grow into their form."

Vannozza grunted. "She has no time. She's already betrothed, remember? We can only hope she's at least proving herself worthy of that fancy education Rodrigo insisted on providing her, not that I understand how any girl needs books and the like."

"I love my books—" I started to protest but was cut off by Adriana's ringing of a small silver bell at her side. Moments later, little Murilla, my favored dwarf, given to me by Papa on my eleventh birthday, hastened in with a pitcher and platter of cheese. She was a perfect miniature with ebony skin; I'd been enchanted by her exoticism, knowing she'd been brought from a faraway land where natives ran naked, and I watched in disbelief as my mother shooed her away like a gnat. Adriana gestured to Murilla to set the things on the table. Ever since Vannozza had arrived without word or warning, Adriana had ignored my mother's overt appraisal of the servants, her pointed stares at the tapestries, at the vases of fresh-cut flowers and the statuary poised in the corners—all evidence of Papa's attention, which she had once enjoyed.

"The nuns assure me Lucrezia excels in her studies," Adriana went on. "She dances with grace and shows a talent for the lute; her sewing skills are also greatly admired, and she's even mastered some Latin—"

"Latin?" Vannozza exclaimed, spraying crumbs. "On top of spoiling her eyes with all that reading, she can chant like a priest? She's going to Spain to wed, not to say Mass."

"A girl of Lucrezia's status must have all the advantages," Adriana said, "as she may be called upon to rule her own estate while her husband is away. Even you, my dear Vannozza, learned to read and write, yes?"

"I learned because I had my taverns to run. If I hadn't, my suppliers would have robbed me blind. But Lucrezia? I cast her horoscope when she was born; the stars dictate she will die a wife. No wife has any need for Latin—unless Rodrigo thinks she can entertain her husband with her knowledge until she's old enough to spread her legs."

Adriana's smile faltered. She lifted her gaze to me. "Lucrezia, dearest, do show Donna Vannozza that embroidery you've been working on. It's so lovely."

I moved reluctantly to the window seat, aghast at my mother's callous pronouncement of my death. The sight of Arancino's empty indent on the cushions sent another rush of anger through me as I retrieved the pillowcase I'd been sewing for Papa. It was the most complicated design I had attempted, employing real gold and silver thread to depict our Borgia emblem—the black bull against a mulberry-red shield. I planned to give it to him as a surprise after the conclave, and

I gasped when my mother wrenched it from me as if it were a soiled napkin.

She ran her fingers over it with deliberate force. One of her rings snagged a loose thread and buckled the bull, marring stitches I'd spent hours perfecting.

"Adequate," she said, "though it looks more like Juno than Minotaur."

I snatched it from her. "Suora Constanza says my embroidery is better than any other girl's in San Sisto. She says I could make rags for the poor and the Blessed Virgin herself would weep at their beauty."

Vannozza reclined in her chair. "Is that so? I should think the Virgin might better weep at your insufferable insolence to your own mother."

"Now, now," soothed Adriana. "Let us not quarrel. We're all on edge, what with this eternal waiting for the conclave and awful heat, but surely there's no need for harsh—"

"Why?" I whispered, interrupting Adriana. "Why do you hate me so?"

My unexpected words shifted something in Vannozza's expression. I caught it for a fleeting moment—a sudden softening of her features, so that a hint of distant pain surfaced under her skin. Then it vanished, swallowed by the pinched line of her mouth.

"If you were still under my charge, I'd bang your head against the wall until you learned proper respect for your elders."

I had no doubt she would. I could still recall the sting of her palm from those times when she flew into a rage, often over trivial mishaps like a grass-stained hem or ripped sleeve. I'd feared her wrath almost as much as her consultations with seers and astrologers, her nightly ritual of tarot readings, which frightened me because they carried the taint of witchcraft and were forbidden by our Holy Church.

Adriana sighed. "Lucrezia, what on earth has come over you? You will apologize this instant. Donna Vannozza is our guest."

Clutching the damaged pillowcase to my chest, I muttered, "Forgive me, Donna Vannozza," and turned to Adriana. "May I be excused?" My mother stiffened in her chair; she knew my request of Adriana was defiant, a declaration that Vannozza had no power over me. I was gratified by the thunderous expression that came over her when Adriana said, "Of course, my child. This heat has us all at wits' end."

I stepped to the door; behind me, Adriana murmured, "You must forgive her. The poor child is bewildered; I fetched her out of San Sisto only two days ago, disrupting her routine because of this unexpected business with the conclave. She misses her lessons and—"

"Nonsense," interrupted Vannozza. "I know all too well her own father is to blame. He has always spoiled her, although I told him it is not wise. Daughters grow up; they leave us and marry. They bear children of their own and put their new families first. But Rodrigo won't hear of it. Not his Lucrezia, he says, not his *farfallina*. She is *special*. No one else has mattered to him since she was born. I daresay, after our son Juan, she is the only thing he truly loves."

The venom in her voice coiled around me. I didn't look back as I left, but once I was in the corridor, I had to grip the staircase balustrade and breathe in a ragged sigh of relief.

I couldn't remember a time when my mother had not despised me. For my older brothers, Juan and Cesare, she'd always had smiles, solicitude, and encouragement; Cesare, in particular, she adored to such an extent that when Papa sent him away to Pisa to study for the priesthood, she wept as if her heart would break—the first and only tears I'd seen her shed. Even my youngest brother, Gioffre, who had done nothing thus far of particular import, had received more affection from her than I ever had. I was her sole daughter, whom she might have taken under her wing, but instead she had been cold and exacting, as if my very existence offended. I never understood it, even as throughout my childhood I longed to escape it. Coming to live with Adriana had been the answer to my prayers. She had showed me that I was important, adored, that I was indeed, as Papa claimed, special.

All of a sudden, I longed to see him. He visited as often as he could, as here in Adriana's house we no longer had to pretend. In my mother's house, we had called him our cherished uncle, because Vannozza was married and appearances must be kept. But there was no need for such subterfuge here. Papa would gather me up in his burly embrace after supper, caress my hair, and sit me on his lap to regale me with stories of our ancestors, for we were not Italian and must never forget it. Though his own uncle had been Pope Calixtus III and our kin had dwelled in Rome for generations, we still were of Catalan blood, born in the rugged vale of the Ebro River in the kingdom of Aragon. "Borja" was our

Spanish surname, and our ancestors had fought in crusades against the Moors, amassing titles, estates, and royal favors that had enabled us to enter the Church and climb as high as the See of St. Peter itself.

"But you must remember, my *farfallina*," Papa would say, using his nickname for me. "No matter how far we rise or how rich we become, we must always protect one another like lions in a pride, for here we are seen as foreigners, whom Italy will never accept as its own."

"But I was born here and I don't look like you," I replied, gazing into his magnetic dark eyes, my hand on his swarthy cheek. "Does that mean I am also a foreigner?"

"You are a Borgia, my little butterfly, even if you have your mother's Italian fairness." He chuckled. "Thank God for it. You wouldn't want to look like me, a Spanish ox!" He drew me close. "Inside your veins runs my *sangre:* the blood of Borja. That is all that matters. Blood is the only thing we can trust, the only thing worth dying for. Blood is family, and *la familia es sagrada*." He kissed me. "You are my most beloved daughter, the pearl in my oyster. Never forget it. One day, this miserable land that so despises us will fall to its knees singing your praise. You shall astonish them all, my beautiful Lucrezia."

While I didn't comprehend exactly how I'd manage to bring Italy to its knees (it was hard enough simply to please the nuns of San Sisto), I laughed and tweaked his large beaked nose, because I knew he had other daughters, sired on other women, but none, I was sure, had heard such devotion from him. I could see it in his gaze, in the luminous smile that came over his strong face, and feel it in the tightening of his embrace. The great Cardinal Borgia, envied for his wealth and tenacity, deemed the most trustworthy servant of the Church in Rome—he loved me more than anyone else. And so I preened on his lap because it pleased him, because it made his laughter rumble like gathering lava, tickling my sides until it exploded from him in a molten guffaw that seemed to shake the walls of the palazzo—ebullient and proud, rough as uncombed velvet, and imbued with an infectious joy for life. I heard his love in his laughter; I felt his love as he lavished me with kisses and teased, "Such a little coquette you are! So like your mother in her youth: She too could dip her eyes at me and make me melt at her feet."

I couldn't imagine Vannozza dipping her eyes at anyone. In fact, all it had ever taken was one glare from her, one sneer, to pulverize any joy I felt.

Except now, for the first time, I understood. Now I knew why she hated me.

No one else has mattered to him since she was born. . . .

I had something she no longer possessed. I had Papa's love.

A plaintive meow startled me into awareness. Bending down, I coaxed Arancino out from behind one of the antique broken statues on the landing. As I scooped him up, footsteps echoed in the *cortile* below. With my cat in my arms, I peered over the balustrade into the inner courtyard and saw Adriana's daughter-in-law, Giulia Farnese, entering in a hurry.

Unhooking her cloak, she flung it at her maidservant. As she ran her hands hastily over her coiffure—disheveled from her cowl—Giulia mounted the staircase to the *piano nobile,* our living quarters on the second floor. Her coral silk gown adhered to her figure, dampened by sweat; she looked flushed, so intent on trying to creep up the stairs that she did not notice me until she was almost stepping on my toes. With a gasp, she came to a halt. Her dark eyes flared.

"Lucrezia! *Dio mio,* you gave me a fright! What are you doing skulking about?"

"Hush!" I put a finger to my lips, glancing to the doors of the room where Adriana's murmur was punctuated by the occasional staccato reply from my mother.

"Vannozza?" Giulia mouthed. I nodded, stifling a giggle. She and my mother had met two years ago, when Vannozza attended Giulia's marriage to Adriana's son, Orsino. After the ceremony, over which my father presided, Vannozza sat at the banquet and glowered as Papa honored Giulia with a ruby pendant. As he fastened the clasp about her throat, Giulia let out a delighted peal of laughter that echoed through the hall. Seated near my mother, I watched her expression darken. When Giulia led Orsino out to dance, her effortless grace making him look even more like a disjointed marionette, I heard Vannozza hiss, "Is this what we've come to? You would forsake me for that girl without a hair on her spoon."

Papa had scowled. I took note of it because he rarely showed anger in public. Through his teeth, he replied, "Vannozza, no matter how high I raise you, you'll always remain in the gutter."

I had taken furtive delight in the shock that spread across Vannozza's face. She had departed soon after, her complacent husband in tow. Before she left, however, she cast a despairing look over her shoulder at Giulia, twirling to the music of tamborette and string as my father beamed on the dais, tapping out the tempo on his upholstered chair arm.

As I now regarded Giulia with perspiration on her brow, her eyes shining in illicit excitement, I recalled how Papa's hands had lingered on her throat as he'd fastened that ruby necklace and how her skin had in turn captured the reflection of his jeweled rings. . . .

Giulia had turned eighteen. She was not a child anymore.

"Where have you been?" I asked. "Adriana thought you were upstairs, napping."

Her response was to grasp my hand and tug me up the narrow staircase to the third floor, where our bedchambers were located. Arancino let himself be jostled against me as we entered my room, stepping over rushes of fresh-strewn herbs. The walls were painted in shades of blue and yellow, my favorite colors. In a niche by my narrow bed, a votive flickered before a Byzantine icon of the Virgin and Child, a gift from my father. In the corner was a pile of leather and calfskin volumes that Cesare had sent me from his university in Pisa: sonnets by Petrarch and Dante, which I devoured by candlelight, long into the night.

"Christ save us, it's an inferno out there." Giulia gestured to the majolica pitcher and basin on the side table. "Be a darling and bring me a wet cloth. I vow I'm about to faint."

I let Arancino down so I could fetch the damp washcloth from the basin. "You went to the piazza, didn't you?" I said, handing her the cloth.

She sighed, her eyes at half-mast as she stroked her throat and bosom with the linen. I waited impatiently for her ablutions to end.

"Well? Did you?"

Her eyes opened. "What do you think?"

I drew in a sharp breath. "You went outside without permission, after Adriana specifically told us to stay indoors?"

"Of course," said Giulia, as if it was of no particular account, as if young noblewomen traipsed through the streets every day without escorts or chaperones, while the entire city smoldered and waited for the conclave to reach its decision.

"And did you . . . see anything?" I asked, my awe at her boldness struggling against a surge of resentment that she had not invited me on her forbidden excursion.

"Yes. Hordes of ruffians storming about, swearing vengeance if Cardinal della Rovere is not elected." She grimaced. "They left filth all over the piazza and robbed the faithful gathered there. The papal guard had to disperse them. It's a disgrace."

"Adriana did warn us. She said it's always dangerous before a new pope is elected."

Giulia paused. "And is Adriana here, pray tell? Or am I talking to my Lucrezia?" As she registered my dismay—for much as I loved Adriana, I did not want to *be* like her—she added, "Of course it was dangerous, but how else are we to hear any news? It's not as though Adriana can tell us." Her voice turned avid. "The conclave is at a standstill. None of the candidates has earned enough votes. By tomorrow, they'll be served only bread and water."

I forgot my annoyance and perched on the bed. I knew that the more time the cardinals took to elect a new pope, the more restricted their enclosure in the Sistine Chapel became. Lawlessness could erupt if the papal throne sat empty for too long, and reducing the cardinals' privileges was supposed to ensure a swift vote. But four days had passed without the announcement, leaving everyone in Rome on tenterhooks.

"They must be famished," Giulia went on, "not to mention roasting alive inside with all the windows and doorways bricked up. But no candidate can win—save your father, whom even as we speak already sways the undecided to his side." She paused, weighting her words. "If all goes as planned, Cardinal Borgia will be our new Holy Father."

I resisted a roll of my eyes. She could be *so* dramatic.

"Papa has lost before," I said. I did not add that he had in fact lost twice. I'd been too young to witness his setbacks myself, but the story of his defeats had been repeated often enough in my hearing. My father had never ceased declaring that one day he must earn the honor of being the first Borgia to follow in the hallowed footsteps of his late uncle, Calixtus III, so help him God. But there'd been other popes since then, including our recently departed Innocent, whom Papa served faithfully, though loyal service had thus far not secured his own accession.

"That was before," said Giulia. "Everything is different now. Really, Lucrezia, don't those nuns in San Sisto teach you anything of the world outside their walls?" She didn't await my reply, ignoring my scowl as she plucked off her hairnet, unleashing damp auburn tresses over her shoulders. "Let me explain it to you: In Florence, Lorenzo de Medici is dead, and Milan is now governed by the Sforza tyrant, Il Moro. Venice remains aloof, while the royal house of Naples is caught between France and Spain, both of which claim a superior right to its throne. Only the pope can prevent chaos. Now more than ever, Rome needs a leader who knows the ways of power and can restore our— Oh, never mind!" she exclaimed irritably, for I had grown bored of her righteous tone and shifted my attention to Arancino, who was stalking a mosquito in the corner. "I don't know why I bother. You're still such a child."

The twist in my stomach caught me off guard. Until this moment, I had never dared question Giulia, whom I regarded as a far more sophisticated, if occasionally irritating, elder sister. We had lived in amiable companionship these past five years, but she was married, proclaimed throughout Rome as la Bella Farnese—while I was still flat-chested, uninitiated into the mysteries of womanhood. But I'd learned something today; I knew that I had a gift even my mother begrudged, and I wasn't about to let Giulia treat me as if I was a silly girl any longer.

"If I'm such a child," I said, "then I can hardly be blamed if I let slip that you went out without permission today, risking your person for common gossip."

Giulia went still, fingers twined in her hair. She regarded me for a long moment before she smiled. "Is that blackmail I hear falling from your lips? How very Borgia of you."

I felt a rush of pleasure. "Well, if what you claim is true and Papa is to become the new pope, surely I deserve to know how it will affect me."

"Indeed." She wet her lips. "What do you wish to know?"

"Everything." To my surprise, I meant it, though I'd not paid any mind to intrigues. I rarely set foot in the Vatican, my lessons at San Sisto keeping me occupied. But momentous changes were happening outside my door, and Papa was at their heart. All of a sudden, my very future seemed to hang in the balance, beckoning with untold possibilities.

Giulia leaned close. "Well, the cardinals went into the chapel, certain that Cardinal della Rovere would win. After all, he's been campaigning for the papal tiara for months, bribing everyone he can to his side. It's even rumored that King Charles of France himself paid twenty thousand ducats to secure della Rovere's election. But once the windows were shuttered and the doors chained, things within the conclave did not go so easy for him. Della Rovere has enemies, more than he thought. Cardinal Sforza of Milan, for one, opposes him. Il Moro doesn't care to have a French toady on the throne, and—"

"How do you know all this?" I cut in. Arancino leapt onto the mattress, purring. I caressed his fur, keeping my gaze on Giulia. "Isn't the conclave forbidden any contact with the outside world so the process of election can remain sacred?"

I wanted to prove to her that I wasn't as ignorant as she thought, but she impatiently waved aside my words. "Yes, yes. Sacred to the multitude that fills the piazza, perhaps, but not to those who know its inner workings. Pope Innocent had been ailing for months; Rodrigo has had ample time to gather allies, though no one thought he had a chance. That is how a *palio* is won. No one sees the slow horse gaining ground until it crosses the finish line."

Rodrigo . . .

It was the first time I'd heard her utter my father's name, and the intimacy in her voice made it sound blasphemous. All this time, he had been Cardinal Borgia to her, our benevolent benefactor. The suspicion I felt when I saw her on the staircase returned, sharpening my tone. "And are you saying that Papa told you all this? He informed you of his plans?"

"Not exactly, but even with the conclave locked away, servants still must serve. They must empty chamber pots and carry messages. And servants, like cardinals, can be bribed."

I went silent. With a few words, she had revealed how little I truly knew.

"And . . . ?" I asked at length.

Giulia went tense, her voice quickening as she described events that by all rights she too should know nothing about, as if she'd been immured in the Sistine with my father and his fellow cardinals. "After the third round of votes was cast, it was clear that della Rovere couldn't win; Cardinal Sforza also lacked the necessary two-thirds. Your father gave a speech that swayed a few to his side, but then he made his move, promising Cardinal Sforza his own office of vice-chancellor." Her smile was triumphant. "That won Sforza over, sure as silver; the man is forever mired in debt, and the vice-chancellorship is the most lucrative office in the Vatican. By tomorrow, it could be over. All your father needs is one vote. One. And if I know him, he'll do whatever he must to obtain it."

I rocked back on my seat, my mind awhirl. No longer did I wonder how Giulia had managed to gain access to such privileged information; all I could think of, all I could see, was my father, clothed in white and gold, the ring of St. Peter the Fisherman on his finger.

"Papa could be pope," I said aloud, in disbelief.

Giulia clapped her hands. "Think of it! There will be so much to enjoy, so much to fill our days from dawn to dusk. You will be the most sought-after woman at his court, His Holiness's beloved daughter." She reached out to hug me. Pressed against her, I heard her whisper, "Tomorrow, Lucrezia. Tomorrow everything will change."

Closing my eyes, I surrendered to her excitement, even if I felt an unexpected frisson of fear. I wasn't sure if being the pope's daughter was something I should welcome.

CHAPTER TWO

Unable to contain herself, Giulia blurted out during dinner what she had learned, eliciting a frown from Adriana and a disapproving grunt from my mother, who was no doubt chagrined that her tarot cards had failed to yield such momentous news. But the import of the revelation could not be ignored, prompting Vannozza and Adriana to closet themselves in the parlor for urgent discussion, while Giulia and I went upstairs to spend a restless night.

As the fifth day of the conclave's enclosure dawned, Adriana announced that we must go to the Vatican. If my father became pope, as Giulia claimed, we had to be there to witness the announcement. But before we did, Adriana hustled Giulia, my mother (who'd stayed overnight in a spare room), and me into the chapel to offer up prayers for his election.

As I knelt before the altar, my eyes burned from lack of sleep. My ears still rang from Giulia's chatter about all the jewelry, dresses, furs, and other wealth that would soon be ours. But a deeper part of me remained somber, attuned to the current that could sweep us up like a flood, submerging the past to reveal an uncharted future.

I had no need to pray. Papa would win. As Giulia said, he'd do anything to achieve it. Afterward, we marshaled the servants, donning cloaks and veils to hide our faces. We had to forgo a carriage or litter, to avoid attention; yet as we traversed the streets, feral dogs and rooting pigs scattering from our path, I barely felt the grit and cobblestone under my soles, so eager to reach the Vatican that I managed to ignore my mother's barbed sidelong looks.

You will be the most sought-after woman at his court. . . .

Crossing the Ponte Sant'Angelo, we took the narrow road up the hill to the Vatican, which was composed of the brick Apostolic Palace, where the popes resided, and a bewildering array of inner buildings, passageways, and courtyards connecting to the Holy Basilica, built upon the crucifixion site and tomb of St. Peter, whose martyrdom had founded our Church.

We were in the heart of Rome, before the ancient structures of our faith. Perhaps because I'd not visited the Vatican often, I was struck by how plain and decrepit it all looked, a sprawl of red-tile rooftops and crumbling façades, festooned with mildew-stained stone angels and faceless saints brooding down upon the cobblestone square. From where we stood, the giant pinecone fountain that gushed in the palace atrium, which provided clean water to nearby residents and where I'd once plunged my bare feet as a child, was hardly visible, but I could see that the open colonnades surrounding it—usually crowded with trinket hawkers and vendors of delicious roast *ceci* beans—stood empty, access blocked by regiments of the papal guard.

It was still early, a rare cool in the morning air, but I soon began to sweat under my cloak and hood. My stomach grumbled; in her zeal to see us here, Adriana had forgotten our breakfast, and I'd have given anything for a bag of those roasted beans. We had taken care to disguise ourselves as pious women, come to see if we would soon have a new Holy Vicar, but the square was deserted, mist unfurling from the un-even paving stones. More guards ringed the outer staircases, I noticed, but they were propped against the peeling walls, with the bleary faces of men who had rested too little and drunk too much.

Then the sun broke through the clouds. People began to appear—black-clad widows fingering rosaries; beleaguered mothers towing grimy children by the hand; men with their caps doffed; merchants and street vendors; and finally the denizens of our underworld, the prosti-tutes in frothy skirts and cinched bodices, furtive thieves and footpads who could filch a purse with a snip of their tiny daggers. Within min-utes, the square echoed with the scuffle of footsteps as everyone congre-gated before the colonnaded entry to the Vatican, south of the crumbling basilica, as close as they could get without disturbing the guards. All eyes lifted to the window of the Sistine Chapel, which reflected only its makeshift wall of hasty brickwork, designed thus so it could be torn down easily to announce the new pope.

We hurried to join them, our servants a barricade around us.

Most of the women dropped to their knees. Giulia shot me a look of consternation from under her veil, making me want to giggle. She was worried she'd soil her lavish azure gown, which she'd insisted on donning to prevent Adriana, often transported by piety, from ordering us to also kneel. It could be hours yet before an answer came, if it came at all. Eyeing the ancient paving stones caked with centuries of residue, I shared Giulia's reluctance, though my gown was plain linen. Between my hunger and the grime before me, I began to wish I'd stayed at home, curled up with Arancino, away from the rabble—

My mother gripped my arm. "Don't think any of this can change your fate. You are betrothed; you still must go to Spain, far from Rome and his side. He will never be yours."

I turned to find her eyes boring into me. "He is my father," I said. "He is already mine."

Fury twisted her mouth. "Not for much longer. Do you think he can keep his unwed daughter about him for all to see? Sons, yes; a pope can always find places for sons, discreet posts of influence to further his aims. But a daughter must wed where he sees fit."

A chill went through me. Adriana and Giulia turned toward us, frowning. Before they could intervene, there was an abrupt swelling of the crowd, a united push forward and joyous cry. My gaze followed the mass of fingers pointing upward; a communal whisper rippled through the square like a gust of wind: *"Habemus Papam!"*

I watched through a daze as the bricks in the window were pulled down in chunks. Within a cloud of reddish dust, the pane cracked open. I caught a glimpse of the shadowy robed figures in the chapel beyond before one stepped to the window, casting out a handful of white feathers. They drifted upon the air, as if about to take flight, before raining upon the cobblestones below. The people surged forth to catch them; only then did I realize, as Giulia lunged forward, they were not feathers at all but small pieces of paper, folded in half.

Heedless now of the filth spattering her skirts, Giulia clutched one of the papers in her hand. My mother and Adriana peered anxiously over her shoulder as she unfolded it and read aloud, *"We have for our pope Cardinal Rodrigo Borgia of Valencia, known as Alexander the Sixth."*

"Deo Gratias!" cried Adriana. Tears streamed down her cheeks.

Around me, the square must have erupted in acclaim, but I did not hear the frantic jostling of the crowd for the remaining papers, the whimpers of pain as hands were trod upon and fingers crushed.

Then, in a sudden rush of sound, I heard the chanting: *"Deo Gratias, Roma per Borgia!"*

The ecstatic cries scattered roosting pigeons from the basilica's eaves. As I looked about in bewildered amazement at the sound of my family name ringing out, Giulia gasped, "Look! There he is, at the window!"

Our servants edged closer as the crowd roared at the sight of Papa's strong figure silhouetted there. He lifted a hand in benediction. The people went to their knees. Beside me, my mother and Adriana went down, too, murmuring prayers of gratitude. Giulia tugged at my hem, saying, "Lucrezia, you must kneel and show your devotion!"

Deafened by the acclaim that greeted my father's first appearance as Pope Alexander VI, our new Vicar of Christ, I stumbled to my knees, a thrill surging in my veins.

"Roma per Borgia! Rome for Borgia!"

The people's throaty shouts overflowed the piazza, reverberating into the city, until I was sure everyone in Italy must hear them. I wanted to laugh aloud; although I couldn't see Papa's face as he stood at the window with his hands raised, I knew he too must be holding back his laughter.

He had triumphed.

Moments later, the clangor of iron-shod hooves reached us. We hastened to our feet as a group of men in the mulberry and saffron of our Borgia livery galloped into the piazza, a group of hired men, or bravos, following on foot. The people veered as the rider at the group's head charged straight through them, oblivious to their frantic scrambling to get out of his way and avoid being trampled.

He reined to a halt before us, whipping off his cap to let loose a cascade of dark-auburn hair. With a cry of recognition, my mother ran to him. "Juan, *mio figlio!* We have won this day!"

My brother Juan shot her an insolent grin, his blue-green eyes gleaming in his swarthy face. At sixteen years of age, he was a man, his velvet doublet straining across his muscular chest. With his aquiline features and strong nose, he exuded a raw virility; physically, he most resembled our father.

"We may have won this day," he said, "but you'll not see the end of it if you stay. Papa thought you might have come here, despite his order that you remain indoors. He sent me to tell you to make haste to the palazzo before this rabble gets out of hand. By nightfall, there won't be a place in Rome they haven't shat upon or looted. Already they gather about his palace to strip it bare."

I was horrified. "Not his palazzo!" Built on the site of an ancient mint, our father's house on the Via dei Bianchi was famous for its splendor; he had filled each of its frescoed rooms with exquisite tapestries from Flanders and antiques dug up from the Forum and had entertained ambassadors, cardinals, and visiting kings there. He often said that, after his children, the Borgia Palazzo was his most treasured possession.

Juan shrugged. "It cannot be helped. We've dispatched retainers to contain the excess, but it's customary to allow the mob free rein. The Holy Father has no need of worldly vanities; he is God's servant now, and all he owns must return to his flock." He cast a disparaging look over the crowd, none of whom dared approach. "Such a waste. This miserable lot will turn it all into kindling or swaddling for their snot-nosed brats."

"Oh, no." Adriana turned pale. "My house: We must go at once."

Juan pointed to his men. "They will escort you. I'll take one of you on my horse." As Giulia eagerly shoved past me toward him, his eyes narrowed. "Not you."

She froze at his icy tone. He crooked a finger at me. "Lucrezia, come."

Juan and I had never been close. In our childhood, he taunted me mercilessly, stuffing worms into my shoes and live frogs under my pillows, until I was afraid to put on my clothes or go to bed. Our brother Cesare said that Juan resented the attention lavished on me, as he had always been Papa's favorite.

But in this moment, I was more anxious to escape the crowd and so didn't resist when one of Juan's bravos picked me up as though I weighed nothing and set me on my brother's saddle. The horse was enormous, a war destrier; as I gingerly wound my arms about Juan's waist, settling myself as best I could (I had little experience on horseback), he whispered, "Better hold fast, sister," before he yelled at his men, "Put my mother and Donna Adriana in a litter! Djem, you see to la Farnese!" I heard our mother's delighted cackle and saw the color drain from Giulia's cheeks.

The Turkish prince Djem emerged from those surrounding Juan. He rode a smaller Arabian steed, his head swathed in his signature turban and a contemptuous grin on his lips. He might have been handsome in his dark angularity, with his astonishing pale-green eyes, had his vicious reputation not preceded him. Having arrived in Rome as a hostage, after his brother the sultan exiled him and agreed to pay a stipend to the Vatican to keep him away, Djem had scandalized Rome with his outlandish garb and penchant for the disreputable. It was rumored he'd killed several men in brawls and then spat upon their corpses; he was also Juan's favorite companion, never far from my brother's side.

Giulia was aghast. "You would entrust my safety to this . . . this heathen?"

"Better a heathen than the rabble," Juan retorted.

He swerved his horse around. With a loud whoop and dig of his spurred heels, he took us galloping from the piazza, forcing bystanders to throw themselves bodily from our path.

As we flew past crowds that now swarmed in anticipation of rapine, I glanced over my shoulder to see Giulia immobile while Djem circled her, like a picador baiting a helpless calf.

It was my first taste of that incipient power Giulia had said I would soon possess. I was the pope's daughter now, while she was but the wife of an Orsini.

Much as I didn't want to admit it, I rather enjoyed the sudden change.

CHAPTER THREE

Juan and I reached Adriana's palazzo before the others, arriving to find people already amassed outside the stout gates. Juan lashed with his whip, raining blows and wedging his destrier through the crowd. I cringed behind him, pressing my face between his shoulder blades, anticipating violence to befall us at any moment.

"Marrano!" a man cursed. "Spanish swine!"

I sensed something fly over my head, hitting the gates with a wet *splat*. I couldn't help but look up at the sound. A pig's head had spattered against the palazzo entrance. After taking a quick glance at the bloodied mess, I turned warily to find a seething mass of ugly faces. It seemed as if a thousand hands strained toward us, eager to rip away whatever they could.

They were going to kill us. Even as our father blessed the city as Pope Alexander VI, his daughter and son were about to be yanked from this horse and—

Juan leapt to the ground, his booted feet making an audible thump. As he jerked his sword from its sheath on the edge of the saddle, he shouted, "Who said that?" Sunlight gleamed across the blade as he jabbed it at the crowd. Those nearest to us took a collective step back, stumbling against one another in haste. "Show yourself," Juan said. "Miserable coward, come here and spew your filth to my face, if you dare!"

A huge man lumbered forth, wiping hands the size of hams on his leather jerkin. He had a nasty scar down the side of his jaw, his close-shaven head pitted with lice bites. "I said it," he growled. "And I'll say it again, to your face or your filthy arse. No Catalan Jew is fit to be pope."

I grappled for the horse's discarded reins as Juan's entire countenance darkened. "We are not Jews," he said in a dead-quiet voice. "We were never Jews. We are of noble Spanish blood. Our kinsman, Calixtus the Third, was pope before us, you ignorant turd."

The man guffawed. "Calixtus was a Jew-loving swine like the rest of you. Just because your family thinks they're noble doesn't mean they are. You are filth. A beggar's pus-riddled cock is more suited to dangle from the Holy See than that of any Borgia."

The mob bellowed raucous approval, though most had already moved back to form a barricade behind the man, affording enough distance to ensure that whatever happened, they'd have the chance to flee.

Juan said, "You will regret that. Whoever paid you to say it will regret it."

Even as the man sneered, I saw his hand shift toward his jerkin. "Paid me? No one pays me to speak the truth, you bastard son of a—"

My voice erupted: "Juan!"

My brother reacted so quickly to my warning, it was almost indiscernible. One moment he was glaring at the man; the next he charged and swiped his sword upward with lethal precision.

A red fissure blossomed in the man's throat. He gaped, eyes bulging, blood bubbling out of his mouth. The crowd shrieked as Juan thrust the sword again, this time directly into the man's chest. With a gurgling cry, he toppled. Juan straddled him, blade raised. With an unearthly howl, he drove the sword into the man repeatedly, spraying crimson arcs.

Agitated by the fresh-spilt blood, the horse tossed its head, whinnying. It began to buck as I clutched at the reins, straining to get my feet into the stirrups while slipping sideways on the saddle.

The crowd stampeded into retreat, all thought of insult or thievery forgotten at the sight of Juan hacking at the corpse like a demon. He was drenched in gore when he finally looked up, dazed, as the others of our party cantered up. The arrival of our servants and his bravos on foot scattered the remainder of rabble like vermin.

The bolts on the palazzo gates were thrown back; our house steward, Tomasso, came rushing out in time to catch me by the waist as I tumbled from the horse. Juan met my eyes; I looked down at the tangled mess at his feet. It no longer resembled anything human.

Peering from the litter, Vannozza gave a cry. She heaved herself out, hastening to Juan. "What happened?" She cupped his chin, heedless of the blood spattered across his face. She was practically standing on the corpse yet didn't seem to notice.

"He . . . defamed us," I heard Juan utter, as if the words cost him effort. He was still gripping the sword, which dripped onto the curled tips of his boots. "He called us *Marranos*."

"And he was about to pull out a knife," I added nervously, though I now doubted if I'd actually seen the man pull out anything. "I . . . I saw him reaching into his—"

"Never mind that." My mother's voice cut me off. Pulling a handkerchief from her pocket, she dabbed Juan's face, wiping away the clots. "Someone search that thing," she ordered.

The servants eyed one another. From the litter, Adriana called out, "Vannozza, *per favore*! Can't it wait until we get inside?"

"No." My mother glared at her. "This dog was hired to bark. There might be something on it that can identify its master. Search it, I say."

I murmured to Tomasso, "You'd better do as she says."

The steward reluctantly left my side. I heard a swish of skirts and half-turned to see Giulia marching toward me, sweat-drenched and pale but resolute. She took my hand as Tomasso bent over the corpse and gingerly peeled back portions of the hacked-up jerkin. Tomasso was grimacing, trying to reach past the jerkin without touching the spilled guts protruding from the dead man's ravaged belly.

"Idiot." Vannozza shoved him aside. Without hesitation, she started to rummage, her black skirts pooling in the bloody mess. I sagged in relief when I saw her toss a thin dagger at Tomasso. She stood with a flourish, brandishing a purse. *"Eccola!"* She pulled its ties open, upending the contents into her palm—silver ducats, far too many for a common thug.

"Who?" Juan's eyes smoldered.

"Think," said Vannozza. "We surely don't need a seer. Who wanted the papacy? Who paid out a fortune in bribes, only for Rodrigo to outbid him? A Borgia has won the keys to St. Peter's kingdom. Now his enemy will seek vengeance. This filth would not have dared confront you otherwise. This is none other than Giuliano della Rovere's dog."

"Was." Juan's smile was terrible, exposing blood on his teeth. "Now he's dog meat."

"There will be others. Curs run in packs."

Adriana cried, "Can we please get inside now before the mob comes back?"

Vannozza's curt nod initiated the rush inside the palazzo's fortified walls.

Only Juan, Vannozza, Giulia, and I remained immobile, until Vannozza jerked her chin at Tomasso. "You: See to this. Throw it into the Tiber along with that pig head. And wash down the road. We have guests tonight. I'll not have them dirty their hems on della Rovere shit." She motioned at Giulia. "Take her upstairs and see her bathed."

Giulia led me away, up the staircase to my chamber. As I stepped over the threshold, I felt suddenly faint. With the assistance of my maid, Pantalisea, Giulia stripped me of my garments. "Fetch water," Giulia told Pantalisea, who raced from the chamber, her soft brown eyes wide as platters. She was just three years older than me, the daughter of a merchant who'd done my father a favor, earning a place for her in my household. She had shared my sheltered existence; she must have seen Juan kill that man, from one of the palazzo loggias.

With a moan of despair, Adriana came into my chamber. Impatience flared in my voice as I heard myself say, "Zia, there is no need to worry. I wasn't harmed."

"Not harmed?" she echoed, incredulous. "Juan has committed a mortal sin on the very day of your father's elevation. It's a terrible omen, another blight on his papacy."

"You sound like Vannozza," I said in exasperation. "That man insulted us and had a knife. Juan was defending our honor. Why should Papa be punished for it?"

"You do not understand. Your father has—" She stopped herself as Pantalisea returned with a sloshing basin of water. Adriana bit her lip, meeting Giulia's gaze. I saw something pass between them, an unvoiced message of some kind.

"Please see Donna Adriana to her rooms," I told Pantalisea, and she went to assist Adriana, who clung to her as if the world were coming to an end.

The door closed, leaving Giulia and me alone. She gave me a pensive look as I removed my shift and took up a cloth, scrubbing myself. When I looked down to my feet, I saw that the water in the basin had turned pink. Blood must have sprayed on me, too. How strange. I hadn't felt it.

"Your robe," Giulia said. "It's there on the bed. Put it on before you catch cold."

I was shivering, wrapping the velvet about me. Though the sun blazed outside, spilling through the window in dazzling shafts, I felt doused in ice.

Silence descended.

"You were very brave," Giulia finally said.

"Brave?" I did not feel as if I had been. "I . . . I just warned Juan. That man—he was reaching into his jerkin and . . ." My voice faded as she gave a firm nod.

"Yet Juan's horse is larger than anything you're used to riding," she said, "and those fiends were all around you. You probably saved his life with your warning, or at least spared him injury. You should be proud of yourself. Few girls would have had the presence of mind to act as you did."

I regarded her in silence. Respect, I realized—that was what I heard in her voice. It caught me by surprise. Times past, she would have chided me for being a silly, helpless child.

"What was Adriana going to say about Papa?" I asked. "What don't I understand?"

Giulia sighed. "I'm not sure this is the right moment, Lucrezia."

"Why not?"

She turned to my mirror. "That man called your family *Marranos.*" She paused, eyeing me in the glass. "Do you know what it means?"

"Yes, of course. A *Marrano* is a converted Jew. But we're not Jews . . . are we?"

"No more than any of these so-called nobles of Italy, who can scarcely stand the sight of one another, let alone a foreigner. *Marrano* is what they call every Spaniard, especially the Borgia, because your father did not content himself to haggle over a meaningless piece of land or dingy castle. He wanted the Holy See and he achieved it. That is why they insulted you: They despise your family's ambition. Vannozza was right: They run in packs. What they need is a strong hand to bring them to heel. Rodrigo will leash them all soon enough, including Cardinal della Rovere."

I sensed she was not telling me everything. "But Adriana called it 'another' blight on his papacy. That must mean there is more." I met her stare, holding my breath as a smile curled her lips.

"That would be me," she said at length. "I am the other blight." Her smile widened. "If I tell you a secret, will you promise not to breathe a word of it to anyone?"

I made myself nod, though I was not certain I wanted to know.

"Very well. Rodrigo and I are . . ." Laughter bubbled in her throat. "We are lovers. And I am carrying his child."

I gaped in disbelief. Before I could stop myself, I blurted out, "But you are married."

"What of it? Do you think because I have a husband I'm incapable of taking a lover?"

I hardly knew what to say. She was right, of course; though I had no experience in such matters, I supposed certain married women did break their vows. I'd suspected something like this already, ever since she told me about my father's machinations in the conclave, a private business she should never have known. But having it confirmed didn't make it less unsettling.

"Does Juan know?" I asked suddenly, and a shadow of fear crossed her face.

"Why would you ask me that?" she said sharply.

"I don't know. The way he behaved toward you in the piazza, I suppose."

She made a moue of distaste. "He might. Rodrigo may have told him. And it would certainly explain why he behaved like a boor, leaving me to the care of that savage Turk of his. Your brother is a jealous man; he wants your father to love only him. He even once made advances to me and I refused. I don't think he's ever been denied before—by a woman, that is."

She turned back to my mirror. As she stood there, straightening her spine to inspect her belly—which to me looked flat as ever—all of a sudden I realized I didn't like her.

"But Adriana must know," I persisted. "She must, if she called you a blight."

"Yes, she knows." Giulia didn't sound the least bit perturbed. "She helped arrange it, in fact. She sent my husband, her son, to live in their family estate in Basanello soon after our wedding." She laughed. "Rodrigo insisted on it. He said he didn't want any squinty-eyed husband getting in the way of his—"

"Stop it." My voice turned cold. "Stop talking about him like that. He is our pope."

She turned to me, a hand at her hip. "Oh, my sweet child. The pope is still a man. Rodrigo isn't going to change just because he now wears the papal ring. On the contrary, he told me he intends to move us to a new palazzo by the Vatican, so he can visit us whenever he likes."

"Us?" I echoed.

"Yes. *Us*. As in you and me. I told you, you'll be the most sought-after woman in his court, but if I am to be the mother of his child, surely I deserve my own palazzo, at the very least." She gave me an appraising glance. "You should rest. You are quite pale, and we have the celebratory feast to attend tonight. You must look your best."

She went to the door. "Oh, and that Spanish betrothal of yours? You mustn't give it another thought. Some minor noble of Valencia will never do now, not for His Holiness's daughter. Already, every noble house in Italy prepares to bid for your hand. Sought after, indeed. You'll be a bride before you know it." Her smile showed a hint of teeth. "Just imagine what a wedding it will be! Do wear your green silk tonight. Rodrigo loves to see you in that color."

I stood frozen as she walked out.

She had seduced my father. I had thought I was the center of his life, his beloved daughter, soon to be the princess of his court, but she had stolen him away. She would bear his child; she would overshadow my every step. It didn't matter if I wed the Valencian or not. She would see to it that I trailed at her heels until another alliance was arranged for me.

Helpless fury uncoiled inside me. I was indeed still a child, as powerless as ever.

Only now I was beholden to a woman I no longer felt I could trust.

CHAPTER FOUR

Flambeaux licked the evening air, their citrus-scented smoke dispelling the hordes of mosquitoes that were the bane of our summers. Remnants of lamb roasted in herbs, of peacock and boar and venison, along with enough wine and marzipan to sate a legion, were being cleared from the tables; the once-pristine but now stained Venetian linens spread on long trestle tables in the atrium had been gathered up by the servants, to be dunked in vats of boiling urine for cleaning.

The guests had begun to arrive at Adriana's palazzo shortly after sunset, a veritable onslaught of cousins and relatives I'd never heard of, let alone met, along with many nobles eager to partake of our family's fortune. Now they reclined on cushions in the loggia, basking in the cool breeze that wafted from the Tiber, or strolled down the garden pathways.

Despite my resentment of Giulia, I took her advice and wore my green silk *camora* and paired it with yellow satin sleeves. Pantalisea styled my hair in ringlets about my face, its heavy length held back by a filet with a single pearl. She told me I looked beautiful, as was her duty; regarding my reflection in the glass, I decided to believe her. While my cheeks were too plump and my mouth too wide, my body still round with childish fat, without discernible breast, I took comfort in the fact that I was well proportioned for my age and my attire complemented me.

Assuming my place beside Adriana in the hall, I greeted all the guests. Juan had stood to Adriana's left, scrubbed clean and clad in black velvet with a gored skirt and gold tasseled belt, from which dangled an ornamental dagger in the Turkish style. He too accepted the guests' effusive praise, charming them with his ready smile, as he could when he had a mind to, as if he hadn't hacked a man to death outside our gates only hours before.

I was relieved that Giulia did not try to engage me, flitting among the guests in her lavish carnation silk gown and diamonds about her throat. Likewise, my mother ignored me; encased in a black velvet gown that was too tight, she elected to lurk in the background and direct the servants, barely acknowledging the appearance of her own husband, Signor Canale, who arrived with my ten-year-old brother, Gioffre.

Little Gioffre's red-gold hair hung in a blunt fringe above his freckled forehead, his sturdy form in a tawny jerkin and hose. He grinned at the sight of me, and I embraced him fondly in return, keeping him beside me as the guests assumed their seats.

"Is Zio Rodrigo coming?" Gioffre asked eagerly, and I smiled to hide the pang I felt at his words. He still lived with Vannozza, who had not yet informed him that his beloved "uncle," whom he idolized, was in truth our father. It must have been confusing. He had heard me call Rodrigo "Papa" but never asked me directly why he wasn't allowed to. He must have suspected, but I assumed Vannozza had told him we shared a mother and had left unexplained who his father was.

"I'm told he will be here soon," I said. "So I'll expect you to be on your best behavior. No chasing after Arancino or feeding the dogs under the table, yes?"

He gave solemn assent, but I made sure to seat him by my side, anyway, so I could cut his meat and water his wine. Though I assured Gioffre that Rodrigo was due to appear, by the time the feast commenced, he had not. Instead, Juan did the honor of toasting our father's health, before giving a long-winded speech about how a new era dawned upon Rome, one in which the corruption of the past would be abolished and Christ's order restored.

If the sentiment was expected, its delivery was not. Juan passed a threatening gaze over the assembly as he spoke, as if to mark the foes among us. I fancied a few of the guests shuddered, apprised of the rampage outside our gates. Though the road leading to the palazzo bore no evidence, Tomasso having followed my mother's orders, I had no doubt that if Juan had been granted his way, the henchman's head would have adorned our table as a grisly warning.

Finally, after hours of feasting, we were excused and I took Gioffre into the gardens, to escape the inevitable gossiping ladies and conspiratorial gentlemen. Toward midnight, as Gioffre and I perched on the rim of the fountain and dangled our hands in the water, playing at trying to catch the speckles of starlight reflected there, a sudden silence fell, like the lightning-charged hush before an oncoming storm.

I stood at once. "Gioffre, quick. Dry your hands." Wiping my own on my skirts, I started with him toward the house. We had barely reached the outer terrace when a large figure loomed in the gallery, his resonant voice booming: "And where is my *farfallina*?"

"I'm here!" I dashed forth, Gioffre at my heels. Papa engulfed me in his embrace, exuding the musk of incense impregnated in his clothes, along with the salt of his sweat. I reveled in his nearness, only now letting myself feel how truly frightened I had been this afternoon at the gates. Nothing could go wrong with Papa here. Nothing would dare.

"Oh, my child." He held me tight, until my bodice dug at my ribs and I gasped, "Papa, I can't breathe." He let go reluctantly, furrowing his broad, sun-bronzed brow. He never remembered to wear a hat, even though at sixty-one years of age he'd lost most of his hair, his bald pate speckled like a robin's egg. His dark eyes were intensely alive despite their small size, examining me as if for visible wounds.

"Adriana told me everything. To think what might have happened . . ." He clenched his fist. "I'd have torn this city down about their miserable heads."

"It was nothing." I forced out a smile. "Juan had it well in hand."

"Yes, that too I heard." He scowled. "I'll have to seek amends with whomever that villain's family is, not to mention reassure the cardinals of our law courts in the Curia that my son isn't about to start skewering malcontents at will. A fine to-do this is, on the eve of my election. By the saints, Juan's too quick with that blade of his. Couldn't he have shouted the wastrel away?"

"He acted in our defense," I said, finding it ironic that I was speaking up for the one brother I cared about the least. "That wastrel defamed us. He was about to pull a knife."

"A knife is no match for a sword. Insults are only words. We can't start killing people for insulting us." He laughed drily. "Were that the case, there wouldn't be a noble left alive in this entire land. Most if not all of them have disparaged us at one time or another." He sighed. "But the most important thing is no harm was done, or at least none that a few hundred ducats in the right hands won't resolve."

I suddenly remembered and turned about, nudging my little brother forward. "Papa, Gioffre is here. He's been waiting all night to see you."

My father's expression went blank as my brother bowed with painstaking care. "Isn't it rather late for you to still be up?" he grumbled.

Gioffre's smile dimmed. "Yes, Zio Rodrigo. Only Lucrezia . . . she said we could walk in the garden until you came, and I—I wanted to . . ."

"Yes? You wanted to what? Stop stuttering and speak up."

"I wanted to congratulate you," Gioffre burst out. "I also wanted to ask if I can live with Lucrezia now. I miss her terribly, and she says she'll be happy to care for me."

My father glanced sharply at me. "Did you tell him this?"

I frowned, wondering why he would be displeased. "Why, yes. We rarely see each other anymore, and I reasoned that since I'm to have my own palazzo, there'll be plenty of room—"

"You reasoned wrong." He returned his gaze to Gioffre. "It's out of the question. You are too young to leave your mother's house. Vannozza would never stand for it. Moreover, Lucrezia will soon have important responsibilities of her own." He punctuated his words with a lift of his right hand, the torchlight catching on a heavy gold ring on his third finger. It bore the crossed papal keys. I knew that when a pope died, his personal ring was broken and a new one cast for his successor; Papa must have been confident indeed to have a new ring forged before he even won the vote.

He extended his hand to Gioffre, obliging my brother to kiss the ring. "Now," he said, "run along to Vannozza and see that she takes you home. The streets are not safe, and I'll not have another mishap."

Gioffre shot a miserable look in my direction before he bowed again, this time with less care. He ran back into the palazzo with the stumbling gait of a boy desperately trying to stave off tears.

Papa turned to me. "I must ask that, in the future, you not fill the boy's head with notions. I realize you mean well, but Vannozza will not appreciate having her last child taken from her."

"He's your child, too," I said. In all my life, I had never openly disagreed with my father, but I couldn't understand why he should treat Gioffre with such disdain. "I see no reason why Gioffre shouldn't live with me or know he is one of us. It's not as if she pays him any mind and—"

"Lucrezia, *basta*." He reverted to Spanish, our *private language*. As he did, he looked over his shoulder, where the cardinals of his court assembled on the terrace, a stone's throw away. "Enough," he repeated in a low voice. "I'll not have you gainsay me. I am the pope now and must show caution in my dealings, especially where my family is concerned. I've enough to contend with, without indulging a boy I'm not sure is truly mine."

"Not yours?" I was astonished. "Whatever do you mean?" Even as I spoke, I braced for another unpleasant revelation. This week seemed destined to be full of them.

My father exhaled a troubled breath. "I suppose you're entitled to an explanation." With his hand on my arm, he guided me farther down the path to a stone bench. "I'm not convinced Gioffre is indeed a Borgia," he said at length. "It pains my heart to say it, but your mother was married when she gave birth to him, and by then . . . well, I wasn't as enamored of her as I had once been. How can I be sure he's not her husband's?"

Was this the reason our mother hadn't told Gioffre about Papa? Did she also doubt his paternity? I thought of my younger brother, always seeking favor in Papa's eyes, much as Cesare had at his age, and how Papa only had eyes for Juan. But Cesare had never doubted he was Papa's son, while poor Gioffre—

"But all you need do is look at him to see he must be a Borgia," I said. "He looks like me."

"And you look like your mother. There we have it. I intend to provide for Gioffre as if he were mine, of course; I'll not see him humiliated. But I cannot put him in your household—" He lifted a finger, silencing me. "Which brings me to another matter."

His expression was somber. I perched on the edge of the bench, watching him tug at his lower lip. I could see he was tired. He had dark smudges under his eyes, and his skin was sallow. In his plain black tunic

and hose, with his scuffed boots hugging his big calves, he appeared as
he always did when not in official regalia, like a frugal tradesman. I always admired how he eschewed personal ostentation. Sighted among
the gaudy red-satin cardinals and purple-drenched bishops, he stood
out in his simplicity. Yet, inexplicably, I now found his simplicity disturbing, as if I had expected a miraculous transformation following his
elevation to the Holy See, some sort of visible change that set him apart
from others, his infallibility marked for all to see.

I recalled Giulia telling me a pope was still a man, and I tensed as he
jutted out his chin and said, "Giulia told me about her conversation
with you this afternoon. She thinks you disapprove. Indeed, she was
aggrieved by your tone."

I bit back the reply that she had no cause for grievance, given her
own behavior. Instead, I muttered, "She is mistaken. I would never
disapprove of you, Papa."

"Not me." He raised his eyes. "She thinks you disapprove of *us*."

I went silent.

"I understand," he continued. "It must have been difficult to learn
your father has been named Supreme Pontiff only to hear that Giulia
and I, that we . . ." He paused, the silence straining taut between us.

"Is it true?" I asked hesitantly. "Is she carrying your child?"

He nodded. A sudden joy lightened his features, so that his eyes
glimmered as they did when he looked upon me. It brought a knot to
my chest. He was happy about this. He wanted this child. It might even
be a daughter, a baby girl, another *farfallina. . . .*

I was so engulfed by this disturbing thought that I almost reminded
him that if he was not sure of Gioffre, how could he be sure of Giulia's
child? Though her husband lived far away, it seemed to me that he
might still be the father. But I held myself back, because I had the sense
that whatever I tried to say would only make him think I sought to
cause more dissension.

"I believed you and Giulia were friends," he said. "She tells me she
thinks of you as a sister. It would hurt me if you did not feel the same."

"I do," I replied uncomfortably, for I did not like lying to him.
"Only when she told me . . ." I swallowed. It was the most grown-up
conversation I'd had with my father. Only days ago, I'd been embroi-

dering a pillowcase for him; now I was discussing his children and love for a woman whom I feared might supplant me in his affections. I longed to halt everything, return to yesterday afternoon on the landing when I saw Giulia enter from her outing, and forget everything I'd learned. I preferred to remain a child, if this was what adulthood entailed.

"Lucrezia, all I ever want to do is to protect you from the harshness of this world, which no girl should experience before her time," said Papa. "But Giulia tells me it is time for you to assume your proper station in life."

"I thought I had. Am I not your daughter?" I couldn't keep the tremor from my voice. I wanted desperately to hear that he still loved me more than anyone else, that I was his most beloved child. But I heard my mother in my head—*Don't think any of this can change your fate*—and it roused a terrible fear in me. What if he could no longer love me as he once had, because he was pope now, and must send me far away to wed a Spanish nobleman?

He looked startled. "Oh, my *farfallina,* do you think I'd ever stop caring for you?"

I averted my gaze. "I don't know, Papa. You love Giulia and her baby. Maybe they're more important now to you."

He reached over to cup my chin. "You are not as smart as the nuns of San Sisto and Adriana claim if you believe that. I could never love anyone the way I love you." He smiled. "But I'm not just your father. I am also a man. And men need different kinds of love."

His echoing of Giulia's words stabbed through me, keen as a knife. "Aren't I enough?"

"My child, of course you are. Never doubt it. But our love is pure; it is not the passion of a man for a woman. Giulia gives me that passion and asks for little in return, much like Vannozza did before her. She pleases me. You want me to be happy, don't you?"

I could not agree. While I didn't care for my mother, Giulia was nothing like her. I suspected she'd not be content to live as Vannozza did, maintaining her distance for appearance's sake. Yet I did not voice my thoughts, because I'd never felt this passion he described. All I knew was that he had compelled me to see him in a new light, no longer the immutable protector but someone with needs I did not understand nor could hope to fulfill.

"Giulia told me you'll refute my Spanish betrothal," I abruptly said. As he looked away, I held my breath, bracing myself for the worst, the news that he had decided to send me to Spain after all. But then he turned back to me.

"I think you've had enough surprises for one day," he said gently. "Let me worry about the future. Besides, you'll be busy in the coming days, for you, Giulia, and Adriana are moving to Cardinal Zeto's palazzo of Santa Maria in Portico." He grinned, as he always did when he gave me a present. "I've ordered the entire palace refurbished; only the most splendid residence in Rome will suffice for my *farfallina*. You'll have your own set of apartments, with an entourage to attend you." He winked, leaning close. "One of the advantages of being pope is I can do as I see fit, within reason. In addition to your new palazzo, I shall build apartments in the Vatican, so there will be enough room for all my children."

Giulia had made it sound as if the new palazzo was entirely for her, but if I was to have my own apartments, then Papa must intend to honor me, as well.

"Can I bring Arancino, little Murilla, and Pantalisea with me?" I asked.

"Your cat, your maid, and whatever else your heart desires. Just say the word and it shall be yours. You can even bring all those books Adriana tells me you hide in your room and Vannozza chides her for letting you read."

I laughed in delight, until I suddenly remembered my other brother, far away in Pisa. Sensing my hesitation, Papa asked, "Is anything else troubling you?"

"You said all your children. Does that mean you'll now summon Cesare home?"

His smile faded. "Eventually. But for now he must complete his studies for the priesthood. He will find joy in service to our Holy Church, as I have, but first he must resign himself to the sacrifices it entails." He glared at me in mock severity. "That means no secret letters relaying the news or messages sent by pigeon to his seminary. I well know how close you two are; since childhood, you've been like twin souls. But Cesare must devote himself to his studies without any distractions."

"It's just that I miss him so much. It's been over two years since I've seen him, Papa."

"Yes, but he still sends you those books, doesn't he?" Papa elbowed me, causing me to giggle. "Forbidden books of poetry that outrage Vannozza." He eyed me. "Books and sisterly devotion are fine things, but you must trust in me to do what is right—for him and for you." He caressed my cheek. "Do I have your promise, *farfallina*?"

I nodded. He kissed my brow. "Good. And will you be kind to Giulia?"

"Yes, Papa," I whispered, and he tweaked the tip of my nose.

"And no more quarreling with Vannozza. No one knows better than me how much of a taskmistress she can be; not for nothing has she turned those inns of hers into gold mines. But she only wants what's best for you. I'll not have it said you failed to show her proper respect."

Dio mio, did he have eyes and ears everywhere?

"Yes, Papa."

"*Bien.*" He brought us to our feet, looking at the torchlit palazzo, from which laughter and music wafted toward us. "I'm surprised they've left me alone this long. I vow I haven't had a moment to myself, even to empty my bladder." He held out his arms. "Now give your old papa a kiss. It's late and you must rest. We'll see each other very soon."

I held him close, drawing in his unique smell. With his whisper of "I love you, Lucrezia," like a balm in my ears, I left him to go up to my chamber.

Perhaps being the pope's daughter might not be such a bad thing, after all.

CHAPTER FIVE

The next weeks passed in a whirlwind as we dismantled our house, filling chests and coffers for the move. Adriana oversaw everything, directing the servants in the proper way to roll up the tapestries and the use of hay to cushion our multitude of fragile plates and statuary.

Giulia and I could not avoid each other; we shared possessions strewn all over our rooms. As we sorted through them, deciding whether to retain this faded sleeve or those tattered slippers, we were barely able to utter more than required niceties—until Adriana burst in unannounced and passed her critical eye over us.

"Did you add lavender to your linen chests? If not, everything will arrive smelly and foul and—" She flung open the first coffer lid. A streak of fur leapt out, making her shriek.

"Arancino, you naughty thing!" I cried, as my cat scrabbled under my bed, spitting fury. I turned apologetically to Adriana. "He must have been trapped inside. I had no idea."

Behind me, Giulia choked back a giggle. All of a sudden I had to bite my lip.

"You had no idea?" Adriana pressed a hand to her chest. "*Dio mio,* imagine if we had arrived in Santa Maria to find that creature smothered to death among your linens."

"It's only across the river," said Giulia. "He'd hardly have smothered, though he might have urinated on everything, lavender or not." She gave me a wry look; without warning, we both burst into laughter. As Adriana watched us in bewilderment, I thought of how Papa had asked me to show kindness to Giulia, and I whispered, "Forgive me."

"Oh, no. I'm the one who must beg forgiveness," she said. "After that terrible incident with Juan, it was insensitive of me."

Adriana harrumphed. "Friends again, are we?"

"Yes," Giulia declared, clasping my hand.

I nodded in agreement, though I was still not so sure I could trust her.

Adriana ordered us to air out the coffer at once, "and repack those linens with lavender—and no cat!" Then she marched out, closing the door on our mirth.

ON AUGUST 26, the feast day of St. Alexander, the servants loaded the last of our furnishings onto carts for transport to Santa Maria, while we donned our brocade and veils to go into the city to witness Papa's coronation as Pope Alexander VI.

We were not allowed to attend the ceremony itself, as women were prohibited from witnessing the sacred consecration in the basilica, during which Papa had to sit in his shift on a special stool, "with a hole in the seat," Giulia told me, "so his manhood can be verified."

"Verified?" I said. "Whatever for? Surely everyone can see he is a man."

"You would think so. But, remember *la papisa:* Everyone thought Pope Joan was a man, and look at how that turned out. Now every pope since must prove he is . . . well, you know," she added hastily, as Adriana shot us a censorious look.

"Are you going to chatter like fishwives all day?" asked Adriana. "Or will you deign to pay attention to this most important event in our family history?"

I turned my gaze to the street below. We sat on a specially appointed balcony in a palazzo overlooking Papa's processional route down the Via Papale to the Lateran Palace, where he'd be enthroned as Bishop of Rome and supreme ruler of the papal states.

The view was breathtaking, as were the smells. Animal ordure and spilled wine from leather flagons turned rank in the heat as cheering multitudes crammed the road; the procession wound its way to the Coliseum, with the rat-catchers leading straining dogs on leashes, which ran ahead to clear the swampy grasses of vermin. Shopkeepers who kept stalls in the ruin's lower levels unfurled colored banners; suddenly the ravaged hulk of an arena, long-since stripped of its marble and travertine to decorate noble palazzos, was resurrected to evanescent life, its cavernous archways returned to a fleeting glory not seen since ancient times. Bronzed plaster angels sprouted from enormous plaster archways straddling the road. The sky could barely be seen among fluttering pennons sporting our colors—an immense sea of mulberry and yellow.

Everywhere I looked, I saw my family name exalted.

Giulia pointed out the most important personages in the procession. "There's Cardinal Ascanio Sforza," she said, indicating a small trim man with protuberant eyes, dressed in ermine-trimmed robes and riding a mule among twelve pages clad in crimson and purple. "Rumor has it, Rodrigo gave him six chests filled with silver after the conclave, but it's a lie. Your father's palazzo on the Corso and the vice-chancellorship are reward enough for any man, even one as greedy as he."

As Cardinal Sforza rode past, along with the other scarlet-clad cardinals and their respective retainers and family members, I recalled what Giulia had told me about him casting the decisive vote in my father's election. "I thought the mob looted Papa's palazzo," I said, thinking Sforza must have inherited quite a mess to clean up.

Giulia chuckled. "The mob never touched it. As soon as he heard the palazzo was his, Sforza sent his own retainers to protect it. He wasn't about to let a single plate escape him. He's become the most powerful man in the Curia, not to mention the richest. And through him, your father has allied with the Sforza of Milan, which means that—"

"Hush your mouth," said Adriana irritably. "You're always filling her head with nonsense."

Giulia scowled. I was about to question her further when a roar from the crowd announced the arrival of Rome's most distinguished families, who had set aside their ancestral hostilities for today to promulgate their shared splendor.

The proud Orsini wore sienna velvet trimmed in gold, led by their patriarch, Virginio Orsini, who oversaw the papal guard. At prudent distance, swathed in equal pomp and velvet, were the Colonna, the Orsini family's tenacious foe. As their servants trod through scrims of dust kicked up by men on horseback, Giulia suddenly leaned precariously over the balustrade to shout, "Alessandro, up here! We're up here!"

Adriana was mortified. "By all that is holy, cease that wailing at once. One would think you had no better manners than a tanner's wife, the way you carry on."

I laughed as I saw Alessandro Farnese looking around in confusion, hearing his name but unsure from whence it came. He finally caught sight of his sister above him, waving; I had met Giulia's older brother once, when he came to visit us before moving to Pisa to study. I thought him rather ordinary compared to Giulia, though he shared her long-lashed eyes, pointed nose, and— I went still. "When did Alessandro arrive?"

"Three days ago." Giulia glanced at me. "Didn't I tell you? I thought I had. Rodrigo—I mean His Holiness—he promised to . . ." She paused, taking in my expression. "Don't even think it. He is not here. You *know* Cesare was forbidden from coming to Rome."

I was no longer listening, already scanning the crowds for my brother. He must be here. How could I have thought he would miss this, no matter what Papa ordered? It was our finest hour, the pinnacle of years of striving, and Cesare and Alessandro were companions in the same seminary at Pisa. If our father had granted leave for Giulia's brother to come to Rome, Cesare must have heard of it. He would have sought the same advantage.

"Lucrezia!" Giulia gripped my shoulder. "There's Juan. Oh, he is a brute, but God save us, there isn't a man here today who can outshine him."

I tore my gaze from the anonymous waving hands and shouting faces, peering through a sudden cascade of rose petals that seemed to materialize out of nowhere. Under that shower of pink and white, Juan rode past us in a mulberry velvet doublet, his broad yellow-slashed sleeves patterned with our bulls in black thread, the sunlight shattering against the inlaid gems of his collar. He clutched a feathered cap in his fist; as he brandished it, he elicited a roar of "Borgia! Borgia!" from the crowd. Tossing his head, his hair rippling past his shoulders, he made the women at the cordons cry out with abandon. He set his gelding to curveting before them, so precise in his control of the reins that his horse barely roused a puff of dust from the road.

I had to smile. The populace went wild, shoving against the barricades. With a grin, Juan reached into a silk pouch at his waist and flung out fistfuls of coins. Even as the people scrambled for his largesse, he cantered onward, followed by his bravos on foot.

Adriana remarked, "He may be beautiful, but he never could learn a lesson. He was nearly killed at my very gates two weeks ago, and still he'd incite a stampede with his theatrics."

I thought my brother magnificent, theatrics or not. Juan had flair, which was one of the reasons Papa favored him. No one knew better how to please the fickle rabble when he had a mind to, his glamour and largesse perfectly timed to ease the taint of savagery that his brutal killing of the man outside the palazzo had engendered.

But my breath actually caught in my throat when, directly after Juan, our father appeared astride a white charger caparisoned in white. Escorted by his retinue of papal guards, Papa wore the triple-tiered azure enamel holy tiara with its teardrop pearls, his robust figure swathed in an ivory-gold chasuble that floated about him like a cloud.

The people knelt. Papa raised a white-gloved hand. Feathered clamor filled the air as pages walking beside him released captive doves from cages. Women began to pray, exultation lightening their careworn faces; men removed their caps in reverence; and children craned their heads eagerly to watch the doves scatter, as bells from all the nearby churches began to toll. I didn't need Giulia to whisper, "He heralds a new age," to understand my father's message.

Rodrigo Borgia was our new pope. Everything was about to change.

Other nobles, papal courtiers, and their personnel followed, until the company disappeared in a fugue of dust. As dirt settled in the air, Adriana rose from her stool. "Come, we must go. Tonight we attend the Vatican feast, and we've only hours to prepare."

I stood reluctantly, unhooking my hand from the balustrade. I hadn't realized I was gripping it; as I felt a sting in my palms from the rough stone, I took another lingering look at the people pushing against the guards, impatient to rush onto the road and scavenge fallen buttons, stray gloves, pieces of ribbon or gilt, anything to take home as a memento.

Following my stare, Giulia sighed. "Lucrezia, I told you. He's not here."

"He should be," I said, without looking away. "I don't understand why Papa insisted that he remain in Pisa when the entire world is here."

"Because if he had invited him, Cesare might never have returned to Pisa. You know how much he detested going there to begin with." Giulia fiddled with her pendant. "Besides, Vannozza wasn't invited, either, and she didn't make a fuss. She has all her taverns to run; with so many visitors in the city, there's money to be made."

"It's not as if she actually serves the tables," I replied, although I was glad my mother had been excluded.

"True. But at least she's not here, devising ways to make us miserable. She was quite beside herself when she realized she'd failed to predict Rodrigo's election," said Giulia smugly, clearly still pleased that she'd been the first among us to glean that momentous news.

"Do you think it's true?" I asked hesitantly, remembering with a shudder how my mother had foretold my own death. "Can she see the future?"

Giulia shrugged. "Evidently not where your father is concerned. Vannozza might look like a *strega,* but all she can see right now is her fury that our time has come, while no one cares about hers anymore."

I forced a smile, but I wasn't so sure. I had lived with my mother; I could recall the winter nights when she sat at the table, laying out her cards. If she couldn't see the future, she certainly thought she could.

"There, now." Giulia pouted. "You are upset. Forget Cesare and your mother; let's go see our new palazzo instead. I hear it's so beautiful, everyone in Rome envies us."

WHEN WE FINALLY arrived in our carriage, we were drenched in perspiration. It had taken hours to push through the rejoicing hordes. But the moment we entered the gates of Santa Maria in Portico, the clamor outside vanished. Here within fortified walls, everything was serene, the celebration beyond our grilled windows muffled by thick brick and mortar.

The palace was enormous, twice the size of Adriana's—a pantheon of polished wood and rose-colored marble. From the large *cortile,* with its decorative fountain and arcade open to an inner garden, we walked into an impressive *sala,* from which forked a warren of intimate *cameras.* Our belongings were stacked everywhere, servants working frantically to set everything in place. The scent of still-damp paint from newly applied frescoes tickled my nostrils. I found myself gazing about in awe while Giulia led me up the staircase to the *piano nobile,* squealing in delight at each discovery.

"Oh, look here, Lucrezia: a privy with cushioned seats *and* drainage!" She peered into the upholstered commode. "No more stink or emptying of chamber pots. Such luxury."

"For the rest of us, perhaps," I said, eyeing her. "You're with child. Don't women in your condition have to urinate a lot? It might be quite a walk from wherever your apartments are."

She pinched my arm—*"Insolente!"*—and proceeded to haul me up to the third floor. Here we encountered more private *appartamenti*, each room flowing into the next, separated by carved cedar doors, with painted ceilings and walls, already set up with our beds, dressing tables, and other necessities.

I found Arancino in my gold-and-blue chamber, meowing in his wicker cage. I rushed to release him. Giulia's voice rang out—"Lucrezia, no. He'll run off!"—just as I undid the latch. He sprang out, slipping and sliding on the polished floor as he fled under my bed.

I looked at Giulia. "See? He knows where he belongs."

"Would that the same might be said of your new betrothed," she retorted.

I slowly rose from my crouch by the cage. "What did you say?"

At that moment, Adriana bustled in. "It's a disaster. It'll take weeks alone to sort through our belongings, and the common rooms aren't even finished yet. There are scaffolds in the *anticameras* and workmen tromping in and out. Whatever was His Holiness thinking to move us here so precipitously? Surely we could have waited until everything was ready."

I glanced at Giulia. Her expression turned icy as Adriana went on, "The staircases alone would strain a horse; and all this paint and dust in the air—it's hardly conducive to a woman in your delicate state."

"I can judge for myself how delicate my state is," Giulia replied. "And I find this palazzo to be perfect. But, if you think it such an inconvenience, I can ask His Holiness to give you leave to return to your own house on Monte Giordano."

Sudden understanding twisted my gut. Adriana had not wanted to move. This magnificent palazzo—it belonged to Giulia, Papa's gift to her. She was mistress here, not me.

"And leave the child to you?" said Adriana. "Heaven forbid."

Giulia glared. Before she could speak, I said quickly, "Let us not argue. I'm sure we'll soon find ourselves at home. It's what Papa wants, isn't it?"

Adriana lowered her eyes. "Indeed."

Giulia arched a triumphant brow. Turning away, Adriana said, "At least these rooms seem to be in order. But wherever is that maid of yours? I specifically instructed her to—"

As if on cue, Pantalisea raced in, red-cheeked from climbing the stairs, her arms full of enameled coffers containing my jewelry and toiletries. "Forgive me, Donna." She curtsied clumsily. "I got lost. This palazzo is so big and . . ." She glanced at the open cage. "Oh, no. I left him here for a moment to go fetch your coffers— Donna, forgive me. I'm afraid he got out."

"No. He's under the bed."

As I retrieved some of the coffers from her, Pantalisea sighed. "I should have watched him more closely, but I didn't want these coffers to go missing."

"Do not worry," I reassured her. "He's a cat. He'll do as he pleases."

Giulia yawned. "Fascinating as this is, I'm exhausted. I must nap awhile." She pecked my cheek. "I'm so happy you like our palazzo. Do tell Rodrigo when you see him tonight."

Her use of my father's name hovered in the air as she walked out. Adriana stared after her. "God save us," she muttered. "*Our* palazzo. And every tongue in Rome wags." She shook her head. "Enough. You too must rest before tonight. Have Pantalisea prepare your gown for the evening. And you"—she jabbed her finger at my maid—"best not get lost again. You are not irreplaceable; we've a hundred noble girls in Rome desperate to serve His Holiness's daughter."

Adriana marched out. As soon as she left, Pantalisea said anxiously, "You'll not see me replaced, my lady?"

"Of course not. Pay her no mind. You know how she hates disorder." I smiled. I was fond of Pantalisea. She served me alone, and loyalty was a quality I must value, as it seemed we were indeed about to live under Giulia Farnese's roof.

"Oh, thank you, my lady. Shall I air out your gown?"

"If you can find it," I said, as we turned to regard the travel chests piled in the corners. We began to unpack, arranging my clothing in the cedar and walnut *cassones*, which protected delicate items from night moths and damp. Little Murilla arrived as we were wrestling with my bed hangings. Together, we managed to heave the damask over the tester, Murilla balanced precariously on a footstool until she tipped it over and tumbled off. Laughing, we leapt onto the bed and threw the pillows at one another until we lay tangled in a heap.

"I'm hungry," I said absently, gazing up at the lopsided canopy. Murilla ran off to fetch food from the kitchens, while Pantalisea and I finished sorting through my belongings, searching for the right sleeves for tonight's gown.

Yet even as I reveled in my surroundings, I did not forget Giulia's offhanded remark about my betrothal or the disquieting sensation that, once again, she knew more about my future than I did.

How long was I supposed to dwell in her shadow?

CHAPTER SIX

The *Sala Reale,* the Vatican's great reception hall, was crowded with guests who had gathered for Papa's celebratory feast. Serene lute music drifted over the assembly, and hundreds of golden candelabra made everything shimmer. This saffron-drenched dream was dominated by my father in his white robes, seated on the dais and accepting congratulations from ambassadors sent by Venice, Florence, Naples, and Milan, as well as the various kingdoms of Europe. At the edges of the hall stood the papal guard, their stony eyes seeming not to see the conniving nobility with their families. Linen-draped tables offered succulent roast boar with applesauce and rosemary; poached pheasant eggs in sweet cream; pickled venison with spicy cloves; and peacock baked with truffles. Pages carrying large silver ewers poured wines from Lombardy and Tuscany into painted majolica goblets; I saw several noblewomen stashing these goblets in their skirts with unabashed cupidity, as keepsakes.

Papa radiated goodwill. With his enthronement behind him—a tedious ritual, which had turned so protracted that he fainted, prompting panic among the faithful—he was now surrounded by those things in life he loved best: rich wine and food, music, laughter, and good company.

Giulia, in turn, looked as though she might never smile again. She had spent hours at her glass, debating her choice of attire before she settled on mauve silk and rubies. Yet as stunning as she looked, she was relegated to the background, charged to act as my chaperone while Adriana entertained the noble matrons. Not that Giulia paid me any mind; she couldn't take her gaze off my father. When he left the hall, she paced until he returned dressed in a black Castilian doublet with a gored skirt, which enhanced his stature and minimized his girth; her eyes stalked him as he roamed the hall with Juan, clapping cardinals on the back and greeting guests by name, showing off his astonishing memory for personal details.

"Look at him," she seethed. "Strutting about in his Spanish velvets while those sows of Rome shove their daughters at him as though he were in need of a harem."

"He must be attentive," I said, watching Papa nod indulgently as each blushing offering was pushed forward to drop in a puddle of silk at his feet. Resplendent in azure damask at his side, Juan also assessed the girls with a practiced eye. Behind him, his companion Prince Djem ran his tongue over his lips as if he were considering devouring the girls for supper.

"Attentive?" Giulia's laughter was brittle. "Honestly, Lucrezia, not even you can be so naïve."

I frowned at her, unsure of her meaning. I'd seen my father and brother charm their way through a crowded hall countless times before. Women invariably reacted to them; how could they not? Giulia, however, interpreted it differently, for without warning she let out a burst of high-pitched laughter and cried, "Why, Lucrezia, how very *amusing* of you!"

I gaped. I had said nothing, and her outburst was so shrill, she made everyone around us stare. A murmur rippled through the crowd, moving like the invisible crest of a wave, past the bishops and nobles and condottiere, all the way to where Papa stood.

He raised his eyes. Juan scowled as Giulia feigned surprise when Papa crooked his finger. I whispered, "I think he heard you," and with a false gesture of startled delight, she clasped my hand and brought us to my father. By this time, I had to clench my teeth to stop myself from laughing at her absurdity. Papa beamed, kissing my cheek and exuding a heady aroma of wine. Giulia rested a bejeweled hand on his arm, whispering in his ear as he led her forth, while I tarried a short distance behind with Juan.

"He should have ordered that bitch to stay in her kennel," my brother growled. "Must we suffer her on the very night of our family's greatest triumph?"

I glanced at Djem, who returned my stare with baleful eyes. "Some might say the same of your Turk," I remarked, not caring if his servant overheard.

"Djem is my companion," he retorted. "He goes wherever I do."

I was about to reply that no doubt Papa thought the same of Giulia, when out of the corner of my eye I caught sight of an unexpected figure leaning against a frescoed far wall, so still he might have emerged from the mural itself, clothed in smoke-darkened pigments.

My heart leapt.

Laughter crashed around me, drowning out the minstrels in the gallery. The hall was full to overflowing, guests spilling into the courtyard. I heard everything as if through a shell, staring at quicksilver flashes of skirts and robes, thinking I must have imagined it. Then I caught sight of the figure again, still at the wall, a large cap shading his features. Even before he reached up to tilt the cap back, his name was on my lips: "Cesare."

He turned heel, moving swiftly away.

Juan paused. "Did you say something?"

"No. I thought . . . it was nothing." I made myself swipe a hand across my brow. "It is so hot in here. I think I'll go into the gardens for a moment. Will you accompany me?"

"Now?" he scoffed. "I'm not leaving Papa alone with that she-wolf."

"Then I'll return soon, yes?" Before he could detain me, I plunged into the crowd.

I could barely see my way as I weaved past clusters of gossiping officials and inebriated nobles, out of the *sala's* double doors into the torchlit passageway. I quickened my steps, seeing the slim figure in black ahead; he moved as he always did, with single-minded purpose, so that I practically had to run to keep up with him, kicking against the weight of my skirts.

He traversed the gardens, sidestepping the lichen-stained statues of long-dead emperors scattered about like bones. The horseshoe spread of the Apostolic Palace reverberated behind me, its clamor growing fainter as I followed his striding figure down the pebbled path.

He came to a halt near the outer walls, under a copse of wind-sculpted cypress. Whipping off his cap, he turned to face me. He did not speak, staring at me as if I were a stranger. He looked too thin in his unadorned clothes, but, still, I reveled at the sight of his startling feline-green eyes under his red-gold brows, his supple mouth and long nose, his pale skin stretched over his angular cheekbones like hollowed silk. But where once his wealth of copper curls had sprung in disarray, shorn stubble now delineated his skull.

"You cut off all your beautiful hair," I exclaimed.

"We have lice in Pisa." His voice was soft, his gaze scouring. I'd opted for blue satin with a gold stomacher. At Giulia's insistence, I even forwent the discreet under-*camicia* favored by adolescent girls and adorned my bare throat with a pearl necklace. I had thought I looked sophisticated when I admired myself in the glass, taking covert pleasure in the slight hint of breast accentuated by my bodice, but now, before my brother's scrutiny, I had to curb the impulse to yank my bulky sleeves higher onto my shoulders.

"I hardly recognized you. Where has *petita meva* Lucia gone?" He used the Catalan nickname he'd given me when we were children, making me sigh in relief. He had looked so angry that I thought he meant to chastise me.

"Don't be silly. You knew me at once, just as I did you. It hasn't been that long, Cesare."

He took a step closer. "It's been long enough. I waited for a letter from you. When nothing came, I feared the worst. I now see that I had every reason."

I laughed. "What did you fear?"

"That Papa had seen you married and sent away to Spain."

"You thought I'd leave without telling you?" I was incredulous.

"Why not? When it comes to our family, it seems I'm the last to be invited—if I'm invited at all."

I gazed into his eyes. I expected to find hurt there, genuine sorrow that he'd been ignored, left to glean the news in Pisa. Instead, I found them shining with his habitual mischief.

"You're teasing me!"

He could not curb that special smile he reserved only for me. He'd rarely smiled even as a boy; Papa often grumbled he was more like a changeling than any son of his, but with me, he smiled often, and it was warm, inviting. It transformed his face from one of austerity to boyish appeal, making him look younger than his seventeen years. Cesare had been my lodestone growing up, the one I always turned to after my mother harangued me for some offense or Juan yanked my braid until my scalp burned.

"Did *you* actually believe I'd let them marry you without my knowledge?" he now said. "I may be ignored, but I'm not without my resources."

"Yes, Mama no doubt being first among them." But I was smiling, too, overjoyed that we were together again. "I'm sorry I didn't write, but Papa forbade it. He said I had to let you be until he summoned you."

"I forgive you," he said, and he reached into his doublet, withdrawing a package. "But if you cannot do what is forbidden, then I suppose that means I mustn't give you this?"

I gasped. "What is it? Let me see! Is it more poems by Petrarch?"

"Better," he replied, but as I reached for the package, he leapt backward in an elegant motion, dangling the book above me. "First you must earn it. Remember how we used to barter when we were children? I gave you a book and you gave me . . . ?"

I burst out laughing. "A dance!"

"Indeed. In Pisa, all we have besides lice is stale bread and prayer—lots and lots of prayer. I rarely enjoy life anymore, much less with my pretty sister." He clasped his hands at his chest, adopting a forlorn stance. "Will you dance with me, my Lucia?"

"Here?" I said, but I was already looking over my shoulder, determining if we were far enough from the palace to not be overseen. "If I do, will you give me that book?"

"Yes!" He grabbed my hand. "I will, though you and everyone else saw fit to ignore me." His arms snaked about my waist, gliding me farther under the trees, our feet crunching over old rubble embedded in the earth as he guided me into the steps of a *pavane*. "No one spared a thought for me," he said, "forced to live in a seminary and share my cell with a farting Medici roommate, nor"—he lifted his voice as I laughed again—"did anyone consider that our father would give Alessandro Farnese a cardinal's hat because of the favors of his wanton sister, while I, a Borgia born, am forbidden to even set foot in Rome?"

I came to an abrupt halt. "You know . . . about Papa and Giulia?"

"Alas. As I said, I have my resources."

I reached out to caress the subtle growth of beard on his cheek. "Does it upset you?"

He gave me a contemplative look. "Should it?"

"I suppose not," I replied, though I'd hoped for a different reaction. If it had upset me, how could it not upset him?

Cesare extended the package. "Open your gift. I brought it all the way from Pisa and kept it hidden from Mama when I arrived. She went through my baggage, as she always does, insisting on washing my dirty hose herself."

I immediately tore open the package, scattering its plain paper wrapping to peer at a book cover made of red-tooled leather. Opening it to the frontispiece, I breathed, *The Decameron.* I looked up. "This is forbidden at the convent. The nuns say Boccaccio is a pagan who extols the pleasures of the flesh over the virtues of the spirit."

Cesare grimaced. "We call her Mother Church for a reason. Just like Vannozza, she likes nothing more than to forbid us knowledge. Best hide it from Adriana, too. She won't approve."

I embraced him. "Thank you, Cesare. I'll treasure it." Although his clothing made him appear gaunt, I felt a lean body underneath, forged of sinew and muscle. Despite his alleged boredom in Pisa, he clearly had not been neglecting his athletic pursuits.

He thawed in my arms. Then he said, "You do realize nothing that has happened can change my fate? Even though Papa now sits on the throne of St. Peter, he'd still grant Juan everything that should by right belong to me."

My stomach sank. I drew back. "Is this why you have come?" When he did not answer, I said, "Cesare, you mustn't make trouble for Papa. You know what he's said—"

"Yes, yes. The Spanish duchy of Gandia is not mine. Queen Isabella and King Fernando bestowed it on our older brother for his valor, but Pedro was killed during their crusade against the Moors, and Gandia belongs to whomever Papa sees fit. I know. I've heard it all before."

"Have you? Because you've never said you agree."

"I don't. But Mama told me Papa has petitioned Queen Isabella to give the title to Juan." His voice tightened. "Five years I have waited, ever since Pedro perished. Five years for Papa to heed reason and acknowledge that what was once his primogeniture's must now go to me, as his second eldest. He does not accept how undeserving Juan is, how unworthy to become a grandee of Spain. All he sees is that Juan must be indulged, while I must sacrifice myself to the Church."

"So you *are* here to fight Juan for the duchy," I said in dismay.

If I'd never been close to Juan, my brothers had always been like foes, their incessant squabbles marring our childhood. Cesare had been an exemplary student, while Juan, keenly aware of his deficiencies when it came to books, dedicated himself to mastering the sword and the bow. But Cesare also excelled in physical feats, so that they were forever challenging each other, wielding staves or wrestling, until it escalated into fighting and blackened eyes. Our mother had been forced to separate them many times, while I did my best to restore an uneasy stalemate by begging them to play with me instead. I had thought it was my fault. I hated to see them at odds, thinking it was because Juan knew I loved Cesare more. But as I grew older, I came to understand that their hostility ran deeper. They were strangers to each other, antithetical in every way, rivals who did not seem to have come from the same womb.

Cesare's smile was bitter. "Fighting him will avail me nothing. Juan has no ambition for himself; he couldn't care less about that duchy. If he had his way, he'd do nothing but tumble wenches and drink himself into a stupor. He only does as Papa tells him."

"Then you won't cause trouble?" I watched his expression. He had perfected the ability to disguise his thoughts; of the three of us, Cesare had been the first to learn that the less he revealed, the less vulnerable he was. "You know how Papa hates it when you and Juan are at each other's throats. And he's our Supreme Pontiff now. He can't afford a scandal."

"No, not more than the one he already has," replied Cesare, startling me. "And while we're on the subject, do you enjoy sharing a palazzo with la Farnese? Are you as eager as Papa to welcome her babe into our family?"

He also knew about Giulia's pregnancy. Of course he did. Vannozza had told him. I couldn't keep the bite from my tone. "Papa says he loves her. He wants me to think of her as a sister."

"Ah. And do you?"

"I did. Only in the past weeks . . . Cesare, there's something about her I do not trust."

"Nor should you. Under that carefree air, you always were astute, my Lucia." He suddenly raised his chin, looking past me. "We have company."

I reeled about to see Juan striding toward us, bulling his way through shafts of moonlight. Cesare stepped forth. "Brother, such an unexpected pleasure."

Juan's eyes were slits. He reeked of overindulgence, as if he'd dunked himself in a wine vat. "Djem told me Lucrezia saw you in the hall. I didn't believe him at first. You are fortunate Papa sent me rather than one of his retainers to fetch her. He'd be furious."

"Who?" Cesare lilted. "The retainer or Papa?"

"You know what I mean! Or did you not receive Papa's message to stay in Pisa?"

"Oh, I received it. But I saw no reason to deprive myself of a visit, given the occasion." Cesare's smile cut across his mouth. "You certainly have cause to rejoice. Our father is now pope and I understand you're soon to be made duke of Gandia. Congratulations. Does this mean we can look forward to the privilege of seeing you to Spain?"

"Who told you that?" Juan demanded. Then, as he took in Cesare's unblinking stare, he sneered, "Mama. She never could keep her mouth shut. Yes, I'm to be made duke once the deed arrives from Castile. What of it? Are you here to challenge me?"

As Juan squared his shoulders, I had a sickening recollection of him hacking the man outside Adriana's palazzo. He was taller, brawnier, than Cesare. My brothers were not so evenly matched anymore when it came to sheer strength; indeed, Cesare looked undernourished next to Juan's robust build. But what Cesare lacked in heft, he made up for in stealth.

Just as I began to anticipate one of them yanking out a weapon, Cesare said quietly, "If Papa has seen fit to give you the honor, who am I to question it?"

I saw at once that his words only increased Juan's suspicion. Juan might be indolent, slow to grasp a certain kind of wit, but he knew as well as I did that the duchy of Gandia was Cesare's last hope to escape the priesthood. With its vast estate near Valencia in Spain, seat of our family's roots, the duchy would make whoever claimed it a wealthy grandee.

Juan worked something between his teeth. He spat a bit of gristle at Cesare's feet. "Do you think me a fool? Gone are the days when you could point out all the errors in my grammar. I don't believe for a moment that after all these years you're prepared to relinquish Gandia."

"Believe what you like," said Cesare. "I hardly see a need to explain myself to you."

As they locked eyes, I interjected nervously, "You mustn't fight."

"I have no intention of fighting," said Cesare. "I'd not wish to be the cause of any disturbance in our family, not at this glorious time."

"As if a cleric in skirts could disturb anything," sneered Juan.

"I'm not in skirts yet." Cesare turned to me. His lips were cold as he kissed my cheek. "Good night, Lucrezia." He looked at Juan. "I trust you'll see our sister safely back?" He didn't await a response. Tugging his cloak about him, he walked away, disappearing into the shadows.

Desolation overcame me. He was alone, without a servant or even a torch to light his path as he journeyed back to our mother's home on the Esquiline, through the city teeming with drunkards, thieves, and ruffians. Concern for him sharpened my voice as I whirled to Juan.

"I hope you are satisfied."

He gave me a befuddled look. "What?"

"You heard me. I hope you're satisfied now that you've humiliated him with that duchy. Is it not enough that he's forced to become a priest, and must slink around instead of being invited into the Vatican to be with us as he should?"

"How is that my fault? I didn't order him to stay away; it was Papa's decision. He thought Cesare would seize the opportunity to renounce his studies at the seminary." Juan gazed toward where Cesare had vanished. "I must admit, he took it well. Maybe our proud brother has finally realized that, like the rest of us, he must do as he is told."

I resisted rolling my eyes. As usual, Juan was oblivious. No matter how it may have appeared, Cesare had *not* taken it well. Indeed, I feared that their encounter marked a new turn in their rivalry, but my worries faded when Juan abruptly shifted his gaze to me. My skin crawled. His eyes were cold; he suddenly did not seem drunk at all.

"You shouldn't have come after him. Papa may choose to lodge you with his whore for the time being, but you are still his daughter. What would your betrothed think if he knew you roamed the Vatican gardens like a stray cat?"

"There was no harm in it," I retorted. "Besides, I no longer have a betrothed."

"Oh? Papa may no longer deem a noble of Valencia suitable, but you do indeed still have a betrothed. His name is Giovanni Sforza, Count of Pesaro."

I went still. "I . . . I have not heard that."

"Because no one knows yet, except Papa, me, and that Farnese bitch, I suppose. It was part of the agreement we made with Cardinal Sforza, in exchange for his support in the conclave. He cast the deciding vote for Papa. We must return the favor."

I was stunned. Was *this* what Giulia had meant?

"Until I'm told otherwise, I am still not betrothed." I lifted my chin. Juan always delighted in bullying me; I could still remember the day he'd crushed a newborn kitten under his heel in front of me just to see if I would cry. Cesare had thrashed him until our mother came running; Juan still bore the scar above his left eyebrow from where Cesare split the skin with his knuckles.

Juan guffawed. "I think our precious virgin sister thinks rather highly of herself."

I tried to move around him. He shifted, blocking my way. "Though I'm starting to believe you're less virginal than we think. You enjoyed watching me kill the other day, didn't you? It must have excited you: all that blood . . ."

All of a sudden he seemed enormous, a barbican of flesh standing between me and the palace. Even as I thought we were alone, far enough away that my screams would go unheard, I knew any display of fear would only provoke him.

"Papa is waiting for me. He sent you to fetch me, remember?"

"Let him wait." He set himself before me, hands on his hips. "I saved you from the mob, so you owe me a reward. Cesare always asked for a dance. Well, I demand a kiss."

Despite his intimidating stance, I was relieved to hear familiar petulance in his voice. It was more of the same, yet another point to be scored in his ongoing rivalry with Cesare. I was not about to concede. "You're a boor." I turned about. "I'll go by myself."

I felt him lunge at me from behind, grabbing my shoulders and forcing me around. "A kiss," he snarled. "Or I'll tell Papa that Cesare was here and you indulged him."

I glared at him. "I most certainly will not. Go kiss a serving maid, if you have such need."

His hands tightened on me, his teeth bared. I had seen that look on his face before—most recently, just before he slaughtered a man. Thinking I'd rather submit than endure this vicious squabble, I gritted my teeth, rising on my tiptoes to kiss his cheek. But he swerved, pressing my lips with his wine-soured mouth. I yanked away from him, enraged. Without thinking, I struck him across the face as hard as I could.

"Beast! If you don't leave me alone this instant, I'm the one who shall tell Papa."

The imprint of my fingers reddened his skin. I braced for his rage, but he only stepped aside with a callous bow. As I inched past him, he said, "You shouldn't feel too bad for our brother. Once Cesare takes his vows, Papa is going to grant him his own cardinalship of Valencia. We cannot keep it now that he's pope, and we need someone in the family to retain its revenues. Perhaps we'll be seeing Cesare off to Spain instead."

"He doesn't need to go to Spain to be a cardinal," I replied icily. "Papa never did."

Without another word, I proceeded to the palace. Though I did not glance back, I could feel Juan's stare following me and hear his coarse mocking laughter.

I hoped he was wrong. I hoped he would be the one sent to Spain.

And I hoped he would never return.

CHAPTER SEVEN

"Donna Lucrezia, you must stand still. How can we get this bodice fitted if you don't stop fidgeting?" The head seamstress let out a frustrated sigh as she motioned to the two apprentices beside the footstool where I perched in my shift, each of the girls armed with sections of my half-finished bodice and little satin cushions bristling with pins.

"Yes." Giulia sighed. "Do let them finish. I have a headache." She occupied an upholstered settle, the nursemaid nearby suckling Giulia's two-month-old daughter, Laura. Since the birth in March of the new year—after a seemingly interminable gestation—Giulia had fallen into a lassitude that kept her confined in Santa Maria, waiting for Papa to visit, though his schedule was so full that he often could only send tokens of love in his stead, belts and shoes and sleeves and jewels, which she left lying about the palazzo, making Adriana glower.

"It's midday." As I eyed the babe at the nursemaid's nipple, my stomach rumbled. "I'm famished. Besides, why should Giovanni Sforza care what I wear? We're already wed."

"Only by proxy. Your actual wedding day is what matters the most. I think you'd want to look your best, if only for your father's sake. Just think—" Giulia slid her gaze to me. "If His Holiness hadn't negotiated this new marriage for you with the Sforza, you might have wed one of King Ferrante of Naples's sons instead and gone to live among the corpses."

I shuddered. Tales of King Ferrante's depravity had flooded Rome the moment the Neapolitan envoys arrived to propose a marriage treaty. The ruling dynasty of Naples was descended from the Spanish kingdom of Aragon and upheld by Queen Isabella and King Fernando, newly titled the Catholic monarchs by Papa. But King Ferrante had supported Cardinal della Rovere against my father in the conclave, betraying himself as an enemy; only now Naples's bid for reconciliation had so terrified della Rovere that the cardinal had fled Rome for his castle at Ostia—an exodus Papa welcomed. Still, judging by the accounts, Ferrante of Naples was an evil man, who kept the embalmed bodies of his executed foes in a cellar under his castle, where he liked to visit them and gloat. When Giulia had taunted me with the news that Papa was considering whether we'd be best served by betrothing me to Naples, I was so alarmed that I went directly to him, barging into the study where he sat in the afternoon to review his correspondence.

"I thought I was marrying a Sforza!" I blurted out. "Are you now planning to send me to Naples instead? What if King Ferrante doesn't like me and puts *me* in his cellar?"

Papa laughed. "Oh, my *farfallina*. Come here." He patted his lap, though I was too old now for such childish indulgence. I perched on his large thigh, anyway, staring at him as he toyed with my necklace and murmured, "You mustn't heed common gossip."

"But what if that common gossip is true? Everyone says he keeps corpses in his cellar."

He sighed. "Has Giulia been needling you again? Women with child: They grow so bored with confinement, they resort to petty amusements. Yes, you will marry a Sforza. I have no intention of sending you to Naples. Heaven forbid. Ferrante is indeed an old vulture, who only seeks our favor because we won the throne, but he'll turn on us quick enough if he gleans another advantage. You mustn't fret. I'd kiss Lucifer before I entrusted a child of mine to him. It's politics. We must seem to welcome his envoys, if only for appearance's sake."

Still, as I now recalled how easily my first betrothal had been annulled, I stood quiescent as the seamstress and her apprentices finished fitting my wedding costume. Better to endure a few hours being poked and prodded than risk becoming King Ferrante's daughter by marriage.

Outside the window, spring beckoned. The winter had been mild, even if we'd spent the Nativity season huddled over braziers, as the palazzo fireplaces had turned out to be more decorative than functional. While Giulia hibernated in her lavish apartments, I rejoiced in her absence, as it left me alone to be introduced publicly as my father's daughter.

Contrary to my mother's assertion that a pope could not keep an unwed daughter about, Papa had delighted in seeing me act as his unofficial ambassador. Together with Adriana—who had recaptured her oversight of me as Giulia's pregnancy advanced—I welcomed envoys from all over Europe and Italy's city-states, who presented me with gifts and requested my assistance. Sometimes they desired entry into the Church for a second son or a cardinal's hat for a nephew; for others, it was arbitration over a land or title dispute. Naturally, I had no power to approve anything, but Adriana took careful notes and later presented them to Papa. Soon, word traveled that the gates of Santa Maria in Portico were the portal through which those who sought favor with His Holiness must pass, and my pile of treasures grew to such an extent, it eventually stirred Giulia from her indolence.

One evening she traipsed into the *sala* as I entertained Alfonso d'Este, son of the duke of Ferrara—a sullen youth, with a preposterous nose and coarse features, who had brought me a falcon. As I warily beheld the hooded bird perched on a pole held by a page wearing padded leather and gauntlets, envisioning what such a sharp beak might do to my Arancino, I wondered if my lord d'Este realized that while women hunted, girls of my age did not. I'd been entertaining him with conversation, trying to find a polite way of informing him that I could not possibly accept his gift, when Giulia arrived, her belly jutting before her, draped in burgundy velvet, and her hair done up in a jeweled caul.

Alfonso d'Este's eyes widened. Standing before the rose-marble hearth (one of the few that actually worked), Giulia shivered in exaggeration. "Oh, it is cold! I fear it might snow."

It was on the tip of my tongue to remind her that it rarely snowed in Rome, but my voice choked as she removed her caul to let her hair tumble about her shoulders. "I washed it this morning," she simpered. "But it takes forever to dry."

I thought I'd enjoy pushing her into that fire. Sitting nearby in an alcove where she acted as my chaperone, Adriana let out a scandalized gasp. Married women, particularly pregnant ones, did not show off their tresses like courtesans.

My lord d'Este could only stare. As I observed keen interest overcome his face—like a cat spotting delectable prey—I excused myself. He had come to see *me*. Bolting upstairs to rummage through my *cas-*

sones with Pantalisea, I returned within the hour to find Giulia giggling over a goblet of wine with the ducal son. I entered on measured steps, my newly donned violet *camora* swishing about my ankles, my own thick fair locks loose under a ruby-studded filet.

He sighed. "There can be no moon without the sun," he said, with unexpected gallantry, and Giulia glowered. After that, she insisted on attending every visit with me, no matter how tedious, enduring the presentation of everything from bolts of samite from the Holy Land to casks of amontillado from Spain and fresh carp from Lake Garda, until the pangs overcame her and she had to enter her birthing chamber, lest she release her child in full view of our guests.

"She envies you," Adriana had told me. "She fears the loss of her beauty and your father's affection. Now that she's given birth, she is a mother like Vannozza, while you, my child, remain pure as an angel."

A dark glow sparked in me at the thought of Giulia's envy. But with the announcement of my own betrothal to Giovanni Sforza, Papa had his secretary direct visiting envoys to his office, until I found myself in my current state—perched on a stool, my legs and arms bruised from the overzealous seamstress, while Giulia, despite her lengthy convalescence, showed no sign of having lost a shred of her allure.

Footsteps coming down the corridor turned my face toward the door. Before he had even crossed the threshold, we all knew who it was, especially Giulia, who managed to snatch her babe from the nursemaid and arrange herself on the settle in time for Papa's entrance.

He had ordered a private passage built between our palazzo and the Sistine, so he could visit us no matter the hour, but it had been weeks since he last used it. His arrival was like a burst of sun-washed cloud—his ermine-lined cape, shoes, cassock, and even his skullcap made of ivory satin, so that the flush in his olive complexion turned ruddy and his eyes gleamed ebony-black. Beaming at the seamstress and her apprentices as they curtsied, he patted Murilla on her turbaned head and then leaned down to kiss Giulia. She thrust little Laura at him—an ill-timed move, for the child let out a wail.

"She's grown since you last saw her," Giulia said.

"So it seems." Papa hesitated. I was surprised he did not kiss the babe, making instead a vague blessing motion over her. I wondered at his disinterest, after he'd taken such a stance about his happiness. Did he regret it? Was he disappointed, perhaps, that she had delivered a mewling girl? Much as I hoped so, for it meant I remained his only *farfallina,* it was still strange; surely Papa must love this child? Not for the first time, I wished Adriana were here to offer an explanation. But she had returned to Monte Giordano shortly after the birth, declaring she had neglected her palazzo but more likely because she was weary of Giulia.

Papa held out his arms to me. "What? No welcome for your old father?" and I leapt from the footstool into his embrace. "My *farfallina,*" he murmured. "Look at you: a bride-to-be. How time passes. It seems only yesterday you were playing with kittens." As he held me, I peered past his bulk to the doorway, where his ubiquitous retainers had congregated. I caught a strange, shared look on their faces. My father's favorite attendant, handsome dark-eyed Pedro Calderon, whom Papa had affectionately dubbed Perotto, hurried forth to retrieve my robe from where it lay crumpled by the stool. He draped it over my shoulders.

"Why, thank you, Perotto," I said. Then, as my father drew back, I saw Giulia staring at me. I pulled the robe closer about me, awkwardly fastening the clasp at my waist.

I had just touched my father with only my shift between my skin and his sacred person.

At the doorway, Cardinal Ascanio Sforza sniffed. He was my bridegroom's cousin, a sleek man in red satin. His slim build and indifferent expression were deceptive; I had the sense he could be brutal and that his mild brown gaze took in more than he cared to reveal.

"And to what do we owe this pleasure?" I heard Giulia ask. She gave Laura back to the wet nurse, all smiles as she rose from the settle to hook her arm in Papa's. "It's been so long; I do trust Your Holiness can stay for supper. We'll dine al fresco on the terrace. Our gardens are finished and so beautiful, aren't they, Lucrezia?" She did not look at me as she spoke, her entire being focused on Papa. "You should see for yourself what your generosity has sown. And I have fresh melon and blackfoot ham, imported especially for you from Spain."

"Oh?" Papa moistened his lips. "A nice ham would be lovely. Alas," he said, "I'm here to see Lucrezia. I promised to take a walk with her today."

He had not promised anything of the sort, and Giulia knew it. She froze as if he'd just announced she was to be evicted. Before Giulia could speak, Cardinal Sforza said, "I'd be honored to accompany Donna Lucrezia. That way, Your Holiness needn't forgo the ham. Or the lovely lady, of course," he added, with a suave nod at Giulia.

"That sounds perfect." Giulia tightened her grip on Papa's sleeve. "Lucrezia understands. Don't you, my dear?"

Again, she didn't look at me. I found myself answering, "Yes, you must stay, Holiness. You haven't had time to spend with—"

"Then it's settled." With a preemptive flip of her wrist, Giulia sent everyone except Perotto and me from the room. Looking bewildered, Papa let me peck his cheek. "I'll make it up to you later," he whispered, and Perotto and I followed the others into the corridor.

I said to Cardinal Sforza, "Thank you for your offer, Eminence, but I expect you have more-important business to attend to."

"Oh, no," he replied. "I must insist. Please change into something fit for a short ride through the city, my lady. Perotto, please accompany Donna Lucrezia and see that she meets us in the courtyard in, shall we say, half an hour?" His smile did not touch his eyes. "His Holiness has prepared a special surprise for you."

Excited, I ran up to my rooms to change. I knew I must bring Pantalisea with me, as Adriana had insisted that I not venture anywhere outside the palazzo without her. After I hastily dressed in a gown of light silk and a hooded cloak, we hurried into the *cortile* with Perotto.

The echo of hammering and shouting workmen issued from the proximity of the Apostolic Palace, where Papa had begun his refurbishments. Cardinal Sforza waited on horseback beside a covered litter and armed escort. Pantalisea glanced at Perotto as he assisted us into the litter. He averted his gaze, flushing to the roots of his tousled black hair.

"He likes you," I teased as we settled on the cushions and the litter jerked forward. "And I think you like him, too. It's not the first time I've seen you make eyes at each other."

"He is comely." Pantalisea peeped through the litter curtains. "Is he of good birth?"

"I believe so," I said absently, though I had no idea. "Part those curtains more." I too was eager to have a view, but not of Perotto, who rode on horseback beside us. I wanted to see Rome. I rarely had the chance to visit the city on my own, and less so since my father became its ruler.

Leaving the Vatican, we skirted the murky Tiber and took the road abutting the old city wall. Bell towers and church spires punctuated every turn. All of a sudden, cacophony surrounded us, as we entered the narrow stone-paved streets. Overhead, drying laundry and jutting balconies hung like a makeshift web. The lowing of livestock being driven to slaughter was a constant ululation against the chattering of goodwives on their door stoops, shrieking children at play, the imploration of vagabonds in corners, and calls of vendors offering everything from relics to tableware. Clerics and nobles on horseback, surrounded by bravos, cantered past with imperious disregard for whomever they trampled. Packs of feral dogs fought over discarded leavings, while hogs rooted in the gutters. The stench of waste and troughs of slimy water brewed a putrid miasma in the air. Everything was loud, filthy, and dangerous.

I adored it.

Rome was my city. My home.

Veering past the market on the west bank, we penetrated the maze of the Trastevere, where affluent merchants resided in fortified palazzos beside tanneries, wine shops, inns, and brothels. As the litter swayed while our bearers navigated the labyrinthine streets, Pantalisea said, "Why on earth are we coming here? Only Jews and thieves reside in this district."

"And rich people," I pointed out. We halted before one of the palazzos—a grim, crenellated structure with an imposing tower and brass-studded gates. As Perotto helped us out, Cardinal Sforza dismounted and the stout gates swung open to dislodge a swarm of pages, who took charge of the horses and litter while we proceeded inside.

A wisteria-hung loggia hugged the main *cortile*, in which pruned trees in ceramic pots held vigil over a fountain. I pushed my hood back, taking in the affluent neglect as well as the band of men loitering in the arcade. Several turned to stare; to my eye, they had the air of hired bravos, like those who surrounded Juan—an observation soon confirmed when one strolled over and bowed.

"Donna Lucrezia, *benvingut.*" He spoke in Catalan, surprising me. He was wiry, though ostentatiously dressed in typical mercenary fashion—his leather doublet caught at the waist with a looped belt dangling a dagger sheath and purse, the ostentatious lacework of his shirt exposed at wrist and neck, his boots sporting wide scalloped edges designed to conceal small weapons. He had strange eyes, neither blue nor gray but a subtle color in between, like dusk. Dark hair curled around his cap. He wasn't handsome. The scar of a crude harelip marred him, twisting his mouth, but he had a certain desultory charm about him as he said, "I am Miguel de Corella, newly arrived from Valencia to serve my lord. You may call me Michelotto. I am at my lady's service."

He had switched to Italian, prompting Cardinal Sforza to say irritably, "And where is your lord, pray tell? Word of our arrival was sent in advance."

"He awaits upstairs," replied Michelotto, but as the cardinal started toward a nearby staircase, he added, "However, he wishes a moment in private with my lady. Refreshments have been readied in the hall, Your Eminence." With a suavity that rivaled the cardinal's, Michelotto stepped between Sforza and the stairs, his touch on my arm so light, I almost didn't feel it.

I gave Pantalisea a reassuring smile, beckoning Perotto. "See that she's not left alone," I told him. He flushed; as I had thought, he had a soft spot for my maidservant.

With Michelotto behind me, I climbed to the second floor, where an upper gallery with painted eaves bordered the living quarters. It was evident that whoever resided here had only recently moved in. Packing straw littered the corridors, along with empty coffers and upended crates; it also must be someone of wealth, judging by the tapestries half-rolled over the walls of the *sala* and woven Turkish carpets on the tables and sideboards.

Michelotto poured claret from a silver flagon. As he handed me the goblet, I said, "May I ask to whom I owe this honor?"

His grimace of a smile tugged his scar. With a slight bow, he backed out of the room.

"Lucia."

I spun about. I could hardly believe my eyes as Cesare walked toward me.

The rounded neckline of his shirt was low about his throat, his black velvet doublet fitted to his body; I saw at once that he had gained weight. He was also growing out his hair. Short dark-red curls were tousled about his head, like those of a Botticelli cherub.

"You're back in Rome!" I exclaimed. "Why did you not tell me?"

"I wanted to surprise you." He motioned about the room. "Do you like my new palazzo?"

"It needs some improvements," I heard myself say, and I winced. It certainly wasn't Santa Maria in Portico, as he must realize. The tile floor was cracked in several places, and there were moisture stains in the corners of the ceiling.

Cesare chuckled. "It does. Are you disappointed?"

"No," I said quickly. "It's beautiful. But how long have you been here?"

"Almost a month—" He ducked as I swiped my hand at him. "Now, now." He smiled. "I wanted to tell you sooner, but Papa insisted I keep it a secret until everything was arranged."

"Arranged?" I stamped my foot. "Exactly what was so secret that I couldn't know my own brother had a palazzo in Rome?" I glared at him, but my remonstrance faded when he lowered his head to my eye level and I caught sight of the small shorn circle on his scalp.

"You took your vows. . . ." Inexplicably, sorrow overwhelmed me.

"Oh, none of that. I had to satisfy the requirements for assuming a new archbishopric and Papa's cardinalship of Valencia. I must *appear* worthy to don the sacred hat."

I blinked back tears. "Are you happy?"

He shrugged. "If happiness means an annual income of forty thousand ducats, I can hardly complain. And it bought me this"—he stretched out his arms—"a slightly used but otherwise glorious palazzo in the heart of Rome's most colorful district, which I am free to do with as I please. She is something, isn't she? I'm going to make her the pride of the city; every noble will beg for an invitation to Cesare Borgia's house once I am done with her."

"So, you've accepted it?" I could not help but doubt his indifference. I felt as I had when Juan came upon us in the gardens: I sensed that Cesare hid his true feelings in order to present the expected façade. "You agree to what Papa asks of you?"

"I hardly have a choice." He moved to the decanter on the table, refilling my goblet and one for himself. "It is my fortune, Lucia. We cannot fight *fortuna,* only try to anticipate her whims and, if we're lucky, bend her to our will." His voice lowered. "I intend to be very lucky."

That sounded more like him, though I couldn't imagine how he might escape the Church. Sipping the claret, which went to my head, I watched him move about the semi-furnished room, trailing his fingers over his belongings. He loved beautiful objects; he had an unerring eye for them. I wanted to ask how he planned to endure this crown of thorns Papa had ordained for him, how he'd manage to stem his passion for the world. There was so much life in him, so much youth and vitality—he would not relish a life of toil in the Vatican, bickering and conniving with his fellow cardinals in the Curia. The vows were the least of it; churchmen had mistresses and sired children—our father's example left no doubt about that—but yoking Cesare into submission was akin to forcing a magnificent stallion to plow a field like an ox.

I kept quiet. What good would it do to say it? He was right; he didn't have a choice. None of us did. We were Borgias. We must sacrifice our needs for the good of the family.

"I have another surprise," said Cesare, startling me from my thoughts. He paused at the window. The thick panes admitted dusty light but were otherwise so grimy I couldn't see past them. I was about to rub the glass with my sleeve when he whispered, "Hush. We don't want to scare our quarry," and pressed an ingenious lever on the side of the window frame. The pane swung outward. The scent of damp greenery drifted up to me.

"You've a garden, too?" I said in delight. He put a finger to his lips, urging me to turn my attention outward. At first, my gaze was drawn to the Trastevere's cluttered silhouette, the cloud-cobbled sky pierced by bell towers, turrets, and spires. Then I looked down, into the private garden abutting the outer wall, where unkempt hedgerows circled a birdbath and an armless Venus, her robes carved into stained marble folds.

And there, for the first time, I saw him pacing the pathway—an uncomfortable-looking man in a blue pleated *cioppa* that hung to mid-thigh, its outer sleeves folded back and tucked into his girdle, displaying the under-slashing of his doublet. His hose was fitted, though not as tightly as my brother's. Or, rather, his legs were not well formed, his dyed-blue boots flopping about skinny calves. Perched on his brow was a ridiculous conical cap with a wide brim; from where I stood, much as I strained my eyes, I could not see his face, only his chestnut hair, cut bluntly at his shoulders. As he meandered around the birdbath, kicking pebbles, a sparrow flittered down to splash in the water. He jumped back, waving his hand to scare the bird away. A sudden tightness in my chest told me who he was moments before Cesare said in my ear: "Giovanni Sforza is afraid of spoiling his clothes. He had to borrow from his relatives to pay for them, you see. That gold collar about his neck is mine. He needed something gold to offset all that awful blue."

I reeled back from the window. "Giovanni Sforza, my betrothed?"

Cesare nodded.

Pushing down on my skirts as if he might actually hear them rustle, I braved another glance. Giovanni had paused to stare up at the window. Even as I froze, I noted in relief that, at least from a distance, he did not appear visibly malformed or scarred, though his features remained shadowed by his cap.

He jerked his gaze away, toward the palazzo. Cardinal Sforza strode into view.

Stepping back again, I shut the windowpane.

Cesare regarded me curiously. "Well?"

I swallowed. "Why is he here?"

"To marry you, of course." He paused. "You don't like him." Before I could respond, he struck his fist into his palm. "I knew it. The moment he arrived, I told Papa it was impossible. Not only is he the bastard of a mere condottiere of the Sforza blood—and a rather poor one at that—he doesn't even reside in Milan. He's a petty count, overlord of that fisherman city Pesaro, dependent on Milanese sufferance. He's also too old, a widower already. You needn't worry. We'll find you someone else—with better legs and taste in clothes."

I absorbed his tirade in silence before I ventured, "How old is he?"

"Twenty-eight. His first wife was sister to the marquis of Mantua; she died in childbed, as did his newborn brat. Even his seed is weak."

I wondered what Giovanni Sforza, Count of Pesaro, might say about me. Surely, he too must question my suitability—an adolescent girl just out of the convent, who was not a Gonzaga, d'Este, or Medici, though my father did sit on the papal throne. I remembered what Papa had told me in my childhood, about how in Italy we'd always be viewed as Spanish-born foreigners.

"How much does he stand to gain?"

Cesare laughed coldly. "A fortune for him. But you needn't worry," he repeated. "Nothing has been promised that can't be undone. I'll tell Papa you found him unsuitable and—"

"Didn't Cardinal Sforza cast the vote that won Papa the throne?" I glanced back to the window. "I don't think he'll want to hear that I found his cousin unsuitable."

"Who cares what he wants? We've already given that viper more than enough. He has our former palazzo on the Corso and the vice-chancellorship, not to mention enough benefices and boys to populate a city-state. A pox on these Sforza."

I met my brother's ardent gaze, then reached for my goblet and drank down the rest of my wine. "Still," I said. "Perhaps I ought to meet him first. That is why I was brought here, yes?"

Cesare's eyes narrowed. "You are under no obligation. Papa asked only that you be allowed to see him. You may return to your palazzo without offending."

"Oh? Has everyone gone blind?" I managed to laugh. "The cardinal knows I'm here, and I believe Giovanni himself just saw me. Come, Cesare." I held out my hand. "I want you to be the first to present me to my future husband."

The cardinal and Giovanni Sforza were standing by the Venus, talking in low voices. I couldn't hear what they said but it must have been important, for they looked startled when Cesare and I emerged from the downstairs gallery.

The cardinal's malleable face rearranged itself into its habitual mask. He glided forward. "Donna Lucrezia, enchanting of you to join us." He glanced at Cesare. "And you, my lord," he said, his gaze slipping to my brother's hand, which cupped my elbow. In a deft move, I unhooked myself, summoning a smile as the cardinal added, "Allow me to present my cousin Giovanni Sforza, Signore of Pesaro. He has been most eager to greet you."

The cardinal motioned. Giovanni sidled forth, his narrow shoulders tense, as if to enhance the narrow breadth of his chest under the pleating of his outer garment.

"My lord, I am honored." I lowered my eyes as I'd seen Giulia do sometimes with my father, particularly when she sought a favor. When he finally spoke, his voice quavered: "I too am honored to make your—I mean, my lady's—acquaintance."

Cesare snorted.

I looked up to see a flush creep over Giovanni's face. He was rather ordinary-looking, but he had a cleft in his chin that offset his large nose and close-set brown eyes and seemed younger than I had expected, his earnest gaze reminding me a little of my brother Gioffre. With words now exchanged, albeit stilted ones, his tension seemed to ease. Still, he fidgeted with my brother's gold necklace as if he was ill accustomed to its weight.

I was relieved. He did not appear to be anything like his manicured relative, Cardinal Sforza.

"Shall we walk?" I suggested. It was forward of me to ask, but I wanted to speak with him alone, without Cesare and the cardinal watching us like falcons.

Giovanni darted an inquiring look at the cardinal, who nodded and withdrew with Cesare to the gallery. My brother looked darkly over his shoulder as Giovanni and I started down the well-trodden path around the birdbath.

The crunching of pebbles under our heels was loud in my ears. At first, I thought he'd taken my suggestion literally and would bring me in a circle around the bath without uttering a word. But when I glanced at him, he appeared to be chewing at his lip. His reticence reassured me. After all, it wasn't as if he had any more choice than I did over this match. Indeed, he had considerably less, as I doubted his family would allow him to declare *me* unsuitable.

"My lord did not expect to meet me today," I finally said.

His eyes widened. I almost giggled. Did he think me a child who did not recognize what was before her? With a quick shake of his head, he mumbled, "His Eminence and His Holiness—they sent word that I was to look my best and be in the garden by Sext. But, no, I didn't think we would meet. I was told you would see me from above. That is all."

He went quiet again before he added, "I've been here for more than an hour. Look—" He swiped off his cap. Sweat had plastered his hair to his head. He was thinning on top; without the cap, he looked his age. "I thought I might faint from the heat. These clothes are . . . heavy."

"I regret the inconvenience." I watched him dab his brow. "You mustn't be accustomed to our climate in Rome. It's only May. Wait until August, when the heat truly starts. Anyone with a villa in the hills leaves before the fever mosquitoes arrive."

"Fever?" He stared at me. "From mosquitoes?"

"Why, yes. I am not sure how it happens, though I assume it's from their bite. Only, we have mosquitoes nearly year-round, because of the marshlands, yet not always fever." I shrugged. "In any event, my father's physician, Dr. Torella—he's a Jew who studied medicine with the Moors in Spain, so he's well versed in such maladies—believes certain mosquitoes carry the fever. Entire quarters have succumbed in the summer and—"

I came to a halt. He had turned an alarming shade of white. "Are you unwell?" I asked, thinking that perhaps he'd recently been bitten by a mosquito.

"I—I've never heard of such a thing. In Pesaro, we've no insects that carry plague."

"No mosquitoes?" This time, I could not contain my laugh. "How fortunate for Pesaro! I get welts whenever they bite me; my skin is so sensitive. But it's hardly plague, only a fever in most cases, and rarely fatal save for the very young or old. Though it can be inconvenient. My brother Cesare caught the fever once and it took weeks before he felt well enough to rise. . . ." My voice drifted off. Not only did I realize I was babbling, but he did not seem placated in the least. In fact, he appeared ready to bolt right back to his mosquito-less city and never return.

"There is no reason to worry." I patted his arm. "As I said, it's still only May and—"

"We'll be gone by August." He pulled his arm away as if he had been scalded. I winced. I'd made a mistake; suggesting a walk was improper enough, but to touch him before we'd been blessed by a priest must make me seem—well, like a Spanish-born foreigner. "Our marriage takes place in June," I heard him say. "So there is indeed no reason to worry, for by August we shall be residing in Pesaro."

"Oh." It would be inappropriate to inform him that he must be mistaken. Papa would never send me from Rome. He had yet to authorize Juan's departure for Spain, in fact, citing the Catholic majesties' delay in sending the requisite patent for the duchy, though everyone knew that in truth Papa was loath to relinquish Juan.

Giovanni went on, "You will find Pesaro most agreeable. It's on the coast, near the Via Flaminia; we have several fine churches and piazzas. I dispose of a palazzo, and my castle, the Rocca Constanza, is also commodious, with four strong towers and a moat."

"You have a moat? And yet there are no mosquitoes?"

He stiffened. "It's dry for most of the year. In the winter, it fills with seawater. We've no need for defense in Pesaro, as we owe allegiance to my cousin Ludovico Il Moro, Duke of Milan, who would send an army to protect us if need be. I am pledged to his service."

"I see." Cesare had called him a poor relation, and he had just made the error of calling Il Moro the duke, when in fact Ludovico Sforza did not own the title by right. He merely acted as regent for Milan's true ruler, his nephew Gian Galeazzo, whom he held in captivity.

But a first meeting was hardly the moment to remark on these entanglements. Maiden brides-to-be weren't supposed to be conversant on such sordid dealings as the imprisonment of nephews by their rapacious uncles.

"I'm certain your city is delightful," I said. He clearly expected my consent, for his expression lightened and he resumed our trajectory. I kept in step, even as I suddenly wanted the business over with. I longed to return to my palazzo for a nap, with Arancino curled at my side, before I decided what to wear for tonight's entertainment. That made me think of Giulia: She would want to hear every detail of my encounter. I would have to avoid her until—

As if on cue, Cesare returned to the garden. "Enough." He stared at Giovanni. "His Eminence awaits you in the hall, Signore."

Giovanni went still. Before Cesare could repeat his dismissal, I turned to him. "It has been an honor, my lord. Thank you for the conversation and the walk."

He bowed over my hand. "My lady, the honor was all mine." Then he slipped cautiously around Cesare and hastened off, his boot tops flapping.

"'The honor was all mine,'" mocked Cesare. "Besides his insufferable poverty, evidently he also lacks any original sentiment."

"Or fever in his city," I mused.

Cesare glanced at me. "Why do you say that?"

"No reason." I yawned. "I am tired. Can you fetch Pantalisea and see me home?"

He took me by the hand, leading me into the house. "I'll have your escort readied and—" Suddenly he halted. "You haven't told me what you feel now that you've met him." His gaze was unblinking, probing, as if he might divine something I intended to keep from him.

I hesitated. What could I say? Cesare seemed determined to hear me disparage Giovanni of Pesaro, when in truth I found no reason to do so. He might not be particularly handsome or engaging, but he did not seem cruel or idiotic, either. I could fare worse, I thought, recalling Ferrante of Naples and his cellar of corpses, and once we wed, Giovanni would of course be told that leaving Rome was out of the question. Papa would laugh at the very thought of me going away to watch some moat fill with seawater.

"He's to be my husband," I said at length. "I hardly think feelings matter."

Cesare regarded me for a moment before a wry chuckle escaped him. "Naturally. How foolish of me. He will indeed be only your husband. And husbands mean nothing."

CHAPTER EIGHT

Less than a month later, as June cast powdered gold over the Tiber and the fruit trees in our gardens shed tattered blooms, I stood at the portico with Giulia and my attendants as Giovanni Sforza rode in cavalcade to the palazzo to formally greet me.

It was supposed to be our first encounter, though I did not see any reason for the pretense. Kept at a distance from Giovanni, I smiled decorously as he bowed from the saddle of his charger—one of five my family had loaned him—and swept off his cap in a rehearsed gesture. Once again, he wore expensive finery, all paid for on credit—as Giulia did not hesitate to inform me once I was swept back into the palazzo to prepare for the marriage ceremony in the Vatican.

"Everything he wears is borrowed; that ruby-and-gold pendant is a Gonzaga heirloom, sent by his former father-in-law, His Grace of Mantua," she said, plucking stray hair from her sleeve. Now fully recovered from her lassitude, she wore luxurious nectarine brocade slashed with purple satin, fitted to her figure. "And I hear Il Moro had to take a loan from his bankers to cover the cost of Giovanni's retinue and such." She let out a troubled sigh. "I do hope he won't have to hire himself out as a condottiere just to maintain your household."

"He won't," retorted Adriana, from where she directed Pantalisea and my women to dress me in my elaborate wedding gown. She had returned from Monte Giordano as soon as the proclamation of marriage was made, determined to reassume her charge of me. "He'll have more than sufficient income now that he's a member of the family. His Holiness has even granted Signore Giovanni his own well-paid commission in the papal army, and Il Moro will uphold his current *condotta* in the Milanese army, as part of the nuptial agreement."

"Oh?" Giulia smiled. "That could prove awkward should we end up at war with Milan."

"Hush your tongue! Would you cast bad luck upon this day? *You* might not take the sacrament of marriage seriously, but to mention war on such an occasion—it's blasphemous."

As Giulia laughed, I resisted stamping my feet in disgust. This squabble between her and Adriana had plagued us for weeks, with Adriana set on having me outshine my father's mistress and Giulia likewise resolved to turn my wedding day into her triumphant public return to society.

For weeks she'd been sequestered behind closed doors, subjecting herself to a variety of beautifying procedures, even as Adriana had me suffer repeated washes of ash and lemon juice to bring out the gold in my hair and subdue its coppery tint. I had nothing to worry about as far as my complexion was concerned, she assured me; but, just in case, she forbade me to set foot outside the palazzo without a veil and preferred that I not go outside at all. Most of my visits to the Vatican had therefore taken place via the passage into the Sistine. The one time I threw aside caution along with my veil to take to the gardens, suffocated from being cooped indoors for days, Adriana had a fit.

Giulia added to the tumult by contriving to undermine Adriana at every turn, until the house crackled with antagonism and I had to interfere.

"Isn't my wedding supposed to be cause for celebration?" I said one afternoon, eyeing Giulia as she reclined naked on unbleached linen, a sheen of rose oil on her skin. Supposedly, the precious attar imported from France at an extraordinary price revived the flesh.

"Why, yes," she said. "Why do you ask?"

"Because Adriana told me that your women confiscated a shipment of Alexandrine silk yesterday that was intended for my nuptial bed."

She flicked a crumpled rose petal from her breast. "She must be mistaken. Rodrigo purchased that silk from Venice for me. I inspected the bill of sale myself."

I could tell she was lying, but it was not worth fighting over. Silk could be reordered. However, given the situation, I had to find her something useful to occupy her time, lest she provoke Adriana to an extreme.

"Very well. Yet as Adriana is doing so much already, perhaps you might help me sort through my gifts? They're piling up in the hall. I worry the servants might be tempted."

As I hoped, Giulia immediately agreed. The only thing she coveted more than my father was evidence of prestige, and there was indeed a pyramid of presents awaiting my inspection. Oversight of the other details of my wedding had so overwhelmed Adriana, she'd let this important task slip.

Thus I sat with Giulia in the evening while Murilla helped us unwrap an astounding variety of treasures sent by Europe's crowned heads. And it was there, as we inspected gold spoons from the sultan of Turkey, twin silver chalices from the king of Poland, and tooled stirrups from Their Majesties of Spain, when I finally allowed myself to voice the one question that until now I had not dared ask.

"Will it hurt?"

Giulia paused in her examination of embroidered hand towels from Paris. "Hurt?" She went quiet before she said, "I imagine it will. But if he knows what he's about, not too much."

Though I did my best to conceal it, anxiety quickened my voice. "How much?"

She shooed Murilla out of earshot. "It depends," she said in a low voice, "on how long it takes him to do whatever he must. Men can have strange appetites."

I contemplated her. "I thought you knew." I did not add that by now I was no longer completely ignorant of what was required of a wife—there was too much gossip around me for complete innocence—but the details, and my expected role in such, had thus far eluded me.

"Of course I know. But I hardly think Rodrigo would want me to—" She stopped. "You. List this as a gift from the queen of France," she barked at Murilla, clearly forgetting, or not caring, that my dwarf could neither read nor write. She wiped her hands on one of the cloths before she thrust them at Murilla, reaching for the next item. "Besides, it's not important."

"It is not?" I was dubious.

"No. Such questions are unnecessary. Your betters have it in hand. God in heaven," she said, flipping open a velvet box, "what has Adriana been doing all this time, if not instructing you?"

"She's been overseeing my nuptial chamber, my gown, my retinue of ladies." I was loath to let the subject lapse, not after I'd finally mustered the courage to broach it. "What do you mean, 'Your betters have it in hand?' I don't understand—"

Giulia squealed, waving diamond-and-topaz earrings before my nose. "Oh, look at these! Are they not exquisite? From Isabella d'Este, Marchioness of Mantua; everyone says she has the most impeccable taste." She clasped the gems to her ears. "They're obviously not right for you: Your neck is much shorter than mine. What do you think? Do they suit me?"

I sighed. It was pointless to continue my inquiry. "Perfectly. You must keep them."

She probably had decided those pearls about her throat suited her more than me, as well; they looked suspiciously like the same pearls sent by the king of England. But I was too agitated to care. I would gladly have let her ransack my entire dowry if she would only answer my questions. With the hour fast upon me, that indifference I'd cultivated was starting to fray, and after that evening I grew so worried that I asked Pantalisea, who, after much badgering, reluctantly told me something of what I needed to know.

"But," she added, as I sat appalled by what she described, "I hear it's not entirely unpleasant. And once you're with child, it stops, at least until after the birth. No gentleman would dare visit such indignity on his pregnant wife. That's what women like la Farnese are for."

I felt nauseous. I could not imagine lying supine while Giovanni Sforza did . . . *that* to me. I almost wished I could consult with my mother. Having borne several children, she must have found some fulfillment in it. But I knew Vannozza would only guffaw in my face.

Now, days later, I stood on the threshold of an unknown future. After today, I would no longer be just His Holiness's daughter: I would be Giovanni Sforza's wife, Countess of Pesaro, and the expected mother of his heirs.

I would belong to him.

"Lucrezia, you look ill," Giulia said. "You could use some rouge. I warned you, crimson satin isn't the right shade for your complexion."

"Rouge on a bride?" Adriana scoffed.

Before they started arguing again, I staggered forward. The result of hundreds of hours of work, not to mention thousands of ducats, my gown weighed on me like armor, the crimson and gold-banded stomacher studded with rubies, my slashed sleeves sprouting like wings from my shoulders, my chemise made of a sheer, scratchy silk. My hair hung in a braid to my waist, adorned with a pearled caul. As I ignored the pinch of my unyielding new slippers, the tears that filled Adriana's eyes made me realize that, while I might feel as though I were encased in plaster, the outward appearance was pleasing.

"Shall we proceed?" I said to Giulia. As my matron of honor, she would lead my escort into the Vatican—another bone of contention with Adriana, who in the end had to submit after Papa commanded it. Giulia's impatient nod made me smile. Envy from her was my reward for all the endless fittings, facial unguents, and hair rinses I'd endured.

Today, all eyes would be upon me.

Giulia swirled to the door, our women bustling into position. Adriana tugged down my veil. Sentries clattered into rank on either side of us as we swept in bejeweled splendor into the palazzo corridors, Pantalisea holding up my train to keep it from dragging on the floor. It was early afternoon; outside, the June sun evaporated the last of the spring rain, but I had not been outdoors in days, and so navigating our way into the Vatican proved an exercise in endurance. But once we reached Papa's apartments, where frankincense wafted from braziers, I had a brief respite for last-minute adjustments to my person.

In his quest to exalt our family's status, Papa had spared no expense. During one of my infrequent visits, I'd watched in awe as a battalion of artists overseen by Maestro Pinturicchio raced to complete the majestic frescoes now adorning every surface. Giulia had laughingly commented about the elder cardinals' disapproval, their muttering of paganism upon viewing Isis and her sibling-lover, Osiris, frolicking among rampant bulls on the ceiling and our emblem of the bladed rays encircled by Moorish arabesques. She had not helped matters, either, by insisting on modeling for a depiction of the Virgin with Child, complete with halo and cherub.

Regardless of what the cardinals said, Papa had taken care to represent the traditional. Ten somber popes stared at me from the walls of the Sala dei Pontefici, including the righteous Nicholas III, founder of the Vatican. Beyond, interconnecting suites displayed scenes from the

Testaments; one chamber was reserved for our family portrait, that most traditional of customs, in which we would appear in saintly guise. I had already posed for Pinturicchio with an unwieldy crown on my head. Juan and Cesare had, too, though Cesare rolled his eyes and later told me that in his eagerness to satisfy Papa, the maestro exceeded his limited talent.

I wished I had time to wander these rooms and delay the inevitable, but my women were spreading my train behind me, preparing me for my entry into the Sala Reale, where the papal court awaited. Only my brother Juan was missing. He was supposed to bring me into the hall.

Without warning, a Turk strode in.

As Adriana yelped and the women gasped in dismay, I scowled through my veil. It was Juan, of course, already styling himself as His Grace of Gandia, though the patent for his duchy had not arrived. Only now he was not clad as a Spanish grandee or even an Italian nobleman; rather, he sported a new beard to complement his outlandish ankle-length tunic of cloth-of-gold, complete with egret-plumed turban and massive gold-and-sapphire collar.

"For the love of God, Juan," I said. "What are you wearing? This isn't Carnival."

He waved my women aside, taking me by the arm. "You should know this collar alone cost eighty thousand ducats, more than your entire dowry."

"As if anyone is counting," I replied, and then my throat went dry as I beheld the crowd.

Papa sat on the dais, enshrined in his vestments and scarlet cap, a fringed brocade palanquin hovering like a storm cloud above his chair. Colored cushions had been strewn on the steps before him, intended for exalted guests, though Giulia and her women usurped the privilege by arranging themselves on these pillows without so much as a reverence in His Holiness's direction. I saw our court master of ceremonies, the German Johann Burchard, who oversaw the arrangement of official Vatican events, gaping at them, mortified by their flagrant disregard of established etiquette. Guided by Juan, I stepped past the twittering women, my train pulling at my waist as I ascended the dais to kiss my father's hand.

"My *farfallina*," he said. His breath was sour—a rarity for him—

and his eyes, usually so lucid, were red-rimmed. "I never thought I'd see the day when I must relinquish my most precious jewel to another." His voice caught in his throat. For a paralyzing moment, I thought he might start to weep. Papa had never been reticent in his emotions, but neither had he said or done anything to indicate my marriage was more than a political arrangement, which would scarcely alter the established pattern of my life. Having taken strength in his nonchalance, now I faltered, turning in bewilderment to Juan. As my brother stepped forth, eliciting Papa's wan smile, I sensed someone else watching.

My gaze lifted, past the clerics alongside the dais, past the stone-faced guards at the wall with their halberds, and past the gossiping courtiers, drawn as if by an invisible cord to a recess under the high windows, where a lone figure stood, just as he had on the night of Papa's banquet. Only this time, Cesare resembled a pilaster of frozen blood, dressed in the crimson of his new cardinalship.

His mouth moved. I thought he was saying my name.

Burchard clapped his hands, startling everyone to attention. I had to look away to Giovanni Sforza, who had moved to the foot of the dais.

In my sudden nervousness, I almost laughed aloud to see my bridegroom also wearing a Turkish robe, Juan's smirk betraying he'd incited Giovanni to it, placing him further in our debt, no doubt, while mocking him in the process. Though he was the bridegroom, on Giovanni the robe looked ridiculous, while Juan carried it with style, despite its unsuitability.

I joined Giovanni. A drop of sweat slid down his temple from beneath his turban as we knelt before Papa to receive his blessing.

With the captain of the papal guard holding the sword above us in symbolic warning of what awaited those who broke their vows, Papa's notary questioned our willingness to enter into Holy Matrimony. After we both affirmed our consent, the officiating bishop slipped twin gold bands onto the index and fourth fingers of our left hands, the veins of which ran to the heart. We then bowed our heads as the sword was removed, remaining on our knees during what promised to be a long sermon by the bishop on the virtues of our married state, until Papa cut it short with an impatient wave of his hand.

Giulia and the other women leapt to their feet to fling showers of white silk petals from the baskets by their cushions. With offended expressions, the exalted guests displaced by Giulia and her ladies queued up to offer Giovanni and me their obligatory gifts, before they tripped up the dais to kiss Papa's satin-shod foot.

The rest of those in the hall broke into applause.

Standing beside my husband, I greeted the line of well-wishers for what felt like hours as my women gathered up their gifts (what was I supposed to *do* with all of it?). When a lull finally came, I immediately turned to search that darkened recess under the windows.

Cesare had vanished.

Juan returned to my side. "Time for the banquet. We are all famished." He reached for my arm; when I resisted, he let out a chuckle. "You needn't bother waiting. Cesare left as soon as the ceremony began. He cannot abide it. He hates everything: the wedding, the Sforza. All of it. He has lost the duchy, his freedom, and now his beloved sister."

"He has not lost me," I retorted. "I would never forsake him."

"You already have," said Juan, and he propelled me into the adjoining hall, where linen-draped tables were set before two daises slung with garlands. Silently, I assumed my seat on the main dais with Giovanni. My father and Giulia sat at the adjacent dais.

The feast commenced—an endless succession of roast fowl, Iberian smoked hams, boar, and venison, along with fresh salads and mountains of fruits, all washed down with decanters of wines borne by pages in our livery. The clamor of laughter as the guests consumed the fare made me nauseous. I could barely swallow a bite as I searched the hall, my dejection building into disbelief as I failed to see Cesare. I couldn't believe it. How could he abandon me today of all days? Surely he must realize how much I needed him, how much I needed to know that, no matter what, nothing would change between us.

Hours later, as a comedic play took place in the center of the hall, the actors struggling to declaim their verses over the din, the most infirm or elderly of the clerics rose and hobbled out. The talk grew less guarded, the merriment bawdier. Papa, in particular, had evidently discarded his sorrow from before the ceremony to now whisper in Giulia's ear, making her simper. At a nearby table, Juan held court with his entourage of overdressed ruffians and Djem; a garishly dressed woman was seated between them, doting on my brother's every word.

Whenever I could, I stole covert glances at Giovanni. Unlike me, he had not lost his appetite. He had consumed three roast capons, his grease-stained napkin tucked into his loaned Gonzaga collar as he deftly peeled charred flesh from the bone. His cupbearer regularly refilled his goblet. The wine was undiluted, but Giovanni did not appear drunk, only absentminded, once returning my look with a vague smile, as though he'd forgotten why we were here.

I wondered at his nonchalance. Anxiety roiled inside me, but he seemed immune to any apprehension of what awaited us, though every minute that passed brought us closer to that dreaded hour of our nuptial bedding. He'd eaten more than his fill yet still looked eager when pages armed with little silver brushes swept the gristle from the tablecloths and a bell chime announced the dessert course; he sat up expectantly as yet another liveried troop marched in, this time bearing platters of sugared almonds, marzipan, and comfits, along with huge flagons of sweet Madeira wine. How could he act as though this feast might go on forever, with no other task before him save to sate himself, never mind that he just taken a new wife?

When I heard Giulia shriek, I turned, startled, to stare at her, as did most of those in the hall. Papa had his entire fist in her cleavage, up to his ringed knuckles. Fishing out a sweetmeat, he popped it into his mouth and smacked his lips, winking at those seated at the table below him, all of whom were cardinals.

"Nothing like a woman's sweat to heat the tongue, eh?" he gibed. The hall erupted in mirth, with all the cardinals taking his lead and tossing sweets into nearby bodices, the women screeching and slapping halfheartedly at the cardinals' roving hands.

Papa reclined in his chair. "Give the rest to the rabble," he ordered Burchard, who gasped as if he had been told to serve up his own leg. Retainers flung open the hall windows, letting in a welcome gust of evening air. Gathered in the piazza, the people stampeded as the pages overturned the dessert platters onto the cobblestones, in a shower of spun sugar.

Papa caught my eye and winked. Then he called out, interrupting the actors: "Music! It is time for the bride to dance! Who here shall accompany my Lucrezia?"

The actors scrambled out of the way, leaving the detritus of their

unwatched performance on the floor—a white mask, several frayed lacings, a fake gilt sword. The musicians tuned their instruments. As the
twanging of strings resolved into the strains of a Spanish *morisca,* I
turned eagerly to Giovanni. It was exactly what was required: some
movement to stir the stuffiness in the air and break the torpor of overindulgence. Perhaps he might even whisper something tender to me as
we danced, to ease my apprehensions.

He shook his head. "I cannot," he mumbled, the stained napkin still
on his neck.

"You *cannot?*" I was confounded. Even the lowliest nobleman knew
how to dance; it was as necessary as learning how to sit a horse or use a
sword.

"No, I mean, I *can.* But these clothes"—he waved a hand about his
person—"this collar: They're too heavy. I will not be made a fool."

It was the second time he'd complained of his garments. I was beginning to suspect it was not their weight that troubled him but rather
concern that he might do them harm. Did he have to return them all
afterward? Was that how credit worked?

A voice rang out: "I shall do the honor," and to my delight, Cesare
strode into the hall with an insouciance that drew every eye to him.

As he passed the mess left by the actors, he reached down and
plucked up one of the half masks, affixing it to his face. The blank
white-cloth shape adhered to his brow, eyes, and nose, exalting the cut
of his jaw and his sinuous lips. He had discarded his robes for hose that
slithered across his thighs, his codpiece dangling silver-tipped points
and the fitted velvet doublet accentuating his narrow waist. His shirt
was of such a dark red silk that it appeared black, its billowing sleeves
ornamented with swirls of Spanish needlework. At his chest hung his
pectoral cross, his sole jewel, its gold chains coiling like serpent tails
across his shoulders.

Coming before our father's dais, he inclined his head.

Papa stared at him. "Your Eminence missed the feast."

"Alas, I beg forgiveness, Holiness, but I was called upon at the last
hour to shrive a sinner."

Now I knew why he'd donned the mask. It was a subtle mockery,
this disguising of his other, non-clerical face. I could hear it in his voice,

too—as could Papa, whose countenance darkened. "A rather poor excuse. Nevertheless, I do not deem it fitting for you to dance with—"

I leapt to my feet. "Please, Holiness! Allow us to indulge you. It may be the last occasion that my brother and I have to dance together."

"Yes," added Cesare, with a smile, "it could be."

"I hardly think that's the case," muttered Papa, but I was already leaving my dais, paying no mind to the hushed murmur rustling through the hall.

Taking Cesare's hand, I let him bring me to the center of the room, close to the fallen sword and coiled ribbons. We positioned ourselves palm-to-palm, so close that I could feel the heat coming off him.

"I thought you had abandoned me," I whispered.

His cat-green eyes gleamed in the candlelight. "I had to change."

"Not out of everything." I directed a pointed glance at his crucifix.

His smile deepened. "The fledgling cannot shed all its feathers until it leaves the nest." He turned aside, booted foot outstretched, a hand cocked at his hip as he began the initial moves of the *morisca*.

The weight of my own garb disappeared as I let him weave me through the intricate pattern of steps we had performed so many times in our childhood, united by the music of our native land, which bound us together as Borgias.

When we finished, I was panting, my bodice making itself felt again, clasping like iron about my ribs. Turning to the dais with our hands still joined, I saw my father regarding us with tears. Giulia was smirking, while Juan, to my surprise, bellowed appreciation. He was the first to bring his hands crashing together, prompting the rest of the assembly to likewise burst into overwrought applause, with a few *"Bravissimo!"* thrown in for effect.

Then Cesare's sweat-slicked hand slipped from mine. The abrupt unraveling of our fingers turned me back to him. He said softly, "Now do you see the power you possess, Lucia?" Stepping back, he bowed. Then he went to Juan's table, where my brother gave him a goblet.

Cesare raised it. "A toast to the Signore and Signora of Pesaro! May they long live in happiness and bear much fruit. *Buona fortuna!*"

Goblets were thrust upward, sloshing wine. In a daze, I returned to Giovanni. His face was shuttered, a hand clenched about his goblet.

Papa motioned to the other guests that they could now take to the floor. Juan was the first, hauling his garish woman to her feet, tackling the dance with exuberance, if little finesse, twirling her around until she was laughing hysterically and the fake pearls from her coiffure were scattered across the floor.

Only then did Giovanni lean to me. His voice was almost timid. "You dance well, wife."

THE CLOCK STRUCK midnight—the hour I had dreaded arrived. In solemn ceremony—Papa had forbidden any ribald jokes or catcalls for good hunting in the bedchamber, as was traditional at weddings—Papa and a select group of cardinals accompanied Giovanni and me back to Santa Maria in Portico.

My heart hammered in my chest. I thought I might faint as we entered the nuptial chamber, which had been prepared on the second floor of a still-vacant wing of the palazzo and was dominated by a vast upholstered bed hung in red silk, its bolster covered in silk petals. I turned anxiously to Papa. His face was impassive; he didn't return my look as Giulia led me behind a painted screen and, together with my women, divested me of my finery. The untying of laces and removal of bodice, overskirts, and petticoats seemed to take hours. No one said a word. By the time the silk nightdress with its embroidered flower motif was slipped over my head, I was biting back tears.

Giovanni was already waiting under the sheets, his nightshirt unlaced at his throat. I couldn't stop staring at the oddly bulbous knob of his Adam's apple as Giulia directed me to use the footstool to clamber into that monstrously oversized bed.

A page handed Papa a single goblet of wine. He stepped forth, the cardinals hovering behind him like red moons. Holding the goblet to each of our mouths, he motioned that we should drink while the page held a cloth under our chins.

The red wine tasted sour. A drop seeped from my lips, soaking like blood into the cloth.

Papa traced the sign of the cross over us. "May no man tear asunder what God has joined," he intoned, and then, without any warning, he stepped back and snapped his fingers.

Giulia came forward. "Lucrezia. Come with me."

I hesitated, not because I wanted to stay but because I was confused. But when I looked at Giovanni, he was staring forward as if I were no longer there. Staggering out of the bed, I shivered—the floor was cold under my toes. Giulia folded a shawl over my shoulders and knelt, sliding slippers onto my feet. I was so taken aback by the rehearsed swiftness of it that I didn't even think to utter good night to my husband before Giulia was steering me out the room. As I left, I cast a glance over my shoulder. Giovanni remained in bed. Papa had his back to me, but I saw tension in his stance, his shoulders squared like crenellations.

Giulia brought me down the passageway and across the courtyard to our apartments, Pantalisea and my other women padding behind with my crumpled wedding gown. All of a sudden I realized I had no idea where Adriana was. I'd lost track of her during the evening entertainment but had failed to notice her absence until now.

"Did I do something wrong?" I finally ventured as we climbed the staircase to my rooms.

"No." Giulia halted at my bedchamber door. "Or, rather, not as far as your husband is concerned. But that dance tonight with Cesare"— her condescending chuckle scraped in my ears like fingernails—"it was charming, but hardly proper. You must exercise discretion henceforth. Albeit only in name, you are now a married woman."

"But he is my brother." I was too bewildered by the abrupt change of events to feel anger at her presumption, though I might have retorted that she was no one to advise me after she'd spent the evening having sweetmeats tossed into her bodice. "He asked me to dance; I saw no harm in it. Giovanni didn't want to, so . . ." My explanation faltered. She was regarding me with the strangest expression. "What is it? What did I do?" I thought my dance with Cesare must have displeased Papa, who had removed me from the nuptial bedchamber as punishment. But that made no sense. He must have known I'd be relieved. Had Giovanni complained, perhaps? I searched my memory for a recollection of him approaching Papa during the feast. No, he'd been at my side the entire time, save when I left him to dance. He even complimented me afterward.

Giulia's voice tightened. "His Holiness expects your obedience. This . . ." She paused.

Despite the balmy night, I drew the shawl closer about me.

"Devotion." She met my stare. "This devotion," she repeated, "that you and Cesare share must not affect relations with your husband. It is vital that we not render insult to Milan."

"Render insult?" Now my anger stirred. "Then I should have been allowed to remain with my husband. Isn't it the custom after one is married?" As I spoke, I wondered if she had stayed with Orsino after their wedding. Or had she instead gone directly to Papa's bed?

Her smile was cold. "What do you know of such things? You are only thirteen; there can be no consummation until you are ready. Your nuptial treaty stipulates it. Do you understand?"

"But if I'm too young to be a wife," I said, "why marry me at all?" I knew about the need to satisfy Cardinal Sforza, which Juan had cited, but I had to wonder whether it had been truly necessary. The expensive feast and gown, the fanfare: It seemed to me quite a lot of trouble.

She made an exasperated sound. "Clearly you do not understand. You have not bled yet. Therefore, you are not a woman. The marriage must remain unconsummated until His Holiness says otherwise."

Humiliation rushed over me. It was true that I'd not yet shed my first blood, but the way she spoke it was like another barbed reminder of her superiority over me. She sounded as if she relished having yanked me from my nuptial bed and pointing out that it was I, not my husband, who was not ready to assume the responsibilities of marriage. I loathed her for it, even if I well knew that marriage was a convenience, an arrangement between families. If love should come of it, it was a gift, not an expectation. Indeed, Papa must have loved my mother once, as he apparently now loved Giulia, but he'd been content to see Vannozza wed to others. Of course, he couldn't marry, because of his vows; nevertheless, marriage had never seemed to me to hinge on desire but rather on necessity—a state that women must accommodate. Giulia alone had shown me how little marriage meant.

"You should have prepared me," I said. "When I asked you about my wedding night, you didn't tell me any of this, though you must have known."

"I did not. It wasn't yet decided. His Holiness had to wait until the final hour before inserting the clause. Had you bled before tonight, it would have gone differently. I am surprised by your tone, Lucrezia; I should think you would be pleased by His Holiness's forethought."

"You still should have told me. You had this entire day to do so." I was deliberately goading her, stung by her insufferable smugness. "What happens when I am declared of age? As you said, I'm thirteen. Surely I will start bleeding soon—"

She held up a hand to silence me, looking past me to my women in the room. Candles flickered in the sconces; my bedcovers were turned down. Adriana must have been here. She had left the hall at some point during the festivities to prepare my chamber for my return.

She had known I would not stay with Giovanni. Everyone had known. Except me.

"When you do bleed, you must tell me at once." Giulia leaned so close, her features blurred. "Only me and no one else, not even Adriana. Your father commands it."

"But what if it happens while Pantalisea attends me or one of my other—"

"Since when do servants matter? If they talk, they'll end up with their tongues cut out. Consider yourself fortunate that Rodrigo has such concern for your well-being. Other fathers do not." She pushed me over the threshold. "It has been a long day. You must be tired."

I was exhausted, in fact. I sat in quiet, tension slowly falling away from me and leaving me limp as Murilla brushed out my hair and Pantalisea stored my things, putting the jewels in a casket, setting the sections of my gown on the press to ease the wrinkles, and folding the smaller articles—stockings, shoes, sleeves, and underlinens—into the *cassones*. Drained, I knelt before my icon of the Virgin to say my prayers, but there seemed to be no point. My most earnest prayer had been answered: For the time being, I'd been spared. I had no experience with which to measure what I'd been denied, but Giovanni must, having been married before. Yet he had not protested. And if he had not, surely I had no reason to.

But despite my relief at having escaped the nuptial bed, I still resented that Giulia had been privy to the intrigue and not seen fit to inform me. It was yet another reminder to me of how she always seemed to know things she should not, forever meddling in my affairs.

As Murilla made up her pallet on the floor, Pantalisea tucked me under the bedcovers. "Shall I stay?" she asked, sensing my disquiet; when I nodded, she climbed into bed.

I cuddled against her breast as she caressed my hair, crooning a lullaby.

As I drifted into sleep, I realized nothing had changed.

I was still more the pope's daughter than anyone's wife—except that now I was determined to break Giulia's tenacious hold over me.

CHAPTER NINE

Although Giovanni took up residence in the vacant wing across the inner *cortile,* we saw each other infrequently. We met most often in the morning, once he emerged from his rooms with his attendants, fully dressed and with his fast broken. After exchanging minor pleasantries, he departed to go hunting or riding, if Papa did not require his presence for an official occasion.

One such occasion was the arrival of a royal embassy from Spain. In the year of my father's elevation, a Genovese navigator named Cristofero Colon had secured Queen Isabella's patronage to sail across the Ocean Sea. He returned in triumph to announce his discovery of a new world. I'd heard about his momentous discovery but had paid it little mind, until Papa had us attend the Spanish embassy's reception and the long-awaited delivery of Juan's patent for the duchy of Gandia.

As always, Spain was in dispute with Portugal, this time over the right to claim this uncharted world, to which the Portuguese king had hastened to send his own explorers. Now the Spanish ambassador conveyed Queen Isabella's petition for papal compromise. Before everyone present, Papa scored the crude map the ambassador presented, allocating those lands west and south of Colon's discovery to Spain and the remainder to whoever arrived first. The ambassador was evidently displeased, muttering something urgent to Papa, who cut him short.

"Much as I esteem Their Catholic Majesties," Papa declared, "I cannot grant them claim to what is not yet theirs," and he retreated to his dais to officiate over the subsequent ceremony of Juan's elevation to the dukedom.

I had the sense that had it been in his purview, the ambassador would have denied Juan the patent. But it was not, and he could only watch in glowering disapproval as my brother signed the deed with a flourish of his quill, not even troubling to peruse it. I had to hide my smirk. Since childhood, Juan had avoided reading anything, pronouncing Cesare's and my love of books "an effeminate foppery." To my amusement, despite this occasion's solemnity, he behaved no differently. He was in fact about to proclaim himself aloud as a grandee of Castile when the Spanish ambassador said tersely, "Her Majesty Queen Isabella would be delighted to welcome Don Juan Borgia, Duke of Gandia, to his estate in Castile. She has but one request."

Silence fell over the assembly. On his dais, Papa scowled. "Request? Have we not just granted Her Majesty entitlement to lands across the Ocean Sea?"

"We are most grateful, Holiness," replied the ambassador, and Cesare, sitting beside me, stiffened at the man's unctuous tone. "However, Her Majesty has heard a disturbing rumor that Your Holiness intends to grant sanctuary to her exiled Jews. She is concerned, as these people defied her edict and took flight to seek refuge in your domain, though she has offered them restitution if they will only comply with her request."

"Which entails renouncing their faith," growled Papa. "We are aware of Her Majesty's edict, which proves her glorious veneration for our Holy Church. Yet it seems to me she needs reminding that she does not rule here. What I choose to do with the Jews in my domain is my own affair."

"They are heretics, damned for the murder of our Savior!" thundered the ambassador, with a startling passion that echoed throughout the *sala*. "Your Holiness is Christ's appointed representative. Surely you cannot intend to allow them entry into the Eternal City."

"Have you seen them?" Cesare bolted to his feet in his scarlet robes. Everyone in the *sala* looked surprised at his unexpected incentive, including Papa, whose countenance darkened further.

The ambassador sniffed. "*Seen* them?" he repeated, as if he'd heard wrong.

"Yes," said Cesare. "Have you seen them? Are you aware of their circumstances? If you were, you would know that Her Majesty has no cause for complaint. Rather, we are the ones who should complain, for she evicted them from Spain to toss them on our doorstep. I have visited their encampment on the Via Appia, Señor; you'll not find a more wretched sight. They cluster in the fields like beasts, with barely enough to keep body and soul together. Some have been here nearly a year, trudging to Rome from every port that allowed them to disembark. We only seek to relieve their plight because they now suffer fever and their waste contaminates the waters that flow into Rome. Or does Her Majesty prefer that every Christian here perish of plague?"

"I do not see how that can be Her Majesty's concern," replied the ambassador. "His Holiness has allowed these Jews in. Is he therefore not also responsible for their welfare?"

Cesare took a furious step forward. "We've sent numerous envoys to Her Majesty on that account, as you well know, Señor, requesting that she cease clamoring and cede our right to assume charge of them. But Her Majesty insists that, regardless of her edict, the Jews of Spain remain her subjects and must abide by her dictates."

"Her Majesty is right," replied the ambassador, with a lift of his pointed chin. "However, if you are so concerned, you need only send them back to us. We have a solution; it is called the Inquisition, which His Holiness's predecessor authorized Her Majesty to implement."

Cesare gave a curt laugh. "Would she burn every soul who does not do as she wishes?"

Papa bellowed, "Enough!" and as Cesare froze, Papa directed his next words to the ambassador: "I fear His Eminence of Valencia is carried away by his compassion. Tell Her Majesty we shall consider her concerns."

The ambassador bowed. "Thank you, Your Holiness. In exchange for your consideration, Her Majesty wishes to extend her appreciation and offer the hand in marriage of Doña Maria Enríquez, cousin to her own husband, King Fernando, to His Grace of Gandia."

And while Juan's face lit up at the prospect of gaining both the title *and* the bride, Cesare stared across the *sala* at our father, in horrified disbelief.

FOLLOWING THE CEREMONY, we retired to dine together as a family.

As the first course was set before us, Cesare said, "We cannot let that worm of an ambassador dictate to us. Queen Isabella banished the Jews by her edict. Those who refused to convert were ordered to leave with whatever they could carry. She kept their wealth and put them to sea on leaking ships. They must now remain under our protection."

Seated at Papa's right side, Juan glared. "Why do you care so much about those Hebrews? They breed like rats. We've too many in Rome as it is. If the queen says they must return to Spain, so be it. She has made me a grandee; we have expectations to fulfill. Defending Jews is not one of them."

Cesare turned to Papa. "Would you please tell my idiot brother that Rome cannot be held subject to Queen Isabella or any other temporal monarch?"

Papa sat silent for a tense moment. Then he said, "I do not appreciate the queen's interference. She's too high-handed. This upheaval she has created in her realm by expelling her Jews will blacken everything she has achieved. But that worm of an ambassador, as you call him, is correct: My predecessor, Pope Innocent, may he rest in peace, granted her inquisitorial authority. And the Jews defied her. Moreover," he added, lifting his voice to forestall Cesare, "this marriage she offers with the Enríquez girl will ensure that Juan has a familial connection to Isabella's consort, King Fernando himself, whose mother was an Enríquez. It is imperative that we accommodate, much as it may grieve me. Isabella has made it a condition for Juan's departure for Spain and access to his duchy revenues. I'll not have my son living in Castile like a peasant."

"Everyone in Castile lives like a peasant," retorted Cesare. He stabbed his knife into his smoked ham. "They're all poor as beggars because of Their Majesties' ten-year crusade against the Moors. You saw the Spanish ambassador; his shirt cuffs are frayed. Isabella is moved only by the need to replenish her treasury; that is why she makes obstacles to the duchy's revenues. She'd gladly let us succor every Jew in Europe if it meant she needn't surrender more than the title to Juan. She commands us against granting sanctuary only to remind us that we are beholden to Spain and that we share a common enemy in France, which conspires with Milan over Naples. She knows should she withdraw her support, we'll be even more vulnerable to Milanese intrigues."

I saw that Cesare had struck a nerve. With a grimace, Papa thrust out his goblet. As Perotto refilled it, anger soured Papa's expression. Florid veins crisscrossed his cheeks; not even Giulia, who sat at his left, dressed in costly silk and too many jewels, seemed able to curtail his temper, for when she leaned to murmur in his ear, he waved her aside. "You presume to advise me, the Holy Pontiff, on how I should manage my affairs?" he snapped at Cesare.

"Only when what I advise is worth hearing," said my brother.

They stared across the table like combatants, the growing strain between them palpable. I had thought Cesare's acceptance of his cardinal's hat and lack of quarrel over Juan's duchy signified that, for better or worse, he had accepted his lot, but I now realized that in truth he already balked at the tethers that bound him.

"You should think before you speak," said Papa. "Accord with Spain must be maintained. Queen Isabella demands it. More important, *I* demand it." He quaffed his wine in a gulp, held out his goblet again. The page behind him hastened to pour from his flagon.

I glanced warily at Giovanni. He was focused on his platter, silently chewing his food as though he heard and saw nothing. I was beginning to think he might be deaf.

Then Cesare said with cold, deliberate precision, "Do as she demands and we will come to regret it. She'll never honor her promises. I'd wager my own palazzo that Juan goes to Castile with our riches in his pocket and by month's end he sends to us for more coin to pay off his debts. Her Majesty won't allow him a single revenue from that duchy if she can help it."

"Oh, yes, brother," said Juan, his fist closing over his dinner knife. "We are all aware of how little promises mean to you. By your own priestly vows, you promised to heed and obey, and I see no example of it here—though your Church benefices pay for the restorations on your precious palazzo, which I hear are not insignificant. How are your needs different from mine?"

I could barely draw in a breath, watching Cesare look slowly at Juan and thinking of the chaos that would ensue should they start brawling here, in our father's private apartments.

"My needs are different," said Cesare, "because what I do serves us all. My palazzo bears testament to our family's prestige. I think of the Borgia first, rather than my own self."

Papa gave a sarcastic chuckle. "Indeed. We forget your altruism— while I myself have had to order temporary halt to my refurbishments in the Vatican to provide for your brother's trip to Castile." His eyes narrowed to slits. "You seem to have forgotten who is pope or that the palazzo upon which you lavish so much of my money is not yours, should I have a mind to take it away."

Cesare clenched his jaw. "I meant no offense, but surely given the situation, all this effort expended on Juan would be better spent shoring up our defenses." His voice rose; I could tell he was losing his control, as he had earlier in the *sala* with the ambassador, and I wanted to yank his sleeve in warning. To try to persuade Papa to reason would only enrage our father more, but Cesare was now beyond reason himself. "While we haggle with Isabella and this enterprise of Juan's sucks up every last ducat in our treasury, our enemies conspire to overthrow us."

"Oh?" said Papa. His voice was dead calm. "Do enlighten us, my lord cardinal."

Again, Cesare failed to heed the fury simmering under Papa's deceptive tone. "You know that since he lost the Holy See to you, Cardinal della Rovere has not ceased to plot. He says you are a usurper who stole the throne that rightfully belongs to him. At this very moment, he is on his way to Milan to persuade Il Moro to join his vendetta against us; my spy in the Milanese court sent urgent word that King Charles of France will also be invited. France and Spain are at odds over Naples; I'd not be surprised that as soon as Charles hears that we've conceded to Isabella, he'll launch an invasion, abetted by Milan, aimed at seeing you deposed and the rest of us imprisoned or killed." Cesare paused. "Is that enough enlightenment? Or shall I go on?"

At the mention of Il Moro—his kin—Giovanni suddenly looked up. He had gone white. But before Giovanni could utter a word, Papa banged his hand hard on the table, rattling the cutlery.

"*Basta!* How dare you lecture me? By God, haven't I enough to contend with, without my own son questioning my judgment? You do indeed think too much of yourself, Cesare Borgia. You are not my better and I suggest you remember it. Remove yourself at once."

Juan gloated as Cesare shoved back from the table in disgust and strode from the chamber. I wanted to go after him. I even slid aside my half-finished plate to beg leave of my father, but then I saw he was trembling with rage and I did not dare.

We finished our meal in silence. As soon as the servitors cleared our plates, Giovanni and Juan left together, having some inexplicable affinity for each other. Before Giulia could rise to escort me back to my palazzo, I excused myself and raced out into the gardens.

I found Cesare pacing there, the citrus-scented firebrands casting wavering light over his robes. He had his skullcap in his fist, his thicket of curls jumbled about his long, pale face.

"It's as though he's lost his mind," he said as I came up beside him, breathless from running through the corridors. "Queen Isabella *demands* it? That woman demands everything—and gives nothing in return. She is not our friend. She would rather see Juan anywhere than in her realm, and Papa knows it. She detests him for openly favoring his bastards, as she calls us, though she doesn't dare say it aloud." He gave a harsh laugh. "Not that Juan cares. Did you know he actually requested a retinue for Djem? He plans to bring that Turk with him to Castile. Imagine the look on the queen's face when our brother steps off the boat with his infidel in tow."

"What about the Jews? Why do you care so much about them?" I was curious as to his response, for his fervor over them had taken me aback. He'd never mentioned any interest in Jews to me, though I knew they lived among us, segregated for the most part in their own districts, and that Papa's personal physician was a Spanish *converso*. But ever since we'd been old enough to learn our catechism, we'd been told that we must shun the Jews, an unbaptized and heretic people who crucified our Savior and practiced pagan rituals.

"I *don't* care about the Jews," Cesare said impatiently. "Did you hear anything I said at dinner? I only care about not acquiescing to Isabella. She exiled them. She cannot now dictate what happens to them. Before we know it, she'll be telling us how to rule Rome, as well. She'll make terms for everything and squeeze us dry in the process to gain benefices for her clergy."

"So, what will happen to them?" Despite myself, I was stirred by his description of the Jews' plight. I did not like the thought of them huddled outside our city walls or the threat of disease they posed.

"They'll have to pay the price for sanctuary if they want to stay. Papa will not lift a finger to help them. Or, rather, he will lift a finger— to take the ransoms our rabbis will offer to save their Spanish brethren. You heard him; he had to stop refurbishing his apartments to pay for

Juan's trousseau. Those Jews are now worth their weight in gold, and Papa will make sure to exact every last coin."

"A trousseau is for a girl," I giggled, and he shot me a brusque look. I sobered, realizing he was in foul temper, for what he believed was good reason. "And this plot by Cardinal della Rovere," I said, recalling Giovanni's reaction. "Are we truly in danger from him?"

"We are always in danger. You should know that by now, after seeing Juan slaughter one of della Rovere's dogs. But I suppose it's easy to forget, sequestered in your fine palazzo all day with Adriana and the Bride of Christ."

"Is that what you call Giulia?" I had to dig my nails into my palms to stop another giggle.

"I call her worse," he said grimly. "That's one of the less insulting nicknames given to her by the people of Rome." He resumed his brisk pace, forcing me to take up handfuls of my skirts to match his stride. "Bride of Christ. The Holy Whore. Curia Slut. She certainly has earned her disdain. Some even call her brother Alessandro 'the Petticoat Cardinal,' because he owes his hat to her favors. Yet Papa would waste his time and wealth on her just as he does on Juan, ignoring the fact that we're being hunted by a pack of wolves that would bring us down."

I grasped his arm, bringing him to a halt. "Cesare, *what* wolves? What are you saying?"

A shadow slipped across his face. He looked at me in silence before he said, "What I told Papa is true. I do have a spy in the Milanese court. He reports that Cardinal della Rovere is indeed conspiring with Il Moro to bring the French into Italy and depose Papa."

Alarm overcame me. "But how can they depose him? He was elected by holy writ. The conclave voted. It is God's will."

"Not according to della Rovere. He accuses Papa of taking the Holy See by bribery. He also says Papa is guilty of simony, nepotism, and—what do I forget? Oh, yes—rampant carnality, courtesy of la Farnese. I warned Papa not to trust the Sforza. They are as faithless as the viper on their shield. Already our friend Cardinal Sforza has made himself scarce, pleading illness. While your husband—well, suffice to say that should Il Moro join della Rovere's vendetta, we won't want that spineless cur in your bed."

"He isn't in my bed," I said, before I realized what I was doing.

Cesare went still. "What did you say?"

"He . . . he's not in my bed." My voice quavered; I was startled by the sudden avid look in his eyes. "Giulia told me that Papa put a clause in our nuptial treaty. Giovanni must wait until Papa declares that I am of age." I watched an indefinable emotion surface on my brother's face. "You didn't know?" I asked him. "You, who have spies in Milan and no doubt everywhere else?"

A hint of teeth showed under his slight smile. "I did not. I had only heard that Papa was considering it when he had the nuptial treaty drafted. I thought the Sforza would never allow it." His smile widened. "Well. It seems Papa is not as oblivious as I feared. At least he made provision for you in case we have played the wrong hand."

"Provision?" I frowned. "Giovanni and I are married. What can Papa possibly do?"

"According to canon law, non-consummation of a marriage is grounds for annulment," said Cesare, and before I could respond to this astonishing statement, he linked his arm in mine, turning us back toward the palace. "But you mustn't let it trouble you. Just follow our counsel and—"

"Stop it." I jerked away from him. "Stop treating me like a child. I know everyone only wants to protect me, but while everyone does, I am but a wife in name alone."

His voice turned cold. "I thought Giovanni meant nothing to you."

"He doesn't. But surely I can't be expected to live like this forever?"

"No, not forever," Cesare murmured. "I promise you that."

I returned to my palazzo in disquiet. Cesare's remark that the clause in my nuptial treaty might represent more than a temporary means to spare me until I came of age had unsettled me almost as much as the terrifying possibility that the French king, abetted by Milan, might march into Italy. We had not suffered such an invasion in hundreds of years; we had our own troubles, certainly—constant skirmishes over titles and lands, violent family feuds, and age-old rivalries—but no foreign power had successfully navigated the treacherous Alps since Hannibal. And history recorded that he had not fared well.

Still, the thought gnawed at my peace of mind, making me restless. When I finally fell asleep, I dreamed of running down an endless passage with blood dripping from my hands and awoke with a gasp to the crash of thunder outside, heralding a storm. My stomach felt sour, as if I had eaten bad mussels. Fumbling at my side table for flint and candle, I knocked both over. From her truckle bed at my side, Pantalisea groggily rose and lit the flame; leaning to me within the wavering light, she whispered, "My lady, are you ill?"

"Yes. It's too hot in here and I have a stomachache." I flung aside my thin sheet, slipping out of bed. "I feel as if I cannot breathe. I think I'll go out for some air."

"At this hour? But it's the middle of the—"

I waved her aside. "It's past the hour when anyone will see me. I'll stay on the loggia."

Pulling my light velvet robe around me and slipping my feet into low-heeled slippers, I felt another vicious stomach cramp as I left my chamber. Pearlescent gloom submerged the passageways and the *cortile* below. Tendrils of mist hung in the cloying air. The day's heat had given way to humidity; even from here, I could smell the pungent Tiber. Sweat dripped down my skin. As I breathed deep to ease the pangs in my belly, thunder rumbled again. I turned my gaze to the lower arcade, expecting to see the first spatters of rain. As I waited, listening to the arid clash of clouds above, I found myself ruminating again on Cesare's words.

If his spy was right and Giovanni's family plotted against mine, my husband had not known. His shock at dinner indicated as much. Although he did not inspire anything approximating affection in me, nor did I believe I inspired any in him, surely he must now be in a state of considerable concern. And if he knew about the clause in our nuptial treaty, which he must, he had every reason to be. Papa could see our marriage annulled. It meant nothing to me either way—until I thought of old Ferrante of Naples and his corpses. I did not want to end up wed to one of his sons. Giovanni of Pesaro might not be ideal, but at least he was beholden to my family, while another husband might have different loyalties.

You must exercise discretion henceforth. Albeit only in name, you are now a married woman.

As I heard Giulia's reproach in my head, I decided to go speak with Giovanni. He had not been rude or unkind, and we were husband and wife. Perhaps together we could reach an understanding that would help us steer clear of our families' entanglements. No doubt, he did not want our marriage annulled any more than I did.

Removing my slippers, I tiptoed down the staircase into the arcade. I knew I was being impulsive and nearly turned back, disturbed by the thunder, by fear that anyone might come upon me sneaking about. I should return to bed. Whatever was decided regarding my marriage, I must accept it. But I proceeded, anyway, ignoring another cramp. Just a talk, I told myself. I was entitled at the very least to hear my husband's opinion.

At the entrance to Giovanni's wing, I paused.

Though he had been residing here since our marriage, it seemed disused, the emptiness amplifying the fading smell of paint and plaster. There were no hangings on the walls. The floors were bare. I saw no chairs or tables, no candles in the sconces. Most disturbing was the absence of servants. Where were the pages on pallets, the chamberlains to stand vigil at the doors during the night?

As I took to the staircase leading to the second floor—where I assumed Giovanni kept his personal quarters—my footsteps echoed. Why had he not hired servants or bought furnishings? Did he prefer to live like an uninvited guest, or was he was simply too impoverished, unable to afford basic comforts? It occurred to me that this too was unsuitable. Must my own husband dwell in privation when Giulia disposed of this entire palazzo?

I reached the second level, where litter from the palazzo's refurbishment—a stack of wood beams, a crusty bucket, broken hammers and trowels—lay scattered about. I did not recall the precise location of the suite where our brief nuptial bedding had taken place, but as I neared a corridor illumined—finally!—by a guttering torch in a bracket, I vaguely recollected being guided through this very passage by Giulia on that night.

I came to a standstill. What was I doing? Even as I considered my foolhardiness, I heard muffled laughter from a nearby room. It awoke something inside me, the festering knowledge of too many secrets kept from me. Though I realized I would be wise to turn back, to remain for as long as I could the ignorant child everyone believed me to be, I stepped forward.

It was time that I behaved like the woman I would soon become.

The door was unlocked. Pushing it open, wincing at the creak of its unoiled hinges, I stepped into a darkened chamber with few furnishings. This was where my husband must live; I discerned faded tapestries on the walls, open coffers, chairs, a long table, an unlit candelabrum. A quiver of arrows, leather wrist guards, and other articles for hunting were tossed in a corner.

The strange laughter came again, louder now. Veering toward a closed door that must give entrance to his bedchamber, I hesitated, wondering what I might find if I opened that door.

An exhalation of breath stirred the hairs on my nape.

"Is Madonna certain she wants to see?"

Whirling about, I suppressed a gasp as I found myself facing Djem, materialized as if from nowhere, his pale eyes glittering in his swarthy countenance, his person inky as the shadows.

"You . . . I did not know you were—" I started to say, but he cut me off by pressing one of his fingers to my lips. It was not an aggressive gesture; it was almost filial, something Cesare might have done to prevent me from saying something I should not.

"If you talk too loud, they will hear," he whispered. He inclined so close that I smelled the musk of his person, the damp of night and tinge of sandalwood clinging to his clothes. I had not had much opportunity to engage with Djem; he was Juan's companion, always at his side, so much like a faithful dog, I'd ceased to see him as anything else. Now, as I stood before him, I caught a feral glint of teeth beneath his full lips, a scornful derision on his face, and I realized I had been more than simply foolish to venture here alone.

He was an infidel. A Turk. His kind had plundered our coasts, spilling blood and capturing women and children as slaves. He was not just Juan's dog. He was his wolf.

"I should go," I said, keeping my voice low but moving past him just the same.

Without warning, he gripped my arm. No one except Juan would have ever dared handle me thus, and as I glared at him, he said, "You came to see. There are many ways to look, my lady."

Turning to the door, he shifted a small metallic latch. A circle of light spilled through.

I found myself drawn to it as if by an invisible hand. It was a spy hole, drilled at eye level so that a vigilant chamberlain could keep watch over his resting lord.

"You must be very quiet," Djem warned. "Unless you want them to know you are here."

Unable to resist the enticement, the furtive conspiracy in his voice, I leaned forward, pressing my eye to the hole.

At first all I saw was a circumscribed view where candlelight trembled and darkness swam. As I focused, details materialized: a decanter and goblets on the sideboard, the stain of wine on their flame-limned rims, and a drunken person slumped on a chair. No, not a person. A heap of discarded clothing.

Straining to the left, I saw that enormous bed where I had lain so briefly with Giovanni, its red hangings pushed back as if to welcome my intrusion. A tripod of tapers bathed the scene.

If Djem had not been beside me, his breath fast in my ear, I would have pulled away.

The tableau before me made no sense. I blinked. A tear, perhaps from a bit of grit caught in my eye, seeped onto my cheek. Everything resolved itself with heart-stopping clarity.

A naked woman knelt on the bed with her pale buttocks lifted, her dark hair in disarray about her face. Behind her stood a man I recognized at once as Giovanni, despite his shocking nudity. As I gleaned his organ jutting before him, I clapped a hand to my mouth to stifle my laughter. I had never seen a man erect before. It resembled an overgrown mushroom.

He set his hands on the woman; she moaned, arching her spine. Giovanni guffawed. His was the laughter I'd overheard in the passageway when I approached the room, only I had failed to identify it because, until now, I'd never heard him laugh. As he pressed his fingers between the woman's legs, she writhed. Then a movement beyond the bed snared my gaze.

Appalled fascination overcame me as Juan stepped forward. He was bare-chested, every muscle sculpted beneath his skin. Incredulous, I saw him nuzzle Giovanni's throat. My husband threw back his head as Juan's hands snaked around his narrow chest to pinch his nipples. Giovanni groaned, began rubbing the woman more insistently. Juan bit him on the neck and said roughly, "Tell me what you want, Sforza pig."

The woman on the bed rocked back and forth, as if in desperate need.

"What was that?" Juan bit again, hard enough to draw a welt. "I did not hear you."

"You!" My husband's voice burst from him. "I want you, my lord!"

A ripple of low, cruel laughter came from Djem. I could not have moved if I had wanted to, transfixed as Juan unlaced his codpiece. Trembling, Giovanni leaned over the woman. Now I distinguished a curve of alabaster cheek within her lush fall of hair, her eyes closed as if in ecstasy when Giovanni yanked her to him, revealing her unmistakable profile.

In horror, I remembered the day Juan killed the man outside Adriana's palazzo and how Giulia had accused him of jealousy. I recalled her coy intimacy when she told me she was with child, and then, with an awareness that incinerated my last residue of trust, I thought of how Papa ignored her babe, though he adored all his children. He doubted her daughter was his, just as he doubted Gioffre's paternity, though he could never have imagined this.

Rage boiled in me. Indulged his entire life, taught to think only of himself, Juan just did what came naturally to him, repellent as it was. But Giulia—she owed us everything. She owed Papa everything. She was nothing without him; all she had was because of his love, and what had she given in return? Lies. Falsehoods. The betrayal of everything he held sacrosanct, his devotion turned to ashes in her mouth as she whispered in his ear and then left his side to deceive him with his son and my own husband.

I tasted metallic hatred in that moment, watching Giovanni thrust inside her while Juan positioned himself behind. My husband bucked his hips. I told myself to leave, knowing I'd seen enough, but Giovanni's gasp as Juan took him became a guttural cry, and I had the sudden sensation that, no matter where I fled, I would never escape this sight. The sensation dug into me, like a blade in my very core. Heat flooded me as Juan turned his head to stare toward the door.

At the spy hole. At me.

A lewd grin broke across his lips. He knew I was here.

I reeled backward, shoving against Djem. The Turk said, "Sometimes, my lady, it is best not to know," and I ran blindly from the room, staggering into the passage and down the stairs, into the arcade, where humid night collapsed around me like a sodden mantle.

Lightning flashed. Rain came pouring down, splashing into the fountain, pummeling the terra-cotta pots. I did not feel it—all that water, rushing over scorched walls, rousing steam. In my mind, all I could feel, all I could see, was flesh upon flesh and that cry from Giovanni that had seemed more like pleasure than pain.

My stomach twisted. I gasped at the force of it, doubling over. I did not hear Pantalisea as she came rushing to me and said, aghast, "Oh, my lady, you are bleeding!"

I gazed at my hands, smeared with blood as they had been in my dream. My robe fastenings had come undone; my nightgown, wet with rain, adhered to my legs. A stain bloomed from my groin like a melting rose. Visceral shame and understanding filled me.

"If you tell anyone about this," I said to her, "I will cut out your tongue."

She shook her head. "Not a soul. I swear it, my lady."

I turned away, trudging through the rain to my rooms, my newborn womanhood and knowledge stoking fiery vengeance in my heart.

CHAPTER TEN

In September, we assembled before St. Peter's Piazza to see Juan depart for Spain.

Papa had provided for him as if Juan were an anointed king, his entourage of nearly three hundred complemented by wagons crammed with apparel for every season, with carpets, platters, ewers, and tapestries. A special galley would transport ten white stallions from Mantua, though the Spaniards were reputed to breed some of the finest horses in the world.

In the Sala Reale, Juan knelt to kiss Papa's slipper. Our father wept unabashedly. "You must do us honor," he said haltingly. "Always wear gloves when you ride, as our people esteem beautiful hands. Heed Their Catholic Majesties and be tender to your wife, as she is of noble birth."

"Maybe he should say, *Don't treat her like one of your slatterns,*" whispered Cesare to me as Juan swaggered toward us. He had grown a luxuriant beard that made him look a satyr from a fresco, who had done too much too young. I had to force away the terrible image of him with Giulia as he gave Cesare a halfhearted embrace.

"I will not ask you to miss me," Juan said, drawing back.

Cesare smiled. "That is good, for I would hate to lie."

Juan turned to me. As he grazed my cheek, he whispered, "We cannot keep you *immacolata* forever, sister. I trust you now know how to best please your husband."

I recoiled from him. As he sneered with sordid intimacy, I said loudly, "Tiles from Seville, like those Papa has in his apartments, and calfskin from Toledo. I would be most grateful."

"Tiles and leather," said Juan. "Yes, I think I can manage." He went to where Papa waited to escort him to his cortège. I caught sight of

Djem among the onlookers, coiled with helpless rage. By Papa's command and the terms of his exile in Rome, he must stay.

Cesare snarled, "What did that fool say to you?"

I kept my voice light, though I longed to wipe the trace of Juan's lips from my cheek. "You heard me. He asked if I wanted anything from Spain."

The carved doors of the Apostolic Palace swung open. A roar rose from the piazza, the populace lubricated on free wine piped from the conduits to pour into the fountains.

"Farewell, brother," I said under my breath. "May we never meet again."

AUTUMN BROUGHT TEMPESTS and portents. In Siena, a statue of the Virgin wept blood. In Florence, an ascetic Dominican friar named Savonarola clamored from his pulpit that a conqueror would redeem Italy without ever drawing his sword. In our own Eternal City, roiling clouds flung lightning into the streets, imploding steeples and striking the old Vatican basilica, sending part of its decrepit roof crashing in, further souring Papa's mood. Now he had to seek the necessary funds to repair the roof, further delaying his apartment improvements.

"He has been despondent since Juan's departure, beset by troubles," Giulia sighed from where she reclined on a settle in the courtyard, while Adriana and I sat on chairs under the colonnade, sewing linens for the Convent of San Sisto, where I'd been educated. We were perspiring in our gowns. Storms might hurl hailstones and cave in rooftops, but the heat did not abate; the air was stagnant, muggy, rousing fears of plague. "Even the cardinals in the Curia were bold enough to challenge Rodrigo over Cesare's elevation."

She paused, to see if we were listening. With an edge in my voice, I said, "I hardly see what they'd have to challenge. Cesare has been cardinal of Valencia for over a year."

Giulia shoved at her neckline, exposing her throat. "They challenged it," she said, "because canon law forbids an illegitimate son from being raised to the scarlet. Only old Cardinal Costa seems satisfied by Rodrigo's decree that Cesare is the son of Vannozza and her first husband, but the others want his elevation annulled. When he heard of their plans, His Holiness threatened to create so many new cardinals in their stead, all Italy would be beholden to him." She laughed. "We should count ourselves fortunate the cardinals don't know about Rodrigo's other secret decree, made at Cesare's insistence, stating that he is in fact a Borgia."

I wanted to fling my embroidery at her, call down a fork of lightning to sear her where she lay. Apparently, so did Adriana, for she gave Giulia a withering look.

Giulia did not notice. "And as if that weren't enough, word has come from Spain that Juan has yet to consummate his marriage. Can you believe it? His new wife has been pining for over a month now, while he spends his nights with his new friends, stoning cats and dogs for sport."

At the mention of Juan, I clenched my teeth. Evidently he had not confided in Giulia before he left, for she appeared blissfully unaware of what I knew. "He behaves precisely as Cesare feared," Giulia went on. "Already he has spent every ducat he brought and had to request access to the revenues of his duchy, which Queen Isabella refused. She sent Rodrigo a letter that put in no uncertain terms what she expects of Juan, should he wish to retain his estate."

My embroidery hoop trembled in my hands as Adriana burst out, "*Dio mio,* do you ever listen to yourself? This constant pretension and knowledge of His Holiness's private business—do you think it does us honor? Do you think we take pride in your utter disregard for your married state, let alone whatever remains of your reputation?"

The color drained from Giulia's cheeks. I resisted a satisfied smile. She and Adriana had been at odds before, but never had Adriana been so forthright. Giulia struggled to find her voice. When she did, she could not curb her outrage. "How—how dare you say such vile things to me?"

"Someone must," said Adriana. "It is only the truth."

"It is *not!*" Giulia came angrily to her feet. Curled in the shade by the fountain, my Arancino stretched out a paw, unsheathing his claws. "I don't care what anyone says. The rabble knows nothing of my sacred bond with His Holiness."

"Oh?" Adriana eyed her. "I wager there is not a person in this city, highborn or low, who has not heard by now of this alleged sacred bond."

Giulia swerved to me. I gritted my teeth. It was not yet the time to confront her, and I feared she might sense the change in me. Thus far she had not, but only because she did not think me capable of hiding anything. How long could my ploy last?

"And you—so demure and complacent," she spat. "Do you condone these aspersions cast on me, after I've been like a sister to you? Or do you only pretend to care because your father ordered it, though you despise me because you want him all to yourself?"

I lifted my face to her. For the first time, I could not conceal my hatred. She must have seen it, she must have felt it, but she tossed her head as if it was of no account.

"Rodrigo loves me. I would have a care if I were you, for now that he's seen Juan to Spain he has no choice but to answer Giovanni Sforza's request to take you to Pesaro by the year's end. It is his right as your husband," she added, "which not even His Holiness can deny."

I froze. Had Giulia sensed my secret? I had done everything I could think of to hide it. Pantalisea taught me how to stanch the blood using bundles of absorbent cloth, which we later burned in the brazier, and how to douse myself in scent to disguise the subtle odor. The first flow was often the strongest, Pantalisea assured, but it lessened with time. Besides the frightening quantity and stomach pangs, I had not experienced much discomfort, but lately I'd begun to feel a dull ache in my breasts and had seen their subtle growth, which I disguised under a slew of new gowns that sparked Giulia's envy. She kept asking me why I needed so many new dresses. And now I waited, on my chair in one of those gowns, dreading the accusation that I was lying to everyone, including Papa, by concealing the fact that I had become a woman.

She snorted. "Or did you not know? The terms of your nuptial agreement stipulate your departure after a year of marriage, consummation or not."

Despite my relief that she'd apparently not seen through my ruse, I was alarmed enough to turn to Adriana. With frigid calm, she said to Giulia, "That is as it should be. A wife must go wherever her husband bids—a fact you seem to have forgotten, seeing as you ignore your own husband, my son, with flagrant impunity."

"As if that deformed son of yours could ever be a husband to me," snarled Giulia, and she stomped off, shouting for her women.

Exhaling, I asked, "Is it true? Must Papa send me to Pesaro?"

Adriana grimaced. "How can we believe a word that comes out of her mouth? She might have a care herself, lest her own tongue send her to perdition. Come; let's return to our task. The prioress expects these linens by tomorrow."

Threading my needle, I tried to tell myself that Papa would never let Giovanni take me away. I debated, as I had since that terrible night, whether I should tell him what I knew and turn his wrath on Giulia. He would see her banished, if not stoned in the piazza; but much as I relished the temptation, I knew I had to wait. I wanted to be the one who brought about her ruin. I wanted to look into her eyes as she realized that I, Lucrezia Borgia, the girl she had disdained and ridiculed, had destroyed her.

Nevertheless, anxiety overcame me. If anyone knew my father's mind, it was Giulia, who enjoyed his company daily, entertaining him at night and hearing his private thoughts. I set myself to uncovering the truth, ordering Pantalisea to eavesdrop in the galleries. I even sent a desperate note to Cesare, but he replied he'd not heard anything of the sort, escalating my concern that no one, save for Giulia, seemed to know what Papa intended to do with me.

Then word came that Papa wished to see me.

Donning a gown in his favorite shade of green, I went to the Vatican with Pantalisea. As we traversed the corridors, I saw unabashed admiration in the sidelong glances of young clerics bustling past me in their cassocks and even a slithering look from an elderly bishop or two. It was not how they'd regarded me before, with indulgence for a delightful child, but rather a furtive appraisal that warned me my secret was not as safe as I thought. Although they could not possibly know, in their eyes I saw the knowledge that I was indeed now a woman.

At the entrance to the papal apartments, I instructed Pantalisea to wait. The guards uncrossed their halberds, granting me passage into Papa's private domain, where he lived behind multiple doors with locks that were changed every week, protected by men with sharp blades and by poison-tasters with sharper senses.

Bejeweled imagery glimmered under the cressets. Maestro Pinturicchio had resumed his work here, despite the lack of funds, or perhaps with the money Papa had obtained from taxing our Roman Jews to rescue their Spanish brethren and bring them into the ghetto, just as Cesare had foretold. Some of the maestro's sketches were not yet finished, charcoal-drawn tableaux awaiting his paint. Yet as I moved farther into the papal sanctum, I saw that those walls and ceilings had been transformed with swirling color. I beheld the Christ swathed in crimson-lashed torment while his apostles grieved against a crushed lapis-lazuli sky and the black-clad Virgin and penitent-blue Magdalene held vigil before his stony tomb, their hands so lifelike, I might have reached out and grasped hold of them.

I slowed my pace. In the Sala dei Santi, I discovered myself as St. Catherine of Alexandria, golden fetters between my hands. Under a scarlet palanquin sat the Emperor Maximus, wearing Cesare's face. Looking outward, in flowing *a la Turca* robes, was Juan. We were only three among a multitude, nearly lost amid disputing merchants, men on horseback, and frolicking cherubs, yet our trinity was all I saw. For a moment, our images seemed more real than our true selves, like reflections in a luminescent mirror.

Then I sensed someone come up behind me.

"So much for doing us honor," Cesare said, motioning to Juan's portrait. "We could have sent my Michelotto to Castile in his stead, and my rogue would have made a better showing."

"Is that why we've been summoned?" I asked. "Because of Juan?"

"It is certainly why I was." He pulled a slim leather cylinder from his sleeve. "Papa ordered me to write this letter, advising Juan to behave according to his rank."

I smiled. "I should think Juan would rather hear advice from anyone but you."

He shrugged. "That's what I told Papa, but he'll not be seen wagging his finger in Juan's face. Still, it is not as if our brother needs to do much, providing he gets his wife with child and does not squander the duchy. Besides, he is gone now and Papa needs me. That is all I require." He paused, sensing as he invariably did my unvoiced apprehension. "I have urged Papa to seek accord with Naples," he added.

I felt a surge of panic. Was the clause in my nuptial treaty about to be used? Cesare had said non-consummation was grounds for an annulment. Had Papa chosen another husband for me? I found myself torn, fervently wanting to see the last of Giovanni, whose despicable acts with Juan and Giulia had erased any hope I might have had for harmony with him. After what I'd seen, I did not want him near me. But I did not want anyone else, either, especially not a prince of Naples.

"Do not worry," Cesare said, reading my silence. "This is not about you. King Ferrante is dying. The moment he does, his heir, Prince Alfonso, will assume the throne—*if* he has our blessing. Naples is a papal fief; Alfonso needs our investiture. So does Charles of France, who has threatened that if we favor Alfonso's claim over his, he will retaliate. I have suggested we marry Gioffre to Alfonso's natural daughter, Princess Sancia. If we do, it may force Milan and France to reconsider their current stance against us."

"Gioffre! But he is not yet twelve years old."

"And you were thirteen," said Cesare. "Papa should have married him first, rather than bind us to the Sforza." He leaned to me. "I have another secret to share: I believe your husband spies on us for Milan. Oh, do not look so alarmed. He will have cause to regret it, have no fear, but for now he must not suspect we know. I need your help, Lucia."

"My help?" I said warily. I did not like the sound of this. I had enough intrigue in my life, between holding my tongue over the scene in my husband's bedchamber and my own secret.

He cupped my elbow, bringing me toward Papa's room. "Giovanni is desperate to return to Pesaro. He claims the expense of living in Rome is ruining him, and he must attend to his court. Papa refuses to grant him leave. I want you to persuade Papa."

"To let Giovanni go?" I said. "Gladly."

"Not just Giovanni. I want you to persuade Papa to let you go with your husband. And I want you to request that la Farnese accompany you." He held up a finger, curbing my immediate protest. "It will only be for a short while. With Giulia gone, Papa will no longer be distracted by her, and I can impress upon him my concerns. And Giovanni will feel more at liberty to betray us once he's in Pesaro with you. He'll have his Borgia wife at his side; he'll think we trust him. Nothing Il Moro tells him must escape our notice. If Milan reaches an agreement with King Charles to bring in a French army, we need to know. Il Moro will no doubt call upon Giovanni to visit him, perhaps even exchange correspondence. You can be our eyes and ears there."

"You mean *your* eyes and ears," I said, even as my mouth went dry at the thought of leaving my home, my city, my family, to live in a strange place with a husband I detested almost as much as I did Giulia. Without fully realizing what I was about to do, I breathlessly told Cesare what I had seen. Once I was done, my urgent whispers echoing around us, I searched his expression for the reaction I expected, for the fury and revulsion that I had felt.

Instead, he said pensively, as if I'd just informed him of a brawl between cats, "Are you certain? The room was dark, was it not? Our imagination has ways of playing tricks on us."

"Of course I am sure. Why would I make up such a horror?"

"Then it's all the more reason to ask Papa to send Giulia with you."

"But I just told you why I don't want to go to Pesaro. They'll be there together! They will humiliate me right under my nose."

"We can only hope," he said aridly. "Listen to me, Lucia. You mustn't let emotion overcome your reason. This situation could serve us well. I assume you want your marriage annulled, yes? Well, so do I; I've never liked Giovanni, and now I like him even less. But we also must separate Papa from la Farnese, to deal with her as she deserves. If they are lovers and you bring her to Pesaro with you, she may fall into her own trap. She'll drag Giovanni into it with her. Imagine the uproar when you inform Papa that not only did you find your husband spying against us for Milan but also bedding his beloved Farnese."

I shuddered. "It's disgusting. Why can't we simply tell Papa? I saw them together; Djem knows, too, that vile Turk. Why must I travel all the way to Pesaro to prove it?"

"You could tell him. But I warn you, he may not believe you." He met my eyes. "You know how much he loves her. He will hate to hear of her infidelity from you, his beloved *farfallina*. She will naturally deny it and may even make him think you're being spiteful."

"Spiteful! She would not dare. It is the truth! I will swear it before the Curia, if I must."

"Calm yourself." He increased his pressure on my elbow, drawing me close. "Yes, you saw them. Yes, Djem knows. But he, Giovanni, and Giulia will deny it. It will be your word against theirs. Are you so confident Papa will believe you? Think carefully," he added, as I gnawed the inside of my lip. "Men are blind when it comes to love. Papa is no exception. He must have time away from her, to regain his reason. Perhaps if we leave her and Giovanni to their own devices in Pesaro, they will do it again. If you can also secure proof that Giovanni is Il Moro's spy, that alone will convince Papa. He'll be so enraged by such a betrayal that he'll believe anything else you tell him. You can destroy them both."

While the very idea made my skin crawl, the subterfuge appealed. Perhaps Cesare was right. Perhaps this was my opportunity to assist my family *and* wreak vengeance on Giulia.

"How am I supposed to find this proof? I only happened upon them one time. I don't think they've done it again, at least not since Juan left. And if I do catch them in Pesaro but have no proof of Giovanni's spying, what then? How will Papa believe me?"

Cesare replied, "You must have another witness, such as Adriana. She too must go to Pesaro; if Giulia attends you, nothing could stop her from going. She'll want to be the one overseeing your household; she will not trust such a task to Giulia. As to how you manage it, you needn't pretend with me. I know you have your wiles. You are a woman now, are you not, despite what everyone thinks?"

My heart stopped for a moment. "You—you know?"

"For some time. You are clever, but no one sees you as I do. All these pretty new frocks and the way you carry yourself . . ." His smile deepened. "You hide it well, and you must keep hiding it, for it too serves our purpose. Let Giovanni continue to think you're too young for the marriage bed. Let him turn all his attention to la Farnese. Bait the trap and you will snare them."

I hesitated. He was now asking me to set in motion my own exodus, the very thing I feared. "I don't think Papa will agree even if I ask," I said. "Pesaro is too far away."

"With a fast horse, I can be there in a day. Say whatever you must to convince him. Tell him the rumors of a French invasion frighten you. I know he's not as oblivious as he feigns; he also fears an impending conflict. He'll want you and Giulia out of harm's way." He reached to stroke my face. "He cannot refuse you. None of us can."

It was on the tip of my tongue to question that if Papa could not deny me, why would he not believe what I knew about Giulia? But Cesare had already turned me to the apartment entry.

"Come now," he whispered, his hand pressing into my back. "Be bold."

Within our father's chamber, a pine-scented fire crackled in the hearth. Copper-and-glass Moorish lamps from Spain swung overhead from the eaves. My nose tickled as I entered, so impregnated was the room with stale perfume and incense. Papa sat on a chair before the fire, head bare and legs propped on a quilted stool. Sparse gray hair fringed his tonsured pate; with one hand, he clutched a shawl about his shoulders as he brooded at the flames. He did not look up at our entrance.

A rustle of silk preceded Giulia. I tensed as she went past me to set a cup in Papa's hand. She assumed her place on a stool at his side, her cerulean skirts pooling about her. As she lifted her gaze, her pupils reflected the fire. "Rodrigo," she said, "Lucrezia is here."

Papa glanced up. "Ah, my *farfallina*. Come here."

Cesare melted away as I kissed my father's cheek. Papa was never the Holy Father to me behind closed doors; as he felt my touch, he let out a long sigh. Up close, I noticed a small, blood-clotted wound on his forehead. "Papa, you are injured!"

He winced. "It is nothing. Just another of my spells—"

"He fainted in the Consistory." Giulia tucked his shawl about him as if he were an invalid. "In mid-session with the cardinals. Fortunately, Perotto threw himself across the floor to cushion the fall. I keep telling him, he works too much. There is no use in berating those who cannot possibly understand reason. You might as well toss pearls to swine."

"Sforza swine, to be exact," said my father, and Giulia smiled at me. "Which reminds me, Lucrezia. Will you not greet your husband?"

With a start, I looked about. To my surprise, Giovanni stood by the sideboard. I glanced at Cesare. He leaned against the door, arms crossed at his chest as if he waited for a spectacle to unfold. I returned my gaze to my father, ignoring my husband. Papa directed his next words at Giovanni. "Well? Will you tell your wife what you said to me after I nearly cracked my head open trying to talk some sense into those fools in the Curia?"

"Pearls to swine," murmured Giulia, and I turned to Giovanni.

"Tell her," blared Papa. "Tell my Lucrezia what an ungrateful wretch you are!"

"I am not ungrateful." The tremor in Giovanni's voice marred his protest as he lurched from the sideboard. Out of the corner of my eye, I caught Giulia's spiteful smile. What I would not have done to wipe that smirk off her face, to put an end to this charade by telling Papa what I knew. I could feel the words ready to spew from my lips. I forced them back. He was unwell. The last thing he needed was to hear that the woman he honored beyond her worth had betrayed him. Besides, though I couldn't yet fully admit it to myself, I wanted to do what Cesare had asked. It was for the good of the family. At last I could prove my devotion to our Borgia cause.

"Your Holiness knows I have no other recourse." Giovanni held out his hands in supplication. "Everyone says you seek alliance with Naples against my family. If so, you put me in an impossible situation, for I bear allegiance both to Milan and to Your Holiness. I only asked that you clarify your position, so I may not act contrary to my obligations—"

The clank of something hitting the floor cut off his voice. Giovanni froze. Cesare had flung a purse at him from across the room. "There," said my brother. "We are tired of hearing about your so-called obligations. Take our payment and go. To Pesaro or the devil, we care not."

"Holiness!" squeaked my husband, even as he nudged the purse with the tip of his boot, as if to gauge its worth. I knew at once that Cesare goaded him, seeking to humiliate him in the hope that Giovanni would assert a shred of pride and stake his claim on me and his right to return to his city.

My father blew a disgusted breath out of his mouth. "You heard His Eminence of Valencia, Sforza. Do what you will. No one here will stop you."

Unexpectedly, Giovanni squared his shoulders. "We have an agreement. By canon and secular law, you cannot keep my wife from me. Not even the Vicar of Christ may stand in the way of those whom God has joined. If I go to Pesaro, Lucrezia must come with me."

Papa half-rose from his chair, stabbing his finger at Giovanni. "Your family plots against me. Your cousin Il Moro would bring the French into San Pietro itself to yank me from my throne. My daughter goes nowhere until you prove your loyalty—to us."

Giovanni blanched. Swerving to me, looking me directly in my eyes for the first time since our wedding day, he said, "They cannot do this.

We are husband and wife, bound by sacred vows. No one can separate us. Tell them."

I couldn't have planned it better. Though I didn't dare look at him, I knew Cesare was smiling. But I was also disconcerted by the apparent sincerity in Giovanni's words. He seemed to mean what he said, despite the perversion I'd witnessed through the spy hole. My resolve faltered. Maybe it wasn't his fault. Maybe Juan and Giulia had forced him to—

As if he sensed my hesitation, Cesare said, "Perhaps we should hear what Lucrezia wants."

"Absolutely not," said Papa. "Lucrezia is a child. She doesn't know her own mind yet. I will not send her to Pesaro with this ingrate."

Swallowing my uncertainty, I turned to my father. "Papa, may I speak?" He shifted in his chair, averting his gaze. "Papa, please?"

He tucked in his chin. "Very well," he grumbled.

"Is what my husband says true? Is it my duty as his wife to accompany him?"

The visible clenching of my father's jaw was confirmation enough. But I could still back away and let my husband escape to Pesaro without me. Only the thought of disappointing Cesare steeled my resolve, making me take my father's hand in mine.

"Papa, I know I owe my obedience to you above all others, but if it is my duty, perhaps we should honor it. All this talk of the French and war—it . . . it frightens me. I could go for a short while to visit my husband's court. I know you wouldn't want me in Rome should the worst come to pass."

My father grunted. As I waited, poised on the edge of his indecision, I wondered what *I* truly wanted. I had never considered it. Certainly no one ever asked me. Did I want Papa to admit now, before everyone, before Giovanni himself, that my marriage was a lie? Did I wish to be relieved of the pretense and return to my comfortable life, unburdened by a husband I did not care for? Or did I want to unleash the hatred inside me and see Giulia ruined, severed from my father's side forever? It troubled me that, despite everything, I did not truly wish Giovanni harm, although I knew that if I agreed to Cesare's plan, it would bring about his ruin. He was weak, I realized, beholden to two masters: Milan on the one side and Rome on the other. He must feel as though he had no other choice; the Sforza were, after all, his blood. He might be spying for his cousin Il Moro, but was I not preparing to do the same for my own family?

I did not know the answers. It was too confusing; everything was happening too fast. When Papa finally looked at me, his eyes gleamed with tears. "What do you want of me, Papa?" I whispered. "Tell me. I will do anything. I would give my own life."

"Oh, no. Never say that. Do not even think it." He caressed my cheek. "Is this truly what you want, my *farfallina*?"

I made myself nod.

He sighed. "So be it. You shall go to Pesaro with your husband."

I went limp. It was done. Gathering my courage, I said, "I . . . I would very much like it if Giulia came with me. I'd welcome her company. And if she stays here, I'd worry for her safety."

Giulia almost recoiled when my father asked her, "Would you?"

She had no choice but to assent. "As Your Holiness commands."

Papa nodded, returning to Giovanni. "I entrust you with their safety. When I order their return, you must bring them at once. You will personally escort them to Rome."

"Yes, Holiness." Giovanni bowed so low, I thought he might grasp my father's hem to kiss it. "Your Holiness is as munificent as he is humble. I will endeavor to serve you always and be a loving husband to your daughter."

Papa scowled. "See that you do. Christ's Vicar may not dare stand in the way of those whom God has joined, but Rodrigo Borgia will, if you give me cause."

As I stood, Giovanni snatched up the purse and pocketed it. Behind us, Cesare snickered.

Giulia gave me a taut smile. "I am honored you wish me to accompany you, Lucrezia. I will naturally be overjoyed to see you presented as the Signora of Pesaro."

My own smile felt keen on my lips. "The honor is mine," I said, as I turned to walk out.

She would learn that, no matter what title I held, I was still a Borgia.

PART II

1494–1495

The Foreign Blade

*I have heard this talk of Italy, but
I have never seen it.*

—LUDOVICO "IL MORO" SFORZA,
DUKE OF MILAN

CHAPTER ELEVEN

The last of 1493, the second year of my father's papacy, had slipped away. Shortly after Epiphany, word came that Ferrante of Naples had died—*sine luce, sine cruce, sine Deo*, reported our ambassador—and the French king issued more threats. Papa maintained a neutral stance, biding his time as blustering winter winds rattled the casements of the Apostolic Palace, blowing hapless birds against the glass. Then, in early March, he gathered the entire court under the musty wood-beamed ceiling of the Sala dei Pontefici to welcome the Neapolitan embassy.

I had the honor of flanking my father and Gioffre, my feet freezing in my ornamental slippers. As our sour-faced master of ceremonies, Burchard, oversaw the protracted ritual of conferring the papal bull that granted King Alfonso II sovereignty over Naples, thereby declaring our stance against France, Cesare watched impassively.

It was his first political achievement, but he did not show it, never once drawing attention to himself as he sat in his crimson regalia among the other cardinals, his handsome face composed. Yet a smile lurked behind his lips as the Neapolitan envoys presented Gioffre with his new title of Prince of Squillace, along with various lands, and Cesare had to lift a hand to his mouth as if to conceal his mirth when Papa declared our younger brother his "Borgia nephew" by his late brother. No one believed it, least of all the Neapolitans. They could barely conceal their own amusement as Papa stamped the decree of Gioffre's lineage upon a portable desk held by kneeling pages, as though the act of tattooing the parchment with his signet ensured its veracity.

All the while, Gioffre attempted to appear older than his years, standing on tiptoes in his azure tunic and jaunty cap, his curly burnished hair (an unmistakable Borgia asset) falling to his narrow shoulders, jewels taken from the Vatican vault weighting his hands and chest. To my eyes, he was charming—a pretty boy who would grow to be a comely man—but he must have seemed a mere child to the envoys. It was a fact not lost on my father, who said, "He's stronger than he looks," and delivered such a hearty clap to Gioffre's back that he nearly sent my poor brother sprawling from the dais.

We sat together at the feast. I had been charged with keeping Gioffre from drinking too much wine, but it proved an impossible feat, given the number of decanters circulating. His freckled face soon flushed with alcoholic excitement as he turned to me in his chair to whisper, "Do you think Sancia will love me as much as you love Giovanni?"

I sat in astonished silence. Even as I struggled for an appropriate answer, Papa's laughter rang out from his own dais, where he dined with Cesare and the envoys. He had recovered from his spell and overflowed with goodwill, even if he had been obliged to leave Giulia sulking in Santa Maria, as this was one of those occasions when he must honor the statute forbidding men of cloth from sharing their board with women.

"Yes," I finally said, with a quick smile. "What wife does not love her husband?" I felt a twinge as Gioffre preened; my words sounded as false as his patent of legitimacy, yet he seemed genuinely pleased, fishing in his tunic to remove an object wrapped in black satin.

"Sancia sent me this. Is she not beautiful?"

It was a miniature of a young woman in an emerald-hued gown, seated before an archway that offered a view of the famed Bay of Naples. Its execution was mediocre, hardly worthy of any Roman-trained artist, but compelling nevertheless, mainly because the subject had such arresting presence. Dusky hair accentuated her piercing gray-green eyes; her strong cheekbones and full lips lent her expression a defiant air. If whoever had painted Sancia of Aragon had stayed true to life, she might not be beautiful but she had undeniable allure, one of those rare women whose overall effect was more powerful than a mere perfection of features.

"She is lovely." As I returned the pouch to Gioffre, I was surprised to feel a stab of envy. Perhaps I had not lied. Perhaps Sancia would love him. Perhaps they would be one of those fortunate couples that found joy in their union. As I pondered this unlikely possibility, I realized how few illusions I had left, and I looked across the table to where my husband sat in his borrowed finery, his pallor revealing confirmation of his worst fears. Our alliance with Naples had indeed placed him in an impossible position, snaring him between loyalty to Milan and Papa's favor.

I sighed. Rather than worry about love, I had a task to perform.

I must discover which side he would ultimately choose.

GIOFFRE DEPARTED FOR Naples after Holy Week, during which he and my husband shared the honor of carrying the gold ewer in which my father had washed his hands on Palm Sunday. We also attended a passion play in the Coliseum, where the noble families outdid themselves staging a re-creation of our Savior's Passion, including banging drums and clashing cymbals to mimic the storm over Golgotha as the unfortunate actor playing Christ hung by ropes from the cross.

As soon as we bid goodbye to Gioffre, who traveled under the guidance of Papa's trusted cousin, Cardinal Francesco Borgia, Vannozza came knocking at Santa Maria's gate. To Adriana's dismay, Vannozza announced she was here to oversee my own departure and installed herself in one of the spare rooms, from which she assumed charge. I suspected Papa's intervention; now that he had made the difficult decision to let me leave for Pesaro, he wanted to preempt another squabble for precedence between Adriana and Giulia. Though my mother had not attended my wedding, she now oversaw the packing of my trousseau with ruthless efficiency, weeding out whatever she considered superfluous.

"I see no reason for her to take things she has no use for or can purchase later," retorted Vannozza when Adriana lifted an objection. "Twenty pairs of slippers are hardly needed when ten will suffice."

I was secretly glad she was here. Though I had no affection for her, the sight of Vannozza marching about with anxious chambermaids at her heels gave me satisfaction, particularly as her presence made Giulia scarce. When they happened upon each other at mealtimes or on the stairs, Vannozza ignored her with a disdain that must have rankled la Farnese to no end. I had no doubt Giulia had plenty to say to my father behind closed doors about my mother's interference, but I had no idea how much so until Vannozza barged in one day during my morning ablutions.

"It is an outrage!" Her voice resounded against the painted walls. "You must tell your father that under no circumstances can he allow that *puttana* to go with you."

Pantalisea and Murilla froze at my tub, soap-lathered sponges in hand. Exchanging a wary look with Pantalisea, I sank into my milky bath, letting the water lap over my chest. My mother took a step forward. I suddenly felt as I imagined a fawn must, caught in a clearing as the hungry predator approached.

"Rise," Vannozza ordered. "Let me see you."

My women cringed. Vannozza snapped her fingers, sending them scurrying out. I had to stop myself from slipping farther under the water as she said, "Either you rise now or I'll pull you up by your hair." She had reached the edge of the sheet-draped tub, hands planted on her broad hips. One look at those coarse, reddened fingers—which plucked grapes from her vineyards and wrung countless chickens for the pot— was enough to assure me she would do precisely that.

I drew a breath and came to my feet. Perfumed water slid off me in rivulets, unspooling over my pink-tipped breasts—which ached so much these days that I found myself teasing them in the privacy of my bed—and dripping over my hips to turn to glitter in my pubis, which also burned with a longing that could only be relieved by the midnight probe of my fingers.

My mother surveyed me from head to toe. "When did you start bleeding?"

I hesitated but knew that my evasion would not placate her. "Eight months."

"That long, eh?" She snorted. "And no one the wiser. Well, well. You have more of me in you than I thought." She reached to a nearby table, took up a towel from the stack, and thrust it at me. The chill of our encounter seeped into my very flesh as she added, "You cannot hide it forever. Rodrigo may send you to Pesaro because he feels it is best, but once you are there, in your husband's domain, Giovanni has every right to do with you as he pleases."

I lifted my chin. "He does not. Papa put a clause in the nuptial treaty that says—"

"I know what it says. Everyone in Italy knows what it says. They laugh at it and at Giovanni for consenting. But he is still a man, and men will have their way when their blood is up. You will be far from Rome, from your father and brothers, from anyone who would protect you. What will you do? Have that woman and dwarf of yours bolt the door? One kick and they will both end up with their legs in the air beside you. He can take all three of you if he likes."

Her callous words roused the memory of the three I had already seen, and I clutched the towel closer. "He—he is not like that. Giovanni would never force me."

"Oh? Have you already sampled him, perhaps, that you know what he will or will not do?" She stared at me. When her smile finally came, it was remorseless. "Can it be this is your doing? Do you actually *want* your father to send his whore to Pesaro with you?"

"No," I said, but my denial came too fast. I knew at once that I had betrayed myself.

"No?" she echoed. "Oh, I think yes. You asked it of him. The question is, why would you deprive him of his bedmate? I know you do not like her—no woman could—but he will be miserable without her. The French rattle their swords; the Sforza conspire; half the Roman barons hate him. He has a thousand troubles, so why be so cruel as to take her all the way to Pesaro, when you know how much it'll hurt—" She stopped abruptly. An expression of incredulity came over her face. Throwing back her head, she let loose a raucous caw. "*Ma, naturalmente!* You do it on purpose. You want your husband to fuck her instead."

I dropped the towel in my haste to vacate the tub. Slipping on the wet floor in my bare feet, I seized her by the arm, my fingers closing about its fleshy circumference. I had to do something, anything, to mollify her suspicions.

"If he does," I breathed, "then I will be safe. I will remain *intacta*."

She pulled her arm from me. "*Dio mio,* you are too naïve to play such games." She flicked her disparagement at me, just as she'd done in my childhood whenever I went to her with a scraped knee or stubbed toe, until I learned how little she cared. I did not mind. Let her insult me, as long as she believed I plotted to create a situation rather than realizing how far it had gone. "You think that slut will keep him from your bed?" she said. "If so, you know nothing of the world. Husbands have plenty of seed to sow." Her mirth ebbed; with a careless shrug, she went on, "But I approve. It is time. That woman will not ruin her figure by giving your father another child, nor would we want her to; I would have to strangle her spawn myself. She must be disposed of—she and that foolish Adriana, who has let la Farnese have her way when she should have locked her up in Basanello with her husband."

Her contempt took me aback. I'd always surmised she had grudging respect for Adriana, if only because Adriana had done Vannozza the favor of taking me off her hands.

She made an exasperated sound as she lifted my robe from a peg on the wall. "Another extravagance: Who needs an entire chamber in which to bathe, with indoor piping no less? La Farnese must have bells in her cunt for your father to have expended so much on this temple for her."

As I tied the robe about my waist, she added, "You mean to put an end to her, I presume. He won't abide being made a cuckold. All pontification aside, he's like every man: He thinks he can stick it wherever he pleases, but heaven forbid one of us should do the same."

"Yes," I said weakly. "That is what I want." It was true, though her perceptiveness so unhinged me that I felt the sudden urge to confess everything. I had to remind myself that, despite our uneasy rapport, I could never trust her. If she found out Cesare had also set me to spy on Giovanni, she would tell Papa. Women's intrigues were fine, but not those of men.

She abruptly wrenched my chin up. "You best know what you are about. Because once it is over and she is disgraced, you must submit. Do you hear me? You cannot remain a virgin. Let him play with la Farnese until you have your evidence, then make him suffer for it. Stamp your feet and shout; throw things and slam your door in his face. But once you have, you will forgive. You will forgive and invite him to your bed. You will spread your legs, shut your eyes, and let him plow you as often as needed until he gets you with child. Only then can you let him loose to wander, because you will be mother to his heir, above all others till death do you part. And who cares where he goes to satiate his lust, providing he does not rub your face in it?"

She dug her fingers under my jaw, her icy-blue eyes so like mine I might have been looking at my reflection, yet also terrifying in their lack of compassion, corrupted by deeds I could not imagine, by sacrifice and compromise and the loss of any innocence.

"A son, born of his seed. Only that will see you safe. Forget everything you may have heard of politics or war; it is not our concern. It has never been. We must endure. Better the man you are married to now than the stranger yet to come." She left the indent of her blunt nails under my jaw as she turned to the door. "Do not make the mistake of thinking you're unique," she suddenly said. "When we are young, we believe we can wrap life around our little finger, but life has a way of teaching us who is stronger. In the end, you are but a woman. If you fail, no one will give you a second chance. Go to Pesaro and be a wife; birth your babies, grow old, and die in your own bed. You never know when Fortuna will turn her back on you. Those who are wise know when to accept while we still can."

She yanked open the door, startling Murilla and Pantalisea, who jumped back, caught eavesdropping at the keyhole. Pushing past them, Vannozza started to tromp away.

"Mama," I called out, and I surprised myself with what I was about to request.

She halted. When she glanced at me, I saw something I had never seen before in her eyes—reluctant admiration.

"My Arancino," I said. "I must leave him behind. Would you . . . ?"

She gave a curt nod. "I will—providing the creature stays out of my larder."

CHAPTER TWELVE

We left Rome in a gusting May wind, escorted by men-at-arms and a train of mule-drawn baggage carts piled high with furnishings and leather chests of belongings.

Papa accompanied us to the Porta del Popolo, the city gate leading onto the Via Flaminia. Surrounded by his officials, he dismounted from his white mule with tears in his eyes and hugged me close, insisting that I must write to him every week, as he'd arranged a special courier service for our correspondence. A knot clogged my throat when Cesare then kissed my cheek; with his breath against my skin, he whispered, "Trust me, it will not be for long."

I returned to my mare beside Giulia. My father seemed to age visibly as he watched us pass under the gate. I kept looking over my shoulder at him, doubting my resolve, almost spurring back when he lifted his hand in a forlorn farewell.

I whispered a prayer for his safety. Then I focused ahead, riding in silence until Giulia said, "I hope we can put all the silliness behind us. I do so want us to be friends again. Your father wants it, too; he is worried that we grow estranged."

"Is he? Well, we mustn't have that. Papa has too much to worry about." I made myself reach out to clasp her hand, to prove I harbored no ill feelings.

At my other side, Giovanni muttered about checking on the vanguard and turned away.

Giulia sighed. "Your husband is trying his best; I was pleased that you asked to go with him to his city. He wants you to be happy, even if he faces this vexing task of having to please two masters."

I resisted the fury her words roused in me; she spoke as if she knew everything there was to know about my husband—which evidently she did. "We must make his house in Pesaro one of gaiety, then," I managed to say, "so he can find respite from his obligations."

"Yes! We must make Pesaro worthy of your presence." She leaned to me with a confidential air that reminded me with a pang of our early days in Adriana's palazzo, when we had truly been like sisters. "Vannozza tried to steal whatever she could from your trousseau, but Adriana put most of it back. We have enough furs, brocades, and silk to clothe an army." She laughed. "We'll make a pageant of it, a new gown for every night and new entertainment every day. You shall earn the envy of Isabella d'Este herself."

Her cheeks flushed. She didn't appear to recall that an army was precisely the threat we faced, should the French actually invade, or that she'd left behind her year-old daughter in the care of servants. All she could think about was diversion. I wanted to remind her of it, but that would spoil the illusion. Instead, I laughed, as well, joining in her lavish plans, even as I anticipated the hour when I would seal her fate.

CESARE MAY HAVE been able to cover the distance to Pesaro in a day, but for us it took two miserable weeks. The roads were in a terrible state of disrepair, pitted with holes, catching the cart wheels and laming our mules. Mercenaries roamed the Apennine passes, making travel perilous at night. We had to reach the safety of walls before dark, causing disorder among eager townsfolk ill equipped to receive us. Finally, on the afternoon of June 8, we reached Pesaro under a downpour that drenched us to our skin, thereby confirming to me that contrary to Giovanni's earlier assertion, there must be mosquitoes in his city.

I rode beside Giovanni. Around us, sodden banners hung like limp rags from balconies; the avenue leading to Giovanni's palazzo was thronged with cheering, mud-spattered crowds. I could hardly find fault with the enthusiasm of my reception, though by the time we entered my quarters on the second floor of his palazzo, I was chilled to the bone. My teeth chattered as my women stripped me of my sopping velvets and Pantalisea tried to arrange for hot water to be brought from the kitchens.

"No," I said weakly, swathed in a fur robe as I clambered into the upholstered bed. The sheets had been freshened with sprigs of rosemary, but the herb barely disguised the pervasive smell of mold and, as

I suspected, my other women went about waving cloths in the air, swatting away the mosquitoes perched in the chamber's corners. "This house feels as if it hasn't been attended to in years," I said. "A bath now would be my death. I just want to rest awhile."

I promptly fell into dreamless sleep. When I awoke, the entire night had passed and bright sunlight speared through my chamber windows. It was a welcome sight after the dreary rain, as were my women awaiting me.

"Donna Giulia has been here twice," Pantalisea informed me as I winced and climbed stiffly out of bed. "She is eager to plan tonight's *festa*."

"A party, tonight? Is she mad? I'm so sore I cannot even think of dancing." I moved to the table where my women had set out fresh brown bread, a hunk of white cheese, watered wine, and a bowl of cherries. I was famished. Once I ate my fill, I felt much improved, though my legs remained wobbly and my thighs were chafed from days in the saddle.

Insistent knocking came at the door. As one of my newest ladies, pretty blond Nicola, went to open it, Giulia pushed past her, radiant in carnation-colored silk, her sleeves slashed and primped with ribbons, her hair done up in pearls and a lawn caul, as though she were about to pay a visit to the Vatican. Rings winked on her fingers; from her earlobes dangled the pair of diamond-and-topaz pendants she had finagled from me.

"So, you are awake," she declared. "I thought you might spend the entire day abed like Adriana. Poor dear. Travel is not healthy at her age. She should have stayed in Rome." Giulia passed her critical gaze over me. "Are you planning on dressing? Your household waits to receive you. Giovanni is with his councillors. We have the entire house to settle. From what I have seen thus far, it's rather gloomy and neglected, but once we set up your things, it will do, at least until we can hire proper artisans to beautify the walls. Your ladies can assist us."

"I think my lady should probably—" Pantalisea started to protest, but I stopped her with a lift of my hand.

"Donna Giulia is right. I am the signora and this is my home. Fetch me a gown." It occurred to me as I spoke that while I had been sleeping, Giulia had been about my new court, alone with Giovanni, but I pushed aside the troubling thought. Even she would not dare, not so soon after our arrival.

Once my women had plaited my hair and helped me into a rose velvet gown with fitted sleeves, Giulia swept me through the two-story palazzo constructed by my husband's grandfather, a fierce condottiere who'd made his fortune fighting Milan's enemies. Compared to Santa Maria in Portico, the house was depressingly provincial, my husband's perennial poverty displayed on its unadorned walls, which lacked any tapestries to cover the chipped plaster. But the *sala grande* had a lovely, if faded, gilt-wood ceiling, and the exterior boasted a handsome portico and upper loggia, with actual glass-paned windows to let in the light. There was also an interior *cortile* and garden with fountains and passable copies of ancient statues.

Giulia sighed. "I am afraid the town itself is not much better. Besides the main piazza and cathedral, Pesaro hasn't had any renovations in a hundred years at least."

"At least it's not raining," I replied, and I marshaled the servants to arrange the furnishings in the *sala* to complement what I had brought. When Giovanni emerged bleary eyed from his council, it was to find fresh tapers in my golden candelabrum, my silk and wool tapestries with scenes from the Old Testament gracing the walls, my Turkey carpets underfoot, and fringed cloths draped over the scarred tables and sideboards.

He said warily, "Do we expect company?"

I took his hand in mine. He flinched. It was the first time since our wedding that I had touched him. "We will," I said. "You must send word to your nobles that you wish to present your wife. We can hire musicians and hold a feast, with wine and dancing."

He drew me toward the fireplace, out of earshot of my women. "I cannot possibly afford it. My council has just informed me that my treasury is empty. All those months in Rome have bled me dry. And my cousin Il Moro refuses to pay a single ducat on my *condotta*." He imparted this last with a hint of accusation, as if I was somehow to blame for his impoverished circumstances.

I sighed. "That is indeed troubling. But Il Moro and Papa are at odds over Naples and the French, so we can hardly expect payment whilst you are pledged to both their service."

"What am I to do?" He raked a hand through his hair. "I can scarcely afford servants, and now you are here. . . ." He shook his head in dejection. "I did wrong in bringing you all this way. I had to leave Rome, but I failed to consider your comfort."

Yes, he certainly had, I thought, just as he had lied about Pesaro's salubrious climate. But I merely said, "Look about you. Are we not comfortable?" I leaned to him, pecking his cheek. It was my second spontaneous gesture of affection, and he went still, as if he was uncertain of my intent. "Let me see to it," I reassured. "I'll write to Papa to request the funds we need. In the meantime, I brought some money of my own. And what is mine is now yours, my lord." I refrained from asking what he had done with the pouch Cesare threw at him in my father's chamber or the most recent installment of my dowry, which he must have received. Papa would never have sent me away to fend for myself, but again I curbed my tongue. Giovanni's penury would keep him in our debt—which only suited Cesare's design. With my husband busy scraping to the hand that fed him, he might be less inclined to re-ingratiate himself with Il Moro.

"Sit." I poured wine from a decanter. "Let me have Giulia order a meal prepared for you, and then you must take your rest." Leaving him by the fire with a dumbfounded expression on his face and the goblet in his hand, I returned to my women.

Giulia regarded me suspiciously, betraying that she had overheard. "You just contended with him as if you had been married for ages. Perhaps you do not require my company, after all."

I rolled my eyes. "Nonsense. How would I manage without you? I don't even know the names of the servants in this house yet. Could you see to his meal and attend to him? I must write to Papa." I lowered my voice to a confidential whisper. "It seems we require funds."

She gave a cautious nod, stepping past me toward where Giovanni sat. He looked up, his eyes widening. Even from across the hall I saw a blush spot his cheeks.

I smiled. Cesare would be proud of me.

A WEEK LATER, after a round of festivities at my expense that kept our guests satiated on quail and claret (and decimated my limited money), the reply from Rome arrived along with a packet of letters from my father, conveyed by his secretary, Don Antonio Gacet. As he bowed before me, his deep-set Catalan eyes appraising my surroundings, I noticed an unexpected figure among his escort. With an insouciant nod, Michelotto acknowledged my recognition.

"His Holiness feels your absence keenly," Gacet said. "He is beside himself that you and my ladies Giulia and Adriana are not accommodated in the manner to which you are accustomed." He extended a heavy leather pouch, along with a sealed envelope. "This is all I could bring for now, but the envelope contains letters of credit. Given the current unrest, our situation with the Medici bank is not as reliable as we would like, but His Holiness has other investments. If necessary, you may exchange those letters to draw on his funds."

"I appreciate it." I handed the articles to Adriana, who stood vigil beside my chair. She had woken from her two-day torpor to pounce like a tigress, only to find I had managed perfectly well without her. Unable to find fault with my household arrangements, she took to shadowing my every move—an irritating circumstance, as I could hardly go about uncovering Giovanni's secret dealings with her treading on my hem, but now the need to be rid of her, at least for a short while, took on significant urgency.

"I trust we have not caused His Holiness undue worry?" I said. "I fear I may have misled him into thinking matters here are more dire than they truly are. Zia, perhaps we should compose a letter, thanking His Holiness for his generosity and assuring him we are quite well, though we do miss him terribly?"

She brightened at my suggestion that she might be of some use other than as a guard dog. "A splendid idea. But first we must read his letters to you and—"

"Oh, no!" I cut her off with a gesture of dismay. "I completely forgot that I promised to see to the arrangements for our upcoming visitors." I smiled apologetically at Gacet. "My lord husband has invited the illustrious Caterina Gonzaga and her husband, Count Ottaviano, and I want everything to be perfect. I fear this house has suffered from a lack of feminine oversight. Might you have any business with Donna Adriana that I need not be present for?"

Gacet assented, as I hoped he would. "Indeed." He said to Adriana, "His Holiness has important recommendations for you, my lady."

"Does he?" Adriana looked as if she might clap in delight. "Well, then, we must hear them at once. Come with me into the study. Lucrezia, we shall attend to that letter later—"

"Yes, yes. As soon as you're finished with Don Gacet, send word to me." I was already rising from my chair, beckoning my women. As we passed the men idling near the casement, I glanced at Michelotto. Tucking his hat under his arm, he followed me out.

Instructing Nicola and Murilla to stay by the garden entrance, I led Michelotto into the enclosed thicket of fruit trees and graveled paths. Pantalisea padded behind, as it would not do for me to be alone with him. I was glad Giulia had retired to her rooms to nap. She wanted to be as refreshed as possible for Caterina Gonzaga's arrival, having heard that Giovanni's former sister-in-law was a fabled beauty. Giovanni was also absent, gone to his Villa Imperiale in the hills overlooking the city to plan a hunting weekend for our guests.

"Though if we are asked," I advised Michelotto, "I shall say you brought me news from my brother the cardinal of Valencia. I assume you have . . . ?"

"Oh, yes." His peculiar slate-colored eyes gleamed. "His Eminence also has important recommendations that he wishes to impart."

I smiled. He looked so out of place in Pesaro's rustic surroundings, in his parti-colored hose, fitted tunic, and wide-topped boots, that no one would ever mistake him for a local. "How is Cesare—I mean, His Eminence the cardinal?"

"I also call him by his proper name, my lady. He does not stand on ceremony in private. Alas, he is not as well as we might hope. The situation grows difficult. Our informants report that the French already begin to prepare to cross the mountains. Their main obstacle thus far was devising special transport for these new cannon they bring—lightweight dragons that can spew iron instead of stone and have greater range. King Charles boasts that he will bring Naples's walls down about Alfonso's ears and bury him in the rubble."

"*Dio mio.*" A pit opened inside me. "Is there any threat to Rome?"

"Who can say? The French are savage; once they're let loose upon us, they could do anything, including marching upon the Eternal City itself. His Holiness has sent King Charles a stern letter, upbraiding him for disrupting the peace, but has also begun to fortify the Castel

Sant'Angelo in case he needs to take refuge. My lord Cesare also does everything he can to rally others to our cause; he had sermons preached throughout the papal states on the Feast of Corpus Christi, warning that if the French enter Italy unopposed, everyone shall suffer. Thus far, only Naples has heeded his warning. King Alfonso rallies his troops, but the barons of our central Romagna region, who are forever lawless, seek only their advantage, while the other city-states are uncommitted. *La Serenissima* is too powerful to fear an invasion. Florence will assist us if it can, but the Medici remain under siege by that devil Savonarola, while Milan, as we know, is willing to spread her legs—begging your pardon, my lady—for Charles."

"Yes," I said, "no offense taken." I took a moment to focus on the pathway ahead, trying to overcome the nightmarish image of the French swarming into our land like barbarians.

"Your assistance is urgently required," added Michelotto. "My lord Cesare believes that once Signore Giovanni receives His Holiness's command from Rome, you shall uncover the truth of his dealings with Milan."

"Command?" I came to a halt. "What command is this?"

"As His Holiness's vassal by *condotta,* he's required to join our defense of Naples."

I let out an incredulous laugh. "My husband? Join with Naples? He'll never agree. He is family to Milan and . . . Or do my father and brother intend to *force* Giovanni to choose?"

"I would not presume to know their intent, my lady. But you show an impressive grasp of the matter, as my lord assured me you would."

As if she stood beside me, I heard my mother's voice: *Do not make the mistake of thinking you're unique. . . . In the end, you are but a woman.* I closed my eyes, shutting out her words. She was wrong. I was not like her. I was above her and all others of my sex, because I was a Borgia.

"What must I do?" I asked.

Michelotto lowered his voice. "We believe there will be letters between here and Milan, advising Il Moro that Giovanni is at his disposal."

"Letters? But how can I . . . ?" My question faded as he removed a purse from his cloak. I untied its cords, peered within to find a jumble of uncut rubies. "This is a fortune!"

"Indeed. Gemstones are less easy to trace and you will require the use of bribes. One of the signore's private secretaries has expressed himself amenable."

I shoved the purse into my skirt pocket, looking over my shoulder. "His staff has served him for years," I whispered, though there was no one near us, Pantalisea having taken a seat on a bench a distance away. "I doubt any of them will prove amenable—"

"This one has." Michelotto's smile tugged at his scar. "His name is Zacapo. He will make copies of the signore's correspondence. Once you review the letters, you must forward all relevant news to us through your usual messenger. Do you dispose of someone trustworthy? You must avoid any appearance of familiarity with Zacapo."

"Yes. My Pantalisea can help." The purse weighted my skirts as we retraced our path.

Pantalisea rose. I extended my hand to Michelotto. "Please tell His Eminence that I will endeavor to satisfy his expectations. I trust you will have a safe trip back to Rome." Then I turned away, concluding our engagement, though not before I saw him wink.

CHAPTER THIRTEEN

Giulia's laughter rang out. Seated at my dais, I watched her take a stool in the center of the floor with her lute, a pack of young-bloods in tight hose gathering about her while Pesaro's cantankerous noblewomen, their faces caked in ceruse, sat on their chairs to stare and scowl.

It had been two weeks since Giovanni's former in-laws, Countess Caterina Gonzaga and her husband Count Ottaviano, had arrived in Pesaro, dispelling the rumor of Caterina's charms, to Giulia's delight. While the countess's manners were as refined as her clothes, she was less Venus than Hippona—too tall, with a square jaw and thin lips, her close-set eyes and mannish hands matching her ardent stride. When Caterina first descended from her carriage, Giulia practically purred; immediately thereafter, she strived to eclipse the countess with her own extravagant attire, whether she was riding the hunt or regaling us with a musical interlude after the feast.

I had thought Caterina oblivious at first, seeming unperturbed as la Farnese whirled about her like an exotic bird, but the countess soon showed her mettle. When we spent a few days at the Villa Imperiale, she outrode Giulia at each of the hunts—no one sat a saddle like the Gonzaga, who were renowned for their horsemanship, no matter the terrain—while ensuring that her husband, who was quite shorter than she was, comically so, but also dark-eyed and virile, was kept at arm's length from Giulia.

Now, as Giulia strummed the lute, her dulcet voice enunciating lyrics of love while she tilted her head to display the gem-studded coils of hair about her face, Caterina leaned toward me to whisper, "I've come to the conclusion that a wife must be either very confident or very foolish to let such a woman remain at her side." As she spoke, she gestured toward our respective husbands sitting across from us on their dais, staring at la Farnese as if she were an angel materialized in our midst.

Startled by her declaration, I took up my goblet. "Donna Giulia is a dear friend. Indeed, she's been like a sister to me since we lived in Rome. I have nothing to fear from her."

"Oh?" Caterina's smile exposed her discolored teeth. "Even the most loving of sisters will compete for supremacy if she feels she has the advantage, as clearly this one does."

I felt a cold start, picturing Giovanni on the bed as he hauled Giulia toward him. I forced out a dismissive chuckle. "Do you imply that she would dare . . . ?"

"You speak as if it is impossible." Caterina's voice was cool. "From what I've seen, your loving sister thrives on attention. A woman like her, living so near Giovanni—well, I've known him for years. He was, after all, wed to my own late sister. He's always too easily swayed by invitation. And, unless I am mistaken, I believe he has not yet received yours." She turned to face me with unabashed candor. "Am I being too forward?"

I shook my head, focusing on Giovanni. He appeared flustered, but didn't he always these days? The expense of the Gonzaga visit was wrecking his nerves. He worried constantly about money, about the French and Milan, all of which caused him to drink too much. As far as I knew, and I'd kept close watch, thus far he had done nothing untoward, staggering drunk to bed every night. I had also discovered that, contrary to his assertion at our wedding banquet, he truly had no skill for dance and attended these soirees reluctantly, knowing he'd be obliged to conceal his incompetence. But was I mistaken? Had he and Giulia found a way to evade my scrutiny?

As I pondered this unsettling thought, Signore Ottaviano pushed back his chair and stood.

Caterina went rigid. Her husband strode past us to where Giulia sat, waiting until she'd finished her saccharine recital before he shouted, *"Bravissima!"* He began to applaud, compelling the rest of us to follow suit. Giulia extended her hand for him to kiss.

"As I said," remarked Caterina, "women like her cannot tolerate being ignored."

"Yes," I replied coldly. "I begin to see your point."

"Do you? I am so relieved. I was wondering, in fact, about that little subterfuge I witnessed this afternoon."

I tore my stare from Giulia to her. "What—what did you say?"

"Oh, *cara,* I too was once a new wife, many years ago. I recognize a bit of intrigue when I see it. That lady of yours, the dark one with the big eyes: She was trying to hide . . . a packet of letters, was it? You chased me out of the room so fast, I did not have the chance to tell you that if you are monitoring la Farnese's correspondence, I approve. I would do the same, if I were you."

"It's not—I wasn't . . ." Inwardly, I cursed my ineptness, as well as Pantalisea's. We had been so cautious with our scheduled rendezvous with Zacapo, to the extent that I didn't even know what he looked like. Pantalisea described him as a thin, fidgety man with beady eyes and sour breath. He was also greedy, pocketing each stone Pantalisea brought, only to report that he had nothing to offer in return. There had been no letters of import arriving at my husband's office, he insisted. Every time Pantalisea returned empty-handed increased my doubt that Giovanni was indeed working against my family—until today after the hunt, when I entered my rooms with Caterina, laughing about how she'd almost sent Giulia tumbling from her mare as they rode in pursuit of a boar, to catch Pantalisea, red-faced and hiding something behind her back. I had not found a chance yet to see what she brought. I had to hustle Caterina out with vague excuses, discard my soiled hunting clothes, bathe and prepare for the feast, all the time berating Pantalisea for her clumsiness. I planned to examine the letters tonight.

Caterina took in my stunned silence. "Oh. I see it is more serious. May I be so bold as to offer a word of advice? To be rid of a rival is one thing, but to betray a husband quite another. He has the right to imprison or execute you, should he believe you impugn his honor."

I could not speak, fearing this perceptive woman had unmasked me.

"But wives must look out for one another," she went on. "We must protect our shared interests. I will not say a word of this. Perhaps I might entreat a small favor of you in return?"

I nodded in relief. "You need only say the word."

"Oh, I will." Caterina returned her attention to the floor, where the musicians had struck up a refrain and her husband coaxed Giulia to dance. "I only need some time to consider it. In the meanwhile"—she stood like a tower, the voluminous folds of her apricot-hued *camora* spilling about her—"I believe it is time we gave our *signori* their due."

She strode forth, forcing Giulia aside to assume her place. I was turning toward Giovanni when the idea stole over me. Giulia stood immobile on the floor, thunderous that Caterina had just ruined her ploy. I motioned to Giovanni, who begrudgingly abandoned the dais; when he reached my side, exuding the stench of wine, I murmured, "I am so tired. I wish to retire. Would you mind? Giulia has no partner, and you know how much she loves to dance."

"If you insist," he muttered.

"Grazi, Signore." I dipped my head, watching beneath my lashes as he offered her his hand and Giulia bestowed him with a brilliant smile. They assumed position beside the Gonzagas, startling Caterina, who, after our exchange, appeared taken aback by my willingness to send my husband into Giulia's ready arms.

I ignored her reproachful glance at me.

Beckoning my women, I left the hall to race to my apartments.

"WHERE ARE THEY?" I said as soon as I burst into my chamber, leaving Nicola and Murilla in the antechamber. Ripping off my sapphire-studded snood, which had been crimping my hair all night, I shook out my tresses as Pantalisea dug between the feather mattresses.

"You do realize that is the first place anyone would look?" I snapped, but my reproof died as she handed me a leather packet affixed with cords for a courier. Opening it, I turned to the candle on the desk, pushing aside my hairbrushes, combs, and vials of scents and lotions.

As I pulled out handwritten pages, Pantalisea looked on anxiously. "Zacapo said the courier arrived only this morning. He copied two letters from Milan and included an original for Lady Giulia that he felt you should see."

I brought the candle closer and peered at the paper in hand, finding to my dismay lines of unintelligible marks. "This is in a cipher. Did he include a key?"

"No. Perhaps my lady is not expected to read it?" she said as she searched the folder.

I frowned. "How am I supposed to send these on to Cesare when I have no idea what they say?" I examined the other letters. "Wait. This one: I can read it." As I did, my breath quickened. "It is from Giulia's husband, Orsino. Her brother Angelo . . . he is dying at the Farnese estate in Capodimonte, and her family gathers at his bedside. Orsino orders her to join them."

Pantalisea crossed herself. "Bless his soul. You must inform Donna Giulia at once."

"Wait. You've not heard the rest. Orsino writes to her directly because her brother Cardinal Farnese approached my father for permission to fetch Giulia. Papa refused. Orsino says . . ." I returned to the passage in question, reading it aloud: *"His Holiness is so transported by his unseemly passion that, now that it is known the French cross the Alps, he refuses to grant you leave to travel and warns your departure from Pesaro will be considered a grave breach of conduct and insult to his sanctity. Nevertheless, both your brother Cardinal Farnese and I, as your husband, command you forthwith, for as the pope may order in spiritual affairs, in temporal ones you owe allegiance to us. We therefore,"* I concluded, with a triumphant lift of my voice, *"expect you in Capodimonte within the week and will send an escort to ensure your safety, should the count of Pesaro not see fit to provide you with one."*

I folded the letter into a square.

Pantalisea said, "You . . . you must tell her."

"I cannot. Papa forbids it. Why trouble her with something she can do nothing about?"

"Oh, my lady. Her brother is dying! She must have the chance to—"

"I said no." I thrust the empty folder at her. "Return this to Zacapo." From my desk drawer, I removed the pouch and shook out six of the rubies. "This is enough for him to buy his own estate. Tell him I expect him to forward any future letters addressed to Giulia. No copies; I want the originals, like this one. I'll dispatch these others with my next courier to Rome."

"Yes, my lady." With a forlorn look, she retreated from the room. I picked up the folded letter from Orsino, holding it for a moment.

Before I could doubt myself, I fed it to the candle flame, watching it curl into ash.

CHAPTER FOURTEEN

We bid farewell to Caterina Gonzaga. She embraced me in the courtyard under a midmorning sun that carried a hint of spindrift from the sea. "Do not forget my advice," she said through her practiced smile, slipping a sealed paper in my hand. "For His Holiness from my husband and myself: a small personal request. I hope it is not too much to ask."

"I'll send it at once," I assured. "Though he might not have opportunity to act upon it."

She sighed. "It is such a nuisance, isn't it, these French coming here like locusts? Naturally, His Holiness has more pressing concerns. Whenever he can attend to it, I would be most grateful." She kissed my cheek. "I do hope we shall see each other again, Lucrezia. It has been a pleasure."

I would not miss her, I thought, as she mounted her upholstered carriage and the entourage rumbled away. Though she had brought me a sense of companionship that I'd not realized I longed for, I did not welcome her petty blackmail. I contemplated the envelope she had given me, stamped with her signet. Probably a request for a cardinal's hat or settlement of a dispute; I seemed to recall her mentioning someone scheming to overtake one of her castles.

I turned back to the palace. The local nobles had dispersed as soon as they realized that free libations were at an end. Giovanni trudged off to meet with his council; the servants were busy washing the floors under Adriana's directions; and though she had waved farewell from the loggia, Giulia retired to her rooms, unaware of her brother's impending death.

I should have felt vindication. After everything she had done, it was the least she deserved. Instead, melancholy overcame me. What was I doing here, in a place where nothing was mine? At this hour, Rome would ring with the church bell, the markets swarming with merchants. Dogs would be yowling from the terraces. My own Arancino would be stalking the *cortile* for mice, while in the Vatican, Papa would sit down to his midday meal of ham and wine.

I wished I could pack my coffers and depart. I had not accomplished anything noteworthy save to keep the news of her brother's demise from Giulia. I had not secured any evidence of spying or adultery, and my sudden regret that I had allowed Cesare to persuade me to come here turned everything gray as I trudged up to my apartments. The afternoon stretched desolate before me—devoid of the bustle of Rome or my family, my sole distractions being an unwelcome afternoon with Giulia, once she woke from her nap, and a round of purloined correspondence from Zacapo, though still none had proven eventful, written in that unintelligible cipher that I assumed someone in Papa or Cesare's employ could translate.

In my chamber, Nicola and Pantalisea were airing out my gowns. "Leave me," I said.

Kicking off my slippers, I fell fully dressed onto the bed. I shut my eyes, tears burning behind my lids. I was fourteen years old.

How could I have known this would be my last hour of peace?

I AWOKE TO wailing.

Groggily, I shifted on my pillows, leaden with sleep. The light in my room had darkened. I must have been exhausted. It was dusk already; I had slept away the entire day.

The cry came again. I staggered up and was moving to the casement overlooking the inner courtyard when Pantalisea rushed in, Murilla and Nicola close behind. One look at them stopped me in my tracks. "What—what is making that awful noise?" In my sleep-addled mind, all I could think of was the French. They were here. They had marched across Italy and over the Apennine range separating us from Rome.

"Zacapo," said Pantalisea. "Signore Giovanni had his office searched. God save us, my lady, he knows everything."

Fear iced my veins. As I spun to the window, Pantalisea said, "No, my lady, please don't look!" but I wrenched back the curtains to stare through the horn pane at the scene below.

Along with the night, mist crept in from the sea. Firebrands were on the walls; in the inner *cortile,* guards in livery held down a small thin man, who struggled as they tore off his sleeves and yanked his tunic to his waist, forcing him to his knees.

Before him stood a wood block.

He cried out again, a desperate lament. I saw Giovanni emerge from among his guards. Beside him was a man holding a poleaxe.

Horrified disbelief flared in me. My breath came in bursts as I frantically fumbled at the window latch, trying to get it open. My fingers kept slipping. I'd barely managed to push it ajar when I saw my husband motion. The guards holding Zacapo forced his arms onto the block. As I felt a cry hurl up my throat, a desperate plea to halt the proceedings, Zacapo wailed and the guard swung his blade, cleaving the secretary's hands from his wrists.

Blood gushed forth in such a torrent that I recoiled, that cut-off wail of terror and pain ringing in my ears. I had to clutch at the sides of the window to hold myself upright as the guards detaining Zacapo leapt back and he collapsed onto the cobblestone, his dismembered hands still twitching. A dark pool began to spread around him, thick and dark as ink.

And as I stood there, petrified, Giovanni lifted his eyes to me.

I reeled back, my legs threatening to buckle as I turned to my women. Pantalisea was crying. Murilla clutched handfuls of her skirts, and Nicola had gone ashen.

I will not faint, I told myself. I will not. I will not. . . .

After a seemingly endless silence, I heard myself say, "Did Zacapo tell them about me?"

Pantalisea nodded. "My ladies Giulia and Adriana are packing. The signore granted them leave to depart for Capodimonte and—"

I did not wait to hear the rest. Ignoring her cry for me to halt, I dashed through my chambers into the passageway, my heart pounding as I raced to Giulia's apartments.

I found the antechamber in upheaval, her women throwing belongings into two large leather travel chests. An unfamiliar Franciscan friar in a cloak stood like a sentinel by the hearth. When he saw me on the threshold, his face turned cold. Giulia's personal maid looked up from where she sorted through clothes. She dropped an armful of items and came to me.

"Donna Lucrezia, I beg you, this is not the time. My lady is enraged and—"

I thrust out a hand, pushing her aside. Ignoring the staring friar, I stepped toward the bedchamber. As I neared, I caught sight of Giulia, dumping unguents and jewels into a coffer on the bed. "How could she have done this to me?" I heard her say. "My own brother died before I could see him. We would never have known had Fra Tadeo not brought word. And all because of her."

"Perhaps that secretary lied," Adriana quavered. "Maybe he wanted to cover up his own treachery by blaming Lucrezia."

"*Dio mio,* how can you still defend her? You heard Fra Tadeo. He came here because we did not arrive in Capodimonte as expected. Your own son Orsino and my brother Alessandro sent a missive informing us that Angelo was ill. That secretary received the letter but never delivered it, because he gave it to her instead. He spoke the truth when put to the question. He said he gave her my letter because *she* had paid him to spy on us."

"But Lucrezia is a child. She couldn't have—"

"A child?" Giulia's laughter was harsh. "When has any Borgia ever been a child? They sprung from Vannozza's womb fully cloven and horned, like the devils they are."

Adriana let out a gasp as I made my presence known, crossing the threshold into the chamber. Giulia looked up at me, her hair tangled about her enraged face.

"If we are devils, then you are the devil's handmaiden." My voice was quiet, assured, despite the fact that I was shaking inside, aware that I had been unmasked. "You can hardly play the innocent, after what you have done."

Giulia flung the vial she held against the wall. It shattered, suffusing the charged air with perfume. "I trusted you! I trusted and cared for you. I loved you as a sister—and *this* is how you repay me." She stalked toward me, her hand raised, ready to strike.

Adriana let out a horrified cry. "Do not touch her!"

I lifted my chin, inviting her blow. She came within inches of me. "Be careful," I told her. "I might do more. I might tell Papa everything I know—about you, Juan, and my husband."

The words came out before I could stop myself. As soon as I spoke, Giulia faltered, the rage fading from her cheeks, turning her skin so pale I clearly saw a blue vein threading her temple.

"You stupid, ignorant girl," she breathed. "You know nothing. You're but another pawn to them, a blade honed to carry out their foul deeds. This is Cesare's doing, isn't it? He set you to the task; he convinced you to ruin me, but you were never a danger to me. The only ones you have harmed are that pathetic husband of yours, whose missives you intercepted, and his greedy rat of a secretary, who lost his life over a handful of flawed rubies."

"Don't dare speak to me of my brother. This is about *you*. I know everything. I was there that night in Giovanni's apartments in Santa Maria. I saw how you betrayed Papa."

She went still. And then, to my dismay, a malicious smile crept over her mouth. "Is that what you think? Let me tell you how matters stand between your beloved papa and me."

Adriana moaned. Sudden fear tightened my chest like a vise.

Giulia said, "Everything I did was at *his* command. Rodrigo sent me to Giovanni that night. Yes, His Holiness, your father, our blessed pope, ordered me to entertain your husband. He already knew what Juan and Djem were to each other and what Giovanni desired. Rodrigo used me to entrap the Sforza—and all to protect you."

I couldn't move. I could barely breathe. Her sordid revelation uncoiled inside me like a serpent, fanged and venomous. "You . . . you are a liar," I whispered. "Papa loves me. He would never—"

She cut me off with a toss of her head. "Oh, yes. He loves you. *La famiglia* is in fact all he loves. I was his plaything; he took me when I was no older than you, before I'd even graced my husband's sheets, and he trained me to be his whore. Do whatever is necessary, he said, to keep my Lucrezia safe."

She paused as I stood motionless, aghast at the enormity of what she described, the obscene deliberation of it. "Or did you think that clause in the nuptial treaty was sufficient?" she said, her voice taunting. "Do you think Giovanni would ever have agreed to wait until you came of age had he been left with any alternative? Blackmail, dearest Lucrezia, is the most powerful incentive that exists. Giovanni would never dare lay a finger on you as long as Rodrigo kept his dirty secret. But you've spoiled it. Your zeal to prove your Borgia worth has unlocked your door to him. I hope you find it worthwhile. You cannot escape him now. Rome stands to fall—and you belong to the Sforza."

"No," I heard myself whisper. "It's not true. . . ." But I couldn't stop seeing Juan in my mind—the way he'd seemed to know I was there, watching—and hearing his whisper before he left: *I trust you now know how to best please your husband.* He had done those vile things with Giulia and my husband under my very roof; he had not tried to hide their depravity, although there must have been dozens of other places to go, although he must have realized how much they risked. But I believed Juan capable of anything. Not Papa. Not this.

"We are not so different, you and I," went on Giulia. "We are both slaves to Rodrigo's ambition—though while you went about seeking your petty revenge on me, I ensured that your precious virginity remained untouched."

"You are lying!" My voice rose to a howl. "It's not true. You did this—you and Juan!"

Her face turned implacable as stone. "You truly are one of them. You deserve whatever happens, because, like every Borgia, you are incapable of recognizing the truth." She met my stare, held it for a blistering moment before she turned away to the coffer on the bed. "But whether you believe me or not is of no concern." Her voice was subdued now, stripped of emotion. "I've had enough of you and your family. It is over. Finished. I will not be their whore again. I will return to my husband to beg his forgiveness and veil my dead brother, whose final hours you have denied me. Take her away," she told Adriana, without looking at me. "I don't want her near me. She means nothing to me."

I began to shiver, even as I said defiantly, "You cannot leave. I forbid it. My father forbids it."

"No, my child, say nothing more." Adriana rose wearily from the bed and stepped to me; her face looked sunken, as if she had aged years. "We must go. Her brother is dead, and my son, her husband, commands her return. He sent the friar to escort us. There will be a scandal if we do not obey. Come, we must return to your rooms. You are without stockings or shoes. You shall catch your death, and then your father will indeed have our heads for it."

"He will," I threatened, directing myself at Giulia. "He will never forgive you for this. When I tell him what you said, he will never let you set foot in Rome again."

Giulia did not answer, did not even glance at me as Adriana propelled me through the antechamber, where Giulia's women stood petrified and the friar glowered. In the passage, we found Pantalisea pacing. She immediately assumed charge of me. As Adriana started to turn back, I grasped her sleeve. "Wait."

She paused. Her expression was full of despair.

"It cannot be true," I said. "Why would Papa do such a thing?"

She lowered her eyes. "I cannot answer for him. I only know that before we left Rome, Rodrigo told me to not interfere should your husband and Giulia . . ." She faltered. When she finally spoke again, the resignation in her voice made me doubt everything I believed, everything that I trusted and cleaved to. My entire world felt as though it were crumbling all around me when Adriana said, "But they never did. He never called for her. I believe that no matter what he may have done, Giovanni cares for you. You must care for him in return; do whatever is required to regain his trust. The French are upon us. They have Milan's support and an army to trample us into dust. You must not lose Giovanni's protection now. He is all you have, should your father fail." She inclined to me, pressed her lips to my cheek. "God keep you, Lucrezia. You are not my charge anymore."

She walked back into Giulia's rooms. As she left, my entire childhood vanished with her, the brittle illusion of safety shattering apart. I couldn't make sense of the void inside me, the terrifying sensation that I had somehow been misled, baiting a snare prepared by others, for reasons I couldn't comprehend. I no longer knew if Giulia had been protecting or deceiving me; I no longer was sure if she had been a friend or a foe. All I knew was that I felt lost in a palace that was not my own, in a world where truth was unfathomable, opaque, and slippery as shadows.

Pantalisea led me to my apartments. By the time she had undressed me, put me to bed, and assumed vigil at my side, I realized that in one thing Giulia had not lied: Giovanni would indeed eventually come to me.

God help me if I tried to resist him.

DAYS TURNED TO weeks.

I stayed cloistered in my apartments, feigning an injured arm from the riding undertaken during the Gonzaga visit. Pantalisea and Nicola tiptoed about the palazzo and brought news of Giulia and Adriana's precipitous departure, followed thereafter by Giovanni himself, who left for his country villa. I avoided looking out the windows; although the *cortile* was scrubbed clean, Zacapo's mutilated corpse hung in the piazza for the gulls and ravens to gnaw, a grim reminder of what befell those who betrayed the signore.

For the first time in my life, I was alone, without Adriana or Giulia, without anyone to give me counsel. It was so unexpected, the solitude, that at first I did not know what to do with myself. I lay awake at night, tormented by Giulia's revelations, by the image of my father sending her to Juan like something he had paid for, which, in some respects, he had.

I found myself doubting. He did love her. I knew he did. As the initial shock waned, I began to think she had only said accusations to hurt me. When had she ever told the truth? She may not have succeeded in seducing my husband here, but Adriana had confirmed it was her charge. Adriana may have advised caution because outside forces gathered against us, but she'd heaped plenty of derision on Giulia in the past. Nothing they said could be believed, I kept telling myself, and even if it could, Papa must have his reasons. He always acted in our best interests, for his family, whom he loved more than life itself.

Still, I could not forget what Giulia had told me. And as the last of summer turned into autumn, as winds rose from the sea to raze the city and fog shrouded the palazzo, I was cast adrift in a world of shadows, where nothing I saw or felt seemed real anymore.

No letters came. I was not surprised. Giovanni had no doubt ordered all correspondence routed to him. Still, the lack of news was unsettling. I had no idea what was happening beyond Pesaro, if Cesare and Papa had sought refuge in the Castel Sant'Angelo as the French

scorched their path to Naples, if the French king had been met in battle, if Naples had triumphed or fallen.

It could not go on indefinitely, this hollow existence; it had to end.
And so it did, shortly before Christmas, when I awoke from one of my
desultory naps to hear horses coming into the *cortile*. Moments later,
Pantalisea brought me the news.

Giovanni had returned.

Within the hour I had bathed, coiffed, and dressed myself in tawny
silk, cut in the Milanese style, with a squared bodice and banded lime-
green sleeves, my hair under a lawn caul, my wrists and fingers devoid
of jewels. I sought to present an image of maidenly innocence, though
heat flared in my cheeks when my husband appeared in my doorway,
his boots brushed clean of mud from the road. In his hand, he carried
a satchel.

I had ordered my women into the first *antecamera,* with strict in-
structions to remain there unless I called for them. I did not want them
to hear whatever might occur. As I faced him, alone for the first time
since our arrival in Pesaro and a year and a half of marriage, I wondered
what exactly he had prepared for me. Fear set my pulse racing, while I
couldn't stop staring at his satchel. Had he brought some instrument of
pain?

"You look well." He moved to the chairs set before the fire; upon the
intarsia table between them, Pantalisea had left a decanter and goblets.
The decanter was full with pale Frascati wine. It was undiluted. If I
must submit, I would dull my senses as much as possible.

I poured from the decanter, trying to avoid another glance at the
satchel at his feet.

Men can have strange appetites. . . .

He accepted the goblet with a curious half smile. "Are you?" he
asked. "Well, I mean? I regret to have been gone so long. It could not
be helped." He paused, as if to lend emphasis to his next words: "I had
to go to Milan to welcome the French king."

Milan. All this time he had not been at the villa. He'd not even been
in Pesaro.

I bit my lip, took up the other goblet. It was not my role; I had
heard somewhere (or had I read it?) that wives must not query their
husbands. I was here to heed and obey.

"I went because of my *condotta*," he said, as if he'd heard my unvoiced question. "And because Il Moro invited me. King Charles has brought thirty thousand men." I gave a sharp intake of breath. "Yes," he added. "That many, along with all the other necessities of a well-equipped army: hundreds of horses and artillery and—"

I could not stop myself. "Is it true what they say about his cannon?"

"How do you know about that?" he asked sharply. When I did not reply, realizing I had once again betrayed myself, he added, "I should have known. They kept you informed until the incident with Zacapo. Yes, it is true; his cannon are unlike any we have seen. His Majesty King Charles organized a demonstration for us outside Pisa. It was impressive." I felt his gaze on me, gauging my reaction. "So impressive, in fact, that should he take it into his head to conquer all of Italy, I daresay there is not a city-state that could withstand him."

I felt sick. He sounded as if he admired it, as if he welcomed this foreign intrusion into our land.

"Charles of France is pious, however," Giovanni went on. "He respects the Holy See and wishes only to stake his claim on Naples, using it as a base for a new crusade against the Turk. He told me it is the infidel, not the pope, who poses the greater threat. But if His Holiness refuses to grant him safe passage through the papal states—"

"Safe passage?" I burst out, horrified by his nonchalant air. "You think my father, ruler of Rome and Supreme Pontiff, should allow this king and his hordes safe passage to raze the Romagna? To trample the very wheat fields that provide our bread, to plunder and pillage as they see fit and scorch their way to Naples to wrest the crown from that realm's anointed head?"

Giovanni sipped from his goblet. "What I think has no bearing. If His Holiness does not, then King Charles has no recourse other than to turn his impressive cannon on Rome."

I loathed him in that instant, more than I ever had. He was *enjoying* it, reveling in our impending devastation. "I suppose what your cousin Il Moro thinks has no bearing, either," I said. "I suppose none of your family is to blame, even though the French king and his impressive cannon are here only because the Sforza invited them."

He lifted his eyes to me. I couldn't tell if it was disdain or relish I saw in his expression.

"We invited them," he said, "because His Holiness, your father, has behaved with utter disregard for the sanctity of his throne. He seized the Holy See by corruption and has turned it into his private trough, which he will drink dry if we do not stop him."

"Your cousin Cardinal Sforza did not complain," I retorted, enraged by his brazen contempt for my father. "Nor, Signore, did you, when offered my hand in marriage."

His face darkened. "You'd be wise to watch yourself. His Holiness has no power over me anymore. He has no power over anyone. In Florence, the Medici have lost. Savonarola has thrown open the city to the French, while the Romagna barons, whose wheat fields so concern you, welcome them with castles and retainers. As for the anointed head in Naples—well, King Alfonso must now defend his kingdom. The Borgia have no allies; your family is doomed."

It took all of my self-control to not spit in his face.

"But perhaps His Holiness believes he can still prevail." Giovanni's laugh was hoarse, cold. He did not laugh often; the raw satisfaction behind the sound made me realize that my family must indeed be in grave danger. "I hear Spaniards are stubborn that way, and his most recent letter does not indicate any fear. All he seems to care about is his whore."

He reached down into his satchel and retrieved a folded parchment, broken seals dangling. I had to clench my hands about my goblet, lest I yank it from his hand.

"From His Holiness, your father." He dropped the letter on my lap. "You will see that, despite his travails, he is enraged over Giulia. The French captured her when she tried to return to Rome, after she went to Capodimonte and your father threatened her with excommunication. He paid her ransom—indeed, the French should have asked for double—and went to greet her at the gates. Alas, she left him only days afterward, to flee to her husband's castle in Basanello. His Holiness now accuses us of not doing everything we could to keep her here, indeed of forcing her to leave. I suggest you write a response assuring him that we tried everything to persuade her of her folly."

I sagged on my chair, overwhelmed by relief as I looked down at the letter. Giulia had lied. If what she claimed were true, she'd never have attempted to return to Papa. He would never have paid her ransom or expressed fury that her departure from Pesaro had endangered her. He *did love* her. What had transpired between her, Juan, and my husband— Papa had no part in it.

I almost didn't notice Giovanni rise to his feet. As I belatedly brought my gaze up, I thought he was ready to depart. He'd said what he had come to say. As soon as he walked out, I would read Papa's letter and then compose a reply to give him comfort. Giulia had deserted him, as she'd said she would; Papa must only read now of how much I loved him, as his family were the only ones upon whom he could rely in this time of tribulation.

"I will write my letter at once," I said. "If you like, when it is ready you can—"

"You will write it later." As I sat frozen on my chair, he added, "Or did you think I would forgive you?" He pulled a pouch from his jerkin, emptying its contents into his palm. "Afterward, if you please me, I'll let you have these set in a bracelet. It would be a shame not to display them, considering how much they cost."

He stood, waiting, the rubies like fragments of bloodied teeth in his hand. Then he threw the gems aside. "I will have what is mine. Go to your bed."

I was so stunned, I couldn't move. He stood over me with the same expression he had shown in the *cortile* before he ordered his secretary's hands cut off.

"Thieving *Marrana*," he snarled. "Get up this instant."

Staggering to my feet, I whispered, "The clause—in our nuptial treaty . . ."

"Do you think anyone cares about that now?" His smile was cruel. "Your father and brother are about to be crushed under France's heel. There is no clause. There is nothing to impede me from taking my due." He took a step toward me. "Must I drag you by your hair?"

Turning blindly, biting back a scream that threatened to erupt from the core of my being, I moved into my bedchamber. My hands felt numb as I fumbled at the lacings of my sleeves. "I must summon my women," I said, as he came up behind me. "I cannot undress without them, and—"

"I don't want you to undress." He pushed me onto the bed. "On your knees."

Crawling onto the mattress with my back to him, my heart pounding in my throat, I waited. A convulsive sob escaped me as he flung up my skirts, wrenching apart my legs to search roughly. He stabbed with his finger. My strangled yelp sounded like that of a bewildered animal.

"Did you think you could escape?" he said, jabbing his finger again and again into me, the pain sharp, piercing, like a talon in my flesh. "That you could humiliate me and laugh about me with your family? You will not speak. You will not move. You will take it as you deserve."

I heard the agitated tugging of laces and cloth as his hose fell, the chill of the tips of his codpiece on my lower back as, with shocking suddenness, he rammed his hips against me.

I closed my eyes, trying not to tremble, even as shudders raced under my skin. I expected a lance of pain, a fiery invasive thrust, but I felt nothing but his groin grinding against me. He cursed, pulling back, one hand pressed upon me while he did something to himself with the other. He was panting through his teeth.

Looking warily over my shoulder, I saw him roughly fondling his *cazzo,* rubbing its limp shaft. He kept rubbing and rubbing before he spat on his hand and said, "You are not ready." Again, he pushed his finger inside me. I clenched my teeth, biting back the sudden urge to ask him if he needed Juan present to rouse his manhood. He wrenched his hand out, wiping something warm on my thigh. "But you will be. When I decide to have you, you will be ready whenever I say." To my disconcertion, he yanked up his hose and strode out.

Moments later, I heard the chamber door slam shut.

I remained immobile, crouched on my knees, waiting for the thundering in my ears and chest to subside. Then I heard Pantalisea venture from outside the door, "My lady?"

Her voice roused me. I righted myself on my elbows, pushing my disheveled hair from my face as she stepped past the spill of rubies on the carpet. "The door," I said. "Lock it."

She came to me, holding me as I retched up watery bile that reeked of wine; I had not eaten any food. My groin hurt. I could already feel how much more it would hurt later.

Pantalisea caressed me. "There, now. It is over."

Not until I looked down did I realize what she believed had occurred. Giovanni had smeared my thighs with my blood.

"*Immacolata* no more," I whispered, and I pressed a hand to my mouth to stem the burst of desperate laughter threatening to engulf me.

CHAPTER FIFTEEN

"He has not returned?" Pantalisea asked. "Not since that night?"

I shook my head, glancing at Nicola and Murilla, who tossed a ball of yarn for a kitten one of the stable grooms had brought me. On the walls, the sconces flickered; there was no hearth in the upstairs apartments of the Villa Imperiale, but we had various braziers scattered about the room to keep us warm. "Not once," I murmured.

It was the sole thing for which I could be grateful; it had been a dismal end to the year. Giovanni had shunned my company as if I had the plague, though we had no choice but to sit like effigies in the *sala grande* during the Epiphany feast for our vassals. Following the distribution of gifts and visit to the manger in the piazza, where children in peeling gilt wings serenaded us, I retreated here to the Villa Imperiale. Though the villa overlooking Pesaro was only a hunting lodge and not meant for winter residence, as January came and went in downpours of freezing rain, I sequestered myself in the tapestry-hung rooms to await any word from Rome.

I had received only one letter from Cesare, given to me by Giovanni just before I departed. It was mud-stained and undated, but I assumed it had reached us weeks after its dispatch. Giovanni had kept it from me, no doubt out of spite, until I mounted my litter. "See what the Borgia pride has reaped," he sneered, thrusting it into my hands.

Every night before bed, I reread its terrifying lines:

My beloved Lucia,

I write to you from the Castel Sant'Angelo, where Papa and I stand our ground. As you may know, Papa refused the French passage through our states, condemning King Charles's invasion and claim on Naples. But now the French are here. They have turned on us like a scourge. We had to flee to the *castel* for our lives, but I do not know how long we can hold out. I can hear their infernal cannon even from behind these walls; they are everywhere, clamoring for Rome's blood. I do not know if this missive will ever reach you, but if it does, know that my every thought turns on you and I would gladly die a thousand deaths to see you safe.

> Your brother always,
> Cesare

I wept, clutching the worn paper to me, spotting its thin texture with my tears.

Fortuna's wheel had already turned. The future I still saw as uncertain had become their past, leaving me in daily dread of the next courier, anticipating the news that we were now under French rule, my father and brother held captive, imprisoned, or worse.

I tried to distract myself with endless rounds of embroidery, recitals from Petrarch's sonnets or Dante's *Divina Commedia*, and meaningless gossip, that time-honored pastime of women to keep boredom or fear at bay. This evening, though, the gossip wasn't so meaningless, reminding me of my husband's persistent—and, to Pantalisea, inexplicable—absence from my bed.

"But why?" she now said. "Surely he does not think you're with child already?"

"God forbid." I threaded my needle. I tried to sound nonchalant. After Cesare's letter, the brutality of Giovanni's assault on me had waned. What I had undergone at my husband's hands was nothing compared to what my father and brother might endure. "I do not care to ponder his reasons," I said. "I'm simply grateful he has chosen to stay away."

But when I thought of him with Juan in that bedroom, I couldn't help but wonder. Giulia had been indiscreet when it came to Vatican scandals; she'd relished disclosing tales of cardinals caught *in flagrante delicto* with acolytes. Men, it seemed, did indeed have strange appetites. Perhaps Giovanni was one of them? Perhaps he was unable to perform with a woman unless he had another man with him? I shuddered at the thought, but it certainly fit with what I had seen. Still, I could not confide my suspicions to Pantalisea. Let her continue to assume the obvious, that I had undergone the usual if overly vehement marital experience—though I knew that what was expected of a wife had most certainly not happened to me.

"Maybe he has a mistress," I remarked. "It's common enough among husbands, yes?"

"Have you any evidence of it?" she replied, in wide-eyed indignation.

"No, but he could still have one." I had to avert my eyes to hide my bitter amusement. I did not believe he had a mistress and prayed that whatever motivated him to keep his distance would continue, for when he did decide to assert his rights again, I would be at his mercy. I dreaded it, my entire life unspooling before me—an endless monotony, punctuated by bucolic celebrations of feast days and the occasional tawdry violation. And children: I must bear his children. God save me from that.

"Does my lady still . . ." Pantalisea said. We had striven to keep my monthly courses hidden for so long that we continued to speak of it in hushed tones, as if it were a permanent secret.

"Why do you ask?" I feigned curiosity to hide my sudden panic. I had bled afterward but hadn't known if it was my menses or the result of his brutality.

"Because a woman can conceive," she said, "if the moon is in its second cycle and—"

A knock at the door interrupted her. My household steward, Lucca, stood on the threshold. "Signora, forgive me, but there is a stranger outside the gates."

"A stranger?" I set aside my embroidery. "Are the gates locked?"

"Yes, my lady. We always bolt them at dusk, as you commanded."

"Then send him away. He could be a spy sent to ascertain my whereabouts." It had been one of my most pressing fears; though I was Countess of Pesaro, a Sforza wife, if my father and brother were held captive, then apprehending me might fetch a hefty ransom. "Wait. Do you know who he is?" I asked, for it also seemed unlikely that a potential kidnapper would appear alone at this hour, without troops at his back.

"No, my lady, but he looks to have traveled a long way. He just sits there on his horse."

Was this the courier at last? With equal hope and foreboding, I pulled on my mantle and gloves and hurried into the courtyard with my women. The black sky hung over us; snowflakes swirled in the frosted air. I could see my own breath as I ordered the unlocking of the postern door set within the massive gate portal. The mastiff kept chained here year-round as protection strained at its tether. Its keeper, a one-eyed veteran of some distant battle, had his hand at the dog's collar, ready to release it. As the door swung open, I thought that no matter what news this man might bring, I would greet it as a Borgia.

Silhouetted outside was a shapeless figure slumped on a horse whose head hung low, every one of its ribs poking out from under its hide. Neither figure moved, as if sketched upon the backdrop of the night. I started to step forward, but Pantalisea held me back. Lucca inched forth instead, brandishing his scythe. We were woefully unprepared, even though the man looked as if he was about to drop along with his horse. If this were indeed a French scout, he'd find nothing to deter him save for Lucca and our mastiff.

Lucca came within paces of him before the man keeled over. He hit the ground with a muted thump, cushioned by his cloak. Pulling from Pantalisea, I hastened to where Lucca bent over the fallen figure, reaching for the crusted scarf about his face. I took in the sprawled limbs under an ox-hide cloak. The man wore common garb—a coarse leather jerkin, wool hose, and squirrel-fur buskins—and his hands were swathed in ragged mittens with the tips cut off, his fingers blue with cold.

"He is dying!" I exclaimed. "He must be brought inside at once—" Then my words choked in my throat as Lucca unraveled the scarf, revealing long, pallid features, finely carved as an icon, a thick red-gold beard like rust upon a chiseled jaw, and heavy-lidded eyes at half-mast, which seemed to see but not recognize me.

I sank beside him to take his hand. "Cesare," I whispered.

He slept for an entire night and day. When he finally woke, wintry sunlight drifted through the casement and across his pillow, the bleached linen only slightly whiter than his skin.

He made a jerking motion. From my stool at his bedside, I reached out to touch his hand, relieved to find warmth in his skin. "There is nothing to fear," I soothed. "You are safe."

His gaze widened. His green eyes were so vivid against his pallor, like shards of emerald in an alabaster mask. "Lucia." His voice was barely audible. "How long have I . . . ?"

"You arrived two nights ago. It's nearly midafternoon." I reached for a bottle on the side table, pouring a measure of thick white liquid into a cup. As I leaned over to place it to his lips, he seized my wrist. Despite his apparent fragility, he still had astonishing strength.

"What is that?"

"Milk thistle, distilled with honey and mint." I met his suspicious stare. "Pantalisea brews it herself; it's her remedy for fever and fatigue. Now, drink."

He coughed at the bitter taste. As I daubed his mouth, cleansing his chapped lips of the residue, he gave me a weak smile. "Foul as poison. You should give some to Giovanni."

I went still.

"What is it? What is the matter?" he rasped. He knew me so well. Even now, after waking from near death, he sensed my turmoil.

"Nothing." I forced out a smile, thinking of his letter as I set the cup aside. "I should be the one asking questions. You come in the night without prior word, refuse to give your name, and then drop from your horse, unconscious." My voice caught. "I thought I had lost you."

"I thought I had lost me, too. Is that nag still alive?"

I shook my head. "She was starved. She died within an hour of your arrival."

"Poor beast." He looked toward the window. The light limned his profile, catching stray threads of gold in his coppery beard. "She was a packhorse. I stole her and rode here without stop from Velletri. It took five days. It's a miracle she held out for as long as she did."

"Velletri? But that's miles from Rome. I thought you were with Papa."

His voice was somber. "I was."

Sudden tears sprang to my eyes. "Dear God. Is Papa—is he still . . . ?"

He struggled up against his pillows. "Yes. Do not worry. He is alive.

I was scheduled to meet with him in Perugia; we agreed upon it before I departed Rome. I just had to see you first."

I blinked back my sorrow. "I don't understand."

"There's no reason you should." He picked at the unlaced opening of his bed smock. It was a spare of Giovanni's, unearthed from a *cassone*, for Cesare's saddlebag had yielded nothing but soiled linens and crumbs. Lucca had undressed my brother, bathed him, and put him to bed; now, as the smock draped to reveal a dusting of fine hair on his chest, I averted my gaze. I still thought of him as the brother who was five years older than me, my childhood companion and protector. I had forgotten that Cesare was a man now, almost twenty.

He broke the quiet. "We had to strike a pact with King Charles. We'll be despised for it, no doubt, condemned throughout Italy, but we had no other choice. We were trapped in the *castel*. The French threatened to turn their cannon on us—"

"Yes," I interrupted. "I received your missive. I still have it."

"It reached you?" He gave a faint smile. "I must reward that courier if I ever see him again. He must have braved hell to escape the city, let alone reach Pesaro." He went silent again, plucking at his smock before he said, "Anyway, the secret passage from the Vatican had collapsed from their barrage. We had no escape. Though the king had promised to deal with us honorably, the moment his army breached our walls they went on a rampage. The Jewish quarter, the Borgo district and palazzos: They looted everything. Mama fled to her vineyard on the Esquiline. They might have torched and raped the entire city if we hadn't agreed to an accord." He grimaced. "I've seen Turks show more restraint. The French are like animals; they pissed on the very altar of the basilica, stabled their horses in the Vatican, and brought their whores into the papal apartments."

"Dio mio." I crossed myself, thinking of the beautiful frescoes, the gilded furnishings and tapestries, now soiled and tainted. "What accord did you reach?" I asked, prepared for the news that we were now subjects of the king of France.

"Don't you want to know what happened before that?" His tone turned mischievous, causing me to smile. "Rome had begun to riot. We don't take kindly to plunder unless we are the ones doing it. Charles was alarmed; his men were being killed in the streets, so he sent an urgent message to the *castel,* asking Papa to meet with him. It was all very regal, very private. Charles rode to the *castel,* and after they embraced, they walked by themselves along the loggia."

He inclined to me. "You've never seen such a ludicrous pair, Papa lumbering like a bear in his *camauro* while Charles hopped alongside him, all twitchy and slobbering. The king of France is a dwarf, Lucia—uglier than sin and no higher than my shoulder. And a fool, too: He had all of Rome in his grip. He could have made us do anything, but by the time he and Papa finished their stroll, their treaty was sealed. Charles vowed obedience to Papa as Supreme Pontiff, renouncing any hope that he would support Papa's dethronement, while Papa sanctioned the king's crusade against the Turk, thereby granting him safe passage through our states."

I considered this for a long moment. "Why didn't Papa grant him safe passage before? By refusing, he put the entire city in danger."

"We never thought it would come to that." Cesare grimaced. "Or Papa didn't. I had a feeling it might. But he was right to refuse them at first. The Romagna territories are part of our holy state: To allow Charles safe passage would have sent a message to every sovereign in Europe that we are open to plunder. And in the end, our refusal helped save us. Most of the Romagna barons had already kissed Charles's *culo* and offered up their fortresses, so our refusal to let the French pass under papal sanction now makes those barons traitors."

"And Naples? Gioffre is there, with his wife, Princess Sancia. Is he now in danger?"

Cesare nodded. "We must pray Naples can escape its fate. It was them or us. Alfonso abdicated in favor of his son, Ferrantino, who is rabid as a dog. He'll no doubt fight the French to his last breath. We can only hope he has enough soldiers to win."

"Is that why you were in Velletri? You left Rome with King Charles?"

"Both Djem and I. I told you, Charles is a fool. He actually agreed to pay Papa five hundred thousand ducats for my company. Having me there lent papal authority to his campaign for Naples. He would have paid even more for Djem, however. Charles wanted the sultan's hated brother in his camp as a hostage because he thinks that when he launches his crusade, Djem might prove useful as a pawn. I traveled as cardinal legate. I brought nineteen mules with my possessions. It must have come as quite a shock when the French opened those coffers and found they were empty."

I chuckled, warming to his tone. "You brought nothing with you?"

"Oh, I did. In the first two coffers. I even displayed my vestments and chalices to Charles, whose eyes popped out more than usual at all the gemstones. He's as greedy as he is venal. Alas, halfway to Velletri, the mules bearing those coffers were intercepted by my Michelotto. By the time I escaped, I had only my robes and skullcap—which I left in my tent." He let out a sudden burst of laughter. "Charles truly believed we would honor the terms of our treaty and let him stake his claim on Naples with our full support!"

My spirits lifted. My brother had just reduced the French menace to a farce.

"Charles has no idea what awaits him. Taking Naples is not going to be as simple as he thinks," Cesare went on. "And while he contends with King Ferrantino, Papa and I will form a Holy League with our city-states. They will heed us now; they have seen what can happen if they do not. And when they do"—he leaned to me, his grin laced with triumph—"we shall make them bow to us. The Medici have already fled Florence, exiled from their own city by that devil Savonarola, who now orders all their precious possessions thrown onto his bonfire of vanities. One great family has fallen; that's one less we have to vanquish. We shall force the rest to their knees, and once we wring from them what we need, we will conquer every one, every petty warlord or haughty duke, every treacherous prince who plotted our downfall. We will make them be our vassals or put their heads on spikes. The time has come for a new age—the age of Borgia. And I shall be its scourge. I shall raise such terror, they will tremble at our very name."

I laughed out loud then, as much at his dramatic declaration as with joy that, despite the circumstances of his arrival, his irrepressible spirit had apparently suffered no ill effects.

"And Djem?" I asked, mirth coloring my voice. "Is he still a hostage with the French?" I thought it was only what he deserved, after what he had done to me that night in my palazzo.

"He is dead." Cesare's reply was flat. "I killed him." And as I gaped at him, stunned by his pronouncement, he added, "It was his life or mine."

Guilt overwhelmed me. "But you—you shouldn't have! I never said I wanted him dead." Even as I spoke, I dreaded Juan's reaction when he was told that his beloved friend was gone.

A slight frown knit Cesare's brow. "I didn't do it for you. That would have been killing a dog because its master had it bark. No, we'd planned our escape, you see; when the French camped for the night, we would steal away in borrowed clothes, take two packhorses, and ride directly to Perugia to meet with Papa. But when the hour came, that damn Turk balked. He started yelling at me, saying Juan would never have let matters reach such a pass that he, a prince, should find himself forced to flee like a thief. I had to stop it. I had to stop him." His voice suddenly quavered. "I thought they'd hear him. He was strong; he fought my garrote. I had to strangle him with the wire I carried in case we ran into any guards."

I sat in horrified silence, unable to utter a word.

"It was his life or mine," Cesare said again, and his quaver deepened. "I had no choice. You must believe me. If I hadn't, he would have given us both away."

"Yes. Of course," I whispered. "You had to save yourself." But I was struggling to reconcile my relief that he had escaped with the brutality of this unexpected act. Then I saw him shudder. He wasn't as indifferent to what he had done as he feigned.

"Please," he said. "Do not judge me. I would never have done it, if there had been another way. But he was shouting so loudly, he'd have woken the entire camp, and I had to—"

"No. Say no more. I understand. Cesare, I would never judge you."

He let out a moan, averting his face. "But you do. How can you not? I killed a man. I shouldn't have told you. I should never have admitted it. I should never have come here."

"Don't say that." I shifted onto the edge of the bed, pulling him gently to me. He melted into my embrace like a disconsolate child. I could feel his coiled muscles. As I realized just how near I'd come to losing him and everything I loved, I tightened my arms around him, trying to impart warmth, my devotion, and reassurance, as he sank his face into my breast.

His arms encircled my waist. "I would have killed a hundred men to reach you," I heard him say, and then he reared up, clasping his mouth to mine, his breath moist as summer dusk. His tongue flickered, probing. As I felt his entire body meld against mine, I struggled but found he had me trapped in his grip. He whispered into my mouth, "No one loves you as I do, Lucia. No one ever can," and I began to succumb to his power, his shoulders unyielding as ivory yet pliant as satin, his bones ridged under his chest, where I could feel his thundering heart.

His lips trailed upward, over my jaw to my ear. "Plato tells us every man searches for his lost twin. But we need never look, Lucia, because we have always had each other."

Desire seared my blood. I let him take my hands, drawing them down to the pulsing strength between his legs. I wanted to resist. I knew in some distant, clamoring part of me that it was unspeakable, a mortal sin, an unforgivable transgression against nature. But sensations I had never felt, never even imagined they existed, overcame me. My body wanted him. My body knew that all along it was here, in Cesare's arms, that I truly belonged—

"*No!*" Gulping air as if I'd flailed to the surface of a dark sea, I pressed my hands at his chest and forced him back. "We cannot."

He cupped my chin. "Cannot? Or dare not?"

"Cesare, please. It . . . you know it would be a terrible sin."

His chuckle was like a purr in the back of his throat. "Since when has sin ever mattered to us? We are Borgias. We were made to love only each other."

"No. You must let me go." I splayed my palms, keeping him at bay. I felt his resistance, his urgent, devastating lust. It was so vast, I felt it would consume me. Even as I fought to curb my own sharp yearning, he abruptly released his hold on me. I could still feel the trace of heat from his fingers on my skin as he gestured with his head toward the doorway.

"Giovanni," he said. "What an unexpected surprise."

I whirled about. I'd not realized until this moment how far I had clambered onto the bed, so entwined with Cesare that for a paralyzing moment I could not distinguish his body from mine. Through a dissipating haze, I saw my husband standing motionless on the threshold, his gauntlets clutched in his fist as he regarded us from under his cap.

"I was told you were here, my lord cardinal, but could scarcely believe it. How is it you came all this way and I was not informed?"

"He arrived only two days ago." I quickly climbed off the bed, tugging at my skirts, cringing inwardly at the distress in my voice and the brittle excuses tumbling from my lips that no one, much less Giovanni, could ever believe. "He was very ill and I—I was going to write to you, but I was tending to him. See?" I spun to the side table for the bottle of medicine and, in my haste, knocked over the empty cup. As it clanked onto the floor, the sound rang too loud to my ears.

"I do see," said Giovanni thickly. "I see that once again I am the last to know."

Cesare laughed. "Come, now! You find fault where there is none. It is true what my sister says. I was in terrible shape. We'd have called for you soon enough." He sprang with ease from the bed, as though he had been in health the entire time, making me wince. His crumpled smock turned translucent in the light, revealing his hard manhood. He didn't seem to notice, or if he did he didn't care, striding to Giovanni and yanking him into a fraternal embrace.

Over Cesare's shoulder, Giovanni stared unblinking at me.

"I'll—I'll inform the servants you are here," I said, hating how I stuttered over the words. As I started for the door, Giovanni stepped away from Cesare. He looked so meager compared to my brother, who, despite his loss of weight, his overgrown cheeks in dire need of barbering, and that borrowed smock, carried himself as if he wore the most exquisite court finery.

"See if you might find me some proper apparel while you are at it," Cesare said. He winked at Giovanni. "Perhaps the signore has something he can lend me? I arrived with the shirt on my back, so to speak. A fracas with the French. Nothing serious. We've had quite a stir in Rome, but the worst is over and His Holiness will summon us soon to join him."

"Of course," said Giovanni, his voice leaden. "Lucrezia, ask my chamberlain to fetch one of my doublets and a pair of hose for His Eminence."

My smile felt taut enough to crack my lips. "I'll see to it at once."

As soon as I left the room, I picked up my skirts and ran as fast as I could down the hallway, not stopping until I burst into my apartments, startling my women at their chores. Pantalisea half-rose to her feet as I dashed past her and slammed my bedchamber door behind me.

With my back against the door, I slid to the floor in a boneless heap.

I did not know whether to weep or pray. I had just discovered the darkness within me; I now knew something forbidden lurked in my heart, held sway over my flesh. How could I ever evade or forget this terrifying hunger, when desire for my own brother scorched my very soul?

And Giovanni had seen it. He knew.

He had looked at me as if I were already damned.

CHAPTER SIXTEEN

We departed Pesaro as the foothills of the Apennines bloomed with early wildflowers and shepherds drove flocks to pasture along the Via Flaminia. The ancient road cut through rocky gorges and dense forest; over its weathered cobbles we rode with eighty guards, our carts loaded with coffers. Cesare stayed close at my side, a gleam in his eye as he remarked, "Should the French happen upon us, I fear you shall be taken hostage as they took la Farnese, for you still ride like a Venetian, *petita meva.*"

I hauled the reins of my mare, causing her to snort at the harsh tug on her mouth. "I haven't much opportunity to practice my riding." My retort was sharp, embedded with resentment for what he'd unleashed between us.

"After all those lively excursions with the Gonzagas?" he said. "I read your letters to Papa; you described yourself as a veritable Diana of the chase."

"My letters were supposed to be private," I said. I knew Giovanni watched us with fervid intensity, though what he expected to see, here on the road, I could not say. Whatever it was, Cesare did not help when he leaned to me to whisper, "I know well how you can ride, Lucia."

I slammed my heels into my mare, as much to get away from him as to disguise the rush of heat in my cheeks.

His laughter rang out behind me as I galloped past my women, catching a glimpse of the fright on Pantalisea's face. She had been after me for weeks, ever since I had come racing into my apartments. Much as she endeavored to force my confession, I only snapped at her that the next time I'd appreciate a warning before my husband barged in on me. She had given me a wounded look in return. Ladies-in-waiting, she murmured, did not receive advance word from the signore, as I well knew.

"But this same lady-in-waiting would like full accounting of how many times the signore has failed to visit my bed," I replied, which put an end to her questions, if not her vigilance. Only this time I was relieved. I felt safer knowing she was observant, as if her scrutiny might restrain me from any other unwitting trespass.

Yet what I so desperately sought to evade had only spurred Cesare. In the months before our departure, he'd contrived to waylay me in the gardens, even as Giovanni watched from the gallery. At night, he took up Giulia's abandoned lute and sang forlorn refrains, making my gullible women swoon at his poetic baritone as I sat with my hands clenched in my lap.

One night, we held a feast. As we dined, he slid his hand under the table to settle his fingers on my thigh, his touch melting through the brocade of my gown while Giovanni sat brooding over the news that the young duke of Milan, held captive for years by his uncle Il Moro, had died—some said from poison at Il Moro's behest. Now duke in title as well as deed, Il Moro had blithely disregarded his past treachery with the French and agreed to join my father's Holy League, leaving my husband in yet another quandary.

"One can hardly blame Il Moro," Cesare remarked. "He must be seen to make amends now that he is Milan's official ruler. He knows Charles's enterprise is a catastrophe—the French may have conquered Naples with their impressive cannon, but it seems they failed to take into account the illicit resistance of its brothels. What do they call this new ailment again?" My brother tugged at his lip. "Ah, yes. *Mal de Napoli*. Though it might also be called the French disease, for who can say who gave it to whom first? Between the rapes and the sores, the French have worn out their welcome. No more talk of a Turkish crusade now!" Cesare laughed. "No, they're eager to put all of it behind them and return home." He looked askance at Giovanni. "Ironic, don't you think? Now it is Il Moro who fears the French might replenish their victuals for their passage across the Alps by plundering his domains."

"What can I do?" Giovanni was so distraught, he was oblivious to how I gulped my wine, feeling Cesare's fingers poised like a spider upon me. "This letter from His Holiness—" He yanked a paper from his jerkin. "It says I must fulfill the terms of my *condotta* to Rome under the league, though surely I must seek my uncle Il Moro's leave, as I also owe him my service. Yet His Holiness warns that if I dare refuse, I risk excommunication!"

"His warning has never stopped you before," said Cesare, and as Giovanni went rigid at the ridicule in my brother's tone, I pushed back my chair and excused myself.

"So soon?" said Cesare. "Such a pity. I'd hoped we might dance. It has been too long since we danced together, sister. Not since your wedding, I believe."

"My head aches," I muttered, feeling my guilt like a rash on my face, the memory of his hand on my thigh like a brand. This time, Giovanni didn't fail to notice my discomfiture when my brother drawled, "Headaches at your age? Young wives should never suffer such affliction; if they do, it is due to an imbalance of humors, which only a dose of affection can remedy." He let his innuendo charge the air; I could not fathom his incredible boldness. Did he actually *want* everyone to know that he desired me in his bed?

"By all means." Giovanni's voice was tight as a fist. "And therefore she should retire and wait until her husband can provide said affection."

Cesare turned to him. Though nothing in his manner changed, he suddenly exuded menace. "And I believe His Holiness would prefer if her husband did not."

I did not wait to hear the rest of their exchange. As I hastened out with my women, I saw in Pantalisea's horrified expression that she'd seen and heard enough to deduce what I refused to disclose. As soon as I reached my rooms, I debated whether to bolt my doors. Giovanni would make good on his threat, and when he arrived after midnight, swaying from too much wine, I greeted him with my chin raised. This time, whatever he did, he would do it while I looked him in the eye.

To my surprise, he did not step over the threshold. Instead he said, with a slur in his voice, "You—you humiliate me. You let him . . . touch you."

"Who?" I asked, even as fear leapt in my veins. When he blinked, searching his wine-sodden brain for a response, I added, "You should be advised, Signore, that regardless of who you think has touched me, if *you* ever do so again, I shall inform my father that you broke our nuptial agreement. I daresay humiliation will be the least of your concerns."

His reddened gaze flared, fury burning off his intemperance. "And lest there be a mistake, let me likewise assure that should I discover you gave yourself to another, all Italy will hear of it. Everyone will learn about Lucrezia Borgia's unnatural lust. I should never have consented to our marriage, knowing now what you are, but I will not be made a cuckold. Defy me and I'll see your family defamed. Do not try me any more than you already have."

Without another word, he turned on his heel and staggered away.

I shut the door and bolted it. He shouldn't frighten me. Fortuna had turned once more in my family's favor. Giovanni might detest me, wish we had never married, but he was beholden to the Borgia hand that fed him, if he wanted to survive.

But I knew what he had witnessed. I knew what he thought he had seen and what he was capable of when cornered; I had watched him order the savage execution of his own secretary. And I found myself fearing what he might yet do to avenge himself.

It now fell upon me to ensure that he did not.

After that evening, I avoided time alone with Cesare, which fortunately did not prove difficult once the summons came from my father, ordering us to Perugia. But now, as I cantered through the countryside toward those distant city walls, I sensed my respite coming to an end. Cesare reached me easily on his black charger, seizing hold of my reins and forcing me to a halt.

"Enough," I cried at him. "Have you gone insane to behave thus?"

His face flushed with color and his brow damp with sweat, he looked fully recovered from his ordeal. Having not lived in such close quarters with him since childhood, I was astounded by his inexhaustible strength. Pantalisea had told me the servants in Pesaro whispered that Cesare Borgia was not like other men, for he ate only once a day and never finished his wine. He slept when the mood took him, as a cat does, and he'd been seen prowling the galleries at night, as if he stalked prey in the moonlight.

"Yes," he said. "I am insane. *You* are making me insane. Would you avoid me forever because of that insipid fool?"

"That fool is my husband."

"He is not worthy of the honor." His voice coiled suddenly. "Or have you had him? Has he already claimed your first blood with his measly Sforza *cazzo*?"

I regarded him steadily, biting back my retort that he had no idea what I had suffered or was prepared to suffer for our family's sake; that I'd already experienced a taste of what bedding my husband involved and would gladly submit to it and more, to protect my brother from calumny. Instinct held me back. If I told him what Giovanni had threatened, Cesare might seek revenge. I had to rely on the fact that I'd always been able to placate him, to coax his rare smile and make him do my bidding. He must heed me now; he must understand how impossible this situation had become.

"You mustn't speak of him thus. He may be a Sforza fool, but I am wed to him. You also know that what happened between us was a moment of weakness. Nothing more."

"Yet you admit there was a moment, though you think us sinners for it."

"Cesare." My voice ruptured. "I beg of you. You were ill. I was so worried for you. We did not know what we were doing. We . . . we erred out of love for each other."

"Erred?" he echoed. Visible hurt scored his face. I ached that I should be the cause of it, but harshness crept into my tone. "Yes. It was a mistake. We never should have done it."

"You do not believe that. I know in my heart that you love me."

"Yes. I do love you—as a sister loves her brother. Cesare, you go too far."

My unwitting echo of Papa's rebuke to him on the night of their argument over Juan had immediate effect. His face took on an ashen hue. "I bare my heart to you after all this time; I offer you my truest self, and you would forsake me as if I were of no account?"

"I do not forsake you!" I cried. But as we faced each other, I realized that I had forsaken him: I denied his heart. It terrified me, his unquenchable longing that gave me no means to escape other than surrender.

And that I could never do.

I glanced over my shoulder. Our company approached; they would be upon us in moments. "I would never wish to cause you any pain," I said, and the anguish inside me came pouring out. "I love you as I love no other—but we are flesh of the same flesh; we share the same blood. Cesare, I cannot be more to you. I will not give you what you desire. If you cannot accept it, then you must leave me. Now."

Above us, a cloud drifted over the sun, casting shadow on his face.

"We must never speak of this again," I said. "You must forget it, as I already have."

Desolation overcame him. I saw the collapse within, so that he resembled less a man in that moment than a boy, my protector and companion who had reveled in our intimacy, in our twin souls that seemed as one, yet had now been torn apart. Tears burned in my eyes; I would have done anything to soothe him, except what he most needed, and as I started to reach out, unable to bear the haunted loss in his eyes, he recoiled from me. With a savage stab of his spurs, he yanked at his horse and cantered off, his departure pounding like invisible nails into my heart.

My women reached me first. Pantalisea gazed at the cloud of dust kicked up by my brother's horse. "Where is my lord going?" she asked, in a nervous tone that betrayed she knew a confrontation had taken place.

I shook my head. I had no words. Giovanni drew to a halt a distance away and stared at me, impassive. I took my place at his side, and we wound our way up the hillside to Perugia.

My father waited on the fortress balcony, clad in white, with his officials about him. Our arrival elicited cheers from the townspeople gathered to welcome us, but I ceased to hear their joyous cries as I gazed upward.

Papa abandoned the balcony even before I started to dismount; I had barely caught my breath before he was sweeping out of the doorway with a fervent *"Farfallina!"* and engulfing me in his sweat and silk. Cushioned in his arms, the travails of Pesaro, the torment of Cesare, slipped from me like a discarded garment. But my throat knotted when I beheld my father's face.

He had aged years. The flesh hung loose on his cheeks and at his neck; stark new lines etched his mouth, and the pouches under his eyes betrayed an eternity of sleepless nights as he'd sought a way to oust the French and save us from ruin. But they were still his eyes, still filled with adoration for me, and my voice quavered. "Papa, I have missed you so."

"And I missed you, my sweet Lucrezia." He hugged me close. "How I missed you! Never again shall we be parted; by all the saints, I swear it."

He did not seem to notice Giovanni standing only paces away. As Papa guided me into the fortress—"Come, you must be exhausted. I've prepared a suite for you"—my husband lurched forth. In his haste, he barely performed obeisance before he blurted out, "Holiness, I am overjoyed to see you safe. I am here to assume my *condotta* with the league, providing I can consult with my cousin in Milan to—"

Papa came to a halt, regarding Giovanni as if he could not understand how my husband had the temerity to address him. "You are late, Signore. The forces of our league, under the command of the marquis of Mantua, defeated the French days ago at the battle of Fornovo. As we speak, Charles and his army flee across the Alps. So, by all means, consult with your cousin in Milan. We do not need you here."

Giovanni's face turned cold. In my mind, I heard again his threat, chilling in its remorselessness: *Defy me and I'll see your family defamed.* . . .

I squeezed my father's arm. "Papa."

His scowl softened as he took in my expression. "Are you certain?" he said. "It's not your duty anymore to protect him. We have other means. We need not placate his kin any longer."

"Be that as it may, he is still my husband. He must be accorded our respect."

My father contemplated me. Then he nodded. "You are right. He is your husband. For now." Without glancing over his shoulder, he barked at Giovanni, "See that you report to my secretary, Signore. I may have a task for you, after all."

PART III

1495–1497

*The Hunger
of Wolves*

Now we are in the power of a wolf. . . .
—GIOVANNI DE MEDICI
(LATER POPE LEO X)

CHAPTER SEVENTEEN

I saw firsthand evidence of the French occupation when we reached Rome in October—the streets strewn with fetid leavings, the churches stained by smoke and fire, and splashes of dried blood upon blade-gouged walls. Devastation had left its mark everywhere, from the torching of inns and taverns to the plundering of the grain mills and storage warehouses along the Ripa Grande and the slaughter of hundreds of livestock and people. The dead were being buried outside the walls, smothered in quicklime lest plague set in. Thieves and other villains who'd sought advantage during the occupation now hung in chains from the Castel Sant'Angelo's walls, while Papa dispatched troops to restore order and arrest malefactors, even as he received the crushing report that more than ninety thousand ducats would be needed to address the repairs.

My palazzo had suffered only minor damage. The courtyard and first floor had been used as stables, the upstairs rooms as barracks. I set myself to putting the house in order, relieved by Giovanni's departure in November: Now an official condottiere of the Holy League, he joined the marquis of Mantua to clear the papal territories of any remaining French-hired mercenaries.

With my husband gone for what I hoped would be a prolonged absence, I looked forward to reestablishing my Roman household and celebrating my sixteenth birthday in the spring.

Then Giovanni's cousin, Cardinal Ascanio Sforza, paid me an unannounced visit.

He appeared on my threshold in his perfumed scarlet, a smile on his face, as if he hadn't fallen into disfavor over his family's support of the French. He'd scarcely ingratiated himself anew in Papa's esteem, and I welcomed him with distaste, watching him run his ringed fingers over my inlaid mother-of-pearl and oak sideboard, as if he were tallying its value.

"Giovanni worries you will be lonely," he explained, when I inquired as to the reason for his visit. "He hopes you'll consider turning to me for any guidance you require."

It seemed my husband had set a spy on me. I kept contempt from my tone as I said, "I appreciate his concern, but I have a family. They have always seen to my comfort and guidance."

"Ah, yes," he assented, displaying the red satin cap on his tonsure. He reminded me of a ferret—sleek, well fed, and fanged. "But sometimes family can be so . . . demanding. I would be honored to act as your surrogate confessor. One can never have too much spiritual counsel, my lady, particularly when one is young and vulnerable to temptation."

A sudden chill ran through me. What had Giovanni told him? Though in truth nothing had gone further than what he'd seen, had my husband dared confide his suspicions?

"You shall be the first to know should such an occasion arise." I came to my feet. "Now, if you'll excuse me, I must attend to my obligations. As you know, His Holiness has summoned my brother Gioffre, Prince of Squillace, and his wife, Princess Sancia, to Rome. They survived the chaos in Naples, praise God, and we look forward to welcoming them. I've much to prepare for their arrival."

His visage hardened. Watching him leave with his hem swishing like an enraged tail, I shuddered. Henceforth, I must exercise caution and avoid any contact with him.

I found myself missing Adriana. I'd always depended on her for advice, though I knew better than to say a word about her. While in Perugia, I had asked Papa how she fared, only for him to snap, "Never mention her to me again. She is dead to me."

I suspected that Adriana had abetted Giulia's penitential return to her husband—a suspicion confirmed by none other than Vannozza, who came to deliver my cat.

As I lifted the lid of the woven basket, I expected to find a corpse. Instead, Arancino sprang out with hackles raised. He scampered under my bed and immediately began swatting at my women's skirts with his claws as they hurried about my rooms.

Vannozza loosened the mantle she wore over her mud-spattered skirts. As usual, she had not taken a palanquin or litter to travel across Rome, despite the recent ravages. Donning an oiled cloak, she walked the streets like a charwoman, trudging through muck with only a man-servant as protection. Despite her soiled attire, she did not look any worse for the occupation, and my relief unnerved me, as if I had harbored some unknown concern for her safety.

"Insolent creature," she remarked, "as everything loved by a Borgia tends to be. I suggest you keep him indoors. With the lack of grain, any beast left alive will be skinned for soup."

I rose from my crouch by the basket. "Thank you for caring for him."

"I would hardly have heard the end of it if I hadn't." She looked about my room, newly hung with my tapestries and velvet bed curtains (I had ordered anything touched by the French given away to the poor), my polished braziers heaped with scented coals. "I see you are settling in. You must be pleased to be back home. Not that Rome is what it was. It will never be the same again, after everything we have suffered."

"Yes. I was sorry to hear of your misfortune."

She arched an eyebrow. "Whatever for? I am still alive."

"I meant your palazzo. I heard it was looted."

"Bah. Houses can be rebuilt, objects replaced. People," she said, fixing her stare on me. "People cannot. Once they are gone, they are gone forever, as you must have learned during your time in Pesaro." She paused, letting her implication sink in. "Do not think I kept your cat alive because I cared. I only did it because we had an agreement. You fulfilled your end of it. Indeed, you exceeded my expectations, for as you have seen, la Farnese is nowhere to be found."

Uneasily, I glanced to where my women stood, lining my coffers with linen. My mother gave an unpleasant chuckle. "Still playing the innocent, are we?" She lowered her voice. "Oh, you did us proud. If there was ever any doubt as to what you are capable of, you disproved it. You rid us of that Farnese *puttana* without him ever realizing you had a hand in it."

"I was told she departed Rome of her own accord," I said, resisting the urge to shove Vannozza out of my chamber. Instead, I motioned to my women to leave. I did not want them overhearing us discuss Papa's former mistress.

As they filed out, Vannozza chuckled again. "There is no need for secrecy. Everyone knows by now of how she stole away in the night, though Rodrigo had made himself a laughingstock, ransoming her from the French and going out to welcome her like a besotted suitor, even as King Charles marched on the city. St. Peter himself must have turned in his tomb to hear them frolic in the apostolic bedchamber that night. Ah, but she did not share his joy in their reunion, it seems, for she fled as soon as the French were sighted on the horizon, taking Adriana with her and leaving your father to face the savage hordes alone. Now she refuses to return to Rome. She implored his forgiveness but insists she must remain with her husband, redeem herself as a wife and mother." She guffawed. "I suppose repentance comes better late than never, eh? As for your father, we can only hope he too has learned that even holy passions have a price."

I avoided her gloating smile. I had no wish to bask in Giulia's disgrace. Though I was happy to no longer contend with her, relieved she'd elected to stay far from us, I could afford to pity her; for my mother, I felt only revulsion toward that stone she had in place of a heart.

"I did not do it for you," I said coldly. "I did it for Papa."

"Naturally. You are nothing if not his devoted daughter. You never think of yourself—which must explain why you failed to heed my warning. Did I not tell you to make your life in Pesaro and be a good wife? Yet here you are, insolent as ever, and apparently unbroken by your husband, who has gone and left you like Eve in the garden to take a bite of the forbidden apple."

I went still, meeting her stare. "You have no idea what I have endured," I said.

"Oh? I suppose you think you're the only woman married to a man she does not love? Let me assure you, what you've endured is nothing compared to what is yet to come." She made a lunge at me, as if to grasp my arm. As I recoiled, she said fervently, "I saw your future in the cards. I know what lies ahead. In the end, *you* shall bear the shame. Is that what you want, a life of pain and regret? For that is what you will reap if you let your Borgia blood have its way."

"I—I have done nothing!" I protested, but I knew what she alluded to, and it horrified me. Somehow she'd divined that Cesare and I had had a falling out. And the reason why.

"Not yet. But it is your curse, a poison you carry inside. You and Cesare will be each other's doom."

I couldn't bear it. Not here. Not now. I had only just returned to Rome; I had not seen Cesare and had no idea where he might be. I had not asked Papa, deliberately. I had told my brother to leave me alone, and he had. Now here was our mother, reminding me again of the torturous pain I had inflicted on him, only she was twisting it into something evil, a curse and a poison, when I knew in my heart that while it was wrong, inconceivable, Cesare never meant to hurt me. He knew no other way to love; he knew no other way because of how *she* had raised us.

"If it's a curse we carry," I whispered, trembling, "it's because of you. Go. Leave and never come here again. I never want to see you as long as I live. I no longer have a mother."

She pulled her mantle about her shoulders. "Do as you will. Banishing me will not help you. If you do not put an end to it, the curse will prevail. Do not come to me when it does. Repentance is only for those who were never warned." As she moved to the door, she said over her shoulder, "Oh, and lest you didn't know, he too is here. In Rome. Cesare has returned," and she walked out, leaving me standing there, frozen.

My brother was in the city.

And suddenly, desperately, I wished I were anywhere else.

"*TE DEUM LAUDAMUS: Te Dominum confitemur. Te aeternum Patrem omnis terra veneratur.* We praise Thee, O God: We acknowledge Thee to be our Lord. All the earth doth worship Thee, our Father everlasting . . ."

The choir's chant rose among gusts of incense, swirling into the bejeweled sunlight piercing the basilica's stained-glass windows. The colored beams fell upon my father, draped in his golden fanon, flanked by youths in white lace, as he lifted the chalice containing the miracle of Christ's blood before the high altar.

Outside in the piazza, the faithful awaited his appearance, having congregated to celebrate our deliverance from the French, weary but defiant after braving disaster as only Romans could. I thought of my mother's words as my father spread his arms and the choir lifted their voices, sending pigeons nesting in the rafters to swoop into the light, their fluttering silhouettes like a flock of shadows, until I fancied I could feel the unseen curse inside me, ensnaring me in its thrall.

It is your curse, a poison you carry inside.

I bowed my head in supplication: "Holy Spirit, come into my heart; draw it to Thee by Thy power, O God, and grant me succor, preserving me from evil. . . ."

Then, without warning, I felt him from across the crowded pews. I looked up, searching the vast space around me that his presence filled.

And I found him; of course I found him. An unmistakable shadow behind the worshippers queuing to receive communion at our father's hand—clad in his crimson robes and standing as if poised under the wing of a stone archangel.

AFTER MASS, AS Papa stepped onto the Benediction Loggia to bless the crowd, Cesare came beside me. "Are you still angry?" he asked quietly.

I shook my head. "You know I could never stay angry with you."

"Then neither am I. I wanted to say goodbye, Lucia. I leave tomorrow for Naples."

My heart sank. He was leaving. I did not know if what I felt was relief or sorrow, only that the thought of him gone carved a hollow within me. When my mother had told me he was here, I'd wanted to flee anywhere to avoid him—but now that he stood before me, now that I saw him . . .

"Are you going to fetch Gioffre and his wife?" I asked, a catch in my voice.

"No, though I'll no doubt see them on their way. Papa is sending me as his official legate, ostensibly to crown Ferrantino as king but in truth to ensure that Ferrantino signs our new alliance and abides by its terms. We have learned we must keep Naples on our side."

"Papa must trust you very much to honor you with such a task."

He sighed. "Or perhaps he's begun to see that I will always put our interests first."

I heard the cardinals behind us muttering, impatient for the benediction to conclude so they could proceed to dinner. Past the archway leading onto the marble balcony, Papa lifted his hands, to the crowd's roaring acclaim.

"Mama told me she went to see you," Cesare said. "She says you quarreled."

"Quarreled?" I glanced sharply at him. "Did she tell you what she said? She was vile, unforgivable."

"Pay her no mind." His voice was tranquil. "Her words mean nothing."

"She knows," I said, and I faltered as something furtive quickened in his eyes, something feral. I shouldn't have admitted it. It only salted the wound still within him.

Then his fingers touched mine. "She only suspects. And I accept your decision. I would never wish to cause you any shame or dishonor. I would rather die a thousand deaths."

My throat tightened as he echoed the closing words from the letter he'd written me months before. "You must stay safe on your journey," I finally said, and I removed my hand from his, shutting my eyes. I let the sounds of the crowd wash over me, forcing his pain deep inside me, into the vault I had made of my heart, to protect us both.

When I opened my eyes again, Cesare had slipped away.

CHAPTER EIGHTEEN

Pools of rainwater speckled the road, muddying the reflection of our company as we waited at the city gate to greet our guests. Two hundred men-at-arms, my pages and twenty women, and the cardinals and ambassadors in their bright silks posed behind me as I sat upon a sure-footed mule, its crimson caparison matching my gown. Nervously, I gauged the procession coming toward us, a glamour of courtiers in cloaks and feathered caps standing out among a sea of colored banners snapping in the breeze, distracting me from the central attraction.

My brother Gioffre rode a white gelding. As he neared, I saw that his features were more angular, though he retained a stubborn spattering of freckles across his nose. His cheeks were wind-chaffed, his grayish eyes lighting up as he shouted, "Lucrezia!" and spurred to me with an effortless control over his mount that I could only envy.

He kissed my cheek. "I missed you, sister," he said, breathless. "But such excitement we had in Naples! The French came and we had to flee to the isle of Ischia, where we hid in the fortress. King Alfonso went mad with grief and abdicated, but his son Ferrantino, our new king, befriended me and had me trained in arms. See?" He reached to his waist, where an elaborate scabbard was buckled, sprouting a gem-inlaid sword hilt. "I am a knight now, as well as a prince. I even killed a Frenchman."

Despite the fact that he was almost fourteen and a husband, I could hear familiar anxiety underscoring his bravado, the eagerness to be seen as one of us. I started to smile and respond when a woman said, "Gioffre, *per favore*. Can't your tales of bloodshed wait? Or must we sit here and risk getting rained upon?"

I looked past Gioffre to his wife, Sancia of Aragon.

As I had surmised when Gioffre first showed me her portrait, the Neapolitan princess was not beautiful. Yet she bore herself as if she was, erect on her saddle, her voluptuous figure hugged by a rich black-and-silver gown. Her eyes were her most arresting feature, fringed in thick lashes and of a startling gray-green hue, like that of a restless sea. As those eyes met mine, she made me think, if only for a moment, that she was the most bewitching creature I'd ever seen. But then I moved past her eyes, taking in the tumble of dark hair escaping the jeweled net at her nape, the hooked nose and wide-lipped mouth, the sallow skin that hugged an oval but square-jawed face, on which the marks of a childhood fever could be discerned. No, Sancia was not beautiful. But she possessed undeniable allure.

"Welcome to Rome, *Principessa*," I said, with a dip of my head. "Your reputation for beauty does you justice."

She gave a satisfied smile. "Donna Lucrezia, you do me too much honor." Leaning from the saddle on her mare to kiss my cheek, she left upon me the scent of her rose attar.

Then she motioned to the retinue behind her, calling out, "*Amato fratello, vieni.* Come greet our sister-in-law Donna Lucrezia," and from among her accompanying nobles appeared a man of such unexpected beauty that several of my women could not control their gasps.

He was like a centaur, his person molded to his horse, the tasseled reins held loosely in his large hands and the musculature of his thighs clenching beneath his black hose as he guided the steed with his legs. His shoulders and chest strained his doublet, emblazoned with the double crowns of Naples. Dark-gold hair spilled from under his jewel-rimmed cap, framing a face bronzed from the sun. Despite his fairness, I marked the resemblance to Sancia in his broad cheekbones and wide-lipped mouth, the prominent nose and deep-set eyes—only his were light amber, a hue akin to honey. And whereas his sister clearly relied on her appeal, he projected only a careless indifference, as though he had no awareness of his impact on others.

Sancia said, "Allow me to present my brother, Alfonso of Aragon, Prince of Naples."

"Donna Lucrezia." He bowed his head, his voice hoarse from the dust of the road. He towered over me on his enormous roan; I had to grapple with my reins as my mule shied away. Alfonso made a clucking sound. His destrier immediately stepped back, picking up its hooves with a precision I'd seen only Juan command from a mount.

"I hope I did not frighten you." His smile revealed ivory-hued teeth. His nose was slightly askew. I found this imperfection as arresting as the rest of him.

I realized I did not want him, a skilled equestrian, to think I had any fear of horses, and I belatedly regretted not having taken a mare or gelding myself. Then, as I wondered why I should even care what he thought, he said, "I meant, frighten your mule. I can see my lady is not easily frightened." His smile deepened. "Or easily flattered," he added softly.

Somewhat flustered, I replied, "Shall we proceed to San Giovanni? We will hear holy service there in honor of your arrival." As I spoke, I turned to Sancia.

"Why, yes, dear Lucrezia," she said. "We must do as you please. We are in your realm."

I dismounted with the aid of a footstool and took my position next to her, with Gioffre on my other side. When Alfonso leapt from his horse and moved to my brother's left side, I discovered he was no taller than me. Much like his flawed nose, his lack of stature only made him more appealing.

After we heard Mass in the Byzantine-inspired chapel of the Bishop of Rome, with its fire-scarred pilasters, we took the Via Laterna along a route hung with banners, where the people shouted their welcome, happy at last after the hardships of the occupation. We rode past the Coliseum and ruins of the Forum, through the Campo de' Fiori to the Via Recta, which brought us past the Castel Sant'Angelo and into the Vatican. As we rode, I sensed rivalry already brewing with Sancia. She tossed her head, bestowing her brilliant smile on the waving crowds. Many seemed unsure of whom to look at first: the vivacious Neapolitan princess, in her sumptuous dark velvets, or me, Pope Alexander VI's daughter, in my costly crimson. I heard calls of *"Bella signora! Bella principessa!"* but to which beautiful lady did they refer? Sancia evidently took it for granted that it must be her, for she ordered her women to toss handfuls of coins from the satin purses at their belts, laughing as she watched children diving for the money.

Of one thing I was certain: As we traversed the newly repaired Pont

Sant'Angelo to enter St. Peter's Piazza, where a riot of bells clanged, I felt Alfonso of Naples's gaze intent on me, and I had to resist looking back at him—though I secretly longed to.

It was improbable, impossible even, but I had the impression that a man like him could make me forget my painful, complicated feelings for Cesare.

⁕

SANCIA'S ARRIVAL IN Rome roused immediate scandal.

From the moment she strode into the Sala dei Pontefici with her head held high and went with brazen confidence to the papal dais, where my father sat enthroned in his regalia, she captivated the Vatican court and our salacious appetite for gossip.

Papa expanded in her presence, his jowls reddening and his embrace effusive after she knelt to kiss his foot. He scarcely acknowledged Gioffre as he bade her to assume a seat on a special cushion beside him, opposite the one appointed for me. He joked and pinched her cheek during the ensuing reception and hours-long feast, offering her the first taste of every platter. By the time she and Gioffre took up residence in a palazzo, recently vacated by a disgruntled cardinal at Papa's request, Sancia had garnered widespread acclaim and poisonous envy; her ability to seduce by setting her fingers just so on a sleeve turned men into gaping fools and their courtesans or catamites into avowed foes. Effervescent and sharp-tongued when she had a mind to be, she had my father doting on her every word, so that he even abandoned his habit of eating ham with each of his meals in order to indulge her appetite for variety. At her request, he also crammed her new palazzo—a musty affair—with enough furnishings, antique busts, and statues to turn the stolid place into an abode worthy of her presence. I thought Gioffre might resent all this attention lavished on his wife, but when I saw them together at banquets or receptions, my little brother was always preening as if he took pride in being the husband of such a coveted woman. Still, I suspected that, much as with my own marriage, their union was in name alone. Was Gioffre not mature enough to provide much in the way of bed sport for a woman of Sancia's evident experience?

I should have despised her, in truth, for she reminded me in a way of Giulia. Yet it was difficult to hate someone who lacked any malice. As competitive as Sancia was—and there was no denying this trait, for no sooner had she cast an eye over one of my gowns than a day later she appeared in a similar creation—she was generous to a fault. When I admired a strand of black pearls she wore one afternoon, she removed it from her throat and gave it at me. "No, no," she laughed when I tried to refuse. "They will look far better on your lovely white skin. On me, they just disappear, dark as a Saracen that I am."

I found she could liven up even the most stultifying gathering with her irreverent wit, but once the guests departed and the candles guttered, she was boisterous and candid, unwilling to take herself or anyone else too seriously. She could also be unusually perceptive, though. It took her little time, in fact, to notice that under my own carefree exterior, I hid secrets.

"What is the matter? I know something is bothering you," she said one morning as we readied to attend High Mass. In the past week, we'd gone hawking on Monte Mario, despite the intermittent spring showers—all we caught were four doves and a chill—then into the city to meet with merchants on the Via dei Pettinari, who were so desperate to gain Sancia's patronage that they gave away their wares, which she gleefully accepted. We even spent one tedious afternoon being sketched by an ugly Florentine artist named Michelangelo. Papa had commissioned him to sculpt a statue, and he had promised to use Sancia as inspiration for his *Pietà*.

"Nothing is the matter," I said, adjusting my veil. "Though I fear we shall be late if we don't leave now, and you know how Master Burchard detests tardiness."

She grimaced. "What he needs is a woman, or a boy, if he prefers. Anything to warm his sour German bones."

"Sancia, *per favore*. It's a holy day!" I had to stifle my laugher as my ladies stared at her in disbelief, unable to reconcile their inculcated notions of propriety with this princess who said exactly what she thought and didn't care a fig for who heard it.

"Well, holy day or not, I only state the obvious. Serving one's master can only please so much." Sancia looked straight at Pantalisea as she spoke, aware that my lady had taken an antipathy to her. In fact, Pantalisea had cautioned me that I must not be too familiar with someone of Sancia's "loose morals," lest her taint rub off on me like an indelible stain.

"Come." I hooked my arm in Sancia's and drew her to the door, away from Pantalisea, before one of them said something she would regret. Pantalisea would stay behind to refresh my chambers, but Sancia could not resist another spiteful look over her shoulder as we left. Using the passage into the Sistine, we hurried to the basilica, where the pews were already full, Papa on his dais with his court in attendance, while the preacher waited impatiently at the pulpit.

Papa winked at me as we assumed our seats. Amid the rustling of our skirts, Sancia whispered in my ear, "Just look at Burchard. Now, does he not seem like someone who's never tasted anything sweet?"

I glanced at where the master of ceremonies stood rigid, with his wand of office in hand, his slightly protuberant gaze fixed ahead and his mouth puckered, as if he were trying to keep down a bout of indigestion. My mirth bubbled up. I clamped my lips, looking back at the preacher—a Spanish Dominican, judging by his ascetic features and white habit—who launched into a monotonous account of how the Holy Spirit had descended from heaven this day to fill our Lord and His apostles with God's light.

Sancia jabbed me with her elbow. "Well? Does he or does he not?"

I shook my head. "I wouldn't know," I muttered, fearing that if I opened my mouth too much, I might burst out laughing. *How* would I know? I was still a virgin, as far as anyone knew. There was nothing I could possibly say about what such "sweetness" entailed.

"You wouldn't know?" Sancia was indignant. "Whatever does that mean? You would not know if he's never tasted something sweet or would not know what something sweet is?"

My embarrassed laughter was starting to choke me. I could feel it in the back of my throat and reached over to grip her hand. She went silent. The preacher droned on. Suddenly she leaned to me again. This time, her breath tickled my earlobe. "I think I know now what ails you. You too have never tasted anything sweet, have you, *cara mia*?"

I could not restrain myself. Even as my hands flew up to cover my mouth, a gush of nervous release that had been pent up for months exploded from me with such force that it couldn't have been more disruptive if I'd set every bell in the basilica to pealing. From his pulpit, the Dominican glared. Burchard shifted angrily in our direction. As I envisioned the congregation—the cardinals and bishops, ambassadors, courtiers, and assorted servants—craning their necks to see what on earth had possessed His Holiness's daughter, I tried to stifle myself, because I knew how disrespectful, how irreverent, I was being.

Sancia seized hold of me and hauled me, gasping and giggling, up the staircase to the marble pulpit, where the canons usually assembled to sing the epistle. Our women clumsily followed, hoisting up their skirts and stepping on the toes of outraged worshippers, the crackling of velvet and silk like a hundred birds let loose. By the time we climbed the stairs to the empty canon stalls overlooking the inside of the basilica, my ribs throbbed from the volcanic release of an emotion I had not realized I'd kept inside.

"May I know what you find so hilarious?" Sancia asked, as if she feared I had lost my reason. "It is a holy day, remember?"

"Yes. I remember." My shoulders shook as I fought back another outburst. Swallowing my nervous, almost hysterical, mirth, I looked askance at our pale women—or, at least, mine were pale. Hers appeared to be enjoying the view, judging by how they shoved at their necklines to expose their cleavage, leaning over the choir railing to encourage those ogling them from the pews below.

"You are right," I suddenly said. I felt as if a stone had been dislodged from my chest. "I have never tasted anything sweet. My body is as untouched as the day I was born."

She did not seem taken aback. "I see. Yet you have been married for . . . how long? Three years?" When I nodded, she gave a sigh. "What are you waiting for? If a husband is not inclined, or if he is but we are not, one needn't take an oath of celibacy. There are alternatives."

"Such as?" I could not believe I dared voice such unseemly curiosity.

"Such as this." Sancia swept out her arm to encompass the vista. The sermon had resumed, promising to be as tedious as I thought, the Dominican enamored of his own tenor even as Papa began to sag on his throne, trying to resist his torpor. Some of the cardinals had already succumbed, heads bobbing against their chests, while the younger men—the pages and secretaries, grooms and ambassadorial assistants, even a few friars—surreptitiously eased off into the shadows under the columns to play dice or gossip with one another.

"Which one?" Sancia said. "If you could choose any man here, who would it be?"

I wanted to play along, if only for the daring fun of it. "None—" I started to say, and then, without any effort on my part, my gaze alighted on Alfonso of Naples. He sat beside Gioffre and the Neapolitan ambassador, appearing to heed the Dominican's sermon. Only as I sat above him, I could glean something in his lap. What was it? A napkin? No. A book! He had a book, which he glanced down at now and then, his fingers flipping the pages with laconic ease.

"He's reading," I said, incredulous.

Sancia chuckled. "Yes, my brother is an avid reader. He adores Dante, Boccaccio, Petrarch, and all the classics. Condemn him to a cell with a book and he would die content." She paused. "So, is it him? If you could, would you select Alfonso as your lover?"

No one had ever asked me such a question. In truth, no one, except Cesare, ever treated me as if I had an opinion worth hearing.

"Well?" said Sancia. "It is a simple answer: yes or no."

I returned my gaze to Alfonso, watching how the light spilled over the polished gilt of his hair, the way he sat with such insouciance, caressing the leaves of his book as if they were skin.

I heard myself breathe, "I believe I would."

"I knew it!" Sancia cried, causing Burchard and those few cardinals still awake to look up. She crooked a finger, drawing me closer. "And he would welcome the opportunity, I can assure you. He has spoken of nothing else since we arrived, lamenting that he's not had the chance to speak with you alone. Shall I see to it? It is fitting, I think. A brother for a brother."

My delight faltered. "Brother?" I immediately suspected she did not refer to Gioffre.

Astonishment widened her gaze. "You did not know? But I assumed, with all the couriers and spies—" Her quicksilver laugh escaped her. "He is, after all, one of His Holiness's sons."

Relief coursed through me. "Oh, you *do* mean Gioffre."

"Gioffre?" She rolled her eyes. "I bed him the one time because it was required of us on our nuptial night, but I'm not entirely without scruple. I desire a man, not a boy, in my bed."

"Then you must—you refer to . . ." I found I could not utter his name.

"Yes. Your other brother. Cesare Borgia, Cardinal of Valencia." When I still did not speak, she added, "We discovered our attraction was mutual when he arrived in Naples to crown Ferrantino. I did so regret I had to leave him to come here, though I'm not so regretful now, because you and I are now friends. He told me I would like you. He said I must look after you until he returns, because you are the most beautiful, tenderhearted woman he's ever known. I must admit, his praise made me jealous. He spoke like a man who cannot forget a lover. But I see why he adores you so."

I sat without moving, waiting for my outrage to surge. I imagined myself slapping her across her face, calling her a *puttana,* for surely it was what she deserved for putting the cuckold's horns on Gioffre with his own brother.

Instead, the relief I had felt earlier returned with an intensity that seemed to flood my entire being. I should be furious with her, and Cesare, too. But he had never dissimulated his aversion to the Church; like so many others who were cardinals or bishops, like hundreds of women forced to enter a convent, he only did what came naturally to those without a vocation. But even more important for me, I thought that we had averted my mother's curse. He had taken a lover. He wasn't pining for me. He had meant what he said about accepting my decision.

"You are not upset?" Sancia asked, with a contrition I would not have thought her capable of. "You must think me reprehensible for marrying the one and bedding the other."

"I do not," I told her quietly. She also only did what came naturally to her. If Cesare must bed someone, at least he'd chosen a princess who would never ask for more than he could give.

"So. Will you do it?" she said, eager to change the subject. "My brother departs for Naples in a few weeks. You'll not have another chance unless he returns."

It took me only a moment to decide.

"Yes," I said. "Let us arrange it. Discreetly."

CHAPTER NINETEEN

I decided to meet him in the Biblioteca Apostolica, the Vatican Library, which housed the priceless papal collection of rare tomes and codices, illuminated manuscripts and ancient scrolls. I thought it the perfect venue, inspired by my sight of him with a book at Mass—but Sancia was taken aback.

"Not a garden, loggia, or even a private house," she said, "but some dusty place full of old papers? Lucrezia, are you certain? It's hardly the setting for a romantic encounter."

"If your brother is the prince I think he is," I assured her, "he'll understand."

On the appointed day, I donned a hooded cape and left my palazzo alone, having told Pantalisea and my other women that Papa wished to sup with me.

I had once paid a brief childhood visit to the cavernous library on the ground floor of the Apostolic Palace, north of the Cortile dei Pappagalli. I still remembered it. My father was then vice-chancellor to Pope Innocent; taking me by the hand, he guided me past the reception room adorned with half-finished frescoes into four vast chambers filled with scriptorium. The vaulted ceilings were grazed by tall rows of shelves that, to my awestruck eyes, appeared about to topple over, laden with books and sheaves. I had noticed a distinct odor, humidity mixed with dust, and a strange arid smell that made me think of a desert, though I'd never seen one. When I commented on it, Papa replied, "That, *farfallina,* is the perfume of knowledge."

The same perfume now welcomed me as I stepped over the threshold and the head librarian in his dark robe and cap bustled up to greet me. Pushing back my cowl, I surveyed the now-finished paintings on the walls and ceiling, colorful sibyls unfurling papyri at the feet of Archimedes and Ctesibius of Alexandria.

The librarian peered at me through his thick spectacles. He said anxiously, "His Highness has already arrived. You requested privacy, Donna, and so I've closed the archives to visitors, citing the need to inventory a new shipment. But, begging your forgiveness, I fear I must ask . . . I must emphasize . . ."

I suppressed my amusement as he faltered. This was a first. Did this fussy little man actually think that I planned to entertain a lover on a makeshift bed of his precious parchments?

He started when I set a hand on his sleeve. "You needn't worry," I said. "I promise we will leave everything exactly as we found it. There shall be no impropriety—though I must ask you to keep this matter between us." I removed a pouch from my cloak. "For your troubles," I added, as his pallid face turned red at the quantity of my bribe.

I moved past him, the brush of my skirts echoing on the floor.

The library looked, if possible, more congested than I recalled; books and portfolios overflowed their berths, spilling in brittle waterfalls into random heaps. There were piles of scrolls along the walls and a pyramid of unpacked crates on a nearby bench, stamped with my father's insignia of the papal keys and bull. As I started to move toward these, a voice came at me, seemingly from nowhere: "I understand His Holiness has a passion for the written word," and I turned about to see Alfonso materialize from between the shelves.

He held a book. He wore a green wool tunic and dark hose, his soft brushed-leather boots bunched about his thick calves. His hair was tousled, wisps of cobweb and shreds of parchment caught in it, as if he had been rummaging through the stacks. His expression captured me—a beatific look of wonderment, as if he'd plunged into a dream he hoped might never end.

"My father has always loved books," I said, acutely aware of our solitude as he neared. He was not as graceful on his feet as he was on horseback; there was a slight awkwardness to his movements and constraint to the way his clothing fit. I realized it was not that he lacked elegance but rather that he had not spent his time polishing his gestures, unlike everyone else I knew. And his apparel seemed ill fitting because it was secondary to him. He must look magnificent naked, I found myself thinking, and I felt embarrassed by my thoughts as he came beside me, his hands extending the book. "Look at this. It is exquisite."

The object he proffered was not a book but a bound portfolio, clearly ancient, which explained the reverence with which he held it. Hand-sewn and water-stained, its ink faded, the portfolio was spread open to a page depicting a giant in a wind-flung scarlet cloak, ensnared by ropes of writhing snakes and with two anguished cherubs clinging to his ribs.

"Laocoön," I said. "He was a Trojan priest who tried to expose the ruse of the Horse; he and his sons, Antiphantes and Thymbracus, were strangled by sea serpents sent by the gods."

"You know the story." His voice was smooth, without that hoarse undertone I had detected on the road, its resonance coming from deep in his chest.

"I do. It's a play by Sophocles, cited in Virgil's *Aeneid*."

"This copy of the *Aeneid* is over four hundred years old." He sounded stunned, as if he couldn't believe it. "I found it all the way in the back, among other manuscripts from the Imperial Library of Constantinople. Did you know you had books here from that fallen city?"

"I did not. But, then, this is not my library. It belongs to His Holiness."

"Yes. How foolish of me. How could you know everything stored here?" His sudden smile crinkled the corners of his eyes. "I fear I lose myself among books. I forget everything."

"So it would seem." I returned his smile, even as I took a step back. I could drown in his eyes. Up close I saw they had no restless green in them, no wisps of gray like Sancia's. Instead, his had flecks of amber, like tourmalines, which in the diffused light looked golden. With his wide cheekbones and mane of unkempt hair, he reminded me of a young lion.

We stood in self-conscious silence, uncertain of what to do next. Then he said, "Shall we sit?" and I followed him deeper into the library, to an alcove where he'd made his perch, the worn cushions indented, books and manuscripts piled on a lectern nearby. The air felt closer here and dimmer, shadows lengthening with the sun's trajectory over the Vatican.

He indicated an unlit hand lantern on the floor. "The librarian offered it to me; he said the light can be hard on the eyes at this time of day, but I cannot imagine keeping a flame here, among all this. One mistake and it could all go up in a conflagration." He shuddered. "Thousands of years of wisdom turned to ashes, like what is happening in Florence."

"You must mean the bonfires ordered by Savonarola." I shifted a few books aside in the alcove. With a murmured apology he retrieved them, and as I sat, thinking I'd done well to wear a simple gown without adornment, he set the books on the floor with care. He handled inanimate objects as if they had sensations.

"It is terrible," he said, "what that friar does, ordering everyone to surrender the most beautiful things they possess. He would burn the very world the Medici built—all that irreplaceable art, lost forever. It is said Botticelli himself was forced to throw some of his own work into the fire. How can anyone order such destruction?"

"Does not Savonarola preach that if we wish to be closer to God, we must relinquish the temptations that lead us into sin? He's not the first to seek to cleanse the world of idolatry; St. Bernardino of Siena preached much the same. Both declare that vanity is mankind's most egregious flaw." As I spoke, I was pleased to see a hint of color surface in his cheeks.

"Do you believe that?" he asked.

"I hardly see how what I believe matters. I am a woman—one of God's lowest forms of creation, according to Savonarola. He has seen those of my gender burned on his bonfires, too, or stoned and hung from gibbets. He has armies of children who march through his city seeking out the impure and iniquitous. Art or flesh—it's all the same to him."

"But your beliefs *do* matter." He inched closer, so I could smell that perfume of knowledge on his person; dust and old paper and his own faint sweat combined to create an ineffable fragrance. He seized my hands, oblivious to the thrill he sent through me. "Women are not thoughtless beings, forged from man's rib to bear our seed. They too can gift the world with knowledge and art; women throughout history have exalted us to higher purpose."

"Is that so?" I looked at our clasped hands. Mine appeared lost within his, tiny ivory reliquaries swathed in russet velvet. I lifted my eyes back to him, relishing the physical impact of his gaze. "Such as . . . ?"

"Well, women like . . ." He bit his lip. "Aspasia of Athens," he exclaimed, "who was cited by Plato, Aristophanes, and Plutarch, among others. She influenced the political and artistic decisions of her lover, Pericles, and wrote her own rhetoric, though none of it has survived."

"Wasn't she also a courtesan?" I said, and he blushed.

"Yes, but she commanded respect from the most famous figures of her age; she alone among women in Athens was invited to dispute at gatherings. And what of Hypatia of Alexandria, who headed the Platonist school of her native city? Socrates tells us she so surpassed every other, she was the greatest mind of her age."

"And was stoned to death by a mob for it." I smiled to ease the pained awareness that crossed his face. "So, we come full circle to St. Bernardino and Savonarola. A woman who expresses her thoughts is a dangerous being."

"Not to me." His hands tightened on mine. I had the sudden sensation that my fingers were dissolving as he drew me closer. "I revere a woman who speaks her mind, who is not afraid to fight for her beliefs or be her own person."

"A woman?" I asked. "Or a wife?" As he went still, taken aback, I withdrew my hands. "As my lord must surely be aware, they are not the same thing, at least not to most men." I started to rise.

He gazed at me. "I am not most men," he said, "as surely my lady must realize by now." He did not reach for my hand again. I had the distinct impression that if I turned and walked away he would not try to stop me. He was offering me a choice, and it sundered my heart to realize he was someone I should fear.

He had the power to overturn my entire existence.

"I have enjoyed our afternoon," I said, resisting the urge to lower my lashes in false reticence. "I owe you my gratitude, Prince Alfonso, for enlightening me in ways I had not expected. I shall always remember it."

He came to his feet. "As shall I. My sole regret is that I must return soon to Naples; I feel as though we have so much yet to discover. May I write to you, Donna Lucrezia?"

Before I could consider it, before I could doubt, I kissed him. He did not startle, though for an instant he showed surprise in his sudden immobility. Then his mouth turned pliant, yielding to mine. When I drew back, I saw what I had hoped for—that look of wonderment, as if he had tasted something he indeed would never forget.

"Yes," I said softly, "you may write."

Pulling my hood over my head, I turned away, knowing that if I dared linger, I might be compelled to surrender what I was not yet prepared to give.

As I suspected, Alfonso of Aragon did not try to stop me.

I returned to find Pantalisea pacing in my palazzo courtyard. As I stepped through the gates, she took one look at me and blurted out, "Wherever you have been, I pray he is discreet. This message came for you hours ago, from your brother's palazzo; the page said it was urgent."

Alarm fired through me as I took the paper she handed me. The magic of my afternoon with Alfonso faded like an illusion.

"I must go to him at once," I said. "Cesare has returned. He is ill."

CHAPTER TWENTY

With Pantalisea and two burly guards, I took a litter to the Trastevere. Night had fallen, blanketing the city in mist, but the narrow lanes and piazzas were awash with thieves, whores, and swaggering condottiere seeking diversion under the low eaves. Acrid smoke wafted from torches carried by armed footmen. The doors and shutters of the taverns were flung wide open to let out raucous laughter and the din of tankards.

At Cesare's palazzo, my guards banged on the gates; after an interminable moment during which I clenched my hands in impatience and Pantalisea glanced around anxiously from under her hood, as if we were about to be assaulted, I heard the bolts slide back.

The postern opened. We slipped inside to find my brother's house shrouded in darkness; a lone firebrand in the inner *cortile* shed light over the coffers and trunks of Cesare's return from Naples, still lashed with ropes and heaped where they'd been left in the arcade.

The page who'd unbolted the gates stood before us. Without giving him a glance, I said to Pantalisea, "Wait here with the guards." I pushed back my hood as I climbed the staircase to the *piano nobile*, hurrying down the loggia to Cesare's apartments.

A figure emerging from the shadows brought me to a frightened halt. "Michelotto!" I pressed a hand to my pounding heart as my brother's manservant bowed. In the gloom, I could barely distinguish his features, but as soon as he spoke, I felt a pang of dread at his somber tone.

"Donna Lucrezia, you were not expected."

"No?" I reached for the crumpled note in my cloak's inner pocket. "I received this missive from—" I suddenly realized I did not know who had sent it. Even as I hesitated, footsteps came hurrying behind Michelotto and he half-turned to reveal Sancia, her hair tangled, her eyes seeming enormous in her drawn face. My fear increased; in the time I had known her, I had never seen her look anything but perfectly poised.

"Lucrezia, thank God!" She thrust out her hand to take me by my sleeve. "Where have you been? I sent that note hours ago. I've been waiting for you all this time."

"You knew where I was," I said. "I was in the library. You yourself helped arrange it—"

Michelotto stepped between us, forcing her to release me. "With all due respect, Your Highness," he murmured to Sancia, "I do not think my lord would wish his sister to see him at this time, not in his current state."

Before Sancia could reply, I said firmly, "If my brother has need of me, then whether or not he *wishes* to see me is of no account." Unclasping my cloak, I let it drop to the tiled floor at his feet. "Please step aside."

Michelotto retrieved my cloak. "As you say, my lady," he said, and Sancia yanked me forward to a pair of wooden doors.

She came to a halt. I searched her face before I said, "You said he was ill. Is it a fever?"

Her voice trembled. "It might be a fever, yes, but unlike any I've seen. He arrived yesterday; he did not want anyone to know. He asked me to meet him here, said he had something important we must discuss. I came at once, naturally. I thought he wanted . . ."

"Yes," I said, growing impatient. "I know what you thought. What did he say?"

"He seemed fine." She kneaded her hands. "Beautiful, as always, with high color in his face from the sun and not at all tired from his travels, but he—he was enraged. No sooner had I stepped into his rooms than he began raving."

"Raving?" I wanted to grab her, forcibly shake out her words. "About what?"

"Juan," she said, and I froze.

"Juan? But he is in Spain."

"Not for long." Sancia exhaled a shuddering breath. "Your father has summoned him; his Spanish wife gave birth to a son, and His Holiness has declared that Juan must return here to lead a campaign against the Orsini barons in the Romagna. They refuse to join the Holy League, so your father will bring the entire family to task for assisting the French and calling for his dethronement. His Holiness intends to grant Juan command as gonfalonier of the papal states."

"Juan? Our captain general?" I almost laughed in disbelief. "*Per Dio,* he cannot be serious. Juan doesn't know the first thing about overseeing an army."

"That's what Cesare said." When she took my hand again, her fingers were icy. "Lucrezia, he was wild. Never have I seen him like that; he said . . . terrible things. He started throwing everything he could get hold of; it was as though he lost his reason. The sweat poured off him. He turned so white that I thought he must indeed be delirious with fever. I still think he is. I think he is very ill. I believe he has—"

"What?" I clutched her hand so tightly that she winced. "You think he has what?"

"The French pox," she whispered.

Everything darkened for a paralyzing instant.

"Impossible," I heard myself utter. "He's always been strong, healthy. Besides that bout of marsh fever when he was a boy, Cesare hasn't been ill a day in his life."

"He threw me out of the room." She drew back, tugging at her bodice to display the mottled bruise on her shoulder. "He did this to me with his hands. I tried to tell him he should not become so irate, that surely, once he expressed his concern to His Holiness, he could compel your father to heed his advice. I even offered to speak to His Holiness myself—you know how fond he is of me. But Cesare threatened to strangle me if I dared say a word to anyone. Then he flung me out of the room as though I were a dog."

Tears swam in her eyes. I could see that the violence Cesare had shown terrified her. As worldly as she appeared, Sancia was barely eighteen years of age. She had lived her entire life in the pampered court, and while it was one thing to play seductress before admiring sycophants, it was quite another to find herself handled like a common *puttana.*

"I love him," she said. "I truly do. He's the most fascinating man I have ever known, but today he frightened me. It was as if I looked into the eyes of a madman. There was a moment as he came toward me—Lucrezia, I thought he would kill me."

I embraced her. "You mustn't think that. He is beside himself, if what you say is true. For Papa to disregard him so completely and bestow such an honor upon Juan—it must have indeed driven him beyond reason. Cesare has tried so hard, for so long, to prove his worth. He cannot abide this. But I am certain," I said, caressing the hair from her brow as she regarded me with the expression of a bewildered child, "that he did not intend to hurt you. He will apologize and make amends, you'll see. He will regret having done this. He already does."

"Yes." She nodded desperately. "I thought the same. It is why I summoned you. You are his beloved sister; he always speaks of you with such admiration. I did not want to interrupt your time with Alfonso, so I sent word to your maid, but I thought . . ."

"I understand. I will speak to him." I smiled to ease her distress, though I felt only mounting apprehension. "Have Michelotto escort you to your palazzo. I'll send word."

Her voice caught as she whispered, "Thank you, Lucrezia," and stumbled down the loggia to where Michelotto stood, watching us.

As Michelotto guided Sancia away, I turned to the doors. I hesitated for a moment, wondering if it might not be better, or at least wiser, to leave Cesare alone until his temper cooled. But Sancia's words—*I think he is very ill*—went through me like a horrid presentiment, so that I found myself rapping upon the wood, my voice peremptory as I called out: "Cesare. It is Lucrezia. Let me in."

Silence fell, the echo of my voice fading into the loggia. I could hear the faint sounds of revelry outside the palazzo walls, the populace in the streets going about their evening without a care.

Then the key in the lock clicked. The door creaked open.

Pushing against it, I entered his chamber.

Though the curtains at the far window were half yanked from their rods, admitting the silvery glow of the moon over the garden, the room was submerged in darkness, causing me to step gingerly. My slippers crunched on fragments of something broken on the floor; as my eyes adjusted, I saw that the entire chamber had been ransacked—tables turned on their sides, heavy chairs toppled, the carpets on the sideboards wrenched down, along with platters, candlesticks, decanters, and goblets.

"Cesare?" My whisper shivered in the stillness.

He stepped into view from a corner sideboard, his back to me, silhouetted against the window with its fallen drapery—his shirt hung about him, a shapeless linen ghost through which the light filtered, outlining his torso within it.

I threaded my way to him. When he felt my fingers on his arm, he said in a low, flat tone, "You should not have come."

"Sancia sent word. She is very worried for you. She thinks you may be ill."

He did not move. As I began to turn him around to me, he abruptly swerved to avoid my touch, inadvertently revealing himself.

I could not contain my shock. He was gaunt, and the bronze hue of his time spent in Naples had turned ashen. Drenched in perspiration, the unlaced front of his chemise clung to his chest as though he had just bathed and put it upon his wet skin. He had shorn his hair again, perhaps to better endure the heat of Naples; his close-cropped skull made him resemble a starving prisoner.

"What do you want?" he said.

"Sweet Virgin, look at you. You *are* ill." I reached out to touch his brow. He flinched. "Cesare, we must call for Papa's physician, Torella. You're burning with fever."

"It is nothing." Again, he jerked away from me. "I have a tertian. It will pass."

"A tertian? Then you should be in bed, under a physician's care."

"I told you, it is nothing. I'm taking some foul medicine for it. I do not need you or Torella fussing over me." He squared his shoulders. "Go back to your palazzo. Go back to playing your silly games with Sancia. Leave me be."

"How can you say that to me? If you are ill, you must be attended; otherwise, I shall be the one who worries about you."

Without warning, he grasped my shoulders, digging his fingers into me. "It is too late for worry," he snarled. "Or have you not heard? I am forsaken."

Though I wanted to push him away, remind him that I was not

some mistress that he could manhandle at will, I kept my reply calm, for Sancia was right: He was sick. "I did hear. Sancia told me. She said you threatened to strangle her for it. Papa is bringing Juan home to lead a campaign against the Orsini. He will name him gonfalonier."

"Yes! While I was in Naples being his lackey, Papa plotted to give our brother a charge that will make us the farce of Italy, never mind that our brother can barely pull the sword from his scabbard—and that's when he is sober. Yet Papa now sees fit to name him captain general of the papal states."

"Cesare." I was struggling to remain composed. "He honored you, too. He named you cardinal. He chose you to represent him in Naples. You judge him too harshly, after everything he has endured. He allows you everything he can—"

"Everything but my freedom. Everything but my choice." His raw burst of laughter chilled me. Sancia had not exaggerated; it truly was as though he had turned feral. "But of course you must defend him. Ever the dutiful daughter, as Mama says, even if you hold fast to your precious virginity before the world while sneaking behind his back to entice that boorish brother of Sancia's to your hallowed bed."

"How dare you?" I had to curl my fist at my side to resist striking him, my concern for his health charred by his reproach. "I would never do such a thing. And who are you to fling such accusations when you yourself would have—" I stopped myself, seeing his malicious smile.

"I myself would have what? Why can you not say it, Lucia?"

"I do not need to. You know well what you desired."

"I do. I desire it still. But you spurned me. You refused me because you must save yourself for one you deem more worthy. Do so. Give yourself to whomever you please, but do not come running after me, because I do not want your concern. I do not want your pity or false affection. I do not want or need you anymore."

I began to step back. The violence Sancia had feared scalded his face, so that in the bizarre alchemy of the moonlight around us, it seemed as if he had no whites in his eyes, his rage swallowing his pupils until a malevolent stranger gazed through him.

"Cesare," I said haltingly, "you are not yourself."

For a terrifying moment, as he watched me inch to the door over the shards of detritus strewn underfoot, I thought he would lunge. I could actually feel his hands upon me, and I braced for his blow. Then he let out an anguished groan. He staggered, doubling over. When I started toward him—for he was crooked somehow, as if twisted from within—he cried, "No, keep away!" Tears streamed down his cheeks, mingling with his sweat, his chemise soaked now, translucent, exposing the contours of his chest.

"Let me help you," I implored. "I love you, Cesare. I cannot bear to see you like this."

Another spasm contorted his face. "You cannot help me. No one can. This devil I suffer cannot be cured; it must have its way. Leave me. Save yourself, instead."

My mother's words lanced through me—*it is your curse, a poison you carry inside*—and my plea was ragged. "There is no devil inside you. You have a fever. You do not know what you say."

He stared at me. "Oh, I know. Hatred is my devil. As long as Juan lives, I'll never escape him. I am doomed to abide forever in his shadow, never becoming who I was meant to be."

"What . . . what will you do?" I whispered.

"Whatever I must. The die is cast. Fortuna shows her cruel hand. And now let the world be forewarned." He wiped his arm across his brow, moving back into the shadows by the sideboard. "You must go. You must leave me now."

Only then did I notice someone in the doorway—a dapper figure in leather, with a plumed cap and black mask over his face, so that I couldn't see anything in his covered visage save for the hint of eyes and teeth. Yet I knew at once that it was Michelotto.

"My lady," he said. "It is time you returned to Santa Maria." He came forward with my cloak and unfurled it across my shoulders. Then he pulled another mask from his pocket and affixed it to my face. As I started to resist, he murmured, "Rome is not safe at night; you must not be seen. I would not have a mishap befall you."

Through the eyeholes of the mask, I searched for Cesare. I could barely see him, crouched by the sideboard, motionless. "Do not bring more harm upon yourself," I said.

My brother did not answer, as Michelotto turned me away.

On the way back to my palazzo, with Pantalisea gripping my hand, all I could hear was the triumphant declaration Cesare had uttered to me in Pesaro, in what now seemed a lifetime ago:

The time has come for a new age—the age of Borgia. And I shall be its scourge.

SANCIA CAME TO visit me a few weeks later. She had apparently recovered, waving aside my explanation that Cesare was indeed ill but on the mend. I suspected her indifference was the only way she knew how to shield herself from the hurt he'd inflicted. In truth, I'd not heard another word from him, my missives to his palazzo gone unanswered. But I surmised that he must be improving or I'd have heard otherwise.

Instead of discussing Cesare, however, Sancia wanted to confirm gossip about my husband. "I'm told he is back, having accomplished nothing of note save to watch from afar, appropriately costumed in armor, of course, while our soldiers chased those hideous mercenaries out of the Romagna. Is it true? Is he here now?"

I nodded, unable to disguise my grimace. Giovanni had indeed returned, and immediately after installing himself in his wing of my palazzo he'd become the object of sniggering, as it was widely known that he'd borne no honor in the skirmishes that were paving the way for our upcoming campaign against the Orsini barons. As a result, he skulked about. I could scarcely abide the sight of him whenever we crossed paths. Fortunately, we rarely did.

"I have scarcely spoken to him," I said. "He avoids me."

"What else can he do? He is humiliated." She paused, eyeing me. "But not so much that he refrained from petitioning His Holiness to let him consummate your marriage. You never told me you had a clause in your nuptial treaty, my sly Lucrezia."

She sounded faintly accusatory. I shrugged, in no mood to give her the sordid details. "It's hardly a secret. And of no relevance now, given the fact that I'm certainly of age."

"You most certainly are. Women younger than you are deemed of age. Yet His Holiness will not declare it and told Giovanni that, after his recent abysmal failure in war, he is not inclined to let him do the same in your bed." Suspicion spiked her voice. "Giovanni of course pro-

tested, citing he cannot be refused his rights as your husband indefinitely, but His Holiness warned that if he dared touch a hair on your
head he'd throw him into the Castel Sant'Angelo to bed with the rats."

I was hardly surprised that Sancia knew of my father's exchange
with Giovanni. She had an infallible ear for scandal. And her news
comforted me, for Papa's dictate would keep Giovanni at bay. Still, I did
not wish to discuss him, so I finally dared to ask if she'd had any word
from Cesare.

She arched an eyebrow. "Much as it pains me, I have not. He's not
called for me once or sent so much as an apology, though you assured
me of his abject repentance. All I can say is that I believe he is as well as
can be expected."

"Why do you say that?" I felt suddenly breathless. Had he fallen
even more desperately ill and I'd been left unawares, thinking him on
the mend?

She shrugged. "You saw him, did you not? When a man's pride sustains such a blow, the only thing on his mind is—well, his pride."

Her words brought back the fear I had felt when I visited my brother.
I realized I shouldn't worry about her mention of the French pox. Cesare only had a bad fever, as he claimed, exacerbated by his disappointment; it was understandable he'd keep to his palazzo until he gained
mastery over himself. Those awful words he'd said to me, the monster I
had glimpsed in his eyes—much like Sancia's indifference, it was how
he had learned to protect himself against the burden he must carry, the
knowledge that while he suffered the shackles of the cloth, Juan was free
to reap glory with the sword. Nevertheless, my disquiet persisted, until
Sancia reached into her skirts and dropped a folded parchment into my
lap.

"From Alfonso," she said, even as Pantalisea, seated nearby, looked
up sharply. My woman had grown even more protective of me in the
wake of our visit to Cesare. "He waits for your reply."

"Since when have married ladies replied to correspondence from a
man who is not their father or husband?" demanded Pantalisea, bringing a glower to Sancia's face.

"And since when have maidservants reproved their betters?" she retorted.

"Yes, since when?" I said, staring in excitement at the letter. I motioned Pantalisea out before she could protest, then turned to the window to crack open the seal.

Alfonso's handwriting covered the page, the practiced script of a man as well versed in penmanship as he was in literature:

Donna,

I write this wishing that I were with you. I have not yet reached my beloved city but have already been warned it is overrun by mercenaries abandoned by the French. Therefore, I am charged upon my arrival with assembling the forces needed to expel this vermin from our domain.

Despite this responsibility, I think of you every hour of every day. At night when I close my eyes, I see your face and relive our all-too-brief time in the library. You may deem me a fool for revealing the simple workings of my heart, which is untutored in courtly arts, but the memory of you sustains me, *bella signora mia,* as does the hope that one day we may meet again.

His letter was unsigned, in case it should fall astray on its way to me. Still, I heard his voice in his words and was amazed that this prince I barely knew could nurture such sentiments for me. I too had felt the magnetic charge between us; I also remembered the idyllic hour we'd spent, lost in our own world, but it had faded into the past, in the turmoil of my encounter with Cesare and with Giovanni's return. Now his letter brought it back to me. Never had I received a missive like this, so heartfelt and candid. After I read it one more time, I turned back to Sancia.

"I must think carefully on my reply."

"Do not think too long," she warned. "He may perish of misery if you do."

But I had no time to compose my response, for soon after, preparations for Juan's arrival overtook us. For weeks through the summer heat, Papa's every waking hour, and thousands of ducats, were lavished on the upcoming reception. Even the cobblestones in St. Peter's Piazza were cleansed of grime, the vagrants and beggars put into jails so they'd not soil the gilded archways built over the road down which Juan would ride.

And as August's pitiless sun poured upon us, baking us in our finery, we gathered on the velvet-bunted dais to witness my brother's return from Spain.

Trumpets sounded in the distance. Looking across the dais from the cushions where Sancia and I sat, I tried to catch Cesare's eye. It was the first time I'd seen him since that day in his palazzo, as well as his first official appearance. I was relieved to find he did not appear visibly sick. He was still too pale, with shadows under his eyes, but he stood tall, elegant in his scarlet robes, his skullcap fitted to his shorn head and his hands bare of adornment, folded before the wide sash at his waist.

"He is coming," I heard Papa's delighted whisper, and I watched in disbelief as he turned to Cesare. "I can hear the cheering. Our beloved Juan is home!"

My sudden impulse to rise from my cushions and harangue Papa dismayed me. All my life, I'd worshipped the ground he trod upon. Yet his disregard for the sense of degradation that must course under Cesare's polished façade made me want to yell for all Rome to hear that Pope Alexander VI had more than one son, and if he failed to show them equal favor, he risked condemning us all to—

A roar of acclaim brought my attention to the procession entering the piazza. A multitude of grooms in our livery surrounded Juan, who sat astride a stallion caparisoned in cloth-of-gold edged with jangling bells, his scarlet cap and sienna-brown velvet doublet so encrusted with gems, he blazed like the very sun. An incongruous entourage of turbaned Moors, somersaulting jesters, and dwarves in matching velvet swirled about him. Close behind him rode Giovanni, who'd gone to the Porta Portese as part of the welcoming reception, arrayed in finery paid for, as usual, by us.

Then I caught sight of Giovanni's expression. I had never seen such joy on his face; he seemed transformed, lightened somehow, even moderately handsome, as though Juan's return had infused him with new life. I stared, unable to believe my eyes, recalling with revulsion his liaison in my palazzo with Juan and Giulia, not feeling Sancia's pinch on my arm until she hissed, "Lucrezia, you must rise. His Holiness is on his feet!" I stood, tugging at my own magnificent, if slightly crumpled, violet and silver *camora,* which clung, sweat-dampened, to my body.

Papa hurtled to the edge of the dais. "My son! Juan, *hijo mío!*" he cried. The crowds, always moved by his paternal abandon, went wild, their cries of "Gandia! Gandia!" thundering throughout the piazza until I thought the echo might shatter the fragile statues of the basilica.

Juan leapt from his horse. The singsong jingle about him grew louder as he mounted the dais to where Papa waited. Sancia said in my ear, "God save us, does he wear bells on his clothes, too?" and I had to curb my giggle as I heard the tiny silver bells chiming on his Moorish-style mantle, which he removed in a dramatic gesture and tossed in a clanging heap behind him.

The crowds let out a roar of laughter. Quite unwittingly, Juan had reduced his triumphant arrival to a comedy.

I shot another look at Cesare. He stood immobile beside the empty papal throne, the angular line of his profile revealing nothing.

But as Papa engulfed Juan in his embrace and the cardinals applauded, as the people tossed flowers in the air and cannon fire exploded from the *castel*, I saw an icy smile unfurl over Cesare's lips.

CHAPTER TWENTY-ONE

"The campaign is a disaster."

Hearing Cesare's voice, I came to a halt before the half-open door to my father's private chamber. Outside, a tempest hammered against the palace, spitting hail and rattling the casements.

I'd decided to pay an impromptu visit to Papa, as he'd been occupied in the weeks leading to the Epiphany festivities. In September, he had seen Juan, newly titled as gonfalonier, march from Rome at the head of our army. I'd barely seen my brother at all; up until the hour of his departure, he'd been sequestered in daily meetings with Papa, Cesare, and their councillors, but I'd heard of no altercations between him and Cesare. Following Christmas, the entire papal court fell into torpor. The Curia took its recess, the cardinals retiring to their palazzos; Papa too should have been enjoying a long-deserved respite, but after several requests for an audience that he failed to answer, I finally took the hidden passage from Santa Maria into the Vatican.

And now I found myself unable to announce my presence. Motioning away the stone-faced guards standing vigil in the corridor, I pressed my eyes closer to the ajar door. In the chamber beyond, I saw Cesare beside a table heaped with what looked like maps and other papers. Papa sat brooding in his large chair, his grizzled chin on his fist. I knew I should announce myself but instead found myself staying hidden by the door, curious to discover why they seemed so intent.

"Don't you think it's premature for these dire predictions?" my father grumbled. "The war is not over yet."

"It might as well be," said Cesare, without a hint of remonstration despite his frown. "No one believes we have any other option than to seek accord with the Orsini and their allies."

"Accord?" exclaimed Papa. "I'd rather pawn my own throne. Your brother may not have excelled thus far, but he has managed to capture twelve of the Orsini fortresses, including Scrofano and Formello. Is that not enough for you?"

I held my breath, awaiting Cesare's reply. I remembered his words to me on that horrible night, about the devil inside him, and his icy smile when Juan arrived. While I knew it was wrong to eavesdrop, I was riveted by the scene before me, for it was the first time I'd found my brother and father alone together, discussing matters not meant for anyone's ears but theirs.

"We both know Juan did not take the fortresses," Cesare said at length. "He may claim thus in his official dispatches, but in reality, it was his first commander, my lord of Urbino, who oversaw those sieges. Unfortunately, Urbino was also wounded during the last one and had to retire from the field, leaving Juan to assume the capture of the main Orsini fortress at Bracciano."

Papa groused, "Yes, yes. We know all that," making me wish I'd paid more attention to Juan's campaign instead of letting myself be distracted by Sancia's constant urging to write my delayed response to Alfonso. I heard a decanter clink; Papa's favored attendant, Perotto, walked past my view to refill my father's goblet. The sight of the handsome chamberlain reassured me; evidently this discussion was not so secret that Perotto couldn't be present.

Cesare was quiet.

"Well?" our father barked, but I discerned a distinct lack of aggression in his tone, as though he tried to rouse an impatience he did not feel.

"Well," said Cesare. I heard papers rustle. "It says here that while Urbino convalesced, Juan made a mess of his charge. The storms turned the ground to mud, so he couldn't employ our cavalry to approach; he also gravely underestimated Donna Bartolomea, wife of Virginio Orsini, who holds Bracciano in the family name and refused Juan's order to surrender. Her obstinacy and the weather kept our army at bay. Then she sent a donkey into Juan's encampment with a message shoved up its tail. Do you want to hear what it said?" My brother paused.

Papa said, "Do I have a choice?"

Cesare's voice was so modulated, so controlled, that only someone who knew him very well would have detected its scathing undertone. "The message was, and I quote, *Let me pass, as I am envoy to the duke of Gandia.*"

I stifled my laughter as Papa spat, "That Orsini bitch will rue the hour she dares mock us."

"Perhaps," replied Cesare, "but for now I fear it is we who must rue, because after she mocked Juan, there was nothing he could do. Word of her defiance spread throughout the ranks, and our men lost faith in him. While Juan harangued them to some semblance of order, reinforcements from the Romagna barons arrived to defend Donna Bartolomea; they chased our entire army into Soriano, where we've been defeated. This latest dispatch is from Urbino himself. He writes that he tried to fight, even while injured, but was captured. He requests payment of his ransom, as is the custom. Juan, it seems, also suffered a wound to his face. Once he's recovered enough to take horse, he requests your leave to return here."

"Impossible!" I saw Papa lumber up from his chair and stride right in front of me, immobile at the door, to snatch the letter from Cesare. As he read, fury darkened his voice. "It cannot be. Juan must not abandon the field. We've not yet struck our blow against the Orsini. If he retreats, all will indeed be lost. I'll be forced to sue for peace. We'll be ridiculed before all of Italy."

It was the hour Cesare had long awaited, confirmation from our own father of Juan's incompetence. Yet Cesare only sighed. "The war is over. Juan is incapacitated and his commander a captive of the enemy. We must swallow our pride, offer the Orsini a truce and negotiate the return of their fortresses before the entire Romagna rises up against us. After what those barons did when the French invaded, we cannot afford to go further in this enterprise. Perhaps later," Cesare added, "once Juan has fully recovered, we can try again. If they are given back their castles and coin to satisfy their losses, the Orsini can be placated."

I was surprised by my brother's magnanimous words but not by our father's reaction. He flung aside his goblet. It struck the far wall with a metallic clatter. In the silence, I clearly heard my father panting. Then he said, "We always have the matter with Lucrezia."

I froze. Cesare did not respond for a long moment. "We do," he finally said, "but I think we should delay. The conversation I had with

Giovanni was not edifying. He refuses to consider any annulment of their marriage on the grounds of—"

A sudden grip on my arm swung me about. Before I could gasp, Sancia pressed her other hand to my lips. "Hush," she mouthed, and she hauled me away into the corridor.

I pulled from her, irate and embarrassed to be caught outside my father's door. Sancia murmured, "I regret the interruption, knowing how much we can learn from eavesdropping. But your husband is in a rage. You should come at once before he tears your palazzo apart."

SHOUTS AND THE crash of something overturning in the antechamber—a table with my majolica decanter or a sideboard of platters—greeted me as I hastened up the staircase to my apartments. I heard Pantalisea cry, "*Signore, per favore!* My lady went to see His Holiness. I must insist that—"

"Get out of my way," Giovanni yelled.

Sancia reached into her cloak, pulling out a small dagger. Her face turned grim. I tasted the brine of fear in my throat as we stepped over the threshold. The antechamber was in shambles, overturned chairs and shards of broken porcelain littering the carpets. My women cowered by my bedchamber door. Giovanni was moving toward them; as he heard Sancia and me walk in, he whirled about, swaying, his eyes narrowed with wine-soaked fury.

"I have the right," he slurred, jabbing his finger at me. "I have the right, damn you!"

An abrupt, cold calm pervaded me. "I am afraid I have no idea to what you refer, nor do I understand the reason for this unseemly display, Signore."

"You should be afraid." He took a staggering step toward me. "Because I have the right, not your conniving demon of a brother or that boar you call a father. You are my wife. Mine! No one can say otherwise. No one can dare say that I am not a man."

Out of the corner of my eye, I saw Sancia unsheathe her blade and palm it. I prayed she would exercise restraint. Despite his threats, Giovanni was far too flown with wine to do much harm. "You are drunk, Signore," I said. "We can speak again when you are sober."

He blinked, as if perplexed by my glacial tone. Then he growled, "You think I lack for counsel in this cesspit? You Borgias aren't the only ones with paid eyes and ears; I too have those who spy for me, and I well know what you and your father plan."

"I do not doubt it. Nevertheless, I have no interest in what your spies say."

Pantalisea stepped behind him. "Signore, my lady does not wish to see you—"

Giovanni threw out his arm, striking her across her face. The impact sent her reeling into the other women, who cried out as she tumbled against them, blood spurting from her nose.

"*Bruto!*" Sancia lunged at him. "You think you are so brave, eh, beating on a woman?" She brandished her dagger. "Let us see how brave you are when I cut off your balls."

Giovanni sneered. "The other Borgia slut is here. Excellent. I will fuck you both, just as Cesare and His Holiness have done before me."

Before Sancia could raise her dagger to him, my hand shot out, detaining her. Stepping past her, I said, "You will leave at once. If you do not, if you ever dare utter such filth again to me or anyone else, I will tell my father and the entire world what you are. Everyone will learn of how you can only bed a woman if my brother Juan takes you from behind like a Turk."

He gaped at me.

"Yes," I continued as his bloodshot eyes widened in horror. "I was there. I saw everything. I used it to destroy Giulia Farnese. I will do the same to you, if you give me cause."

His voice seemed to choke him. "It's . . . not possible. I did not— you could not . . ."

I smiled. "Oh, but I could. I did. Have you forgotten there was a hole in the door? Djem was there; he showed it all to me. And although he is dead, Signore, I am not."

He did not move. He did not speak. I felt our mutual hatred, our loathing for each other, cresting before he whispered, "You will regret this."

"I do not think I will regret anything where our marriage is concerned," I said, recalling what I had just overheard in Papa's chamber.

He may have refused Cesare's request to concede an annulment, but if I threatened to reveal his sordid secret, he'd be in no position to refuse again.

His hands bunched; I glanced at them. "Harm me," I added, "and I shall ask His Holiness to have you plead more than non-consummation of our vows."

With a strangled sound, he lurched about, shouldering past my women to trudge out the door. Only then did I feel my resolve weaken, as I turned to Sancia. "He will never forgive me."

"If what you told him is true," she replied, "you do not need his forgiveness. Giovanni Sforza may be a drunken fool, but even fools know when to submit."

✑

WINTER EBBED. SPRING tiptoed in, bringing larks and buds to the trees in time for Holy Week. On the morning of Good Friday, Giovanni arrived unexpectedly at my door. I had not seen him since our confrontation months before, and I barely acknowledged him now as he stood in my antechamber with his cap in his fist, dressed in a somber tunic, boots, and cloak.

"I am going to the Church of Sant'Onofrio in honor of our Savior's martyrdom." He paused, awaiting my response. I thought he looked haggard; if I'd cared anything for him, I would have told him as much and suggested he consider the state of his immortal soul on a daily basis, not just on sacred ones like today.

Instead, I refused to look up from where I sat with my women. Having finished my morning prayers, I was passing the time embroidering. "That is good," I said, wondering why he felt the need to announce his intentions, when he never had before. "I wish you a good day."

"You should come with me. You are my wife."

With a pointed glance at Pantalisea, whom he had struck, her bruise taking days to fade, I replied, "I will attend Mass this afternoon with His Holiness as scheduled. You are welcome to join us," I added, "as my husband."

He made a sudden move, but something in my gaze, perhaps my

undisguised contempt, stopped him from stepping over the threshold. Reaching into his jerkin, he removed a paper, folded over and stamped with a lump of wax. He lifted his arm as if to throw it at my feet. Murilla leapt off her stool to intercept it. My dwarf boldly blocked his passage, daring him to come any closer.

His mouth twisted. He handed the paper to her. Turning about, he left my rooms without another word. Murilla brought me his missive. I started to set it aside in disdain when Pantalisea ventured, "Perhaps my lady should read what he has to say."

"Oh? Why would anything he says interest me?" But I broke the seal, anyway, and unfolded the page. He had written in a brief scrawl: *When I summon you, you will come.*

Crumpling it, I tossed it into the hearth. "As I supposed. It has no interest."

HOLY WEEK CAME to an end with all its solemn magnificence, although a series of unexpected storms turned Rome into a quagmire. Together with Papa and the Vatican court, I took part in the release of a hundred white doves to commemorate the Resurrection and then I retired to my palazzo, fatigued by all the endless processions and Masses. I had not seen Giovanni again, to my relief. I was worried about Papa, who had suffered several fainting spells, aggravated no doubt by Juan's furtive arrival after Easter Sunday, with only a few attendants and a bloody bandage swaddling his face. This time, there was no reception or triumphal arches; my brother was immediately sequestered in his Vatican apartments to be treated by Torella for the slash across his cheek. But I knew how dejected Papa must be, for as soon as his ceremonial obligations were over, he also retreated to his apartments to be examined by his doctors, who ordered him to remain abed until he recovered from his exhaustion.

More than a month passed before he sent me a summons. I felt immense relief as I walked through his doors to find him wrapped in a lynx-trimmed robe and seated on his great chair. He still looked tired but he had sparse color in his cheeks; I also realized our meeting was private, for he had only his trusted Perotto in attendance. The young man gave me a quick smile as I entered, as if to reassure me that my father's indisposition had not been too serious.

"Come sit by me, *farfallina*," Papa said. I hurried to his side, settling on a stool by his knee and reaching for his large, veined hand.

"Papa, are you feeling better?"

He let out a sigh. "In body, I am as well as any man of my years can expect. But my spirit these days is another matter."

"Yes. I am sorry," I murmured, knowing that this time he could not avoid the disappointment Juan had caused him, as he had so often avoided it in the past.

"Why should you be?" He cupped my chin. "It is not your fault that I'm obliged to sign a treaty with the Orsini that puts us again at the mercy of their intrigues. Nor is it your fault that Their Majesties of Spain complain of the dishonor caused by Pope Alexander the Sixth, who favors his son above all others, or that Savonarola cites our misfortunes as a sign that God has turned His wrath upon the Borgia." His fingers trailed down my cheek. "These are my burdens to carry."

"But you are not to blame for Juan's failure," I said, and as soon as I spoke, I regretted it. Though by now everyone in Italy, indeed in all of Europe, must have heard of Juan's disastrous campaign, I did not want to rub salt into a smarting wound.

Papa's hand went still on my face. I tensed, thinking he'd reprove me, but instead, he said, "You do not understand. You have no son. Or a husband, either, now that Giovanni has fled."

"Fled?" I said in surprise. I had grown so used to avoiding contact with Giovanni, and he with me, that I never questioned his disappearances. "Where has he gone?"

Papa's voice hardened. "It must indeed be a grave matter if the wife is left unawares. According to my informants, he rode for Pesaro shortly after Good Friday, arriving in his city with his horse near-dead under him and crying out foul accusations against us."

I felt sick, but before I could summon my courage to ask, my father added, "He has shown himself unworthy of every honor I bestowed on him. I've written to demand an explanation for his unauthorized departure, but I don't expect a reply. He'll cower in Pesaro and seek the support of Milan, as he always has." Papa paused, staring at me. "It seems your marriage is not a happy one."

"No," I admitted, averting my gaze. "It is not. We have nothing between us."

Papa withdrew his hand, his gaze clouding over. "I am sorry for it. I'd hoped to see you settled as a wife and mother. You cannot know true joy until you hold a child of your own in your arms, seeing it through its first years and watching it grow, planning for its future. Such dreams—" His voice snagged. "Such dreams we have for those who will follow us."

I knew he was thinking of Juan and watched him blink back tears as he directed his gaze to the marble hearth and the fire crackling in its depths. Then he said, "With matters as they now stand, we cannot delay further. We must decide what to do. I'll not have you unhappy any longer. But before we decide, I would know if there's truly nothing between you. You've been married nearly four years. Did he never . . . ?"

He knew that Giovanni had not, as he himself had forbidden it. I had the disquieting sense that he was asking something different of me, probing for proof of any misdeeds. Had he heard unsavory gossip about Giovanni? I debated how much to reveal, for Giovanni had ignited a scandal with his departure. By abandoning Rome, he'd laid bare our estrangement for everyone to see. No doubt, there would be questions as to why I had not gone with him, why he'd felt such urgency to escape. I recalled the note he had left me, which now seemed like a threat. Yet he had not called for me, and I'd overheard Papa and Cesare discussing the annulment. Surely, any claim of mistreatment at my husband's hands would only bolster their case before the Curia. But I also knew about Giovanni and Juan; with my brother recovering from his wound, I didn't want Papa to be forced to admit that Juan was as guilty of abnormal sin as was my husband. Then I remembered that Sancia had heard me threaten Giovanni with his secret. Had she kept quiet or did Papa already know and was testing my willingness to tell him everything I knew?

"Well?" he said, with a hint of reproach. "Did he or did he not?"

I shook my head. "He never touched me."

He let out a sigh, but I could not tell if he felt relieved or more troubled. "And would you welcome the chance to end your marriage to him? Speak plainly. I'll not ask you again."

"Yes, I would. We . . . we are incompatible."

His chuckle was arid. "I understand it's more complicated than that. Cesare seems to think Giovanni does not love women." He went silent again, searching my face as if to uncover the very secret I stubbornly concealed. "Have you seen or heard anything of his unnatural desires?"

"He . . ." I swallowed. Again, I struggled against the admission seething inside me and had to clamp down on the urge to let it erupt. What good would it do to defame Giovanni now that our annulment was a given? He'd only throw back the accusation at Juan, who already was sunk in a mire of calumny, and the last thing Papa needed was another problem to resolve.

"I do not know, Papa. But he was never tender with me as a husband should be."

"Yes. That, too, I know. I forbade it, and I heard he made quite a scene in your rooms not long ago because of it. A Sforza to his core, with no better manners than a peasant. Shall we see him disposed of?"

His request was so unexpected, it took me a few seconds to grasp its meaning. When I did, a knot filled my throat. "It can be arranged," he added. "No one will ever know how it happened."

Giovanni's fate now rested in my hands, requiring only a word to see him pay for the humiliation he had inflicted. It unsettled me that, in some dark place inside me, I relished it. I relished knowing that I now had the power to bring about his demise.

"No." Fighting back my impulse to make Giovanni disappear forever, I took my father's hand again. "I could not live with such a deed on my conscience."

"It would not be on your conscience. I did not ask if you wished to dispose of him personally but rather if you want it done. It is not the same thing, as any villain in Rome can tell you."

"No, I do not want him . . ." I glanced over my shoulder to the far wall, where I had seen Perotto. The shadows had thickened there. I could barely see him, unmoving in the corner.

"He will not tell." Papa's voice brought my gaze back to him. "Servants never tell, if they value their lives." He lifted his chin. "Am I to understand you are firm in your decision?"

"Yes," I said quickly, before I had the chance to reconsider. "I want an end to our marriage but no harm brought upon him."

"I thought he had harmed you. He would only receive what he has given: *And thine eye shall not pity; but life shall go for life, eye for eye, tooth for tooth.* So ordains Deuteronomy." My father went quiet, as if he too relished the thought of Giovanni's death. Just as I thought I might have to plead for the very life of a man I detested, Papa pursed his lips.

"Very well. When I return from Ostia, I will petition the Curia for an annulment based on non-consummation. It won't be easy. He is stubborn; he'll fight to keep you *and* his honor. He will not explain himself but rather demand that I send you to him forthwith. Naturally, I shall refuse. If that Sforza wishes to make demands, he can come here to me and do so—on his knees."

"He won't," I said, and I knew then that I had truly seen the last of Giovanni. If nothing else, the shame of the secret I harbored would guarantee it. "Honor means more to him. If you grant him dignity and do not drag his name into spectacle, he'll do as you ask."

Papa snorted. "An annulment based on impotency is a spectacle. And I thought you said you were incompatible. How can you be so certain of what he'll do?"

"Because I know he has his pride. Proceed with discretion and he'll oblige."

To my relief, he grunted his agreement. My fears about Sancia were unfounded; she had kept my confidence. If my father had known everything, he would not have been so accommodating.

His expression turned distant, his mind already moving on to other matters. "I will see you upon my return," he said, as I leaned over to kiss his cheek. "I'll only be gone a week. Cesare has already gone to prepare my arrival; Juan insists on accompanying me, though he is not yet fully healed. Should you need anything, my staff can send a courier. Unless you'd care to join us, too?"

"No, Papa." I forced out a smile. "I have plenty to do, now that the rains are over. All that damp has ruined my garden, and there is a leak in the palazzo's east wing."

I left him in his chair, gazing into the fire. As I slipped out, Perotto eased from his post at the sideboard to prepare my father's nightly ablutions. He smiled at me again. I nodded in return. I had no sense of foreboding, no inclination of impending disaster.

There was no warning that everything I trusted was about to shatter.

. . .

THE CORRIDORS WERE empty save for the ubiquitous papal guard standing vigil at doors and stray menials fulfilling tasks for their masters. Leaving Papa's private quarters, I moved into the echoing Sala Reale, making my way to the Sistine, where the passageway to my palazzo was located. I had come alone to the Apostolic Palace, not knowing how long my father would wish to see me and not wishing to have Pantalisea or other women tarrying in the Vatican at night. Now I regretted it. My skirts swished over the cold marble floors, like disembodied whispers in this vast hall yawning before me, its vaulted ceiling and thick pillars submerged in darkness. The scent of old incense and mustiness tickled my nostrils; when I paused to sneeze, the sound ricocheted about the ancient hall like a fall of crumbling rock, startling me.

As the echoes subsided and I gathered my composure, I caught sight of movement by the archway leading into the Sistine. I paused. A large figure began to walk toward me, his cloak billowing. At first I felt no alarm, thinking him a guard or other servant, but as he neared, his bulk so imposing that he seemed to have dislodged from one of the columns, I started to back away. A cowl veiled his features; as a scream welled in my throat, he lifted a gloved hand to push back his cowl. I stared at the large reddish wound marring his right cheek, puckering the side of his mouth and distorting his once-handsome face. My brother had not only been injured; he was disfigured.

Trying to hide my shudder, I said, "Juan, what are you doing here?"

"I might ask the same of you." His sardonic smile became a grimace on his scarred face. "I see that I have scared you. You look pale."

"You caught me by surprise, is all. I was visiting with Papa. I thought you were . . ."

He tilted his head. "What? An assassin, come to kill you?"

"Don't be a fool," I retorted, and his smile vanished, his eyes taking on a harsh glitter. I realized that, after his recent fiasco, ridiculing him was the last thing I should do. "I only meant that I didn't know you were already up from your sickbed. Papa said you were not yet healed."

"I am not." He motioned to his face. "And you have kept so far from me, you haven't yet had the opportunity to behold my new visage."

"That is hardly fair—" I began to say, but he was right. Circum-

stances had been such that we'd had no opportunity for contact, and I
had done nothing to initiate it. Still, my own remorse that I'd not even
inquired after him made me say, "How can I be faulted when you came
back from Spain only to go to war shortly thereafter?"

"I suppose you can't."

As he spoke, a sudden shift in his expression, an unexpected vulnerability, made me ask, "Does it hurt?"

"It did. I thought I might go mad from the pain at first, but not as
much now. It will leave this scar, I'm told, though Torella insists that if
I apply his poultices every night as instructed, the mark may lessen in
time. Perhaps I should grow a beard, like an old Jew."

"Dr. Torella is skilled. You should heed his advice."

He laughed. "What difference can a poultice make? Look at me: I
am ruined."

I did not know what to say. I could not tell if he referred to his
physical appearance or his reputation; either way, he spoke the truth.
With an awkward nod, I said, "It is getting late. My women are waiting
for me. Perhaps we can visit when you return with Papa from Ostia?"

Juan nodded, stepping aside. As I began to move past him, I felt his
touch, a tentative pressure on my arm. "Lucrezia."

I glanced at him. Up close, I could see that his wound had been
deep; it was healing, yes, but he must have taken the brunt of the blade
and was correct in thinking no poultice would restore his beauty. Our
virile Juan, apple of our father's eye, would bear that visible mark of his
humiliation for the rest of his days. I could only think that Cesare
would find some justice in it.

"Those tiles and leather you requested," he said. "I brought samples
with me from Spain."

"Oh." I had completely forgotten. "I shall look at them when we
next visit."

He did not take his hand from my sleeve. "No."

"No?" I echoed.

"I mean, yes, you can." His smile was timid, almost nervous—
something I had never seen in him before. "But as I must send for some
belongings of mine from Castile this week—or rather my secretary will,
for I'll reside here longer than anticipated, because of this wound,
and . . . Perhaps you could look at what I've brought now? If you like

them, my secretary will place a full order for you. My wife will send whatever you need with my things."

I felt a ripple of concern. "Now?"

"Why not? We could sup together in my rooms." He removed his hand. "I'll have my servants bring us cheese, bread, and ham. And wine—I brought Papa the best vintage from Jerez."

Something made me hesitate. He no longer seemed like the brother I had known: the prodigal son protected by our father; the privileged youth who overshadowed Cesare; the arrogant man who swooped me out of the piazza on the day Papa won the papacy and hacked a hireling to pieces outside Adriana's palazzo. I had heard that war could change a man. Had it changed Juan? I thought it unlikely, yet all of a sudden I felt that refusing him would be cruel. Changed or not, he would never again be the man he had been. He could not erase his own blunders, and spending a few hours with him now was surely a small kindness I could afford to give him as his sister.

Still, I was uncomfortable and demurred. "As I said, it is late. My women will worry."

"Then no supper," he said. "Just come see the samples. It will only take a moment." The imploring note in his voice had to be unintentional, but as I took in that hideous scar that would forever remind him he was not infallible, not only on his skin but also in his soul, something I had never felt for him stirred in me.

Pity. I pitied him. Juan had not been allowed to fail or triumph on his own terms. Everything he suffered was because too much had been expected of him. Unlike Cesare, he hadn't been given a cross to bear, save for our father's unrealistic belief that he could do no wrong.

"Very well," I said, "but only to look at the samples. I cannot tarry any longer."

"I understand." He took me by the hand—like a brother should but he never had before—and brought me through the palace, up a back staircase into the levels above Papa's apartments, where Cesare also kept a suite. Lanterns hung from braces on the walls, the exposed beams of the ceiling blackened by their smoke, for the roof was lower here. Coming before a door, Juan fumbled in his doublet.

"You keep it locked?" I asked in surprise.

"I have the samples and other things from Castile in here, as well as my armor and weapons." He fitted the key in the lock. I was about to remark that surely he did not worry about thievery here, in our father's own palace, when the door swung open onto his large chamber.

The room smelled of sour linen and soiled chamber pots, of burnt wax and embers in the hearth. Discarded clothing was scattered about the floor; my gaze fell at random upon crumpled hose, mismatched muddied boots, various sleeves with their points tangled, and cloaks flung on chairs. I had to smile. Even as a child, Juan had acted as if his possessions would store themselves, never picking up a single thing that fell from his person. When our mother rebuked him for his sloth, he always replied, "Isn't that what servants are for?" Yet he evidently had not allowed a servant inside here in days. Was he so ashamed of his appearance, he didn't even want a groom or page to see him?

But the chamber itself was luxurious, with a four-poster bed adorned in rumpled carnelian brocade and a fresco covering an entire wall, depicting a fanciful landscape of swaying trees, saffron skies, and a shimmering city. As I picked my way to the mural to examine it, I heard Juan say, "The samples are in my antechamber," and I realized he must have brought me through a back door rather than the proper entrance, which would explain why I had not seen any guards. I had to smile again. Back staircases and back doors: Juan was indeed a changed man.

Then I froze, staring at the mural. It was a desert scene, with its whitewashed city like a mirage on the horizon, dominated by a high minaret and shaded by leaning palms. Turning around slowly, I espied a jumbled pile of belongings by the bed. I started to inch toward them, recognizing an odd-looking brazier with a peaked lid that was not of Roman design, as well as a quilted leather pillow embroidered with crescent moons. I had seen one just like it in my mother's house, when Pope Innocent's Turkish hostage first arrived after fleeing his brother the sultan, bearing a multitude of gifts that Papa purloined for Vannozza.

Djem. I was in the dead Turk's rooms.

As horrified understanding swept over me, the door opened behind me, and Giovanni said, "Did I not say you would have cause for regret?"

CHAPTER TWENTY-TWO

He shut the door, turning the key in the lock. As he stood there, a taut smile on his lips, I felt every nerve in my body start to clamor. I had to grasp the bedpost to stop my knees from giving out beneath me. I watched him enter, my mind unable to grasp that he was even here. He couldn't be. He had left Rome. I must be imagining this.

"What . . . why are you here?" Despite my struggle to remain composed, my voice betrayed my mounting fear. "I was told you had gone to Pesaro."

"I did." He took a step toward me, his hands reaching to the lacings of his codpiece. "You are still my wife. I told you in that note that when I summon, you will come—willingly or not."

I threw a desperate look over my shoulder, at the doorway through which Juan had disappeared. "Juan is here with me. He's in the next room. I will scream if you—"

"Do so." Giovanni pulled off his codpiece. I backed away as he approached, until I was fully against the bed. I could retreat no farther. He must have read my intent as I looked again to the other door, for he moved swiftly, lifting the dagger in his other hand.

"Resist me," he breathed, "do anything except what I tell you, and I'll make sure you bear the same scar as your brother—on your face and everywhere else I can put this blade."

His eyes were dull as pebbles—unvarnished, unblinking. Unfeeling. I had seen that look before, on the night he came to me in Pesaro. On that night, I had felt this same paralyzing fear and I had not fought back. I had not been prepared. But our circumstances had changed. He must have returned like a fugitive, skulking into the city and the Vatican without anyone knowing. Papa would have his head for it. If he dared lay a finger on me, he'd never leave Rome alive.

I swallowed the metallic tang of terror and said, "Sancia was right. You are a brute."

He lunged at me, clamping a hand over my mouth and smothering my shriek as his other hand came up. The chill of his blade was a sudden cold shock against my skin.

I bit down as hard as I could into his palm; I tasted his blood and felt the recoil in his body, pressed against mine. He did not let go. With a savage thrust, he rammed me against the bed, the hilt of his knife on my throat, cutting off my air. I thought he would kill me. He would slit me open and I would die here, in Djem's rooms. By the time Juan came back from wherever he had gone, he would find me lying in a pool of my own entrails.

Giovanni snarled, "Do not make me do it. Do not make me ruin that pretty, lying face. Because I will. I will carve you in pieces like a spring calf."

He pressed harder on the hilt. As blood pounded in my temples and my lungs shrieked for breath, as the room and everything else in my world darkened and faded into a terrifying eclipse where all I saw, all I heard or felt, was his contorted face, his other hand grappled and tore at me, rucking up my skirts.

"Spread your legs. Now. I know you can. I know you have done it before, for your brother Cesare and your father and God knows who else. *Do it!*"

I was gasping, drawing in desperate breaths through my nose, while his fingers poked at me, digging like splinters.

"Dry as sand," he grunted. Seizing hold of me by my bodice, he hauled me around and flung me onto the bed. It was all I could do to cling to consciousness. My throat felt crushed; I knew that if I screamed, I would barely make a whimper. But I was not about to succumb. I was not going to lie here and let him violate me. Kicking out my legs, I felt the impact and heard his sudden groan as my heels connected with his groin. I longed for anything sharp. I wanted to stab him with it again and again, until he lay bleeding at my feet.

"*Si cagna!*" He clouted me on my temple. My ears rang as if cymbals crashed inside. Pushing his hand firmly between my shoulders, he started hitting me, anywhere he could, and as he did I sensed his excitement, his pleasure in the pain he inflicted, and I struggled even more, knowing what was about to happen, what he was about to do—

"You idiot. What is this?"

Everything went quiet. I was suffocating, my face pressed into the bed; as I jerked my head to one side to gulp a draft of air, slow footsteps came toward us.

Juan. He had come back in time. He was here, and Giovanni was doomed.

I must have made a sound, a frantic plea, for Giovanni hit me again. As I fought to stay awake and not tumble into the churning darkness in my head, Juan drawled, "Is this how you intend to do it? Everyone will know she was unwilling. She'll be bruised as a Trastevere slut after a brawl."

"I cannot," panted Giovanni. "Look! I have no manhood. She—she does something to me. She is a *strega*. A witch. She has cursed me. She steals away my vigor."

Juan let loose a derisive guffaw. "No wonder she has cursed you. Is that all you have to show for yourself, that flaccid little worm? Why, you're barely at half-mast. I could get a rise out of you, though. I remember how you used to beg me for it."

Giovanni bleated; I heard him stumble back as Juan growled, "Let me show you how this is done. Hold her down."

Panic erupted in me, white-hot and searing. I had hoped Juan would save me, strike down Giovanni and drag him off to be arrested, imprisoned, garroted in the piazza like the common thug that he was. Yet even as I started to writhe, trying to turn myself over and use my teeth, my fingernails, anything I could to stop them, Giovanni's hands slammed down, immobilizing me.

"Let's turn her over," he said gleefully, and Juan replied in a cold, cruel voice that cut into me like fangs, "No. I don't want to see her face. I'll take her from behind."

When I felt my brother move behind me, kicking my legs apart, I let out an inchoate wail that I could not believe had issued from my lips, from those of any human being.

And as he leaned over me, Juan whispered, "This is for my Djem.

For what Cesare did to him," and a terrifying wave of understanding crashed over me. Somehow he had found out that Cesare had murdered his beloved companion. Djem had been more than an exotic pet he'd tethered with his leash—they must have been lovers, as he'd been with Giovanni and Giulia. Djem had not been waiting outside that door on the night I happened on them; the Turk was there because he was about to join them.

My very soul fled my body as Juan plunged into me. I felt nothing. I became a shell, a hollow piece of flesh as he bucked against me and Giovanni howled with delight.

After what seemed like a nightmarish eternity, I felt Juan shudder in release.

Blinding pain overcame me as I felt him yank his member out. I was back inside my ravaged body, cowering in a raw corner of my being and hearing myself whisper, "No. God, please . . ."

"Let me," Giovanni said. "I am hard now. See? Let me at her."

"No." Juan's hands were on my garments: arranging, smoothing, settling—gentle, as if I were a child who'd taken a tumble.

"But you said— What about me?" Giovanni cried. "I'll be made a fool, my name dishonored throughout Italy! As soon as they return from Ostia, your father and Cesare will petition the Curia for the annulment. *She* will accuse me of not consummating our union. She told me so herself!"

"It is the truth." Juan gathered me up in his arms as if I weighed nothing, setting me on my feet. As my gown fell about me in rumpled folds, I swayed, blinking rapidly as the room spun around me. He was holding me upright. I felt poised on the edge of a precipice.

"But you said you would help me! You said you—" Giovanni halted, seeing something in Juan's face that I did not, for my hair was a tangled curtain through which I could only discern fractured images: the guttering flame in the candlestick, the squashed shape of a heel-flattened tunic on the floor, the crescent moons on the pillow in the corner.

"Listen to me." Juan's inflectionless tone reminded me of my father. "You will leave tonight. You will return to Pesaro and hide in your stingy palazzo that reeks of fish and poverty. You will hide and you will pray, with all your might, that she does as I tell her and doesn't seek revenge through Cesare, my father, or any rogue she can hire. Pray she only accuses you of non-consummation and you survive with dishonor on your name instead of a Borgia blade in your gut. Now, get," Juan said. "Get from my sight before I kill you myself, you miserable Sforza."

With a sob, Giovanni turned, unlocked the door, and staggered out.

"Can you walk?" Juan asked me. When I did not answer, he added, "Here, let us try," and he let go of my arms and slid one hand about my waist. My knees buckled. Horror washed over me, a blackness so deep it was like a refuge. His grip on me tightened. Fighting to retain the last of my shattered strength, I made myself stay upright.

"Now stand still and let me see." Juan stepped in front of me, parting the scrim of my hair, tucking its disarray behind my ears so that my face was exposed. "Oh, no. That idiot broke your lip." His fingertip touched me. "Can you feel this?"

Every part of me, every sinew and nerve, recoiled. I wanted to whirl about and flee, shrieking, into the corridors, rousing everyone from their beds and gaming tables or seductions, so that the guards and courtiers, the cardinals and my father himself, came rushing from behind their doors to discover that Juan Borgia, Duke of Gandia and beloved of Pope Alexander VI, had violated his own sister.

Instead, primal instinct took hold, something more powerful than the mindless urge to escape, making me stand quiescent while he probed my lip.

"If you do not feel it," he said, "then it looks worse than it is. But we should still tend to it. Wait here." He started to step away. Then he paused, glancing over his shoulder. "Wait," he repeated, as he might instruct an impatient hound or one of his horses. When he saw that I did not move, he went into his antechamber.

My eyes lifted to where Giovanni had left the key in the other door. I saw myself running to it, throwing the door open. I could hear my cries for help already sundering the quiet of the Vatican. Papa was still here; he hadn't left for Ostia yet. I still had time to—

Juan returned with a basin and cloth. "Sit," he said, and I perched on the side of the bed, aware of a dull ache between my legs. Kneeling before me, he wet the cloth and cleaned my lip. As he dipped the cloth again to moisten it, blood swirled in the water, threading it with pink.

"Now you must do as I say," he said, dabbing the edges of my mouth. He glanced into my eyes, which I kept fixed on him. He smiled.

"Oh, I know you want nothing more than to go to Papa. I know you want Giovanni and me to pay for this with our lives. I understand. No one knows more than I how we crave revenge when that which we hold dear is taken from us." His hand wiping the cloth on my face trembled. "But you will not tell anyone until we know for certain. You will wait and abide, no matter what. Do you understand?"

The relentless intensity of his stare was making me sick. I swallowed again. When my voice finally crawled its way out my throat, it was a whisper: "Why?"

He cocked his head. The gesture gave me a jolt. It reminded me again of our father. It was uncanny, terrible, in truth, how much he had come to resemble Papa—and I despised him all the more for it. He had no right to look anything like the man who had given us life, who would see him torn him apart limb by limb for what he had done this night.

"Why?" His chuckle tugged at the wound on his face. "Because you may conceive." He did not look away from the sudden fear that must have flared in my eyes. "It can happen. It certainly did with my wife. My seed is potent: I gave her a son with one thrust. Should the same happen to you, you'll have to explain who the father is. You'll have to admit you bedded with me or that Giovanni Sforza actually did what Papa and Cesare are so eager to say he did not. It will change everything—for you. Should word get out that you're with child, it will wreck any plans they have for you."

"Plans?" I heard him through a dull roar in my head, as if he were a thousand miles away.

"Yes. Another marriage. Or did you think they'd free you of Giovanni and leave you alone? You are too valuable, their new alliance. But in order for them to use you, you must remain a virgin—*la immacolata* Lucrezia, on auction once more. Who shall bid the highest?" His acid mirth faded. "But if you fail to do as I say, if you cross me in any way, I will tell them myself. Only they will hear how you came upon me and asked to visit my rooms to see the samples. And how, without any provocation on my part, you put your hands on me. I am but a man, weak of flesh, confused by battle and my wound, so alone and far from my wife's comfort. You, so lovely, so sweet, offered me solace; you assured me it was not a sin, not between us. *Mea culpa.*"

His words dug like talons into me. "Who do you think they will believe?" he said. "His Grace the Duke of Gandia and Gonfalonier, appointed by His Holiness himself to lead his army? Or the wayward daughter whose own husband ran away from her, whom they must keep pure? Perhaps it doesn't matter who is to blame. It is still incest. They will lock you up in a convent until you die, and once the scandal fades and I do my obligatory repentance, I will still be Papa's son."

My mouth tasted of ash. Gathering whatever spittle I could, I spat in his face. It hit him on his wound, dribbling down the side of his damaged cheek.

"When Cesare finds out, he will kill you," I whispered.

"I suppose he will try, *if* he finds out." Juan sat back on his heels, dropping the cloth into the basin. His face hardened, so that any similarity he had to Papa vanished, revealing another face under that insouciant one he displayed to the world—the one I'd once seen dripping with gore outside Adriana's palazzo.

He gripped my wrists. "But let me warn you now, sister. If he finds out, you'll have only yourself to blame. I have no compunction about killing Cesare. I'll grant no quarter this time. None. Just as Cesare gave none to Djem, just as he never gave me any when we were growing up, always whispering behind my back and ridiculing me."

Although I knew it was dangerous, even lethal, although my entire body reeked of him and his seed was still wet inside me, I had to smile. "You did this to hurt Cesare?" And something cold and implacable forged inside me, like a new blade. "This is how you take revenge against him, by violating your own sister?"

"Fitting, isn't it? Cesare thinks he's so sly, advising Papa that I am a fool, a useless profligate who cannot even take a castle from that Orsini sow. He plots to see me stripped of my rank and my duchy, of everything he's always wanted and Papa gave to me. But now I have paid back every insult, every time he made me feel as if I were unfit to call myself a Borgia. Now I have taken the one thing he desires more than anything else but could never have: you."

I saw his true hatred then, the virulent lifelong rivalry he could never purge. It reminded me of an evening a lifetime ago, when Cesare slipped into Rome unannounced and Juan came upon us, determined to humiliate, demanding that I kiss him.

Juan pulled me to my feet, yanking my arms behind me and pushing me to the door. "But only you and I will ever know. We have our own little secret now, Lucrezia. Every day our brother looks at you, thinking you so innocent, cherished and protected, only you and I will know how soiled you truly are." He put his mouth to my ear. "And don't think of trying to rid yourself of it or confiding in your women. All those back-alley crones with their herbs and amulets—more often than not, they end up killing the mother *and* the child. A bad death, too, by all accounts; I've heard of whores puking poison or drowning in their own blood after the hook got stuck in their womb."

He released me. "Open the door." When I did, he gathered a cloak from the pile on a nearby chair and draped it over me. "Walk." He stayed behind me; I could feel the tip of his dagger through the cloak, poised at my back. As he took me down the stairs into the deserted halls, my footsteps echoed in bitter mockery of my own carelessness. I'd willingly gone with him. I had known who Juan was since our childhood, and still I had let sympathy overrule caution. I had stepped into the very snare he baited. Now I had to live with the consequences.

For he was right, I thought, as he led me in a stunned haze to the Sistine and the door that led to the hidden passage to my palazzo. In the end, it did not matter whom they believed.

When it came to our family, the truth meant nothing.

CHAPTER TWENTY-THREE

I remained in my bedchamber, tended only by Pantalisea. I would not allow my other women near me, not even Murilla, who tapped plaintively at the door and refused to believe Pantalisea's explanation that I had contracted a fever and did not wish to expose others to it.

"But you are in there with her." Murilla's protest reached me all the way in the refuge of my bed, where I'd huddled under furs despite the warmth of spring in the air. I felt as though I would never be warm again. "Why is my lady not worried for you, if her fever is so catching?"

"Because I've already had it," retorted Pantalisea. "Besides, what matter is it of yours? Step aside. This tray is heavy."

"Why do we not call for a physician? If she is so ill, we must summon Torella." My dwarf was persistent; she knew there was more here than anyone would admit, and she was not about to make it easy on us.

"*Madre di Dio!*" Pantalisea stomped her foot. "Am I to stand here all day with a tray full of dirty dishes? Move from the door this instant and let me pass."

Rousing myself, I drew back the sheets, which felt heavy as wool, and slid from bed. The air clung to my ankles like icy fingers. I heard Murilla's gasp from where she peered past Pantalisea: "Madonna is up!" The dishes on the tray clattered as Pantalisea swerved around, her own gasp escaping her as she caught sight of me, one hand clutched about the post of the bed, the other cradling my midriff as I swayed, trying to get my bearings.

I knew I looked terrible, though I had not dared glimpse myself in a mirror since the night I staggered into the palazzo, battered and bruised, with blood drying on my thighs. Pantalisea had not said anything as she undressed me, bathed me, and enveloped me in my robe and put me to bed, as if she knew her questions were futile. Perhaps she had guessed what had befallen me. She couldn't help but see the bruises; she had wiped away the blood and applied salves to my lip, which grew so swollen I could barely sip gruel. Now the bruises had started to fade, from virulent purple to sickly yellow; my lip had almost healed, too. My private parts no longer throbbed, and the rest of my young body, while still weak, was beginning to resent this enforced hibernation.

Still, I imagined the savagery of the deed must be seared onto my face as surely as it was in my body, and the way Pantalisea now exclaimed, dumping the tray onto the nearest table, "Oh, my lady, it is too soon for you to rise. You must not force yourself!" told me everything she would not say. As she started to steer me back to bed and Murilla slammed the door shut on my gawking women in the antechamber, planting herself in front of it, I made a token gesture of resistance. It was nothing Pantalisea could not overcome, if she had a mind. She did not try, however, pausing to look at me with such fierce concern that I almost started to weep.

"How long . . . ?" I whispered.

"Nearly three weeks." She lowered her voice. "You needn't worry. His Holiness and your brothers have not returned from Ostia. There was some delay; I have no idea why, but they sent word through Princess Sancia." Irritation notched her tone. "She's been my bane, sending messages here every afternoon, demanding an audience with you. I've kept her away thus far, relaying that you are ill with fever and cannot be disturbed. But I do not know how much more I can—"

I held up a hand. "There is no need. I want you to do one more thing for me."

"Anything," she said at once, and I had a sudden recollection of a day that now seemed a lifetime ago, when we traveled together by litter to Cesare's palazzo and I teased her about Perotto. That same day from an upstairs window, with Cesare at my side, I had first seen Giovanni, in his stiff new clothes, pacing the garden.

He's to be my husband. I hardly think feelings matter.

The memory clutched me. I bit back my anguish, thinking that if I had known then what I did now, my answer would have been so different; the trajectory of my life to this moment would have been diverted to an unknown but surely less arduous path than the one I now must tread.

"My lady?" said Pantalisea. "What is it? Tell me what I can do for you, please."

"I must be gone from here before my father and brother return," I said. "Send urgent word to the prioress of San Sisto. Tell her I wish to seek sanctuary behind her walls. As soon as possible."

❧

I HAD FORGOTTEN how quiet it was.

As a child, I had spent so much time here, my days punctuated by the tolling bells of the Romanesque tower calling the nuns to prayer, my ink-stained hours divided by lessons, and my nose forever in a book, drowning me in words, so many words that it seemed the entire world was but an unexplored story, waiting for me to turn its pages.

San Sisto was a wealthy convent. In the centuries since its founding, the Dominican house had benefited from papal generosity. Innocent III paid for its restoration and a series of frescoes in the chapel, celebrating the New Testament. The relics of Sixtus II had been transferred from the old catacombs for display here, to attract pilgrims and their offerings. Noble widows seeking placid finales, surfeit daughters whose families could not afford a dowry, unfortunates who'd sowed insurmountable scandal in their wake—all paid for peace within these cream-brick walls, where vanity was eschewed and former names renounced in favor of appellations like Annuziata and Magdalena. Here, the inviolate rule of St. Dominic brought order to the unpredictable chaos of life.

Nevertheless, I was certain San Sisto had never seen anyone arrive as I did. I scarcely allowed the prioress advance warning before I was at the gates facing the Via Appia, shrouded in my cloak, valise in hand, and my maidservant at my side. The prioress knew me; my education here had been overseen by her. She was too self-contained to show any consternation that I had returned after years of absence, but I gleaned in her stance that unexpected guests were rare. Other convents might be open to visitors, their barricaded façades and grilled windows mere foils to disguise illicit brothels that peddled novices like bottles of olive oil;

but not San Sisto. Here, no impropriety must soil the house's holy repute.

I knew this. I depended on it. No man, not even my father, would reach me here.

"I trust these rooms will suffice," said the prioress. She led us into a small apartment composed of a sparsely furnished chamber with a small sleeping area separated by an archway without a door, hung with a gauze curtain that would discourage any unauthorized entertainments.

"Perfect," I murmured, even as Pantalisea stiffened. "Please," I told her, "give Mother Superior the gifts we brought."

"Oh, you should not have, my child," protested the Prioress, her seamed face creasing as Pantalisea set the valise on the table to remove a bundle of scented beeswax tapers. I had remembered at the penultimate hour, as we were about to abandon my palazzo, recalling Adriana's adage that I must never visit a sacred place empty-handed. "And the cloth," I said, ignoring Pantalisea's scowl. I did not care if our surroundings were stark to the point of austerity, if I slept on a pallet with nothing but moldering linen to cover me. To obtain the safety I needed to determine my fate, luxury must be sacrificed.

Pantalisea reluctantly extended the folded blue Venetian velvet with its golden pomegranate motifs, which my father had given to me.

"For your Virgin's mantle," I said.

The prioress sighed. "Thank you, my child." She made a slight motion; from the passageway outside, a nun slipped in to retrieve the gifts, leaving as silently as she had appeared. "You must be weary," said the prioress. "I will leave you to rest. But"—she lifted her gaze before Pantalisea could usher her out—"first I think we should speak alone."

I nodded. After Pantalisea had trudged out, closing the door behind her, I faced the prioress. "I have not come here to make your life difficult," I began, "nor do I wish to be an imposition."

"And yet you will do both."

My throat knotted. "Yes. I am afraid I will." I stood quiet, hands folded at my stomacher, my cloak falling about me. My stance conveyed what I could not bring myself to admit; I saw it in her gaze as it rested on my midriff and then lifted again to my face.

"When are you due?" she asked. There was no judgment in her

voice. Had I not known better, I would have thought she had asked the same question innumerable times before.

"I may not . . ." I faltered. "It might not be what I fear."

"But you are here nevertheless." While she did not smile, her expression softened, in the manner of a woman who might dwell apart from the world yet was not ignorant of its vicissitudes. "To seek refuge within these hallowed walls."

"Yes." I struggled against the sudden urge to confide everything. "I need time, a place to rest. Until I know for certain." Even as I spoke, I wondered at my own deceit. Though nothing had happened in my body to confirm my supposition, though I had no sense of what a woman in my assumed state should feel, I knew it already, as I had known nothing else.

Already, my brother's seed grew inside me.

The prioress remained quiet for a moment. Then she assented, turning to the door. As she reached for the latch, she said, "You have requested sanctuary, and we must do everything in our power to uphold it. Should what brought you here turn with time into a desire to renounce the world and take the veil, we will uphold that, too, as we must for any sinner who seeks redemption. But we cannot endanger ourselves. We cannot put this house and our fellow sisters of Christ in harm's way, not for you or any other. Above all else, we must protect our sanctity."

"I understand," I said.

"I hope that you do. For should this fear that brought you to us come to pass, you must stay in this room and a designated section of the cloister. It will not do for the others to see you in such a state. Once the child is born, if you choose to remain, you must surrender it. It cannot stay with you under any circumstance. Should you decide to leave, then you must go with the child as soon as possible. We cannot have our order disrupted for too long. There are those among us who would find the sight and sound of a babe too harsh a reminder of what we have renounced. Temptation must be removed for the safety of all."

She did not wait for my reply. Opening the door, she left me to contemplate the choices she had given me, neither of which I could even start to consider.

Pantalisea returned. "Are we staying?" Her undertone of anxiety betrayed that she still was not sure I was making the right decision. She had not yet realized the precise reason for my exodus from my palazzo and my family, though she knew Giovanni had left for Pesaro and something terrible, unspeakable, had befallen me in the wake of his absence.

"Yes," I said. "We are staying. Or I am. You are free to leave."

"Leave? Why would I leave? Are servants not allowed to serve their ladies here?"

"No, it's allowed, if you abide by their rules. We both must abide by the rules." I sighed, unclasping my cloak and dragging it from my shoulders to drape it across one of two hard-backed chairs in the room. I glanced at the uninviting woven seat; in a few months, I would need an upholstered cushion if they expected me to spend my days here, sewing and waiting—

I shook my head, forcing these thoughts aside. There would be time enough to reflect. Instead, I said, "If you stay, however, you must know the reason. It would not be fair, or safe, otherwise. When Cesare and my father find out where I am, they will not be pleased. There will be questions—difficult questions. If they cannot ask me, they may try to ask you."

She frowned. "But I thought my lady came here because . . ." Her voice drifted into abrupt awareness. "It is not because you seek to flee the signore?"

"No." I beckoned her close, clasping her hands in mine. I'd never had a sister. I had never known another woman in whom I trusted enough to confide, not with the truths I kept deep within my heart. Giulia had been an idol turned rival, and Sancia, while delightful, was too recent a companion. Perhaps if we'd had more time together, Sancia could have helped see me through this trial; I had no doubt she had the courage and strength. But it would put her at odds with my family, and I did not want that for her, for anyone. Pantalisea, on the other hand, had been at my side since I was eleven. She had been my most loyal servant, upon whom I had come to rely, always knowing that if ever I had a secret to entrust, she would keep it for me, regardless of the cost. Or so I now desperately needed to believe. For this secret could get us both killed. I did not doubt Juan's threats. After what he had done, I must never doubt the extent of his malice again.

I drew her to the other chair and quietly, without any tears, I told her everything. By the time I finished, her face had turned white. I added, "As I told you, you need not stay. I know how much I ask of you, how dangerous this could be." I heard myself trying to soften once more my harsh reality, though this time it was for her sake, not mine. "I may not be with child. If I am, however, nothing will be the same. You must choose now. If you stay, if you share this with me, then you put yourself at risk, from Juan, certainly, and perhaps from others, as well."

"Others?" she echoed.

"Giovanni," I said. "He left by Juan's order, but our marriage is not yet annulled. He may try to stop Papa from petitioning the Curia, claim we indeed consummated our union. He's a coward and a villain, and if he suspects I am with child, he will try to claim it. I must do whatever is necessary to protect the babe. Giovanni can never have the opportunity to call it his."

"But you speak as if you *want* it. There must be another way. Surely here in Rome, we can find someone we can pay, a midwife who knows how to rid you of it."

"And how do you suggest we find this midwife without alerting Juan or having rumor make its way through the city? I am His Holiness's daughter; I have no coin to purchase such enormous silence. No," I said, making my decision in that moment. "I will not destroy it to save myself, nor will I remain shackled to Giovanni."

It was the first stance I'd ever made for myself, the first time I stood on my own, without anyone to cajole or persuade me. After everything I had endured, I felt as if I were sloughing off the skin of one existence to become someone new.

"I too am a Borgia," I said. "The time has come for me to show it."

Pantalisea whispered, "What shall we do?"

The smile on my lips felt as cold as the price that I knew I must exact. "What would any girl do in such circumstances? When the time comes, I must send for my mother."

⤜❦⤛

A FEW WEEKS later, Vannozza arrived swathed in her antiquated black, although in the convent garden where we met, seated before a table with sugared fruits and a decanter of light wine, she seemed appropriately dressed, if overlarge, in the delicate symmetry of our surroundings, the spidery arches of the cloister enclosing us as starlings darted in the sky above.

I did not have to say anything at first. "I thought you never wanted to see me—" she started to declare, and then she paused, scouring me with her gaze. "*Dio mio.* You are with child." How she knew so easily was unimportant; she'd always cultivated a keen eye. Or perhaps her painted cards had given her a sign. That, too, I no longer doubted. She had known things about me that she never should have. When it came to her children, she indeed had the sense of a witch.

I reached for the decanter. "Perhaps."

"There is no 'perhaps' about it," she barked. "You are. I see it on you. Have you been sick?"

"Sick?" I poured wine, began ladling refreshments onto the plates, keeping my voice and expression calm. "How so?"

"Do not play the fool with me." She thrust out her hand, detaining me. I sat still, the plate I held extended between us. "I mean sick, as in nausea and vomiting; as in malaise. Women often feel ill when they first breed. I never did, but it happens. The bleeding stops and they feel sick. Even the smell or taste of certain foods can send them rushing to the privy. Has any of this happened to you?"

"No." I pushed the plate past her on the table. "But, as you say, *you* never felt ill. I am your daughter." I met her stare. "Do you want to know how it happened?"

I knew it was dangerous, summoning her like this. I'd spent the days before her arrival planning our meeting to the last detail: how I would act, what I would say and, more important, what I would not. I must be clever this time, more so than she. It would not be simple, I realized, now that she sat before me, with her preternatural capacity to see past my every ploy.

With a chuckle, she popped a candied apricot into her mouth. "I assume it happened in the usual manner. What I want to know is, why come here instead of staying in your palazzo until Rodrigo returned? He's very unhappy. He says you have engaged in such a public act of renunciation by entering a convent, you set every tongue in Rome to wagging. By now there isn't a vagrant on the street who hasn't heard of how your husband left you, forcing you to seek refuge to ease your anguish." She went quiet for a moment. "Or is this your plan? To leave your father with no choice but to proceed with the annulment, regardless of how much those Sforza threaten?"

She went on before I could answer. "Not that I fault you. A wife so neglected: Where else can she turn but to her faith?" She retrieved the goblet of wine I'd poured for her. "When Rodrigo petitions for the annulment, your retirement here, however temporary, can only support his claim that your husband was unable to perform as he should."

I remained silent, watching her empty the goblet.

"But as you're surely aware," she chided, "there can be no such claim. A pregnant wife cannot accuse her husband of neglect, at least not in the bedchamber. As soon as he hears, Rodrigo must cancel the proceedings and dispatch you forthwith to Pesaro. Hiding will only spare you so much. Slim as you are, you'll start showing within a few months, and then the blessed sisters themselves will send you packing."

"I think not." When I finally spoke, I kept my voice as smooth as the goblet stem I caressed. "I've confided in the prioress, and she has agreed to let me stay until after the birth. And," I added, "this child, if indeed I am to bear one, is not my husband's."

My revelation thickened the air. Then she breathed, "*Puttana.* Whose is it? Which lowly stable groom or page did you lure into your bed?"

I detected anxiety in her insult, an unvoiced trepidation. Much as I welcomed it—for it betrayed that she was fully cognizant of how complicated the situation was, which only suited my designs—I said, "It is not Cesare's, if that's what you fear."

She swept her goblet aside. Half-rising from her chair—"Whosever it is, I will feed the *bastardo* to my dogs!"—she flung up her hand.

Before she could strike me, I said, "Juan," and she staggered back, her hand flying instead to her chest, as if I had dealt her a mortal blow.

"He brought me to his rooms," I told her, surprised by how emotionless I sounded, as though I recounted an event that had happened to someone else. "He took me there so Giovanni could violate me. But when my husband failed to manage it, Juan did it for him." I watched the color seep from her face. "He did it to avenge himself on Cesare, to make sure that we all bear the shame of it. Will you still feed the child to the dogs now—your own grandchild, twice over?"

Vannozza collapsed back onto her chair. For a fleeting moment, I almost pitied her. I had never seen her look so devastated, so wretched or old. Every line in her face came to the surface, like cracks in brittle parchment.

"No," she whispered. "It cannot be."

"If you do not believe me, ask Juan yourself, though you should consider that he threatened to see both Cesare and me dead if I dared reveal it. He also said Papa would keep me in a convent until the day I die, which I presume would not suit whatever plans he's made for me once this annulment is granted?"

She regarded me as if she couldn't decide whether to scream or kill me herself. "Why should I believe any of this? I know well that Cesare concocted that plot to rid us of Giulia; he told me himself how he enlisted you to do his deed. Why shouldn't I believe that now you and he seek to cast aside a husband you detest? This child you carry: It might not be Juan's at all but rather some other by-blow you got yourself with to ruin Juan and see Cesare reap glory in his place."

I smiled, reclining in my chair even as I resisted a rise of fear. This was the gambit I must win. I had only my word. There was no proof that I'd been taken by force, other than testimony from Pantalisea, who'd seen my bruises—and she could be silenced. Vannozza could make it seem I was deluded, mad even. God knew, she would do anything to safeguard Juan over me.

"Juan has done nothing glorious. He cast asunder Papa's favor and has proved his unworthiness," I told her. "Cesare doesn't need to seek revenge. All he needs to do is give Juan enough time to hang himself."

Vannozza went quiet, glowering like a basilisk.

"And even if this were a plot, as you say," I continued, "are you willing to risk it? Are you willing to risk having Papa's wrath fall upon us? For that is what will happen if I tell him the truth." My hands went to my belly, where I did not feel the slightest swell. Doubt made me hesitate. I shoved it aside. "But I could be mistaken. My monthly course may be late. Or, if I am not mistaken, perhaps I'll lose it. Many women miscarry, yes? But until then, I am in Rome and so is Juan. And wherever he dwells, it is too near for me."

"What do you want of me?" she growled. "He is my son. I'll not see him defamed because of you." Her voice turned vicious. "You forget that I know how you and Cesare circle each other like curs in heat. You forget I know of the poison you both carry; if you couldn't have Cesare, for whatever reason, why not Juan? Perhaps you enticed him. Perhaps you did this to yourself."

"If I did," I replied coldly, "surely you are the last person I would trust. No," I said, as her shoulders crept about her neck, as if she were fighting the urge to lunge at me again. "What I want of you is simple: You shall see to it that Juan leaves Italy. Tell Papa he must return to Spain and his wife and son, where he belongs."

An incredulous burst of laughter escaped her. "You think I have the power to persuade the pope to send his cherished son away?"

"No. But Juan made a disaster of the Orsini campaign. He now has mortal enemies in the Romagna barons, who will not take lightly his incursion into their domains, no matter what truce Papa proposes. Juan's life could be in danger; the barons have killed men for less. And while you might not have power to see him gone, you are still his mother. Papa must heed your concerns if you present them as such. The alternative, of course, is the truth. But no matter which punishment I reap, it's still a grave dishonor on our name. The pope's own daughter, violated by his cherished son . . ." My threat hung between us. "I will not lie. I will tell Papa everything. I have nothing to lose. I have already lost everything."

The bones of her jaw protruded as she clenched her teeth. "I see," she said at length. "You think you can blackmail me. You are mistaken, however, if you believe Rodrigo will capitulate so easily. He adores Juan. He plans to send for Doña Maria and their son so they can live here together. He told me so himself."

"Plans change," I said.

"Indeed. But not because of you. You overestimate your father's affection for you. This is not the first time a daughter has strayed. There are other ways to see dishonor averted."

I pretended to consider this. "Then it seems I must appeal to someone else," I said, and I did not flinch as she bolted to her feet in a fury of black skirts, rounding the table to seize my wrist, nearly yanking me from my chair. I heard as if from a distance the clang of the decanter tipping over as my knee hit the table, then she was snarling: "You dare threaten me? *You dare?* Because if you do, let me warn you that I will win. I *always* win. I will cut that bastard out of your insides, grandchild or not, if you dare breathe a word of this shame to Cesare."

I wanted to laugh aloud, bellow my own rage back in her face. She had taken my bait. She did not think for a moment that my rape by Juan was something I'd devised or that Cesare had any knowledge of it. Her threats could no longer hide her terror; she exuded it like a stench. I had gambled to perfection. Cesare was the key. He had always been the key. She knew as well as I did that if Cesare discovered the truth, Juan's safety, indeed his very life, would be forfeit. Cesare would never forgive him. He would avenge me. He would disembowel Juan with his bare hands.

I pulled my wrist from her. "Do as I say and Cesare will never know. I swear it."

"And if I do not?" Her breath came in shallow bursts. "What if I refuse?"

"Then let it be on your conscience. All I want is to never set eyes on Juan again. I leave it to you as to how you go about ensuring that. Because if you do not, I will."

She took a step back, her hands bunched at her sides. "Even if I agree to persuade your father and he complies, I promise you, when the time comes, there will be a reckoning. Juan is the future of his dynasty, the glory of his family. Rodrigo will not forsake him for a mistake."

Her callous declaration twisted my gut. "Be that as it may, I cannot imagine any glory will be found in an accusation of incest. And my mistake could be a son. If so, I will give him over to be reared as Papa sees fit, a new Borgia prince to exalt our name—providing he never knows who his father is."

She snorted. "You think to hang this sword over our heads? A game like this—it has no end. You will never know a moment's peace. You can still escape it. There is still a chance, if you will only do what is required."

"Are you suggesting I dispose of the child and pretend it never happened? Is that my escape?" I shook my head. "Never. I will not bear the sin of having killed my own flesh."

"Then *you* are forever cursed! I warned you. I told you you would be each other's—"

"Enough." The anger in my voice was like a whip cracked between us, silencing her. "Do not say another word. I want Juan and Giovanni gone from my life. If I'm never happy again, if I never know a moment's peace, at least I'll not have to endure their presence. As for my child, should it survive, it must never carry the taint of my sin." I lifted a hand, cutting her off. "We have nothing more to say. I am prepared to send word to Cesare, so I suggest you do what I ask."

Whirling about, Vannozza seized her shawl. She marched off, her heavy footsteps fading away into the tense silence.

I looked down at my hands, saw I was trembling. Leaving the table in disarray, I returned to my rooms, where Pantalisea sat by the narrow window, her dark head bent over her sewing. She looked so serene, engrossed in her task, as if we still dwelled in Santa Maria in Portico and she repaired a rip in one of my sleeves. I wanted to embrace her, reassured by her presence as I'd never been before. She'd already breached the rules, going out to my palazzo to fetch luxuries—quilted pillows for the chairs and narrow bed; extra counterpanes, blankets, and cotton sheets; carpets for the table and floor; a candelabrum and braziers. When the prioress lifted protest, she snapped, "She is to bear His Holiness's grandchild. Unlike our Blessed Virgin, she need not give birth in a manger."

The prioress had pursed her lips.

Now Pantalisea stitched a new velvet hanging for the archway to my bedchamber, having torn down the old one, remarking it harbored lice; the smell of the lye used to wash down the cloisters had become a permanent stink in our nostrils.

"Well?" she asked as I entered. "Did that harridan agree?"

"She hates me more than ever, but she'll tell Papa whatever she must to see Juan sent back to Spain. She has no choice; she'd prefer that Juan left, rather than expose us all to infamy."

Pantalisea looked doubtful. "And if she succeeds? What about the infamy to follow? Your marriage still must be annulled, while you are here, most likely with child. How are you going to explain it when they summon you before the Curia to testify to your virginity?"

"I do not know. I cannot foresee the future. I did not ask for any of this!" My voice ruptured. Without warning, my pain burst forth in a deluge that startled me almost as much as it did Pantalisea. Until this moment I had not cried, not a tear, not even when I was alone. It was as if the savagery of Juan's assault had calcified inside me, a fetid pearl, but as I heard my own anguish, all I could do was crumple into Pantalisea's arms and weep like a disconsolate soul.

I had lied to my mother. I *did* want to pretend this had never happened. I wanted to believe that if I refused to accept it, I could leave this self-imposed exile and begin my life anew.

Instead, I kept hearing her voice in my head: *You will be each other's doom.*

I had thought she meant Cesare and me.

Now I feared that her malediction would engulf our entire family.

CHAPTER TWENTY-FOUR

"Madonna, wake up. My lady, you must wake up!"

I groaned, shoving my head farther under my pillow. Only weeks after my mother's departure, I began to suffer nausea that sent me hurtling to the porcelain pail in my room, until my stomach heaved and my head pounded; all I could manage was to stagger back to bed as Pantalisea set compresses on my brow and forced chamomile infusions past my lips.

"There can be no doubt now," she declared drily. "You are most certainly with child."

The confirmation turned me into a cowering thing. Once I knew I indeed nurtured Juan's seed, dark lassitude overcame me. I huddled under my covers, barely stirring even when the prioress summoned Suora Paulina, the herbalist, who prescribed various remedies along with moderate exercise—though I could barely keep her drafts down, much less make the circumscribed circle around the cloisters in my exhausted state.

"Nine months," I moaned. "How will I endure it?"

"You will endure it because you must," said Pantalisea. "Because for you, the alternative is unthinkable. Besides, we dare not risk ridding you of it now, not when you are showing signs. The cure for what ails you could also kill you."

I cursed her then, because she spoke the bitter truth. I cursed her, my mother, and Giovanni—but, most of all, I cursed Juan. I wished for death to befall him; I cursed him to hell, before I doubled over and retched again.

Now, only hours after Vespers, just as slumber finally claimed me, here was Pantalisea, shaking my shoulder and uttering inconceivable demands.

"I tell you, you must rise." Her urgency pierced my misery. "Someone is here. You must see him."

I opened my eyes. Cesare. He had defied the rules of my exile and come to me. I did not care that his arrival and discovery of why I was immured would be catastrophic, did not think of anything except that he was here at last and I could seek comfort in him, as I had so many times.

Cesare would know what to do. He always knew what to do.

Yet as I righted myself, blinking away the grit of sleep, Pantalisea said, "It is Perotto. He came knocking at the gates. The prioress refused him admittance at first, but he insists he has news you must hear. She gave him entry into the courtyard. He will speak to only you."

Perotto was Papa's favorite servant; I threw off the sheets, wincing as my feet hit the cold floor. "Quickly," I told Pantalisea. "Fetch my slippers and cloak."

THE CONVENT WAS dark, quiet. Torches in brackets crackled on the walls; our shadows leapt before us as we hurried to the courtyard— a small flagstone space right inside the gates, with a fountain and trough for horses, where merchants could deliver supplies. It was a sliver of the outside world that never penetrated the heart of San Sisto.

The prioress was waiting, along with Suora Leocadia, the convent's gatekeeper. Suora Leocadia's beefy arms crossed at her chest as the prioress said, "I fear this is most irregular. Indeed, were you any other guest, it would be out of the question for you to receive a visitor at such an hour, and a male one, at that."

I should have murmured something appropriately repentant, but my gaze was already straining past her to the cloaked figure. He stopped his pacing near the mossy trough and swerved at the sound of my approach. My heart quickened. What news did he bring?

"Yes," I said, wanting to push the prioress aside. "I understand. I will hear what he has to say and send him out at once."

"See that you do," said Suora Leocadia. "Because ever since my lady came to this house, we've been in a state of unrest, and now, with these ungodly rumors of—"

"Hush, Sister." The prioress kept her eyes on me. "He cannot stay," she said. "No matter what the situation is, we have our reputation to consider."

I nodded, shivering as she motioned to Suora Leocadia; they moved into the cloisters, leaving me in the courtyard with Pantalisea and Perotto.

He did not move; consternation froze me likewise where I stood. Then he suddenly came before me, bending as if to fall to one knee. "My lady Lucrezia, you must forgive me, but I had to come."

I set my hand on his shoulder, though I knew that if Suora Leocadia saw me make physical contact with a man within the sacred precinct, she would campaign mercilessly for my eviction. "Just tell me." My voice sounded so thin, as though it were about to fail me.

Perotto lifted his gentle brown eyes, which glistened with tears. My throat constricted. "*Dio mio,* what is the matter? Is it my father? Has something happened to him?"

"It is his lordship the duke of Gandia. He . . . he is dead, my lady."

I blinked, confused. "Gandia?" Then, with the force of a hammer blow to my chest, I understood. Behind me, Pantalisea let out a stifled cry. I glanced over my shoulder to where she stood under the cloister archway, a hand pressed to her mouth. She did not need to say what was writ plain on her face. I had cursed Juan only days ago.

I returned to Perotto. Tears slid down his cheeks. I should have felt the same grief. I should have felt the loss crack open inside me. Juan was still my brother; we were flesh and blood, no matter what brutalities he had inflicted. Yet I felt nothing. Until I thought of my father.

"Where is Papa?" I said anxiously, knowing his grief for Juan would be terrible.

"In his apartments in the Vatican: That is why I'm here." Perotto's voice quavered. "After the duke's death was confirmed, His Holiness shut himself up in his rooms. He will not let any of us attend him, and his cries, my lady—he was heard all over the palace."

"And now?" I dreaded his response.

"He has not made a sound in hours. We bang on the door, but he refuses to open it. My lord of Gandia now lies in state in the *castel;* he's to be interred tomorrow in the chapel of Santa Maria del Popolo, if His

Holiness allows it. They pulled your brother's body from the Tiber, after an entire night of searching. It is feared that after being in the waters he cannot be kept above ground much longer and—"

"Please, no more." I pulled up the hood of my cloak. "I must go to Papa at once."

THEY PULLED YOUR brother's body from the Tiber. . . .

Perotto's grim words tumbled in my head as we rode through sulfurous mist, a sickly scrim camouflaging the streets, muting the snarls of skulking dogs, the shouting of drunkards and laments of beggars, the scampering of emaciated children and rodents in the middens. Arid thunder rumbled overhead; when I heard the muted hiss of Perotto taking his dagger from its leather sheath, I began to think I should have waited in the convent. Pantalisea had stayed behind at my insistence; I needed her to keep to my rooms, in case it was necessary to defend my absence, though the prioress had lifted no protest when I informed her why I must go.

As we neared the Apostolic Palace, which loomed out of the fog like the skeletal remains of a long-slain dragon, a flurry of unanswered questions overcame me. My brother Juan, esteemed child of privilege, favored son, and experienced man about Rome, found dead in the Tiber. Only those who perished of plague or violence were consigned to the river; only beasts, the poor, the criminal, the unwanted, or the unlucky ended up in those murky depths.

What had happened to him?

I almost detained Perotto as we entered by a servant gate, to ask how Juan had died, but my voice lodged in my throat. I could not bear to know, lest I begin to falter, the ice encasing me thawing until the sheer horror of it, the pain, overwhelmed me and I confessed to this loyal youth what Juan had done and why I fled and how I now feared I was somehow to blame for his death.

Inside the Vatican, the clergy amassed to whisper. The unexpected demise of a papal son was an event; even the most indolent among them felt called upon to tend His Holiness. Perotto managed to guide me with expertise through the frescoed maze, employing secret passages and hidden doors to avoid the maelstrom of speculation that my arrival would cause.

Guards stood outside the papal apartments. At my father's private door, we found cardinals gathered, including Cardinal Sforza.

I had not seen him since Giovanni and I separated, though I suspected he continued to advise Giovanni even from afar. As he turned to me, I hid my trepidation.

"Maestro Perotto," he said, "it's in rather poor taste to bring a courtesan at such a time."

Behind him, portly Cardinal Costa grunted. "Poor taste or not, it may be just what the physician ordered. After all, if the scent of a woman cannot rouse His Holiness, we might have to consider calling for a new vote of the conclave, eh?"

The others guffawed. Seeing a smile slither across Cardinal Sforza's mouth, I lifted a hand to cast back my hood. Astonished silence fell. But I focused only on Cardinal Sforza's expression, thinking I must imagine how his gaze lingered for a moment on my belly, though I did not yet show; my gown was concealing, fitted at the waist and flowing loose to my ankles, according to the current fashion. Still, he must have heard by now of my abrupt retreat into a convent and, of course, he knew Giovanni had left me. Perhaps my husband had even shared some of those foul accusations of his that Papa mentioned, for the cardinal seemed to sense what I had gone to lengths to hide as he murmured, "This is indeed a surprise, Donna Lucrezia. We thought you indisposed."

"My indisposition is nothing before this tragedy, Your Eminence. My brother the duke of Gandia has been found dead; my family and I are bereft."

"Indeed." He dipped his head. "All Rome, I assure you, is bereft."

His proper tone carried an unmistakable hint of mockery. It was apparent to me that he and these others had gathered outside Papa's door in the hope that the loss of his beloved son would signal the end of my father's ambitions, if not his own life.

I gestured to Perotto. "Tell His Holiness I am here."

Cardinal Sforza said, "I fear you have come in vain, my lady. We have been here for over five hours and His Holiness shows no inclination to reveal himself, though he has important business to attend to, not the least of which is the burial of his son."

"He will see me," I said, as Perotto passed between the guards with their halberds. I heard him rap on the gilded door. "Your Holiness, please forgive me, but her ladyship Madonna Lucrezia is here. She begs an audience with you." I held my breath, not looking at the cardinal, though I could feel his stare fixed on me.

It seemed I stood there forever, waiting. I began to think the worst, fear smothering me until I could barely draw in a full breath. My father had fallen ill with grief. He would not let anyone in until we had to break down the doors, and by then it would be too late—

The metallic creak of bolts drawn back caused the cardinals to recoil. Cardinal Sforza made as if to detain me. I went still, daring him to set his spidery, ringed hand upon my person. "With due respect, my lady," he said, "perhaps I should enter first."

"Why?" I replied. "You have never loved His Holiness."

His gaze turned cold. "And my lady should have a care," he murmured, so low only I could hear him. "Your marriage to my cousin Giovanni is not annulled yet."

"And if this were any other moment," I said, "I would remind my father of how you connived to see me wed to your cousin, though you know well that he is unfit."

The cardinal's mouth turned inward. I swept past him, the guards, and Perotto, through the half-open doors into my father's chamber.

I came to a halt. A scuffle of footsteps behind me, an indignant "We must speak to His Holiness"—all cut off by the swift closure of the door. Perotto had barred the cardinals' entry.

Before me, the chamber swam into focus: frescoes in shadow, the Moorish lamps hanging motionless from the eaves, costly Turkey carpets on the heavy walnut and oak furnishings, and my father's bed, shrouded in purple and white like a barge submerged by its own sails. I began to walk toward the upholstered chair with its footstool, facing the hearth. My soles crunched on something underfoot, but I paid no heed. There was no fire in the hearth's deep well; instead, a terra-cotta pot of ferns sat there. Light spilled from a lone candelabrum.

I looked around me. "Papa? Papa, where are you?" My voice faded into inky recesses. "Papa, please. Answer me."

"I am here."

I whirled about. He crouched in a puddle of white robes under the large window overlooking the piazza, its curtains pulled to form a blank canvas. I began to move to him, overwhelmed at the sight of him, alive and speaking.

He said, "Do not come any closer. I cannot bear it."

I went to him, anyway, as he let out a moan and I saw his arms, draped in crumpled sleeves, rise to cover his face. "No. Go away, I say. Leave me."

"Papa, please. I want to be here for you." I sank before him, reaching out a tentative hand. Though he did not remove his arms from his face, a strangled sob caught in his throat and he whispered, "You should not have come. They should not have called for you. There is nothing here for you. There is only death."

"No one called for me. I came because I had to. Papa, please look at me." I set my hand on his shoulder. It felt like a mass of boneless flesh. I knew it was impossible, as it had been only hours since the tragedy, but it seemed as though he were dissolving before my eyes, his robust muscularity, his invincibility, pooling at my feet.

He lowered his arms. He was pale as wax, his fallen face scored with tears. His eyes were haunted, sunken in the hollows of his skull, helpless with disbelief. "Why?" he whispered. "Why does God strike at me now? Why take my Juan? What did he ever do to deserve such a fate?"

"I do not know," I whispered, even as in that terrible moment, as I beheld his bewilderment, I saw that Vannozza had not told him. Papa did not know what Juan had done.

"No," he said, "you do not know the reason, but I do. God did this because He must punish me for my presumption, for my vanity and arrogance, for believing I am equal to Him. He must prove that I am nothing. *We* are nothing. We are dust under His heels. Dust and bone. He can grind us up and cast us to the winds whenever He chooses."

"Papa, no. You mustn't say that. God would never punish you. It was an accident, a horrible—"

"NO!" His roar rocked me back on my heels. He came to his feet, looming over me like a mountain of soiled ivory, crashing his fist against his chest. "It is my fault. Mine! I am to blame, for I did not abide by His commandments. I forgot that I am His servant, a vessel for Him to fill with wine or blood. I trod His halls and sat upon His throne and gorged—yes, gorged like a pagan—on His wealth. I never showed a moment of humility. I never showed Him that only by His grace can I claim to be His pontiff. Now He reminds me that I too must sacrifice, as He once did before me. I must surrender that which I most loved—my son."

He fell back to his knees; I smelled the tang of spilled wine on his robes as he uttered, "Do you know how they killed him? They stabbed him nine times. I counted the wounds myself. Nine. Their blades pierced his cloak and doublet, into his flesh. They stabbed him until he could no longer fight, and then they slit his throat. They threw him into the river, used rocks to sink his corpse. They did not even pretend to be common villains; they left thirty ducats in his purse, his dagger and sword. They killed him because I loved him and God wished it so."

"Who . . . ?" I almost couldn't speak. "Who did this, Papa?"

Tears welled again in his eyes. "Whoever they are, wherever they hide, I will find them. I will hunt them down. Oh, how will they pay— with their torn and flayed skins, which I will hang over the altar of the basilica itself. God is not the only one who can seek retribution."

Forcing myself to inch closer, resisting the urge to run out the doors and down the halls, to run and never look back, until I reached San Sisto, I embraced him. As he felt my arms about him, he leaned into me to whisper, *"Vae illi homini qui cupit."*

Beware the man who covets.

I had no sense of what he meant, what he was trying to tell me, and I had no time to ask. Behind us, the chamber door crashed open. Perotto cried, "My lord cardinals, I beg of you! His Holiness is not to be disturbed—" and I turned with my father's cryptic words still echoing in my ears, to see the cardinals striding toward us, Cardinal Sforza at their head.

"Your Holiness, we implore your forgiveness." The cardinal's pliant features conveyed dutiful reluctance. "But the situation cannot wait any longer. News of the duke's death is spreading; the populace will soon gather in the piazza to hear words of reassurance from Your Holiness. At times like these . . . alas, there are too many who might resort to vandalism and looting, should they believe Your Holiness is incapacitated by grief."

I glared at Sforza, loathing him so intensely in that moment that I wanted to strike him. Papa tensed in my arms. Then he pulled away and stood. Though his robes hung crumpled about him, his voice did not waver. "I shall compose an address to be read to my people. My son—" He paused, swallowing. "The late duke of Gandia is to be conveyed to his tomb before the altar of Santa Maria del Popolo with a full procession of honorary guard and interred with all obsequies due to his rank. Thirty days of mourning will be instituted throughout the city. I will not tolerate lawlessness; anyone who dares seek advantage in this tragedy will be arrested."

"Yes, Holiness," said Cardinal Sforza. Behind him, I saw a mixture of relief, consternation, and, on those less practiced at concealing their emotions, disappointment.

They had not succeeded. Papa remained unvanquished, but in that instant I began to understand how much they truly reviled us, how they longed to see the Borgias fall.

As the cardinals turned away, Perotto rushed forth to attend my father. Suddenly Papa's voice rang out: "Where is His Eminence the Cardinal of Valencia?"

Cardinal Sforza halted in mid-step. "I believe my lord Cesare veils his brother's catafalque. Shall I send for him, Holiness?"

My father assumed the remote consideration of the Supreme Pontiff, who must transcend personal travails to fulfill his duty. "Yes. Tell him his sister, Lucrezia, is here. He must return her at once to the Convent of San Sisto, by my command."

"Papa, no," I started to say. "I must stay here with—"

"You will go." He did not look at me. "You will go and remain there. No daughter of mine shall suffer the days ahead; this cross is mine to bear. Mine, alone."

CHAPTER TWENTY-FIVE

Cesare arrived at the Vatican clad entirely in black; I marked at once the shadow etching his cheeks, pronouncing his aquiline nose and supple mouth. He did not speak as he escorted me to the waiting horses and our escort of men-at-arms. For a time, neither could I. It felt as though Juan's death had stolen our lifelong ability to find succor in each other's presence, no matter the cause.

As we rode down the Via Appia, dawn chased away the mist, melting upon the cupolas and spires. Overhead, pigeons flocked to the piazzas, to watch for the tradesmen and vendors with their food carts. It was just another day, I found myself thinking. A day in which the word of the pope's loss would spice the marketplace gossip, bringing out goodwives to mutter on their stoops; others would begin to congregate in the Piazza San Marco to await confirmation of the tragedy and reassurance that, despite his overwhelming sorrow, Papa would not allow Rome to descend into chaos. Then the people would return to their lives, to their own losses and travails; they would forget. Juan's name would become another byword for the senseless violence that plagued the Eternal City, another unfortunate recorded in the daily ledger of death.

Yes, everyone would forget—except Papa, who now had Juan's death carved upon his heart as viscerally as if he himself had been stabbed nine times.

I kept returning to what he had said to me before the cardinals burst in: *Beware the man who covets.* I had thought it a warning, something he needed me to know. But now, riding back toward the convent with Rome awakening around me, I doubted. Perhaps he'd only whispered words that held meaning for him, an obscure message that was more a warning to himself than to anyone else. For he had coveted: He had craved the papal tiara and the power it entailed more than anything else. He had schemed to obtain it. Did he believe that he must now beware of his own self?

"Do you . . . ?" I started to say.

Cesare glanced at me—a quick stab of his feline eyes. His brow lifted a fraction, waiting for me to find my tongue.

"Juan," I said haltingly. To speak his name felt strange on my lips. "Do you know what happened to him?"

"Didn't Papa tell you?" In the golden light spreading around us and evaporating the mists to reveal a dazzling summer sky, I saw a nerve twitch in his temple. Something about that tiny sign of life in his otherwise sepulchral appearance made my heart race. An immediate queasiness overcame me. I gritted my teeth, praying I would not be sick, not here, not in front of him.

"He did," I managed to say. "He . . . he told me about the body, that it didn't appear to be a random act. But how did they take him? How could he have ended up in the river?"

Though he wore the guise of mourning, Cesare's expression was reflective, as if he considered the fate of a stranger. At length he said, "Juan was with me that night."

I gripped the reins so tightly, my mare bucked her head in protest. "He was with you . . . ?"

He nodded. "It's not a secret. We were together most of the day, in fact. First at Papa's beck and call, as usual, because . . . well, because Juan felt the need to trail us like a shadow, suspicious of everything I might say, and me because I'm due to return to Naples now that King Ferrantino is dead." He gave a bitter smile. "Ruling that rock of a kingdom must be arduous indeed. How many kings of Naples have we seen since Papa took the see? Two? Three? In any event, Federico of Aragon, uncle to our late Ferrantino—who can tell those Neapolitans apart?—will inherit the throne. Papa wishes me to act as our legate for the coronation."

I regarded him in appalled disbelief. He spoke as though nothing had occurred, as if our own brother had not been slain and was not soon to be conveyed to his tomb. I was about to say as much when I recalled that Juan had told me he'd have no compunction killing Cesare.

"So," I said, "you were with Juan all day and then . . . ?"

"We dined together that evening, along with the cardinal of Monreale. Afterward, Monreale and I returned to the Vatican, but Juan said he had business elsewhere. We assumed he was going to a courtesan or one of those seedy taverns he liked to frequent. I did advise him to take precautions, given the late hour. Evidently he heeded me, for he had his sword and a groom. They met with a masked companion in the Piazza degli Ebrei, a ruffian Juan may have hired as a bodyguard. He told his groom to wait in the piazza and went on with the masked man."

"The Piazza degli Ebrei? Isn't that close to Cardinal Sforza's palazzo?"

"Indeed." Though Cesare's impassive tone did not alter, it sent a shiver through me. "We only know it was that particular piazza because we found the groom there, knifed several times and near death; he told us about the masked man. When Papa heard, he immediately had every possible location searched for Juan. Eventually, a Dalmatian boatman, of all persons, who'd been fishing by the Ponte di Ripetta, led us to the body. He said that sometime after midnight he saw two men arrive with another on a horse, bearing a corpse wrapped in a cloak across the crupper. The men hauled it into the river, loading stones onto the cloak to sink it. They were not very thorough; our guards dragged Juan out at low tide, entangled in reeds. He was bound to be discovered, though the boatman insisted he'd seen a hundred bodies disposed in the same manner and no one had ever come looking for them before."

Cesare sighed. "Whoever did this wanted us to find him. They must have taken Juan shortly after he left the piazza; they were on his heels, so to speak. His murder was planned in advance."

A terrifying chill crept through me. *Who* could have orchestrated such a deed? Who would have dared stalk the pope's son through the night and kill him so savagely? Nine wounds, I suddenly thought. Nine. Just like nine months, the same number it took for a pregnancy to yield fruit . . .

"They must have known Juan would visit that district," added Cesare, bringing my startled attention back to him. "They were lying in wait for him. If he hired that masked man to protect him, it did him no good. Either the man fled during the attack or he was part of it."

"Does anyone know who this man is?" I asked, even as a memory of when I'd gone to see Cesare while he was ill in his palazzo raced through my mind. Michelotto had been wearing a mask when he came to fetch me. But many men went about masked at night in Rome; it was as much a disguise employed by criminals to hide their faces as an affectation among the rich, perfumed masks shielding sensitive nostrils from the putrid air. It did not mean . . . it could not mean that—

"He could be anyone." Cesare shrugged. "The city doesn't lack for hirelings: a disfigured condottiere plying his trade in the alleyways, as so many do, pretending to be a bodyguard-for-hire to gain Juan's confidence. Our brother was always befriending scoundrels, consorting with the worst riffraff Rome has to offer. I doubt we'll ever find the man, if he's still alive—and he is not the only one we suspect. Accusations started to fly even before the water had drained off the corpse." He turned to me with a cold smile. "I believe even your husband is thought to be a possible culprit."

I had to focus on keeping my gaze steady, to not let him sense the anxious suspicion cresting inside me. "Giovanni? How can that be? He's in Pesaro."

"We heard otherwise. Not long ago, one of our informants reported that a man matching Giovanni's description was seen slinking into Cardinal Sforza's palazzo. Juan may have gone to meet him there; perhaps Giovanni was this masked stranger, though that seems too obvious a ploy for someone of his limited intelligence. Still, as you say, the piazza lies next to Palazzo Sforza. If Giovanni was hiding in Rome and didn't want anyone to know it, where else could he lodge? But he's not there now. We had it searched. He is gone, no doubt already back on his way to Pesaro." Cesare paused, staring at me with an unsettling curiosity. "You've not seen him since he left? Cardinal Sforza was most emphatic when questioned that Giovanni had not come anywhere near the city since he made his cowardly exit."

"No," I whispered. I swallowed, strengthening my voice. "No. I have not seen him."

"Well. There we have it. A report from an informant hired by us is hardly evidence, and if no one actually saw him in Rome at the time, then—"

"He'd never do something like this." I cut him off before I could stop myself, wincing to hear the urgent need to inject incredulity into my voice. "Giovanni and Juan were friends. They liked each other. Everyone knew it. What would Giovanni gain from killing him?"

Cesare gave a chuckle. "Yes, we both know how well they liked each other. I thought quite the same: Did Juan arrange to meet your husband as a lover? Anything is possible." Again, his disconcerting gaze fixed on me. "It might work, in fact. If you tell Papa what you saw that night in your palazzo between him, Juan, and Giulia, it would certainly spare us a protracted petition for an annulment. We could prove with one arrest that Giovanni is not only a catamite who never bedded his wife but is also a jealous one who killed Juan. It's not as if our brother was faithful to anyone. He slept with half of Rome, if the rumors are to be believed."

I was aghast. "But Giovanni would never . . . he had no reason to—"

Fleet as a raptor, Cesare rounded on me, grabbing my reins from my hands and tugging our mounts so close, his thigh pressed against mine. I heard the jangle of stirrups behind us as the escort likewise drew to a precipitous halt, keeping their distance.

"What do you know of Giovanni or what he will do?" he hissed. "Why do you defend that vermin, when by your own account you are well rid of him?"

"I do not defend him. I don't defend anyone!" My own anger surged. "Unhand me."

He released my reins. The vein in his temple now pulsed under his skin. He was hiding something. I knew it with a cramp in my stomach that reminded me of my intolerable condition and made me want to retch.

"Giovanni might be vermin, but he'd never dare," I said, tasting bile. "He's desperate to stay in Papa's good graces. He'd never consent to such an act, while he still hopes to save our marriage."

"Oh?" Cesare eyed me. I wanted to look away, but I knew that if I did he would realize at once that I too hid something. "If I recall correctly, your husband not only fucked Juan—or was it the other way around?—but he also ordered his own secretary's hands chopped off for abetting your intrigues, not to mention that we're about to charge him with impotency in your bed. It seems to me that a man in his position is quite capable of anything."

Doubt assailed me. I thought of Giovanni's brutal assault on me and how Juan disdained him for his botched effort, sending him away with an earful of threats. Had Giovanni obeyed or only pretended to do so, remaining in the city to plot his revenge, fearful that his role in my violation might be revealed? Juan had proven he cared for no one but himself; moreover, he was the only other witness. If Giovanni had paid for Juan's death, it was just my word against his. He could counter the claim of non-consummation, demand an examination by midwives to refute my virginity, and then all of Italy would discover that I was in fact—

This time, I couldn't hold back. Leaning to one side, I spewed onto the road. I gagged, my stomach heaving. With one hand clutching my saddle and another at my mouth, I gazed up in horror at Cesare, bracing for his denunciation that I'd concealed something so momentous from him.

He sat quiet on his horse, his eerie calm reminding me of the meeting between him and Papa that I had spied upon, when his very serenity had become a weapon Papa could not evade.

"You did not ask where Juan and I dined that evening," he said at length, and he reached into his doublet, extracting a red silk handkerchief. He handed it to me. As I clutched it to my lips, inhaling the aroma of his scent on the cloth, he went on in a velvety tone, "We were with Mama at her villa on the Esquiline."

The world capsized around me. "You were at Vannozza's? Did she . . . ?"

He leaned over in his saddle, retrieving the silk from my hands. Folding it over once, he proceeded to dab my lips. His breath smelled of cloves as he murmured, "She did not say a word. Ah, no. Wait." His fingertips pressed harder, stifling my voice. "I am not finished. I knew she had visited you. I set Michelotto to watching San Sisto and he saw Vannozza leave, clearly distraught. He'd also seen your Pantalisea coming and going with linens and coverlets, as if you prepared for a long stay. I didn't need Mama's cards to divine what was afoot." He paused, the soiled handkerchief clutched in his hand.

"Cesare . . ." My voice faded as he clicked his tongue, shaking his head.

"No, no. There's no need for apology. I'll not tell a soul, though you do realize that at some point Papa must be informed. This would ruin his plans, should it come to light. At the very least, he cannot claim you are untouched. At the worst, Giovanni will demand your return and we'll have to oblige him." He went silent for a moment. "Is the child his?"

Tears burned behind my eyes. "No. Juan, he—" I could not speak the words, not aloud.

The darkening of his face revealed that he didn't need to hear the words. "Did you tell Mama?" he asked, and when I nodded, he still showed no visible upset, though I expected rage, his avowal to see Juan's corpse dragged through the streets. Instead, he licked the edge of the cloth to wipe a trace of spittle from my cheek. "Juan forced himself on you. Is that it?"

I recoiled at the cadence of mistrust in his tone. "Do you think I would lie?" He did not answer. My voice rose, shrill. I was so incensed I no longer cared if the guards accompanying us overheard, if all of Rome overheard. "*How* could you, Cesare?"

He leaned back. I exhaled a furious breath, about to haul my mare about and proceed to the convent, when he said, "I've never believed for a second that you would lie to me about anything. If you say Juan did this to you, then he did. I suspected something terrible must have befallen you. Why else would you flee into the convent while we were in Ostia?"

"And you," I retorted, "would you lie to me? You don't seem surprised by any of this." As I spoke, a horrifying notion surfaced. "*Dio mio,* was it Juan? Did he tell you? Did he boast of it to you?" The very thought tore at the pit of my being. Juan was capable of it; I imagined him drunk, taunting Cesare before our own mother at her table, exulting in his prowess, hoping to incite confrontation, as he'd so often done. I heard him as if his ghost hovered at my side: *I'll grant no quarter this time. None. . . . I have paid back every insult, every time he made me feel as if I were unfit to call myself a Borgia.*

And in return, Cesare would have killed him for it.

He startled me when he suddenly tossed his head, letting loose his familiar laughter, tinged with mordant wit. "You insult me. If he'd boasted of it and I sought to avenge you, do you think I'd have made such a mess of things?" His fingers, twined with the red silk, tapped his thigh. "Well? Do you? Of course not. Because you know well that if I had done it," he said, his voice icy, "there would be no evidence—no moribund groom or tattling boatman. No corpse in the Tiber. Juan would have disappeared, which is all he deserved—anonymity and an empty tomb, not a martyr's funeral and public laments. Gone forever, as if he never existed."

He turned away, nudging his horse. In the distance, sunlight shimmered upon San Sisto. The convent offered only the illusion of refuge now—this world I had sought to escape, if only for a brief time, could not be kept at bay even from within its walls.

Beware the man who covets.

As Papa's cryptic words came back to me, I called out, "Cesare."

He paused, casting a glance at me over his shoulder. His eyes were hooded. "Yes?"

"I . . . I am glad he is dead," I said, and I felt my own revulsion at my callousness curdle inside me, like a taint of poison on my tongue. "I threatened Mama with the truth so she'd make Papa send him away. I cursed Juan; I longed for his death. I know you have only ever wanted to protect me, so, please . . . tell me the truth now. It will be our secret, ours alone. Did you kill him?"

He tilted his head, as if he were amused. "Alas, I did not. But had I known this, I assure you I would have."

PART IV

1498–1500

A Cry of the Flesh

Per pianto la mia carne si distilla
(The flesh melts away with weeping)
—Jacopo Sannazaro

CHAPTER TWENTY-SIX

"Another push, my lady," urged Pantalisea. "This time with all your strength."

She bent over me as I straddled the upholstered birthing stool, my body aching, my womb pummeled from within. Suora Leocadia stood like a sentinel at the door, while Suora Paulina, convent herbalist and now apprentice midwife, knelt at my feet as I drew in another shallow lungful of air, tensed, and bore down, every muscle shrieking.

"I cannot," I gasped. "Please, no more. Just let me die."

I spoke through a sweat-drenched veil, which Suora Leocadia had insisted I wear to cover my shame. Only she, the herbalist, and Pantalisea were permitted to attend the birth, which began a day ago with a sudden pang and gush of bloodied water. Now, after an agonizing night spent in this smothering room, during which the being within me defied every effort to coax it out, I sat with my chemise plastered to me like a suffocating second skin, longing to howl like the demented captive thing I'd become.

"You will not die." Suora Leocadia thrust her mole-pocked chin at me. "I forbid it. Our Holy Mother forbids it. You will deliver this babe first. You will bring it into this world and then we shall wait on the Almighty's will. Now, push."

The sound that came out of me then was like the frantic cry of the slaughterhouse animal that knows it is doomed—half sob, half shriek, fraught with despair.

"I cannot!"

As Suora Leocadia flinched and drew back, Suora Paulina murmured, "Madonna must not dwell on the pain. Cast your thoughts elsewhere and let your body do its work."

"Cast my thoughts elsewhere?" I gazed at her in disbelief, for I had never felt more imprisoned within my body. "What do you suggest I think about?"

"Anything," interrupted Pantalisea. "Only do not fight it."

Suora Paulina was already reaching again to my bruised private parts, eliciting a moan of pain from my lips. I shut my eyes and tried to be anywhere but in this fetid room I'd come to despise, pretending I had taken wing to soar above this convent that had been my cage.

At first, all I felt were Suora Paulina's fingers probing me. Clenching my teeth, I cast my mind further away, remembering how slowly time had passed, my days regimented by the unassailable hours of the liturgy, my belly swelling until I no longer fit into my clothes. Pantalisea had made furtive trips to purchase cloth, fashioning new gowns in a voluminous style that concealed my girth and accentuated my enlarged breasts. She laced me into one of those gowns on the day the Curia summoned me to declare myself *virga intacta*, unspoiled by man.

Seated before the cardinals, my hands clasped demurely across my lap as I took in their prurient gazes resting, as if transfixed, on the creamy mounds of my chest, I delivered a speech that astonished even me with its sincerity. I knew from letters smuggled into the convent by Pantalisea—who met weekly with Perotto, suborned by Papa to deliver important news—that the annulment proceeding had turned acrimonious. Giovanni had declared our marriage consummated "many times over" and railed to his cousin Il Moro in Milan—who wasted no time in maliciously relaying the accusation to his envoy in Rome, thus ensuring all Italy heard of it—that His Holiness had other unspeakable motives for wanting to separate me from my husband. I trembled when I learned this, thinking of the time when Giovanni came upon Cesare and me, entangled in each other's arms in the villa above Pesaro. But his bid to defame our name only succeeded in rousing Papa's wrath.

"Do people say I am both her father and lover?" Papa railed before the Curia. "Let the common vermin of this world, as ridiculous as they are feebleminded, believe the most absurd tales about the mighty! Our good or evil can be judged by only the highest power."

He left the cardinals of the Curia without any doubt as to which verdict he expected them to deliver. Papa had no patience for obfuscation. He threatened reform, Pantalisea informed me, culling gossip from Perotto. He refused to grant any requests that carried a hint of corruption; he condemned venality and abolished indulgences. He even went so far as to send Sancia and Gioffre along with Cesare to see the new king of Naples crowned, to prove he was repentant, depriving himself of the solace of his own family. Every cardinal had something to lose from Papa's new stance; none could afford inquiries into their private affairs. By the time I appeared before the Curia in my new gown to attest to my virginity, their sentence was a foregone conclusion.

Couriers galloped to Pesaro, carrying the Curia's official dissolution of my marriage and Papa's ultimatum: Giovanni could retain my dowry—a considerable sum—providing he pleaded impotency. Already in negotiations for a new wife, offered by his former in-laws the Gonzagas (who evidently were undeterred by his dishonor), Giovanni agreed. For the first time since Juan's death, I burst into laughter when I received the news, scandalizing the sisters toiling in a nearby herb patch.

Papa had wiped clean my sordid past. Publicly, I was *immacolata* once more.

"It's almost here! Push, my lady—I can feel the crown of its head!"

Suora Paulina's excited cry brought me hurtling back into my body. As my screams erupted, loud enough that surely they must have reverberated throughout the convent, my legs flew apart to welcome a release so vast it was like a flood washing over me.

I sprawled on the stool, breathless. I could not lift my head as movement burst around me—a blur of stained hems and clogs clapping along the floor. Suora Paulina barked for scissors, the witch hazel, and a basin of water. Through my half-closed eyelids, I glimpsed a bluish tail that bound something to me. Then I heard splashes of rosewater, its scent drenching me.

"Is it alive?" Pantalisea asked anxiously.

A fraught silence fell. More whispering, followed by an abrupt *thwack* and an outraged wail. I finally looked up. Suora Leocadia flung the door open and marched out, letting in for a moment the sound of rain pattering upon the cloister. From where she knelt by my feet, Suora Paulina offered me a squirming bundle swathed in white linen.

"A boy, my lady," she said. She set the baby in my arms, resting him on the still-distended bulge of my belly. "My lady must stay seated awhile longer," she advised. "The rest of the birth must come out. If it stays inside, you will sicken. I'll fetch a robe and fresh chemise."

"And a mop," muttered Pantalisea as the nun left. "When it comes to anything more than brewing chamomile or taking honey from the hive, they don't have the sense of a mule."

I wanted to laugh, but everything hurt. Peeling aside the swaddle, I revealed a tiny, puckered face, eyes like slits, and the toothless pit of a mouth. Another impossibly loud cry issued from that mouth, causing me to gasp. "*Madre di Dio.* He looks like an old man."

"He looks like His Holiness," said Pantalisea. "Sounds like him, too." She smiled at me. "What are you going to call him? He will need a name for the christening."

A lump filled my chest. "I made my decision. He must be reared by whomever Papa chooses. He—he cannot stay with me, nor can he ever know I am his mother."

"You'll never be able to do that now," Pantalisea said softly. "You may not feel it yet, but I can already see it in your eyes. He is entirely yours."

I started to look away, but the babe began to kick, crying and beating his fists. Instinctively, I hoisted him higher upon my chest, parting my sodden chemise to release my breast. The clamp of his mouth on my nipple sent a jolt of pain-laced pleasure through me.

"See?" Pantalisea sighed. "You cannot resist."

My arms cradled him. I felt a near-imperceptible shift in my heart, where something stirred to fragile life, unfelt until now.

"My son," I whispered. "I have a son. . . ."

As I pressed my lips to his still-soft and misshapen head, I realized what I felt was not only the joy of unquenchable love but also the awakening of inescapable fear.

A Borgia, twice over. What would be my child's fate?

CHAPTER TWENTY-SEVEN

They left me alone with him for almost three weeks. Three endless blessed weeks, during which I woke every morning to find my boy blinking at me from his makeshift crib by my bedside. The wintry light seeping through the grated window turned to rose upon his flawless skin, his hands opening and closing as if he were attempting to show me something, before his hunger erupted in a bellow that was music to my ears. Drawing him into my bed, which I had piled with wool coverlets and furs, I unlaced my nightdress so he could clasp onto my breast to suckle with a single-minded fervor that left me in no doubt that he was indeed a Borgia.

I resisted naming him. I thought I could not love him. I even feared I might hate him, fruit of a savagery that had shattered my trust. I had told myself I'd be happy to relinquish him, if he did not die first, as many newborns did. While I awaited his birth, I'd complained to Pantalisea innumerable times of how much I longed to be free of this burden. I wanted to return to my palazzo, to my silks and jewels; I longed to forget and be Lucrezia Borgia once more, the pope's beloved daughter.

Yet here I lay in my rumpled bed, which smelled faintly of mold from the incessant rain, with my child feeding from my body, warmer than a kiln as he curled against me. As I caressed his wisps of dark-copper hair, I felt that I could stay here forever; I couldn't imagine being anywhere other than where he was. I chattered Pantalisea's ears off whenever she returned from errands outside the convent, about how he'd gurgled or farted ("All babies do that," she said); of how blue his eyes were, like mine ("That might change"); and how I thought he was already trying to talk ("At his age?"). But she also fussed over him and helped me change him, washing his soiled swaddles in the courtyard

trough, which the prioress had allowed us to use, despite Suora Leocadia's objections. Pantalisea slept on a pallet on the floor, always on her
feet at the first whimper from his crib.

In my joyful exhaustion—sleep was an elusive balm I had to snatch
whenever I had the chance—I forgot the prioress's warning: that the
cries of my child would set teeth on edge; his very presence reminding
the nuns of San Sisto that new life, conceived in sin, was among them.

In February, the reminder came. I sat in the cloisters, swathed in
shawls while he slept after nursing. I was starting to doze when footsteps jolted me awake. I turned to see the prioress, her face somber
within its wimple. She extended a folded parchment to me.

"From His Holiness."

I could not move, as doing so would disturb my child, so she bent
down stiffly to tuck the paper near my buttocks. "I have already sent
my reply," she said, and she was turning away when I asked in a low
voice, "What reply?" though I knew. I knew and dreaded it, for it sig-
naled that my respite had come to an end.

"He wishes to pay us a visit," the prioress told me. "He has asked
that we accommodate his need for absolute privacy. I told him we shall,
as we owe him our obedience. But once he departs, I expect your decision. If you wish to remain, you must prepare to take the veil and relinquish your son. If not, then you must depart." With a nod, she went
back down the cloister with the same brisk indifference with which she
had delivered her message.

Clutching my son, I stared into the barren winter garden.

I had to protect him, no matter the cost.

I DRESSED IN the same gown I'd worn to the Curia, though now it
hung loose on me. I wore no jewels save for a gold crucifix about my
throat. At the last minute, I wrapped a few articles I had brought during
my hasty departure from my palazzo—a modest bracelet of pearls, a
ruby-studded comb, and a sapphire pendant—and thrust them at Pantalisea. "Pawn these. Find a way to hide him in safety until I can send
for him."

She gave me a sad shake of her head. "If we could not pay to end
your pregnancy out of fear of discovery, how do you expect us to hide
the child now? Besides, Perotto warned me that your brother Cesare has

set spies on every corner of the road leading from the convent; he is told of every time I venture outside these walls. If I steal away with the babe, he will know."

I kneaded fistfuls of my skirts. I had made the bargain; Juan's death had sealed it. I need not fear him anymore, and Giovanni was no longer my husband. Why did I feel such an overpowering need to safeguard my son? Papa would never harm him; nor would Cesare or even my mother. They would cherish him, for he too shared our blood.

Sensing my distress, Pantalisea said, "You have a new mother's nerves; it is to be expected that you'd fear for the child. You have more reason than most. But His Holiness will understand." She coiled my hair at my nape. "Your father loves you. Tell him you cannot do it. Tell him you have searched your heart and you must raise your son as your own."

"Yes." I seized on this fragile shred of hope. "We are his family. He belongs with us."

Nevertheless, when I stepped into the dining hall with its stained-glass windows depicting the Annunciation, the sunlit panes casting translucent colored lozenges at my feet, I had to force myself to smile: Papa was seated at the scarred table where the nuns ate their mutton. He wore a plain black tunic and hose, his thick legs sheathed in riding boots. As I neared, I saw sagging skin under his chin, lines bracketing his mouth and scoring his brow, his grief etched permanently upon him. His brooding eyes met mine before he motioned with his hand for me to approach. His papal ring glittered, sole evidence of his pontifical splendor.

"I thought it best to meet alone," he began. "I let it be known about the Vatican that I rode out to hunt. We cannot afford any more scandal, as I'm sure you would agree."

I found the imperviousness in his voice disturbing. Then he said, "Cesare told me everything. I am very disappointed, Lucrezia."

Not *"farfallina."* Not "my beloved daughter."

My temper flared. "Surely you do not think I am to blame?"

"I did not say that. I am saying that I am disappointed you didn't confide in me." When I did not speak, he sighed. "Come here." I took a wary step forward. He reached for my hand, enfolding it in his fingers. I let out a small sound of relief; all of a sudden, I was on my knees with my head in his lap as he set his palms on my head and whispered, "I know it is my fault. You were so vulnerable, married to that lout, and I left you to fend for yourself, like a doe set upon by wolves."

"Papa—"

"No. Do not make excuses for me. I am an old fool. I did not want to see it. I didn't want to believe he was anything less than perfect. I thought the best of him, always. I knew he lacked the talents that you and Cesare have in such abundance, but it endeared him to me. He . . . he reminded me of myself, of my own struggles in my youth, when I labored to find a place to call my own in this wretched world. But Juan was not like me; he had no aptitude for anything beyond his own pleasures. Still, I gave him everything I could, because I thought he would change. Despite my disillusionment, I thought in time he'd become the man I wanted him to be."

I had never known this; I had never paused to consider that the overwhelming love he'd lavished on Juan welled from a hidden aspiration that his son could never fulfill. It explained so much about why he'd favored Juan over Cesare, unwittingly sowing their enmity. Cesare had always been his rapier, keen and capable, a true Borgia through and through, while my dead brother—he had been the clumsy ax which Papa tried in vain to hone to his exacting standards.

I reached up to caress his cheek. It felt rough, grizzled, as though he had not had a razor taken to it in days. "Papa, you could not have known. No one could. I do not blame you. I don't even blame him anymore." As he choked back a sob, I stood and embraced him. "Papa, please do not cry. I hate it when you cry." I could feel his shoulder blades indenting the wool of his tunic; he had grown alarmingly thin, and any fears I had of his intentions melted away. "It's over now, Papa. And my child, your grandson—he is so beautiful. Just like you."

He snorted through his tears. "I should hope not. I am not beautiful. I never was."

"You are to me." I drew back. "Do you want to see him?"

He nodded, but as I turned around to fetch my child, I heard him say, "Before you bring him to me, we must reach an understanding."

I went still.

"You told Vannozza you wished to surrender the boy. Do you still want that?"

I turned back to him and said quietly, "No. I want to keep him."

He went silent. Something hardened in his eyes, as in times past when I'd asked for something he was unwilling to give.

"I am his mother, Papa. Surely, he belongs with me."

"He does. A child should always be with his mother. But you must realize how impossible it would be?" He lifted a hand, staving my protest. "*Farfallina,* let me finish. I did not come here to chastise you. Nor am I saying you must never see him or be a part of his life, but we cannot let the world know the truth about him, not only for your sake but also for his."

"But he is my son. He . . . he is everything to me."

"And we both know who his father was." He watched me struggle to gain control of myself. "Think of your future," he said. "You are not yet eighteen. You have your entire life to live. You will bear other children, God willing. Would you sacrifice everything, let yourself be branded like this for the rest of your days?" He paused, his tone softening even as his words twisted an invisible noose about my throat. "We have annulled your marriage, declared you a virgin before the world. Would you say now that we deceived, that I, the Supreme Pontiff, lied? We will never live it down. It will be our end—yours, mine, Cesare's. And the child's."

I was finding it difficult to breathe. I could not imagine giving away my son, no matter what happened. The thought that I'd not see him every day, not smell his milky skin and hear his cry, made me want to grab my child, flee Rome, and never look back. "I do not care. I will sacrifice everything if I must. I can go away, live in the country. Just, please, Papa. Do not take him from me." Tears broke my voice. "I could not endure it. He is all I have."

"Hush, hush." He had his hands clasped before him, his eyes now moist with his own tears. "You do not have to sacrifice everything, save these first years of his life and the freedom to call yourself his mother. I am prepared to strike a pact with you—one that will benefit you and the child, if you will only heed me."

I fought against the urge to run, to plunge into the teeming streets, where I might lose myself: another anonymous woman with a babe. Yet even as I imagined it, I knew how utterly naïve I was. I had nothing. Everything I had was because of my family. How would I survive in a brutal world I'd never set foot in, save for when I stepped from an up-holstered litter surrounded by guards? To indulge my sentiment, I would risk my child's very life.

"A pact?" I echoed.

"Yes." The sadness in his face vanished, replaced by that vibrancy I always associated with him. He was eager now, as he always was when negotiation came to the fore, no matter the subject. He could not escape the politician inside him even if God Himself commanded it.

"I will declare the child mine," he said, "the fruit of an unfortunate indiscretion. I'll draw up an official bull proclaiming him as such, citing his mother to be an unwed woman, one who must remain nameless for her reputation. He will be entrusted to Vannozza's care; she will oversee his rearing." He saw me grimace. "I realize you and your mother are at odds, but I think you both can agree that your son must grow up know-ing that Borgia blood runs in his veins. Only we must never divulge his true parentage. A child of such sin: He would carry the stain always."

Every part of me rebelled against it. My mother raising my child, after how she had treated me? My son growing up never knowing who I truly was? It was unacceptable.

"You can visit him," added Papa, "within reason, of course, and with the utmost discretion. He will adore you—his beautiful sister. And he'll have brothers to look up to—Cesare and Gioffre—who can teach him to be a man. On my word, he will lack for nothing."

"Except the truth," I whispered.

His sigh was heavy. "What good can it do him? We know the truth. Is it not enough? This world would never understand. They will use him to strike at us; you and your son will become living proof of our evil. I know what the truth can do. Best if we keep it to ourselves."

I did not answer at once. I let the silence stretch between us, so it would not appear as though I capitulated without deliberation. I knew it was indeed for the best, the only option open to me, unless I wanted to find myself in a pitched battle of wills against my father, which I was certain to lose. I also knew in my heart, though it pained me to my core, that it was best for my son. He would be privileged, a prince of our house, which was all I could wish for him. Yet still I hesitated, un-willing to concede, because Papa must know that I was no longer that eager girl who would do whatever he asked of me.

Finally, I assented. "Under one condition: If she harms him in any way, he must return to me. He must live with me, the truth be damned."

"Naturally. Though she would never. He is her grandson, too. That means everything to Vannozza. *La familia es nuestra sangre.* The family is our blood. Nothing is more important."

I resisted a bitter smile. "Then let me bring him to you."

When I returned with the babe in my arms, fretful and hungry after his nap, Papa came to his feet in awestruck wonder. At first he seemed uncertain as I set the kicking bundle in his arms, but then I saw instinct take over, his large veined hands enveloping the little body, the joy in his face easing his pain, so that he again resembled the robust man who had never let tragedy or failure defeat him.

"Such a gift," he breathed. "A Borgia grandson. What shall we name him?"

"Rodrigo," I said quietly, as if the answer had always been in me. "I would name him after you, Papa."

❧

I RETURNED TO my palazzo in the spring.

Nicola and Murilla were elated to welcome me home. Every furnishing in my apartments had been polished with linseed oil; every vase and hearth overflowed with greenery. Even my aloof Arancino meowed plaintively and curled about my ankles until I scooped him up. As he purred in my arms, I gazed about my rooms. It unsettled me, the orderliness, as though I had only just stepped outside for air. There was no indication I'd been gone nearly a year, during which so much about who I was had changed. How could I return to being the girl who had twirled about this palazzo, enamored of her position in life, unaware of the savagery awaiting her?

I felt I did not belong here anymore. And there was more trouble yet to face: my upcoming reception in society. No matter how well kept my secret was, there would still be widespread speculation over the dissolution of my marriage, and every eye would be upon me, the daughter who had fled and hidden away for months while her marriage was declared invalid.

Nevertheless, I was relieved to leave behind the frugal crust of the convent. My first bath was a decadent affair; I spent hours luxuriating, until my fingertips wrinkled and Pantalisea scolded me for drying out my skin. "What will they say when they see you looking like a sun-dried prune?"

"That at least I am clean," I replied, as Nicola and Murilla giggled. "And still a virgin, remember? Virgins are eternally fresh. Besides," I added, leaning to her, "perhaps you should be the one who worries over appearances, after all those rendezvous you kept with our gallant Pe-rotto while we were immured in San Sisto."

Nicola burst into laughter; Pantalisea tried to look scandalized but it did not take. Instead, she blushed, gathered up my wet towels, and marched out.

Murilla said, "We missed her, too, my lady, oddly enough."

"And I missed you." Throwing my arms about her tiny person, I swung her around as she squealed; my attendants outside the bathing chamber rushed off to spread the word that Madonna Lucrezia was certainly in high spirits for a woman who'd entered a convent because her impotent husband had forsaken her.

Laughter was healing, the company of my trusted ladies a solace, but every night after I retired, I pushed my face into my pillows to stifle my sobs over my Rodrigo, for I missed him so much it was a constant loss inside me. I had surrendered him to my mother outside San Sisto in the dead of night. She took him in her arms and had started to turn away when I grabbed her by the arm. "He may go off his milk. He's accustomed to me, not a wet nurse, and—"

She gave a brusque laugh. "I've given birth to six children, four of them by your father. I think I know by now how to care for a babe."

Before I could demand that she return my child, which I was about to do, she clambered into her litter and rode off, leaving me with furious tears in my eyes.

"She is his grandmother. She'll watch over him like a hawk," Panta-lisea kept saying that night, our last in San Sisto, while we waited for the escort from the Vatican to arrive. I wanted to believe it. Neverthe-less, in the next weeks as I resumed life in Santa Maria in Portico, I sent Pantalisea to my mother's house on the Esquiline with a variety of flimsy excuses, bidding her to act as my spy, until Vannozza put a halt to her visits by declaring, "Tell my daughter if she is so concerned, she can come see for herself. Otherwise, I'll thank her to stop sending others to meddle in my affairs. As you can see, the child grows fat as a bishop. Tell her one teat tastes much like another and he does not miss her at all."

Pantalisea looked askance as she relayed this message, uncomfortable but confirming that my son indeed seemed both healthy and happy. I hated the very idea that he could forget me so easily but took some solace in the fact that he'd adjusted to the change. I could have slipped out to see him anytime I wanted; by now, I had perfected subterfuge. But the moment I made the decision, I balked. I feared that if I set eyes on him again, nothing would stop me from taking him back.

Thus I wept at night and smiled by day, as word of my return spread and I was besieged by offers to dine with the noble families. Every morning when I woke, there was another invitation waiting, a puzzling development that only became clear when Sancia came to see me.

She and Gioffre had recently returned from their two-month visit to Naples, and she pranced into my rooms clad in green velvet that brought out the color of the sea in her eyes, her exuberant *"Cara mia!"* trilling from her lips before she halted. "Is that you? I can scarcely believe it."

I went to hug her. She held me at arm's length, appraising me. Behind me, Pantalisea coughed. All of a sudden I was aware of how much I had actually changed, having shed the slimness of girlhood, my hips rounder and breasts full, as I was still binding them to aid in the painful drying of my milk. To Sancia, who had not seen me in many months, I must appear quite transformed.

"Why, you are grown up," she said, almost in dismay. Her gaze narrowed. "It seems every woman must seek retreat in a convent more often, if these are the results."

My laughter sounded too high to my ears. "You exaggerate." I surveyed her in turn. "I see you are still as beautiful as ever."

She warmed at once, as she inevitably did to compliments. "Love can be as beneficial as the cloister—and is far more enjoyable." Hooking my arm in hers, she added, "I want to hear all about it. I was beside myself when you left. And after Juan was found dead—" Her attempt to adopt a mournful tone failed. "I wanted to write to you, but no one would allow it." She shot a menacing look at Pantalisea. "I did send for news of you every day when you had that dreadful fever. I trust you were informed?"

"I was. Thank you." I drew her to the door. "And I will tell you everything, I promise, only I must rest before tonight's reception in the hall and—"

"Yes, of course! Everyone will be here tonight to receive you."

I frowned. "Everyone? I was told that I was dining with Papa and a few nobles."

"A few nobles?" She rolled her eyes. "Surely you know that every nobleman who is not already married or on his deathbed has made a bid for your hand."

As I stared at her, incredulous, she said, "How can you not have heard? His Holiness has been fending off proposals ever since he announced the annulment. You are now the most coveted bride in Italy. Let us see. . . ." She held up her hand, ticking off the names on her ring-laden fingers. "There's Antonello Sanseverino, son of the prince of Salerno, though his family favored the French during the invasion. And Francesco Orsini, Duke of Gravina, who is far too old. Oh, and Ottaviano Riaro, son of the countess of Forlí, but he's a child; and Piombino of Appiani, who is too poor, and—"

I turned away, repulsed.

Sancia asked, "What is it? Did I say something wrong?"

I tried to smile. "I truly had no idea."

"So it seems. I thought—well, never mind what I thought. I clearly thought wrong. Oh, but you've gone white as death. Lucrezia, are you quite certain you are not ill?"

I felt faint. I had to sit. Pantalisea came to me with a goblet of watered wine, glaring at Sancia, who ignored her and floated onto the upholstered footstool nearby, waving a peremptory hand at my attendants. "Leave us."

Begrudgingly, the women departed for the antechamber—all save Pantalisea, who planted herself at my side. Casting a scowl at her, Sancia said to me, "You must have realized you are expected at some point to take another husband?"

I clenched the goblet. "*Dio mio.* I've only just been freed of Giovanni, for which I spent months sequestered in San Sisto to—to stay out of sight while they finalized the annulment," I said hastily, flustered by Sancia's keen expression. "And my brother Juan was only recently killed. I've not yet recovered from the shock. I cannot possibly consider another marriage at this time."

"Indeed," said Sancia, as if my litany were of no account. "Nevertheless, His Holiness is obliged to consider for you." She looked again at Pantalisea in warning. "And though this must stay between us, I have it on excellent authority that Cesare will petition the Curia to be absolved of his vows. With Juan gone, Rome is in dire need of someone to defend the Holy See's territories in the Romagna, where those quarrelsome barons continue to defy papal authority. Were it up to them, we'd have another French incursion, now that Charles the Eighth is gone. He left no direct heir, so his cousin will take the throne as Louis the Twelfth. . . ."

Her voice faded. She was still talking, but I barely registered the news that Charles of France, who'd caused us such anguish, was no more. All I could think was that Cesare had finally achieved that zenith he'd strived toward all these years. Juan's death had freed him of his shackles. He could now divest himself of the hated scarlet to assume charge of our defense, as only he could fill the vacant post of gonfalonier.

"Are you listening to me?" demanded Sancia, startling me.

"Forgive me. What were you saying?"

"I was saying King Louis seeks to claim Milan. He also wants an annulment of his marriage now that Charles's queen, Anne of Brittany, is a widow. Louis's own wife, Jeanne, is, by all accounts, both homely and pious. She's also barren, which makes her fit only for a nunnery."

My head was reeling; I could barely absorb this maze of events, much less how it might affect me. Sancia tapped her foot at my silence. "You do realize what this means? Once Cesare is no longer a cardinal, he must have a title. But the duchy of Gandia is beyond his grasp; it belongs to Juan's son in Spain, and his widow fights for it with her every breath. She went so far as to accuse Cesare of having had a hand in your brother's demise."

She paused dramatically, gauging my reaction. My mouth went dry. I had no desire to hear more, abruptly wishing she would leave, much as I cared for her. I did not want to think that Papa had dissuaded me from raising my son because he already had another husband waiting for me, though I'd been warned already, by both Juan and Cesare, that it was my fate.

"Of course, His Holiness will not abide such malice," Sancia went on, for she was never one to be deterred when there was gossip to impart. "He sent an envoy to Spain, denouncing the widow and her accusation. But their Catholic majesties have decreed the duchy must go to her son, and there is nothing anyone can do about it. However, don't you find it strange that His Holiness also ordered a halt to the investigation into Juan's death? He still vows vengeance, but how can he have it if the assassins are never found? In any event"—she sighed, clearly not expecting me to answer—"Cesare will require a suitable wife once he's released of his vows. And satisfying the French king's request for an annulment will put Louis in our debt, which can only suit Cesare's plans."

I finally realized her prattle had a purpose. "He has . . . plans?" Even as I spoke, I thought that of course he had plans. When did he not?

"Why, yes. He plans to marry me."

A taut silence fell. Before I could find the right words to reply, Pantalisea threw up her hands in disgust. "I hardly think my lord Cesare would stoop so low."

Sancia whirled on her. "How dare you!"

Gripping my chair arms, I ordered Pantalisea out.

"You should dismiss her," Sancia spat. "She is a trull who thinks too highly of herself. If she were my servant, I'd have her flayed."

I measured my tone, for Sancia was acutely protective of her rank. "She is my most trusted lady, but I assure you, I shall reprimand her for her disrespect."

As Sancia glowered, I belatedly discerned a change in her, as well— less overt than the one she'd seen in me, perhaps, but one that had nevertheless hardened her in some indefinable way.

"How can Cesare marry you," I ventured, "if you are already Gioffre's wife?"

My question caused her to avert her eyes, her fingers plucking the rich embroidery on her skirts. "Gioffre can't be a husband to me. He . . . he is too young. Cesare loves me. He told me so when we were in Naples."

"Did he?" I wasn't surprised he'd taken her again to his bed, even if it seemed callous in the wake of Juan's death. But he was not in mourning. He never had been. I also detected a frailty in her avowal. Here was the change I had perceived: the covert falsehood she told herself to hide her vulnerability. Sancia of Naples, siren of the court, was the one in love, so much so that she'd transformed her liaison with Cesare into a quest for permanency. Did Cesare feel the same? Much as I wanted to believe it, I could not. My brother had only ever loved two people in his life: Papa and me. I'd not seen any sign in him that Sancia meant more than a bedmate whom he had discarded once before and would no doubt discard again when it suited him. "You might be careful where Cesare is concerned," I said softly. "He often promises what he cannot fulfill."

Sancia squared her shoulders defiantly. "This promise he will keep. He told me he would move heaven and earth to make me his wife and defend Naples from the French, though I doubt either will require much effort. His Holiness now has France on his side. As for my marriage to Gioffre, well, His Holiness had yours to Giovanni dissolved easily enough, did he not?"

I had to stifle sudden laughter. She thought it had been *easy*? She believed my annulment had required only the stroke of Papa's quill? Then again, why wouldn't she? To anyone not mired in the lurid details, it must have seemed the simplest thing in the world.

"It wasn't quite as easy as you think," I said, and as her expression faltered, I added, "Perhaps it will be for you, however." I patted her hand. "I am happy for you. Truly, I am. For you and Cesare. But I must excuse myself. I really should rest before tonight if, as you say, I'm expected to entertain half of Italy. Would you mind terribly?"

"No, no. You've quite an ordeal ahead, with all those envoys sent by your suitors to impress you." She kissed me on the cheek, swirling to the doorway. "Oh, I almost forgot. There is one other who seeks your hand."

I forced myself to widen my smile, thinking I couldn't bear to hear the name of another stranger. "Let us keep it a surprise," I heard myself say.

"I'm quite sure he will be," she replied, and she pulled open the door, tossing over her shoulder, "I'll return after you rest. If that scold is your most trusted lady, then you'll need my help in selecting the appropriate gown. Your Pantalisea dresses like a peasant."

THE SALA DEI Pontefici was crowded to capacity, with smoke from the multitude of standing candelabra and wrought-iron chandeliers adding to the stuffiness. I was perched below the dais on a cushioned stool, watching the courtiers, ambassadors, and nobles parade before us. Papa ambled about the hall, sipping from a goblet, while a page carried the decanter behind him. It disturbed me to see him thus; since Juan's death, Papa drank too much, when he had always shown abstention. Tonight he was visibly intoxicated, jovial and waving his hands, a benevolent Bacchus who kept calling out to various envoys and motioning them over to the foot of the dais to greet me. I sat rigid, my smile taut as I returned their compliments. Sancia had spoken the truth. I was being ogled like a prize calf.

"Try not to look so dejected," Sancia murmured beside me, her crimson gown exposing her shoulders. "I told you, you needn't worry. It's all for show; none has the prestige to win your hand."

I was about to retort that I hardly saw the reason for all this fuss if that were the case, when Cesare suddenly appeared, striding directly toward us.

I had not seen him since his return from Naples. He looked fit, his black hose and doublet adhering to his physique like a silk pelt. A silver chain embedded with garnets was draped across his chest. He must be confident indeed to have eschewed his official robes for such an occasion, considering he had not yet shed his vows. For the first time that evening, I felt a genuine surge of delight—until he neared and I saw his expression.

His eyes blazed. "Where is she?" A few paces behind him, Michelotto sketched a bow in my direction. Inexplicably, his obeisance sent a chill racing up my spine.

Sancia drawled, "My lord, is this any way to greet your sister after so long an absence?"

Cesare clenched his jaw, glancing to where Papa engaged an ambassador in conversation. "I have no time for games. Where is she? You must tell me now."

"Oh, my. Such impatience." Sancia turned to me. "Lucrezia, where has that haughty maidservant of yours wandered off to? Evidently, she is not in your palazzo."

"Pantalisea?" I frowned. "I told her she need not attend me tonight. She requested leave to stroll in the gardens and—"

Cesare turned, pushing his way back through the crowd. I stared after him. My heart started to race. As I rose from my cushion to follow him, Sancia said in a fierce whisper, "You must not interfere. Let your brother do what must be done."

Papa's laughter rang out from across the room; without warning, something about his hollow mirth curdled my blood. "Interfere?" I said angrily. "What are you talking about?"

At that moment, Papa beckoned me. "Lucrezia, come greet His Excellency Signore Capello of Venice." He gestured to the elegant Venetian he'd been speaking with, who bowed.

"Go." Sancia pushed me forward. Stumbling against my hem, I went to my father and stood at his side, directing my attention to the ambassador, though I barely heard his speech. After what seemed an interminable length of time, he bowed again and Papa escorted him away. I suspected it had been a distraction, but when I looked around to search the *sala,* I did not see Cesare anywhere.

I have no time for games. Where is she?

Apprehension flooded me. I began to weave my way toward the far doors leading out of the *sala,* smiling and fending off queries from overdressed matrons and their inebriated husbands, sidestepping cardinals and bishops until just as I reached the doors, someone snagged my sleeve.

It was Sancia, out of breath from following me. "I told you not to interfere," she said, but there was a tremor in her voice, as if she'd feared she might not reach me in time.

"Tell me what this is about. Why does Cesare seek my servants?"

"Not 'servants,'" she said, and her quick glance about us escalated my worry until I felt the tight fit of my bodice squeezing the very breath from my lungs. "He seeks only one."

"Yes, my Pantalisea. Is it because she insulted you today in my chambers? Honestly, Sancia, it was hardly cause to complain to Cesare and have him—"

She whispered, "Don't be a fool. This is about *you*. They must protect you and your son."

I froze. She looked around us again, though there was nothing casual about her dissimulation as she checked for eavesdroppers. "Lucrezia, you cannot think you deceived me. All the rest of Rome, perhaps, but never me. I know you too well. Why else would you have fled to a convent for nine months? Though I must say, *brava* for that performance you put on for the Curia. It is a pity, really; your Pantalisea must be quite adept with her needle, to have disguised your belly so well." She paused. "She knows too much. She was in the convent with you."

I heard my father in my head—*I know what the truth can do*—and I whirled to the passageway into the gardens, even as Sancia grasped me again, yanking me close. "Have you not learned by now that everything we do has a price? They plan a new marriage for you. No one can know your secret. *No one,* do you understand?"

"No," I said. "She will not tell a soul. She'd die before she betrayed me." As soon as I spoke those words, terror engulfed me. I clutched Sancia's hand. "We must stop it. We cannot let him do this!"

She bit her lip. "It is already done. He is determined to—"

Shoving her aside, I took up my heavy skirts and began to run down the passage, my breath burning in my lungs. The entrance to the gardens yawned before me, illumined by flambeaux. The air was moist, redolent of jasmine. It was such a lovely night; nothing bad could happen on a night like this, I thought in a daze, remembering when I'd followed Cesare out here on the evening of Papa's celebratory feast, how we had danced under the moon—

A scream shattered the air.

I whirled to my left, toward a copse of willows draping over fragmented statuary, and saw furtive movement. Every pebble in the path poked the thin soles of my slippers. I sensed something horrible there and tried to quicken my pace, my gown weighing upon me like stone, so that I feared I might fall before I reached the trees.

Cesare appeared, loping toward me. Behind him, Michelotto rose from a crouch; something thin, taut, and gleaming was stretched between his hands—a length of wire.

All of a sudden I could not take another step.

Cesare likewise halted when he saw me, his motionless figure slashed by the flicker of the torches. Then he started to walk slowly, and as he came closer, and closer still, the light picked out the crimson garnets on his neck chain.

He looked exactly as he had in the hall. No blood on his hands or clothes, though it was, I realized, too dark to be sure. Relief made my knees sag. I would have fallen to a heap on the path had he not darted forward to slip an arm about my waist.

"You should not be here," he said, and I smelled his sweat, a pungent musk, and realized the front of his doublet was ripped, as if someone had grabbed hold of it and—

"No." I struggled against him, slamming my palm into his chest. "I want to see." I struck his chest again, harder this time. "I want to see what you have done." But I did not need to see. I knew I had arrived too late. My Pantalisea was already dead.

"You must not," he said, almost in regret. "Trust me, Lucia."

"Dear God." I brought my hands to my mouth and staggered from him, from his handsome face, watching me. "Why? Why would you do this?"

"I had no choice. If I hadn't, Papa would have sent someone else. At least this way, they did not suffer. It is quick, almost painless, when you use the garrote."

Like Djem. He had strangled Pantalisea as he had the Turk. The horror rising in me was so vast, so unbearable, I did not realize at first he had spoken in the plural until he said, "Your maid and Perotto knew too much." I let out a choked wail and began to stumble down the path. He rushed to my side, pulled me back by my arm. "Lucrezia, look at me."

I slowly lifted my eyes. He was still my brother, still Cesare, but in that moment he was like a stranger to me—a malevolent stranger in an inescapable nightmare.

"They had to be silenced," he said. "Rome may speculate about why you remained so long in the convent; they may not believe you stayed out of sight solely because of the dishonor cast on you by Giovanni and the annulment—but only she knew for certain. She witnessed the birth. She also saw Perotto outside the convent; she may have told him about the child—and who sired him. You confided in her, did you not? You told her everything."

"But Perotto is Papa's favorite servant! He would never have—"

Cesare cut me off. "As I said, Papa gave me no choice."

"No choice?" I shrieked. *"You killed them!"*

He flinched. "I did it for you. Hate me if you must; insult me; blame me if that will ease your conscience, but it was done for you. Now only our family will ever know."

"Sancia is not our family." Tears spilled down my face. "She knows. She told me. Must she die, too? Shall I bring her to you so you can silence her with your garrote?"

"Sancia *is* family: She's married to Gioffre. Moreover, we cannot threaten a princess of Naples. She asked Papa about your time in San Sisto; she guessed why you were there, so we felt it best to tell her about the child. She would never have stopped asking, or looking for answers, if we hadn't. But it is all she knows. She has no idea who the father was, and we strongly advise you to keep it that way."

"*We* strongly advise?" I wrenched my arm from him. "Even if that same princess of Naples will soon wed you instead?" As his face registered disbelief, I spat out, "Yes. She told me that, as well. You plan to disavow yourself of the Church and take her as your bride because you need a new title—our brother's own title of Prince of Squillace."

"Lucia," he said haltingly, "you mustn't believe everything you hear—"

Raw laughter erupted from me, seething with rage. "Tell that to Rome! Tell that to everyone who speculates about why I tarried so long in the convent. Post a warning in the piazzas: Woe to those who dare question. Cesare Borgia will silence anyone who utters a word against us." I took dark satisfaction in the pallor that spread across his face as I stepped away from him. As he began to reach out again, I said, "Do not touch me. I do not want to ever see or hear from you again. You should not have done this. I will never forgive you for it."

Turning blindly, I walked back to the palace, not seeing or hearing anything around me, moving in a haze past courtiers spilling out from the *sala,* through the Vatican into the torchlit piazza, crossing to my palazzo and up the staircase to my rooms.

My women waited for me. "Pantalisea has not yet returned," Nicola said anxiously. "She left hours ago to meet with Perotto, but she hasn't come back."

Without a word, I went into my bedchamber and closed the door. Not until I was finally alone did I allow the grief to well up in my throat, shoving my knuckles into my mouth and biting down hard, breaking the skin until I tasted my own blood.

Burying my face in my hands, I wept until I had no more tears left to shed.

CHAPTER TWENTY-EIGHT

Days passed. I stayed sequestered in my palazzo, where Nicola and Murilla fluttered about me, trying to entice me with fruit, slices of cured ham, and *manchego* from Castile. I could barely swallow a mouthful. I grew thin, listless, my eagerness to return to my former life a horrible delusion, a cruel trick of fate. I longed for the placid routine of San Sisto, where I knew what was expected and Pantalisea was always by my side. If I could have, I would have returned to the convent, renouncing all worldly comforts and locking myself inside. But I still had my son, now in my mother's thrall, and the world outside my doors refused to wait.

Within the week, Sancia returned to regale me with my father's excommunication of the friar Savonarola in Florence, whom he'd ordered arrested and condemned to burn at the stake. As I sat silent in my chair, she set my women to airing out my gowns and polishing my jewels while she detailed the friar's terrible demise, how he'd been torn apart on the *strappado*—the rack—and forced to renounce his heresy before he was strung above a pyre and roasted alive. I half-expected to hear the indignant stomp of Pantalisea's foot, her snort of disgust and muttering under her breath about frivolous princesses with too much time to spare and no manners.

But Pantalisea's body had been dragged from the Tiber, found tied up in a sack. A few days later, Perotto's corpse surfaced near an embankment. I paid for their funerals—Perotto consigned to a common grave, while Pantalisea was interred in a local church, her family compensated by Papa for their loss.

Nicola and Murilla were bereft. Sancia assumed the explanation, telling them that my maidservant and her lover had gone into the city and been beset by thieves. It was a paltry excuse; Pantalisea would never have ventured out after dark, given the perils, nor would Perotto, my father's intimate servant, have allowed it. Nevertheless, my women accepted it. So many died at the hands of villains and rogues. Hadn't my brother Juan perished in a similar manner? If violence could claim His Holiness's own son, why not two servants?

Finally I bestirred myself, at Sancia's insistence. "Come," she urged. "You must get dressed and come outside. Let me take you to Vannozza's house. It will do you good."

I realized that in the horror of the past days, submerged as I was in my grief, I had ceased to miss my child. The fear that in some awful part of me, I blamed him, too—had I rid myself of him before his birth, as Pantalisea had suggested, it might have saved her life—compelled me to agree to Sancia's suggestion. Enveloped in a cloak, I went with her to my mother's house, where I beheld my son playing on a blanket in Vannozza's trellised courtyard.

He was beautiful, paddling his plump feet and entranced by the lacings of my sleeve, tugging and tugging until one snapped and he tried to stuff it into his mouth. My sorrow boiled up then, remembering how much Pantalisea had cared for him. I might have wept as I leaned over him, had Vannozza's rebuke not fallen on me like a fist.

"No tears in front of little Juan. He will feel your distress."

I whirled to her. "His name is Rodrigo."

She shrugged. "I changed it for his christening. Juan, or Giovanni in Italian, is now his official name. Your father has claimed the child as his; he would never name a bastard after himself, so it was necessary—as necessary as that unpleasantness with the servants. I assure you, no one took any pleasure in it, but sometimes we must do what is against our nature to protect those we love." Her eyes took in my appalled silence. "Now it is done and we should never speak of it again." Without awaiting my response, she returned to her tasks, leaving me to cradle my son until he drifted off to sleep in my arms.

Then Vannozza came to take him from me.

Sancia was uncharacteristically subdued during our return to my palazzo. As I bade her good night, she said softly, "I never meant to deceive you. I overheard Cesare talking to that manservant of his with the flat eyes: Michelotto. I tried to dissuade him, but he told me to not meddle in matters that did not concern me. He ordered me to keep you occupied in the hall while he and Michelotto went to find them. You were never supposed to know. They were supposed to disappear, their bodies found later, as if it had been an anonymous act."

"But I did know," I said, angrily turning on her. "If you'd deigned to tell me while there was time, I might have prevented it. Instead, you kept silent and now they are dead."

She gave me a despairing look. I wanted to reassure her, for I now realized that nothing we might have done would have changed it, short of whisking Pantalisea and Perotto away from Rome, and even then my father would have found a way. But I did not tell her this; she had betrayed me, just like Papa and Cesare, and so I went into my palazzo alone.

WEEKS LATER, AS I paced the *cortile,* restless and at odds with my own refusal to return to the Vatican, Cesare came to see me.

I did not hear his approach. One minute I was alone, kicking at fallen blossoms from the potted fruit trees; the next, I turned to find him standing under the colonnade, a shadow among the pilasters. Despite everything, the sight of him moved me, even as I affected an impassive stance when he said, "Word is you will not come to see Papa. He says you may as well not have left the convent at all, seeing as you're intent on living cloistered here like a nun."

"Does it surprise him? It shouldn't, after what he ordered you to do."

He made a deprecatory gesture, taking a step toward me. I lifted my hand. "If that is all you came here to say, then you have said it and you may go."

"Lucia," he said. I went still. "Lucia," he repeated, and he moved so swiftly, he was like a streak of dusk, dropping to his knees before me. "Forgive me. I beg you. I will do anything you ask, only do not deny me your love. I cannot bear it."

I tried to resist his imploration, his magnetic proximity. I had vowed to myself since that horrible night that he'd strayed beyond even my capacity for forgiveness. He had hunted Pantalisea and Perotto like prey, killed them in the very gardens of the Vatican. His henchman had bound up their corpses, flung them into the Tiber. I could not reconcile the horror of it with the brother I loved, whom I'd adored even more than my father. He had become someone I did not know, did not want to ever know; and yet, as he knelt before me, his head lowered, I longed to caress the copper curls on his nape, to confess that he knew, as no one else did, that no matter what he did, I could never deny him my love.

"You should have never have done it," I finally whispered.

He lifted his eyes. "I know. . . ." His voice faded into uneasy silence. "If I could change it, I would. I should have persuaded Papa to another recourse. Only he was so determined . . ."

He spoke as though he had broken one of my toys, not cruelly taken two lives. I made myself draw back. He stood, brushing bits of grit from his hose. For a moment, I saw the boy of our childhood, so clever yet also so secretly insecure, always eager to do Papa's bidding, to win the approval our father had lavished on Juan. Papa commanded it and Cesare obeyed. All my thwarted rage and sorrow should have been directed at my father, in truth, for he too had known what would happen that night and given no thought to how it might affect me.

"Why are you here?" I said. "You cannot have come solely to implore my forgiveness or chastise me for denying the Vatican my presence. Papa must want something. What is it?"

He sighed. "You know we've had numerous offers for your hand?" He paused; when I did not confirm or refute his question, he added, "We believe there is one best suited for you."

"Oh?" I felt a terse smile cross my lips. "What if I do not wish to marry again?"

He frowned. "Surely you know we must fulfill our duty, now more than ever. Papa has suspended the inquiry into Juan's murder, against my advice. I told him we must find the culprits, lest the speculation further tarnish our repute, but he says it has become too painful, and it will not bring Juan back. Our enemies rejoice at our loss and seek every advantage in it. The Romagna in particular has become a cesspit of intrigue, abetted by Milan. We cannot let our foes see us weak."

"Yes." I turned away. "I see only that nothing has changed. I want no part of it."

I heard him move closer; I shut my eyes, as if in pain, as he touched my shoulder. "This is why we chose this suitor. I think he will make you happy." I felt his hand tremble. "I want you to be happy, Lucia. You must believe that, even if you believe nothing else."

Without warning, the memory buried deep within surfaced, of his hands upon me in the Villa Imperiale, the strength of his desire, so urgent, like a forbidden rush in my veins—

"Who?" I heard myself say. "Who have you and Papa chosen for me?"

He was silent for a moment before he said, "Alfonso of Aragon."

I couldn't move, turning back around to regard him in incredulity.

"I hear you like him well enough," Cesare went on. "Sancia told me that when he accompanied her here, you found each other agreeable. He's also your age, and King Federico has agreed to make him duke of Bisceglie, so he'll be more worthy to take you as his bride." He paused, frowning at my silence. "Would he please you? Papa says this time, you must not be forced."

I didn't know what to say, let alone how to feel. I had not thought of Alfonso in so long, he almost was like a stranger to me. I'd consigned him to the past, to a brief halcyon moment from a time when I'd not yet understood what it meant to be a Borgia. With a pang, I remembered my joy at meeting a man besides my father or brother whom I might come to love, and then the letter he wrote to me, which I had failed to answer. To marry him now, after everything—it seemed incredible. Impossible. An unexpected gift I no longer deserved.

"Would it please Alfonso?" I managed to ask. "Or has no one bothered to ask him?"

Cesare removed his hand. "He seemed enthused enough by the prospect during my visit to Federico's court."

"You discussed it with him in Naples?" I recoiled. "While I was in San Sisto, awaiting the birth? But my marriage to Giovanni had not yet been annulled."

"And?" He gave me a puzzled look. "Papa instructed me to make overtures. I told you that we've learned to keep Naples on our side. But I promised nothing, if that's what concerns you."

"I see. And with Sancia as your bride, which will keep Naples further on our side, shall we make it a double wedding, brother?"

He gave a derisive chuckle. Then, when he realized I was serious, he said, "I may have ridden the mare, but I have no interest in stabling her. Sancia is Gioffre's wife. So she shall remain."

Though I'd suspected as much, his indifference still took me aback. "Does she know? Because she thinks you love her. She said you promised to move heaven and earth to wed her."

"Did she? She misunderstood. Love cannot serve me. King Federico, on the other hand, can—by giving me his legitimate daughter, Princess Carlotta, currently serving as lady-in-waiting to the royal French widow, Anne of Brittany."

"The same widow King Louis wishes to marry," I said, recalling what Sancia had told me. "Only Louis needs an annulment. And Papa is the only one who can grant it."

"I see you have not completely forgotten the art of politics."

"I am my father's child. It's not something we can easily forget," I replied coldly, even as I thought of Sancia and how wrong she had been. She would not take well having been lied to. Though Cesare might not care, he'd make an enemy of her for this.

"Did Papa truly say he would not force me?" I said.

"Yes. He says he learned his lesson with the Sforza. He wants you to be happy. We both only want you to be happy, Lucia."

I ignored his attempt to appease me. I was not yet ready to return to that place of safety where he had been my protector and confidant—my stalwart brother, who could do no wrong.

"Then tell Papa I shall pray on it," I said, unable to curb the sarcasm in my tone.

His brow arched. "Pray?"

"Yes." I met his stare. "Have you forgotten how? You shouldn't. You have much to atone for."

Without another word, I walked away.

ALFONSO ARRIVED IN mid-July, as the *ponentino* wind stirred the noxious heat of summer. There was no fanfare this time, no extravagant escort or trumpets, no horseback ride in borrowed finery to salute me at my balcony. My bridegroom slipped into the city unannounced, with only a small group of servants, and was greeted at the gate by Cesare and Gioffre, who escorted him to the Vatican to his reception in the papal apartments.

Perhaps it was the surroundings, the windows shuttered by intricate celosias, turning the light saffron as it sifted through the apertures. Or perhaps it was my awareness of my appearance, clad in black velvet with a jewel-studded stomacher, my girdle edged in pearls, the symbols of chastity. I'd twined my hair in a gold-filigree caul and refused Sancia's attempt to paint my face—"You're sallow as an invalid," she exclaimed, "after all these weeks indoors!"—because I did not want him to think me frivolous. But I knew that no matter how much care I had taken, he must have heard the rumors even in Naples, of my failed marriage and confinement in a convent.

Whichever the reason, the moment he stepped into the room in his gray doublet, broad-shouldered and with the sheen of sweat still on his brow, his short stature made taller somehow by his confidence, all I could see, all I could feel, was him.

I wanted nothing more than to be his.

Dropping to one knee, he kissed Papa's foot. He did not seem to have changed in the two years since we'd seen each other, and I had to remind myself, as Sancia elbowed me and he turned to greet the cardinals, that there was no reason he should have. He had gone home to fight for Naples; he had not suffered the collapse of a marriage, a violent attack, a forced refuge, or the birth of a child he could never claim. . . .

Then he came before me. The scent of him—of velvet and salt, of the tang of horseflesh clinging to his clothes—overwhelmed me. His eyes were darker than I recalled, a deeper brown than the mellow honey hue I remembered, but they still riveted me, so that I could not look away as he bowed and Sancia chided me, "Your hand. You must give him your hand."

I quickly extended my fingers, devoid of rings. His lips were soft as they brushed my skin, the slightest touch of warmth before his eyes lifted again to mine.

"My lady Lucrezia," he said.

"My lord Alfonso," I replied.

My heart was beating so hard, I thought he must hear it. The whole room must hear it, a thundering announcement that betrayed my desire.

"Well?" Papa grumbled, and only then did I realize Alfonso and I were staring at each other, our hands entwined in the space between us.

Cesare drawled, "I believe they approve, Holiness."

Papa beamed. "Good! Then let us proceed to the ceremony and the feast. I see no reason to delay what the Almighty has ordained."

Around us, a burst of movement—the cardinals and others were making haste to the double doors to secure seats in the chapel. My fingers felt melded to Alfonso's; I had to make a conscious effort to not clutch at his hand like a child who had finally been found after wandering for years, lost in a tangled wood.

He could be my savior. While he was beholden to Papa for the privilege of marrying me, he had royal blood, with the power of Naples at his back. He was not like Giovanni, dependent on whichever crumbs his relatives tossed his way. Alfonso was respected, cherished by his family. He could make me happy, I thought, staring into his eyes and seeing myself reflected there. But the mere hope of happiness terrified me. He might be a prince in his own right, but could that protect him from my family's exigencies and caprices? Or, like Giovanni before him, would he find himself trapped, forced to choose between pleasing or enraging us?

I made myself push aside any thoughts of my first husband, wondering if Alfonso could sense it upon me, my tumultuous past like a dark shade at my side. He did not know—indeed, must *never* know—the travails I had undergone to reach this moment, but he must be aware, for his hand tightened on mine, and though he did not say a word, I felt his strength in his grip, the silent reassurance that emanated from him.

He was trying to tell me I was not alone anymore.

But could I do the same? Could I in turn keep him safe?

Then he said, his voice low but strong: "Are you certain, my lady?"

He offered me the choice. If I told him I was not, he would indeed depart. Nothing Papa said or did would deter him. I did not have to relinquish him, after all, because he would enter our union only if I, and I alone, allowed it. This was not about family alliances or political convenience: It was about us—him and me. And I felt a surge of relief, because I knew he would never permit himself to be lured into something he was not fully prepared for.

"If you are," I whispered.

He smiled. "I've been certain from the very hour I first met you."

THE CEREMONY WAS simple. As Botticelli's melancholic angels watched from the walls, the Spanish *capitan* of the guard, Juan Cervillon, held the symbolic sword over our heads and we recited the vows that bound us in Matrimony.

We heard Mass, and then the assembly filed into the hall for the nuptial banquet. All the while, it felt like a dream from which I must soon awaken. I kept glancing at Alfonso's profile, at his strong, slightly askew nose and sculpted jaw, his tawny hair loose upon shoulders that strained the fit of his doublet. I remembered how I thought he would look better unclothed and realized I would soon have opportunity to verify it. I actually felt heat flood my cheeks and must have squeezed his hand involuntarily, for he turned his head to me and winked.

Our companies crammed into the *sala,* where linen-draped trestle tables bunted with wreaths of sunflowers had been set up. The sounds of chatter and clacking heels on the floor deafened me; it was not until I was upon the dais that voices raised in dispute from across the room reached me.

I looked up. My stomach knotted as I saw Sancia, confronting Cesare at the hall entrance.

"Enough!" my brother snarled, loud enough for us to overhear. "I will not have a fracas at my own sister's wedding."

"What about *us?*" Sancia shot back, even as Gioffre cringed at her side. "You promised me. You said we would—"

Cesare caught her by the wrist, "I said, enough," but by now everyone had stopped to stare. "This is not the place or time. We shall discuss it later."

Beside me, Alfonso tensed. Sancia thrust out her chin, lifting her voice even more. "I think not. I think we shall never speak again." She marched to her table, her women scuttling behind. Gioffre cast a miserable look at Cesare before he trudged after his wife.

With a mien of distaste, Cesare returned to the dais he shared with Papa.

Alfonso remarked, "I wonder what the trouble is?"

I glanced warily at him. He really did not know, after Sancia and Cesare had frolicked at his very court?

He smiled. "Whatever it is, no doubt Sancia is to blame. I am afraid my sister has always had a foul temper. She must have provoked my lord Cesare beyond reason, as she's apt to do with every man who is not her brother or a saint."

I found myself saying, "She might have a sharp tongue, but I do not fault her in this instance." I tested his willingness to admit that he knew of Sancia and Cesare's tangled history.

But he only said, "Perhaps," and motioned to the page behind us to pour wine. "But whatever the cause, our grandfather indulged her too much. He often said that what she really needed was a whipping to show her her proper place, but I don't recall him ever giving her one."

"No woman, no matter how sharp her tongue, should ever be whipped," I retorted, but my hand trembled as I reached for my goblet. For a blinding moment, I saw Giovanni thrusting a knife against my throat as he shoved me onto the bed.

Then I felt Alfonso touch my leg under the table. "Forgive me," he murmured. "It is only that Sancia can test the patience of any man."

"She is your sister, my lord. Regardless of her behavior, you owe her your respect."

"Yes." He nodded solemnly. "I do, indeed. I spoke out of turn." A slight smile crinkled the sun-bronzed creases at his eyes. "God help anyone who ever dared raise a whip to my sister."

I laughed uneasily. "She has my admiration for it."

The music began, an unobtrusive accompaniment to the procession of roasted meats, sauced fowl, and heaving platters of sugared fruits, though more than half of the fabulous creations paraded before us were so thick with gilt that when Alfonso started to request a serving, I had to stop him. His brow creased. "Why not?"

"Because those dyes are poisonous," I told him. "The dishes are for display. A guest at an Orsini wedding once ate everything set before him and perished of it. His servants also nearly killed one another fighting over his corpse, as it was full of precious metals." I saw his frown deepen. "Do you not serve ornamental dishes in Naples?"

He shook his head, as if amazed, then suddenly let out an uproarious laugh—so loud and unrestrained, it reminded me of Sancia's.

"What do you find so amusing?" I asked, and he said, "Ornamental dishes that are also poisonous. It is rather fitting, don't you think?"

I stiffened. "You find the possibility of death fitting?"

He leaned to me. "Surely you have heard what they say, that the Borgia invite foes to dine and then they sow death in their food? Now we can confirm the falsehood of such rumors. The poison, in fact, is quite visible."

I stared at him, appalled.

His amusement crumbled. "It was but a joke," he said hastily. "I would never believe—"

"I should hope not." My spine flattened against my chair, my displeasure so overt that I saw Papa out of the corner of my eye frowning from his dais. "I never heed rumors, my lord," I added frostily. "I would not countenance such defamation of my family." Even, I thought, if they might sometimes deserve it.

He gulped his wine. "Yes, that too was most insensitive of me. It would seem I am determined to make a disaster of this day."

His evident discomfort thawed me. I knew from Sancia that Neapolitans were more carefree in their demeanor, less given to the subtleties of Rome. As Alfonso struggled to say something that would not offend, I realized that while he'd been reared in a dangerous court and surely understood what others were capable of, surprisingly it had not censured him.

Unbelievable as it seemed, my new husband said precisely what he thought.

It occurred to me that an idle afternoon in the library could not predict a lifetime. As with Giovanni before him, I knew almost nothing about this man I had wed.

I attempted to hide my consternation. To my relief, I heard the music livening: A trilling of pipes preceded the appearance of dancers clad in white, wearing magnificent headdresses with masks fashioned in the shapes of mythical beasts. The dancers leapt into a *saltarello,* the favored dance of the courts of Spain, but I recognized Cesare at once among them.

His ivory satin hose enhanced his sculpted thighs and narrow waist, and his flowing shirt was open to his chest; he pirouetted and knifed his legs back and forth. He wore the mask of the unicorn, its water-stiffened velvet horn jutting from his forehead, his eyes flashing within diamond-sequined holes. His partner was a flame-haired woman with a bejeweled domino resembling a griffin, her cleavage exposed by her low-cut silver bodice. As she whirled about Cesare, skirts frothing over supple insteps, he snatched her by the waist and kissed her suggestively on her throat, all the while looking directly at me.

I went rigid. As the dance proceeded, I finally dared to glance at Alfonso. He reclined in his chair with an indulgent smile, tapping out the melody on his goblet. If he took note of Cesare's brazen display, my husband did not reveal it. But as I then surveyed the hall, where most of our guests lolled, gorged on meat and wine, I saw Sancia with Gioffre at the table by Papa's dais.

She looked enraged. Flinging her napkin aside, she came to her feet. Gioffre darted a confused glance at our father, clearly uncertain as to whether he should follow his wife's example; from his throne, Papa flicked his hand, ordering my little brother to stay put. He then turned his face deliberately away as Sancia yanked at her gown peremptorily and, with her women in a dejected file behind her, stormed from the hall.

"She doesn't like being made a fool," said Alfonso, bringing my gaze back to him. "The only thing worse than her temper is her pride." His hand crept over mine in my lap, braiding my fingers. "But we do not need to concern ourselves with such upsets, do we?"

With those words, he betrayed that he knew perfectly well the reason for Sancia and Cesare's altercation. He also was saying that, unlike them, he and I did not have any need for temper or pride.

"Your father has stipulated we must reside in Rome for a full year after our marriage," he went on. "I agreed, naturally, but once the year is over, we shall return to Naples to set up our own household." He paused, lifting his other hand to my cheek. "That is, if you do not object?"

"No," I said immediately, although after my experience in Pesaro, I had every reason to inform him that all the horses in his kingdom could not drag me to Naples, which was an even greater distance from Rome. But I did not. Because in that instant, as he took my hand under the table while his other hand cupped my chin, I would have agreed to go with him to the New World on a leaking galleon if he had asked it of me.

"I think the time has come for us to retire," he said, and I nodded, voiceless, as he brought me to my feet and the cacophony of talk and clinking cups and swirling dancers came to a halt, like a pantomime frozen in mid-revelry.

I glanced at Cesare. Beads of perspiration slipped from under his mask, his curls plastered to his skull; I felt his gaze stalking us as we went to Papa and made our obeisance. Papa assented with a beatific smile, motioning for an escort of guards to accompany us to my palazzo.

"Is no one else coming with us?" I asked Alfonso, as we moved to the hall doors.

"His Holiness made stipulations," he replied, "and thus so have I. There will be no public bedding or proof of consummation. This night, wife, belongs to us alone."

No ONE HAD thought to prepare a nuptial suite for us, but Nicola and Murilla, bless their hearts, had lit scented tapers in my bedchamber and waited outside, curtsying with barely suppressed giggles as Alfonso and I stepped past them. I cast a chiding look at them; Nicola's eyes gleamed with mischief, while Murilla puffed out her little chest in imitation of Alfonso and lifted her eyebrows in saucy approval.

The door clicked shut. Alfonso stood behind me; I felt his stomach, hard and flat, pressed against the small of my back. "At last," he breathed. His mouth was at my throat, his hands unraveling my hair, undoing ribbons, removing the latticed hairnet, tossing it all aside like so much tinsel as I stood, motionless. Though I tried to subdue them, fractured images of the night Juan had assaulted me returned, paralyzing me. It was the first time a man had touched me in this way, and my terror was such that I could scarcely draw breath.

He paused. Desolation grew inside me as he took a small, deliberate step back. I had feared his touch, but now that I did not feel it, I feared its loss even more.

"I have no wish to force myself on you," he said, "if my caresses displease you."

I turned around too fast; my apprehension must have shown on my face even as I said, "You—your caresses do please me."

"Do they? Because if I had to hazard a guess, I would say you are terrified."

"I am most certainly not." I tried to sound defiant. "Lest you forget, I've been married before, my lord. I know well what is expected of me."

He sighed. "And I know well that you are not what they claim."

My throat tightened. "I told you, I do not heed rumors. I therefore have no idea who they are or what they say," I replied, but I did know. While I'd been kept isolated from the rabble and their vicious gossip, I suspected all too much what had been said about me—the Borgia daughter, whose own husband had forsaken her, declared her the object of her own father's lust, and in retaliation been obliged to admit his impotency. In the end, Giovanni's shame had been less than mine, for he had wed anew and could prove he was not incapable with another wife, while I . . . I must live with the scandal of his insinuations for the rest of my days.

"No?" Alfonso looked down for a moment. When he lifted his eyes, his face was somber. "You should. Everyone, especially those like us, should know what is being said."

The atmosphere in the room shifted; I crossed my arms at my chest, warding off a sudden chill. "I . . . I do not want to know. What good can it do me?"

I heard Papa in my voice, his warning about the evil perceived of our family, and dreaded what Alfonso might say next. I could not bear to hear how they spoke of me in Naples, the garish speculation, the lewd innuendos that might carry seeds of truth.

Instead, he moved closer. "I know your first marriage was not of your choosing. Nor can I imagine it was pleasing. I do not know the details, but I promise you, on my life, that I will never harm or oblige you. If you prefer to bed alone tonight, I will leave without dishonor. I am willing to wait as long as is necessary until you are ready."

Gratitude eased my fear. He did not ask for the truth, though he must have suspected I was not the innocent my father had proclaimed, that we'd in fact lied and perhaps not only about my virginity. He merely awaited a response, inviting but not insistent. I remembered when I'd kissed him on impulse in the library, and as I thought of how marvelous it would be to love freely, not out of obligation, I heard myself say, "I think I have always been ready for you."

After that, there were no more words. The pain of the past melted into sensation, a slow-building rapture that made me feel faint as he peeled away my garments until I stood naked before him, my hair coiling to my waist. He gazed at me with that same wonderment I had first seen in the library. I made myself stand still, as if he were about to draw me, not raising my arms to cover my nipples, which were teased by his gaze and by the air on my skin, not using my hands to shield the golden triangle between my legs, which until this moment no man had fully seen.

"My God, you are beautiful," he said, his voice thick. "Like that work by Botticelli, the one of Venus on her shell, all white and pink and gold, as if you have just risen from the sea."

My mouth went dry; I felt the heat of my flush. He dropped to his haunches before me and reached behind to cup my buttocks, bringing me to him. When I felt his tongue like a current of lightning, I could not curb the moan that came from my lips.

I threw my head back. My knees began to buckle. My fingers tangled in his hair as he went deeper, deeper, and I heard myself gasp and cry at the same time, exploding from within. He drew me to the carpet, his fingers everywhere, his clothing seeming to dissolve on its own. As he reared over me, I beheld a Herculean chest so very different from my brother's, wide and heavy with muscle, matted with dark-blond hair that felt like coarse silk. His arms, hewn of granite, braced on either side of me; he seemed enormous, a giant. Against my thighs, his hard member pulsed. With my eyes fixed on his, I reached down and grasped its length. He surged in my palm.

"I cannot . . . wait," he groaned.

Rearing my hips to meet his, I welcomed him inside.

As he plunged, as his mouth met mine and fused our breath, I discovered I was indeed still a virgin—in every way but one.

CHAPTER TWENTY-NINE

We spent the next weeks in bliss.

He taught me all the lessons he knew, and I was eager to show him how much I could learn. I must have proved adept, judging by his moans and the eager spill of his seed. He tasted just as he smelled, of spindrift, and my taste in his mouth, he told me, was like powdered aniseed. Even after we bathed and ventured out to take our meals (during which my women could not stop giggling, no doubt having been entertained through the keyhole by our frolics), he vowed he could still smell me on him like an indelible perfume.

That summer of 1498 was the happiest I could remember. My new husband did more than show me about the passion and candor that could exist between a man and his wife. His love of nature and books, his delight in afternoon strolls in the gardens after a day spent digging through the library or a ride to the pine-forested hills about Rome, where he liked to fly falcons or hunt quail, made me realize I had not loved until now, not truly, not like those who knew they were deeply cherished. I had thought my family was enough, that I was such a part of them that we could never be separate. Alfonso chipped away at my belief. He broke it piece by piece, like a brittle carapace that revealed pliant silk within, which he molded to his image. As we lay satiated, sheets tossed about us, I saw myself in his eyes like a goddess incarnate, and I could have wept in joyous relief that at last I had found the one I belonged with, the companion I had yearned for without knowing it.

"I am yours," I whispered, my head on his shoulder, his arms enveloping me. "Yours forever, till death do us part."

He always fell asleep quickly, like a child without worries. "Do not speak of death in bed," he murmured, tightening his hold. "I am Neapolitan; for us, it is bad luck."

I smiled. I could not wait to see Naples. I longed to leave Rome and the past behind, to embark on our new life. It was only as I started to drift off, buoyed on spent lust and his gentle snores, that I remembered my son. I wondered what he was doing in that moment, if he was asleep in his crib with his little fists bunched at his face, if he was warm and loved in my mother's house. It seemed a crime that I could feel such happiness without him, that I could contemplate going to Naples and leaving him behind. Dread crept through me then, a ghost I could never fully exorcise. I could not keep this secret forever. I would have to confess. Alfonso must be told that, in addition to being his wife, I was a mother who desperately missed her child.

Yes, he must be told. Just not yet.

❧

IN AUGUST, PAPA obliged the cardinals to return to Rome from their summer retreats. Before their begrudging faces, Cesare, fully armed with papal approval, requested leave to renounce his holy vows. He symbolically set down his crimson cap and bowed his tonsured head to become a secular man once more, free to pursue a carnal life, including marriage, if he chose.

"Naturally, the Spanish ambassador had to raise a fuss," he told me as we supped al fresco in my palazzo. Alfonso had gone into the city with his bodyguard, Tomasso Albanese, and Cesare had arrived unexpectedly. Though we had not been alone in some time and I was wary of him, he seemed not to notice my reserve, regaling me with news of his latest imbroglio. "He rebuked Papa for letting me 'shed so lightly' the honor bestowed upon me by Christ"—Cesare rolled his eyes—"though I rather think Their Catholic Majesties are less concerned with my lack of religious devotion than they are with my choice of a French bride."

"So you are going to wed Princess Carlotta?" I said, taking a bite of bread stuffed with smoked ham and trying to maintain my reserve and not display my flare of interest in his affairs. "Papa has agreed to let you travel to France to pay suit to her?"

He nodded, twirling his goblet. He reclined in his chair, his long body at ease, but I could see traces of his recurring ailment. He had a new sore at the corner of his mouth, and a few recently scabbed spots on his throat and cheeks. His hands too were marred; to me, it appeared as though his fever had resurged with an alarming new virulence, but he made light of it when I asked, saying it was less severe than the first bout he'd suffered. He still referred to it as a tertian, but to me he did not look well, and those spots were troubling, even if his spirit seemed unaffected.

"Papa wants to send me as soon as possible," he now said. "The French wait to receive me. King Louis has offered me an estate and the title of Duke of Valence; they already call me Il Valentino. It has a nice ring to it, don't you think?" Downing his wine, he immediately reached for the flagon. His fourth cupful in less than two hours, I noted, when in the past he would rarely have finished one. "But we still have some challenges to overcome, mainly persuading all the cardinals to put their seals on the decree for Louis's annulment and convincing that weasel Federico to make good on his promise to support my suit."

Disquiet stole over me. "But I thought King Federico had expressed himself in favor of you marrying his daughter?"

Cesare scowled. "He did. I was there to crown him at the time; he would have said anything. Yet now he reneges, citing that unless we can arbitrate the disputes in the Romagna—which we've no intention of doing right now—he cannot support seeing his daughter wed to me. These Neapolitans are all the same. You cannot trust—"

"Is that so?" said Alfonso. I turned in my seat to find him standing in the gallery, still in his cloak, his manservant close by.

"My lord," I said, flustered. "We—we were not expecting you so soon."

"Evidently." Alfonso unfastened his cloak, handed it to Albanese, and waved him off. Drawing up a chair, he began to ladle olives, slices of cheese, and cold chicken onto a plate. He ate with his hands, his appetite hearty. "What is this about mistrusting my uncle Federico?" he asked Cesare, who regarded him with unconcealed disdain. "Perhaps I can be of help."

"I doubt it," my brother said, slamming his goblet onto the table.

Alfonso chuckled. "You doubt what, precisely? My specific ability to influence my uncle or my general inability to influence anything?"

"Both." Cesare stood abruptly, startling me, as he had always been courteous to Alfonso. His change in attitude reminded me of how he'd treated Giovanni Sforza. "I believe I have been misled, my lord, by said uncle and indeed by your own self. Had I known in Naples that your family would throw so much dust in my face, I might not have been so eager to see you to my sister's bed."

Alfonso shrugged. I found myself gripping my chair as he chewed his food before he said, "I did not mislead you when we spoke in Naples. I did indeed wish to marry Lucrezia, and I believe she wanted to marry me, as well—which, as it turns out, she did. As for this matter concerning my uncle, he is within his rights to decide who is best suited to wed his daughter, as you would agree if you only took a moment to consider his purpose rather than your pride."

"Meaning?" Cesare's voice was taut.

"Meaning she is a legitimate princess of Naples and—"

"I am but the bastard of the pope." He threw out his hand, sending his goblet crashing to the tiles. "I am well versed in Naples's ploys, Signore. I came to manhood whilst your ogre of a grandfather, Ferrante, schemed and plundered his way to his grave; I know how much you esteem your own words. And lest you forget, some might say you are as much a bastard as I am, seeing as the French claim to that rock you call a kingdom could be declared more valid than your family's, should His Holiness my father set his mind to it."

Alfonso's smile did not reach his eyes. "I never denied that my father sired me out of wedlock or that I bear no legitimate claim to the throne." He paused. "But you appear to seek such a claim for yourself through marriage to Carlotta. How can you not see that the situation might prove somewhat vexing for her father, who also has his heirs to protect?"

Cesare's expression grew so icy, I actually began to rise from my chair, my hand held out as if to ward him off. "Come now. Is this necessary? Surely Alfonso can assist by at least writing to his uncle to ask that he reconsider—"

"No." Cesare spat out his refusal as if it were a seed stuck in his teeth. "I forbid it. If Federico chooses to refute his promise, then let him learn what comes from it." He glared at Alfonso. "I will thank you, my lord, not to interfere," and with a terse incline of his head in my direction, he left us.

I heard Arancino wander under the table, purring. "He is . . . not himself," I said to Alfonso. "He has been ill and at Papa's side constantly—he did not mean what he said."

Alfonso reached down to pet my cat, who, perversely, after having disdained every other male touch, had discovered he could not resist my husband's. "I think Cesare knows exactly what he says. He despises me."

"Why would you say that?" I protested. "Did he not negotiate our own marriage?"

"He did, but now he finds cause to regret it." Plucking a sliver of chicken from his plate, Alfonso fed it to Arancino. "If Cesare Borgia does not get his way, the alliance that binds us could sour." He turned pensive. "Should that occur, you may have to choose whose side you are on."

"Side? But he is my brother. His Holiness is my father."

"And I am your husband." He wiped his hands on my discarded napkin. Rounding the table, he kissed my cheek. "As I said on our wedding night, I would never oblige you. Yet neither shall I sit by and wait for them to do to me what they did to the Sforza of Pesaro. Should it become necessary, I will fight them—with or without you."

He did not await my reply. Turning away, he retreated to the wing Giovanni had once occupied, which had since been appointed for Alfonso, though he never used it save to store his possessions and provide a place for his servants to sleep.

Arancino leapt onto the table and began to tear at the chicken carcass. I let him eat his fill as I stared after Alfonso, not able to decipher if what I felt was fury that my husband dared doubt me or foreboding that he might have reason to do so.

For the first time since our marriage, that night we slept apart.

As AUTUMN WINDS set the pennants depicting our bull, rampant against a scythed sun, snapping, we gathered to bid Cesare farewell. He was departing for France, accompanied by an escort that not only eclipsed the retinue that had accompanied Juan to Spain but also made him the talk of Rome, with rumors running wild that even the shoes of his horses were made of silver and his pages' livery fringed in real gold.

It was not true, of course. His horses and pages, plentiful as these were, wore the usual trappings, though the same could not be said of their master. Determined to have Cesare arrive in France like the prince he would become, Papa had sold the benefices of his forsaken cardinal-ship for a profit of two hundred thousand ducats, now turned into the bejeweled accessories that filled Cesare's caskets. My brother himself wore white damask studded in pearls, his sumptuous velvet cloak girded off the shoulder in the French style, his plumed cap sporting a fiery brim of rubies, under which his features were covered by a half mask of fine gauze to hide the scars of his ailment. I had wanted to express my concern that he should leave while still obviously unwell, but with him and Alfonso at odds, it was better for all if he did. As he held my hands tight, Cesare said, "You must take care, Lucia. I expect to read only hap-piness in your letters." He sidled closer. "I shall not be gone long. When I return, I will have everything we need to ensure that no one challenges us again."

He referred to the supremacy of our family, to which my husband now belonged, yet I heard a threat in his voice that caused me to draw back. We stood paces from Papa, who sat on his dais overlooking the piazza. The papal court congregated around us, while the populace lin-ing the barricaded route guffawed and drank free claret flowing from the fountains.

"You must take care, as well," I finally said. When I looked into his eyes, they were like scorched holes within his mask. "*Forza e in bocca al lupo.* Show moderation in all things, for the sake of our peace of mind and your own continued health."

His gaze narrowed. Then he smiled and bent to me for our goodbye kiss. I stifled a gasp when I felt his teeth nip my lip. "Do not stray too far from the fold," he whispered. "I am finding it more difficult than I imagined to see you love another."

Before I could utter a response, he turned to Papa with a swirl of his cape and knelt to kiss the papal slipper. Papa embraced him. As Cesare proceeded into the piazza, where his Mantua steed awaited, I glanced at my father. Cold satisfaction slipped over his face, in startling contrast to the tearful sorrow he had shown at Juan's departure.

I had the unsettling impression that, rather than celebrate the son he had just exalted, Papa still grieved for the one he had lost.

THE NATIVITY FESTIVITIES came and went in a blur of frankincense and Masses. With the taste of the host still on my tongue, we welcomed the new year of 1499 and advent of Carnival, that time of hedonistic indulgence that preceded Ash Wednesday and the austerity of Lent. Together with Alfonso, Papa and I donned beaded masks and stood on the balcony of the Castel Sant'Angelo to greet revelers. But the winter had been harsh, with biting winds and incessant rain swelling the Tiber to overflowing, and we saw few people, though we remained for over an hour under the dripping canopy. Finally we retreated indoors, soaked to our skins.

"Your famous Roman carnival leaves much to be desired," declared Alfonso, shivering as we undressed in our suite and plunged into the large linen-lined copper tub prepared for us. He ducked his head under the hot rosewater, surfacing with his hair slicked like liquid gold from his brow, his newly grown beard glistening with slivers of petals as he eyed me with that lazy gaze I had come to know so well.

We had not spoken about our dispute. Although months had passed, I remained uneasy over his suspicions of my family. It seemed pointless now, with Cesare gone to the French court for what would surely be months, if not longer; still, my uneasiness prickled me as he crooked a finger and said in a husky voice, "Come here."

I floated to his arms, his hardness sending a startled thrill through me as he drew me to him. "I am freezing. You must warm me."

"You do not seem very cold to me." I flattened my hands on his chest, pushing him away.

He growled. "Would you refuse your husband?"

I pointed at his chin. "Your beard scratches. It feels like I'm being kissed by a bear."

"What, this? I would have you know, Madonna, that beards are the latest style among fashionable lords. Any man who can grow one does, and if he can't, he—"

"Buys a face wig?" I teased, and Alfonso yanked me to him, my body slippery as an eel caught in his net. "Kiss me now," he demanded, and I did. As I felt him pulsing against my thigh, I finally ventured, "Are you still angry over what Cesare said to you that day?"

"I had forgotten about it," he replied, but the tightening of his brow told me he had not. "And I was never angry. Your brother is a Borgia; he has too much pride. He and Sancia, in truth, would have made the perfect couple." He chuckled. "Or ended up killing each other in their bed."

"Yet I share the same Borgia blood," I persisted, needing to hear what he truly thought. "It stands to reason that if you doubt him, you must doubt me, too."

He took my hand, brought it under the water to his erect manhood. "Does this feel as if I doubt you?" He lifted me up, sliding me upon him. A moan escaped me. He thrust upward. "I do not doubt you, sweet Lucrezia," he whispered. "I want and desire you—always."

The water splashed in waves over the sides of the tub, wetting the floor. His groans grew so loud that I started to giggle, pushing my hand over his mouth to shush him, lest the servants outside our door (forever eavesdropping) overheard.

He did not care, and by the time we were done, neither did I. But I did not fail to note that he had not fully answered my question.

THE WINDS WANED. A sullen sun emerged from the brooding clouds and we repaired to the countryside, to hunt and dine in a cardinal's villa. Alfonso was full of vigor, having taken down a brace of quail and five rabbits earlier in the day with the white goshawk that Papa gave him for Christmas—an exquisite creature, brought with great expense to Rome from the northern wastes of Iceland. Alfonso had fallen in love with the falcon at first sight, naming her Bianca and letting her reside in a silver-chased cage in our rooms, feeding her chunks of raw meat with his own hands, and adorning her with jesses of gilt and a sapphire-studded hood that brought out the azure shadows in her plumage.

"I'm beginning to think he loves that bird more than me," I remarked to Sancia as we strolled through the vineyard, past trellises hung with winter-shriveled vines. "Look at him. He cannot keep his eyes off her."

"He does seem infatuated, doesn't he?" Sancia laughed. She had reverted to her ebullient self, obsessed with gossip, clothes, and impressing every man she met, just because she could. I'd had opportunity to observe her at numerous feasts and ceremonial occasions in the Vatican, and she seemed oblivious to Cesare's absence or the humiliation she'd endured at his hands, thrown aside for another Neapolitan princess whose legitimate birthright promised more than she could ever deliver.

"Gioffre wants one, too." I couldn't help but smile as I watched my younger brother venture to the imperious goshawk perched on Alfonso's gauntlet. "I think I shall ask Papa to buy him one for his seventeenth birthday. Does that sound agreeable?"

I let my suggestion linger. She nodded absently. "Whatever you deem best."

I sighed. "Are you still not . . . ?"

She gave me an exasperated look. "Must we discuss it?"

"Well, it has been almost five years since you and he wed, and—"

"I know how long it has been." Sancia picked up her skirts, exposing the wood patens we both wore to avoid muddying our satin slippers as we navigated the rain-glutted path. "His Holiness has already spoken to me about it. He scolded me for not bearing him grandchildren." I heard the edge in her voice. "Gioffre is willing enough, but I cannot endure him pawing at me."

"I am sorry to hear it," I mumbled.

"Yes, well. We cannot all be so fortunate in our husband as you. Now, let us forget my woeful state. Have you heard the latest about your other brother?" Her voice turned avid. "No? Oh, you do need to get out of your marriage bed more often. It is the talk of Europe! King Louis received our Valentino with due pomp, but it seems the French court laughed at him behind their sleeves for being *so* overdressed." She smiled in cruel delight, for which I could not fault her. "And despite the king's promise to hasten Cesare's marriage to Carlotta, he has kept our lord entertained yet unfulfilled, as she apparently refuses to even consider it."

As I cringed inwardly, imagining how enraged Cesare must be, Sancia added, "Louis now seeks alliance for him with another princess, though I hardly think that after all the effort and expense, Valentino will be willing to settle for— Watch your step!"

She lunged for my arm, but I was already slipping, my muddied hem tangled about my patens, tripping me on a stone in the path. I barely felt the fall, cushioned by my cloak and gown, but it knocked the air out of me, so that I lay flat on my stomach, gasping, partly amused by my own clumsiness and partly mortified as I heard frantic footsteps racing toward me.

Alfonso knelt beside me, his face white. "*Amore,* are you hurt?"

I shook my head. "Help me up." Taking his hand, I let him haul me to my feet, my surroundings swimming about me as I grappled for my bearings. His men looked on in concern; I saw Papa rise up from his chair on the villa's terrace, a hand at his brow. At his side, Gioffre struggled to hold my husband's flapping goshawk on his arm.

"Such a fuss." I turned to Alfonso. "I only stumbled and—" A sudden cramp cut off my voice, and I grimaced, tried to draw breath. All of a sudden I heard my own whimper, followed by Alfonso's urgent cry—"She is injured!"—and, to my horror, I felt something hot and liquid seep down my thighs.

"No, my love. Do not weep." Alfonso cradled me in his arms. We lay in the villa's rumpled bed, which had been hastily prepared by the stunned cardinal and his servants, for by the time Alfonso carried me into the house, blood dripped off my soiled slippers. After I was brought to the strange room, Sancia had barely loosened my stays before the unformed mass gushed from me onto the floor.

"I did not know," I whispered. "If I had, I would have done anything, everything, to safeguard our . . . our—"

I could not say it. I could not believe I had miscarried something so precious, so easily, when I had carried Juan's seed to fruition. I desperately wanted to tell Alfonso everything in that moment, as I felt his chest convulse and knew he too struggled to keep grief at bay. I wanted to reassure him that I had brought a babe into the world before and had felt, almost from the moment of conception, the sacredness of the life inside me.

Yet when I summoned the courage, all that came out was an admission I did not realize I also carried, like an incurable canker: "Maybe I am to blame."

Alfonso cupped my chin. "Blessed saints, why would you say that?"

"Because of my family . . . God has cursed me."

"Their sins are not yours." He drew me back to him. "Do you hear me? You have been wronged. God must look upon you with great compassion for everything you have endured."

Had he finally learned the truth? For a terrible instant, I thought Sancia had told him out of vengeance for what Cesare had done to her. She must suspect who had sired my child, though she'd not mentioned it again since the night of the murders. I felt ashamed to doubt her, but I did. And as I sought Alfonso's gaze, I dreaded something else I could not admit: the fact that, while I had known I carried my brother's child, I had not felt Alfonso's. I had not sensed new life in me at all. Sancia had breathlessly reassured me in those chaotic moments as my women cleaned the blood from the floor: She said I could not have known, for it was too early; there wasn't anything recognizable as a child at all. But I averted my face as she left to fetch Alfonso, who waited anxiously outside the door. I heard her murmuring to him before he came in, and I wondered that I could have been so oblivious, that I failed to heed any signs.

Had I ignored his child because a new life would supplant the one I had forsaken?

Now, as he regarded me tenderly, dabbing my tears with his fingertips, I searched his face for signs of that first corrosive doubt he would surely feel upon learning I had deceived him by bearing a child out of wedlock. I couldn't endure the thought, the questions that would follow, which would only lead to more tangled lies, until he took it upon himself to find out the entire truth.

To my relief, I saw nothing but sorrow and worry for me. I knew then the real reason I could not bring myself to tell him: I could not risk him trying to forgive me and failing, could not risk that in time he'd grow to hate me for it, turn against me and never look at me like this again. I would die before I could bear to see loathing for me in his eyes.

"We will make others." He pressed his lips to my brow. "We are still young. You will bear our children, I promise you. A first miscarriage is horrible, yes, but not unusual, sweet wife. Many women suffer the same yet go on to have healthy broods."

Laying my head on his chest, I absorbed his words like absolution.

I needed to believe them. I had no choice.

I had to believe his love could make me pure again.

CHAPTER THIRTY

My hopes were not in vain.

In early March, less than a month after my miscarriage, to our joy I discovered I was pregnant again. I resolved to not do anything to endanger the child this time and sequestered myself in my palazzo, refusing all social invitations and insulating my apartments from the daily foibles and scheming of the world outside.

However, this turned out to be more difficult than I imagined. News came almost by the hour of Cesare's troubles in France, where he endured King Louis's quest to find him a wife; several suitable candidates, like Carlotta before them, had refused, causing Cesare to threaten to depart—though he could not do so without the king's leave. Finally, Louis found a willing bride: Charlotte d'Albert of Navarre, princess of that small Pyrenees-riven realm between France and Spain, which acted as a bulwark against its neighbors' mutual aggression. Spain lifted immediate protest, sending a volley of rebuke to Rome, citing Papa's unholy treaty with their ancient foe and menacing an alliance with Milan, Naples, and Venice against us—to no avail. Cesare wed Charlotte in a grand spring ceremony, with word of his prowess at the subsequent consummation dispatched to the Vatican with such urgency that the courier rode six separate horses to death in the process. When the news arrived, the Spanish ambassador confronted my father before the entire court, to Papa's outrage, advising him to seek reconciliation with Their Majesties of Spain before it was too late.

But it was my own husband's reaction that took me by surprise. He arrived one morning in July as I basked in the gallery, my eyelids at half-mast and hands about the bulge of my stomach. His clearing of his throat startled me. "*Amore,* you are back from your hunting so soon," I said, and then my delight extinguished as I recognized the slim scarlet figure at Alfonso's side.

"Madonna." Cardinal Ascanio Sforza inclined his head. He always wore his sanctity like armor, behaving as if my separation from Giovanni were of no account to him, though it had cast aspersion upon his family.

My greeting was icy. "Eminence. You were not expected."

"No, I should think not," he said, as Alfonso looked to where my women sat nearby, occupied with sewing, while Arancino batted dangling threads from their hoops.

"Wife, let us go into your antechamber," said Alfonso. "We have important news."

We? Since when had he and Cardinal Sforza become familiar? I bit back my immediate retort, gesturing at my women to stay put. "Shall I have Murilla bring us refreshments?" I asked Alfonso, and his hesitation increased my concern. Then he nodded and I imparted my order before following them into the stifling antechamber. Though it was only midmorning, the heat was insupportable. Had I not already been in my fifth month, I would have insisted on departing for the countryside, away from the stink and fever-infested swamps of the city.

Murilla delivered a decanter of cool cider; I shut the door and turned to see Alfonso and the cardinal regarding me with such gravity that my heart clenched.

"Dear God, what is it? Has someone died?"

"If only it were that simple," said Cardinal Sforza, reaching to pour himself a cup.

Alfonso said, "Cesare. He is coming back."

"Is that all?" I was bewildered. "But surely it is to be expected. He is all anyone has talked about for weeks, and now that he's married, why would he stay in France?"

The cardinal sipped from his cup, his delicate mannerism at odds with the steel in his eyes.

Alfonso said quietly, "You do not understand. With King Louis's own marriage to Anne of Brittany now secure, he and Cesare found accord. They have declared they shall join together to bring another army into Italy, this time with Cesare at its head. They intend to take Milan."

"I see," I said, resisting my dread as I looked pointedly to the cardinal. "You cannot ask me to feign concern for the Sforza cause."

He had the presence of mind to avert his gaze as Alfonso claimed my attention, urgency imbuing his voice: "It is not only Milan that is at risk. Naples cannot withstand another invasion; it would be our doom. Your father keeps saying he'll never give the French leave to loot the south, but he's ordered festivities to celebrate Cesare's return. He flaunts caskets of jewels before the Spanish envoy and declares he will use them to finance Valentino's enterprise, intimating that he will not stand in either your brother's or Louis's path. Even Sancia had bitter words with him recently, after Gioffre was arrested by the Vatican guard for brawling."

"Gioffre was arrested?" I said. "When?"

"A few days ago; it was nothing. He was drunk. Lucrezia, listen to me: When Sancia went to see His Holiness to demand he punish his guards for arresting her husband—who is also his son—do you know what your father replied?"

I shook my head, a knot in my throat.

"He said Gioffre might be her husband but was no son of his, and if she did not like how he treated those beneath him, she could return to Naples. He also said that Cesare would be here soon enough to set matters right. Sancia says it sounded like a threat."

I could imagine it did. Indeed, none of this boded well, and I regretted that I'd elected to remain ensconced in my palazzo, for I knew how easily disharmony in our family could turn dangerous. All the hopes I had nursed crumbled around me, as I once again faced the unthinkable possibility of my father and brother arming themselves against my husband.

"Sancia is beside herself," Alfonso went on. "She insists that we leave before Cesare returns and takes our heads for King Louis to gloat over. She believes he will wreak vengeance on our uncle for not allowing him to marry Carlotta and will invade Naples, no matter the cost."

"What do you want of me?" I asked, with as much calm as I could muster. I felt the cardinal's stare and knew they had come here with a purpose. "I cannot stop Cesare—"

"Not Cesare," interrupted Cardinal Sforza, as if he corrected an inept child. "We are all aware no one can stop him once he decides upon a course, but His Holiness may yet be persuaded. If you plead our case, he might reconsider this ill-advised alliance with France."

"You're asking me to advise His Holiness?" I was incredulous.

"We would not ask if there were any other way," replied Alfonso, though I could see he was as discomfited by the request as I was. "But we need someone whom he will heed. His Holiness has always trusted his family above all others."

Not always, I wanted to say. He had rarely heeded me. And I was a woman with child, not yet twenty years old. How could I presume to advise my father on matters of political expedience, particularly when it pertained to Cesare?

"You must try, Lucrezia," Alfonso urged. "For us and the future of our child." For the first time, I heard actual fear in his voice—a fear he must have harbored all this time but had kept to himself. Before, he had only expressed determination, to fight back if necessary, but now I realized he must truly believe Naples and his kin were in peril. The revelation jolted me to my core. I had defended my family. I had evaded Alfonso's suspicion, done my utmost to demonstrate we were not everything said of us. Now, by their own actions, Cesare and Papa refuted me. They proved that when it came to their interests, everything, and everyone, was secondary. I could not allow it. I had to put a halt to this constant strife that now threatened my very marriage.

"Yes." I lifted my chin. "I will speak to him."

I HAD TO wait a few days until Papa finished his obligations with the Curia and sent word that he could receive me. I went to see him at supper time, finding him quartering his favorite smoked ham with his fingers, layering it on chunks of thick peasant bread. He expressed delight at my arrival.

"It's been too long since you spent some time alone with your old Papa," he chortled. "So busy have you been with that gallant husband of yours, eh? He must make you happy and I'm glad of it. My *farfallina* deserves every happiness."

I swiveled my Venetian-glass goblet, the watered wine within banking at its sides like a tiny red sea. It angered me that he would pretend my happiness was all that concerned him, when I knew he plotted mayhem with Cesare. Yet now, as he sat in his linen robe, his sparse hair askew on his liver-spotted pate, and his fleshy cheeks rubicund with drink and relaxation after a long day, I felt like a child again and had to brace myself to dispel his good humor.

My very silence, however, gave me away. He abruptly said, "Well? Are you just going to sit there biting your tongue?" He took a swig from his goblet. "If," he added, "you're here at your husband's behest to talk me out of the French alliance, I'll not hear a word against it." His affability vanished. "I'll not hear Cesare disparaged, not when your husband sees fit to slink about in the company of that viper Cardinal Sforza."

My fingers clutched about my goblet.

Papa went on, "I have a mind to throw the cardinal in the *castel* until he learns his place. I might feign reconciliation with him but only because, as a famous emperor once said, 'He who is prudent and lies in wait for an enemy who is not will be victorious.' And much as it pains me, your husband has been anything but prudent."

I widened my eyes, as if in surprise, even as I suppressed a rush of icy doubt. Had Alfonso not told me everything?

Papa eyed me. "You look bewildered. Can it be your husband keeps secrets from you? It is common knowledge among my informants that, since word came of Cesare's return, Alfonso has been running around in a panic, listening to—indeed, one might say *encouraging*—every poisonous word the cardinal spews in his ear. By now he and his sister, Sancia, must be of the firm belief that Cesare's sole purpose is to raze their beloved Naples to the ground."

"Is it?" I asked.

Silence ensued. When Papa tried to look away, I said angrily, "Then it is true! You plan to strike at Naples because King Federico denied Cesare his daughter."

"I never said that. Nor is it my intent, no matter what Cesare might desire. Milan, yes: The Sforza must pay. Il Moro will not hold his sword over me any longer. And those bloodthirsty wolves of the Romagna—we must see them brought low, too, which means a dungeon or the scaffold in most cases. But not Naples. Destroying it serves no purpose."

I set my goblet aside, placing my hands on my stomach. "Swear it to me, Papa. On this child's life, swear to me that you will not allow Alfonso or his realm to be harmed."

"I don't believe Naples is his realm. He does not rule there," Papa retorted, "while I sit on St. Peter's throne. Would you doubt my word as Supreme Pontiff?"

I made a move, as if to slip from the chair to my knees. "Swear to me, anyway, for my child's sake, as he—"

I was halted by a rapping at the doors, followed immediately by the arrival of an anxious chamberlain: "Holiness, forgive me, but Her Highness Princess Sancia insists she must be seen and . . ." He blanched, backing away as Papa stood in fury.

Behind the chamberlain, Sancia swept in, her hair disheveled about her face. Without a glance at me, she said to Papa, "Does she know what you and Cesare will cost her?"

In a dizzying haze, I struggled to my feet.

My father glared. "You interrupt a private audience with my daughter. Remove yourself at once and we shall speak later, at an appointed time—"

"Later?" Sancia's wild laughter pealed. "There is no later, as far as Lucrezia is concerned. He is gone already, because of you and that demon you call a son."

"Gone?" About me, the room began to recede. "Who is gone . . . ?" But I already knew; I could see it on her face and I turned, trembling, to my father. "It cannot be. . . ."

Papa said through his teeth, "Am I to understand that my son-in-law, your brother Alfonso, has left my city, forsaking his own wife when she carries his child?"

"And are you saying you did not know?" Sancia countered. "Mother of God, how devious can you be? It is what *you* desire. Everyone in Italy has heard by now that Cesare marches from Asti with over forty thousand Frenchmen and mercenaries, not to mention enough cannon to bring down the walls of Jerusalem. Louis of France has proclaimed that as neither Rome nor any other city-state will defend Milan, the conquest of Il Moro's domain will be a minor task, at best. So," she said, thrusting out her chin, "what does Cesare intend to do with his army after such a minor task is concluded? Where will he take his army next, if not to the very gates of Naples?"

"You dare come into my holy presence, into my very rooms, to utter such blasphemy?" he bellowed. "Get from my sight. Go! Run after your brother. Run to Naples and hide with him under the stairs, and pray to God that your uncle Federico is not caught off guard like Il Moro."

"Papa, no!" I cried as Sancia recoiled, but when I moved toward her, he flung out an arm, detaining me. "Go," he ordered her. "You will never connive in Rome again. Go. Now."

"I will not," she said, though her voice began to quaver.

"Oh, but you will," said Papa. "You will depart this very hour, for if you do not, I will see you thrown into the piazza in your chemise to walk barefoot to Naples."

She cast a defiant look in my direction and swung around to the doors, where the chamberlain stood petrified to his spot. "See that Her Highness has the appropriate escort," Papa called out to his servant as Sancia neared. "Under no circumstances is Gioffre to go with her. If Naples does not care to leave its kin with me, then neither will I send any of mine to it."

Sancia did not turn back. After the doors closed on her, Papa muttered to me, "I did not know. Alfonso is a villain and a coward to have believed such lies of us—"

"Not me," I whispered. "He did not believe them of me." I pushed past him, walking to the doors, which seemed to loom an eternity away.

Behind me, my father shouted, "I will not have it. You will not go after him. I forbid it. Do you hear me? *I forbid it!*"

Like Sancia before me, I did not turn back.

"LUCREZIA, IT IS your turn. Are you going to play or not?"

Reluctantly, I turned from the mullioned window to the table and the ivory-and-gemstone chessboard. Gioffre slumped in his chair, tugging at his lower lip as he waited. My hand hovered over my white queen; as I started to move it, he exclaimed, "Not there. Look at my bishop; he'll take her and you will lose the game." He pouted, emphasizing the sparse beard he was trying to grow, no doubt to hide the eruption of pimples on his chin. Though he neared his eighteenth year, he still had the gangly appearance of a pubescent youth, not like Cesare or Juan had been at his age. "You do not care. You're not paying any attention. I thought this was supposed to be a fun excursion for us, coming here to Spoleto, but all you do is sigh and look out that window."

"That is not fair," I said, stung by the truth in his words. "Papa sent me here to oversee the city, because we face imminent war. It is an honored post and I must fulfill my obligations."

I had indeed done that, accepting Papa's appointment to be governor of this Umbrian city and spend the last days of summer within the impressive fortress perched above the cluster of houses and streets at its skirts, overlooking fields of wilted poppies and chestnut woodlands. Here I exercised power authorized by my father, delivering his papal briefs to the city notables, arbitrating complaints, and hearing petitions, all the while ensuring Spoleto's position in Rome's defense. I held audiences in the great court under its portico, was regaled by speeches, compliments, and banquets; I heard deference in the aldermen's greetings and saw awe in their plump wives' enthusiasm to serve me, and none of it mattered.

Gioffre rolled his eyes and slid his bishop over to take my queen. He knew as well as I did that we'd been dispatched here as privileged pawns in the struggle between Naples and Rome—a struggle that had escalated as soon as Sancia arrived at King Federico's court, breathing fire.

Initially, I refused to heed my father's explanations. I shut myself in Santa Maria in Portico and tore up his notes, sending away his placating secretaries with his appeals. I knew every doorway was watched; I could not even sneak out to visit my son at my mother's house, though I longed to, as the sight of him might bring me some solace amid the excruciating tumult.

And as my belly enlarged and reality sank in—that I was a wife abandoned, locked up in the sumptuous cage of my palazzo—my anger was such that when Papa sent me the decree to act as the governor of Spoleto, conferring upon me both the title and means of escape, I did not hesitate. Papa had Gioffre accompany me, along with a cortège. I departed in silence, hiding my fear that Cesare might indeed get his way, despite Papa's assurances to the contrary and my devastation that Alfonso had fled from me without a word. I'd wept in my rooms, railed and cursed my husband, accusing him before my women of playing me for a fool, of using me to cajole my father even as he slipped out the back door. Still, I clung to hope. Spoleto was just a two-day ride from Rome, far enough away to ease my humiliation but not so much that, should the situation change, I could not quickly return to the Eternal City. It had crossed my mind to simply ride to Naples and demand an explanation from Alfonso, but, of course, the notion was as foolish as it was impossible. Even here, Papa had set spies on me. If I set foot outside the fortress, his informants would be on my heels.

Nor, I thought now, would the situation ever change. Every evening after our repast, if not required for some provincial event in the hall, we repaired to this tower room, the highest point in the castle, where I could brood at the window, looking out in vain for a messenger, while my brother yawned and griped about how dull everything was. Unlike me, he seemed oblivious to his spouse's absence, though he did express pining for his horses and hounds, his new falcon, and the rabble of rogues he had taken to roistering about with in Rome, drinking too much and throwing rocks at the sentinels on the *castel,* which had precipitated his brief arrest.

"Just admit it," he now said, stretching back in his chair and propping his booted feet on the table. "You hate it here as much as I do. Why don't we ask Papa to let us return home?"

"No." I paced again to the window. "I was sent here to act as his representative, and I will not have it said that I shirked my duty."

"No one thinks you shirk your duty. Your husband has shirked his—but not you."

I glanced at him over my shoulder. "Do you not miss Sancia at all?"

He shrugged. "Why should I? She doesn't miss me, I can assure you." I saw fleeting pain cross his face, but before I could probe deeper, sudden movement caught my eye. Swerving back to the window, I strained to see through its warped panes.

Dusk hung over the road winding to the castle. When I saw the approaching shape on a horse, I let out a cry that nearly sent Gioffre tumbling off his seat.

"Come!" Grasping his hand, I hauled him down the steep stone staircase, ignoring his breathless warning—"Be careful!"—and pulling him through the hall into the garrison forecourt before the massive main gate. A moment later, the messenger appeared, just as I'd prayed he would—exhausted, coated in dust, the colors of our Borgia livery barely visible as he dismounted, dropped to one knee, and removed an oilskin packet from his satchel.

"My lady." His voice was coarse with grit from the road. "Word from His Holiness."

Gioffre groused, "You might have killed us on those stairs, and for what? More papers from Papa."

Disappointed, I reached for the packet. I was glad of the darkness settling over the forecourt, even as the servants raced to light the torches now that I was present. I did not care for my father's servant to see my dejection.

Then he pushed back his hood. With a start, I recognized his strong-featured face, the long, pointed nose, and the salty brows over deep-set Spanish eyes—Juan Cervillon, captain of the papal guard, a man so highly regarded by my father that he'd had the honor of holding the ceremonial sword over Alfonso and me at our wedding.

"Captain Cervillon," I said in surprise. "What reason would His Holiness have to send you from Rome at this late hour, when a common messenger would have sufficed?"

"I do not come from Rome." His smile shone on his dirty face. "I come all the way from Naples, my lady, where I spent some time visiting my family."

"Naples?" I clutched the packet to my chest. "Did . . . did you see my husband?"

"I did, indeed. His Holiness sent me there to negotiate terms for my lord the duke of Bisceglie to return. That folder you hold contains his letters to you."

I WAITED IN the courtyard, dressed in my most resplendent gown—emerald green, the color of constancy—with jewels threaded in my hair. I had decided to wear it loose, though I was married and six months' gone with child; it shimmered like a golden veil, floating past my waist, my afternoon strolls on the parapets without a coif having polished it to a sheen.

At last, I heard the clip-clop of hooves coming up the road. Rising from the chair under the canopy, I waved aside Nicola and the linen parasol she held to protect my skin. September's sun pressed on me like an anvil as I stepped forth. The approaching company resolved itself—a small group in unlaced doublets, loose shirtsleeves pushed up to forearms. It might have been a company of local merchants or men-for-hire, certainly not the escort of a prince.

My heart quickened.

At the gate, the men stopped. I heard ribald laughter, a catcall such as between men in a tavern—then he dismounted, handed the reins of his horse to one of his companions, and strode to me, his compact, muscular legs moving with incredible swiftness. All of a sudden he stood before me, exuding that pungent scent I had missed so much, and raised my hand to his lips.

"You have no beard," I said. As overjoyed as I was to see him, I wasn't about to admit it.

"Yes. I was told my wife does not like it." His complexion was bronzed from his travels, highlighting the amber in his eyes and tousled mane.

I wanted to touch his cheek, knowing it would feel as smooth as it looked. Instead, I said with asperity, "Your wife would have preferred the beard to your absence."

He let out a soft exhale. "About that . . ."

Before he launched into what was certain to be an uncomfortable explanation, I said, "There is no need to give me your apology. I read your letters. All of them."

"All?"

"Yes. It seems your previous correspondence did not reach me." I gave a biting laugh. "I should have known. But Captain Cervillon gallantly brought not only your letter from Naples but also stopped in Rome on his way here to obtain the others. My Murilla gave them to him."

His jaw tightened. Without having to say it, we both understood it had been my father's command that I should not receive any of the letters he had sent.

"I came back because I was promised restitution," he said, "including full dominion over my household and wife, and the city of Nepi as recompense, to be deeded in our name. His Holiness assures me we can live where we please, once our child is born, and that Naples will not be overrun by the French, but—" He stepped so close, only a drift of air could have passed between us. "Lucrezia, I do not trust them. Not any-more. You must understand that, if we are—if our marriage is to . . ." He faltered. "I could not bear it. God help me, I could not endure an-other hour without you."

"Nor I without you," I whispered. I melted into his arms, felt them close around me in a protective circle that I vowed nothing from that day forth would ever break.

WE SPENT THE end of summer in Spoleto, until the leaves of the oaks turned brown and the Umbrian wind began to stir. In mid-October, we returned to Rome with Gioffre, riding into the city to the music of pipes and the antics of jugglers, who greeted us at the gates and accom-panied us to our palazzo. Here, Papa himself greeted us, arrayed in his secular dress of black Spanish velvet, looking trimmer than the last time I'd seen him, less florid about the face; when I espied a striking young woman among his entourage, sheathed in carnation satin and ostenta-tious jewelry, I held back a smile. She resembled la Farnese, which ex-plained the improvement in my father's appearance.

We had not been back a week when news arrived that Louis of France had crossed into Italy to join Cesare, who won singular victory over Lombardy and conquered Milan. That northern city, prize of the Sforza domain, flung open its gates to receive its invaders. Destitute and deprived of allies, Il Moro fled with Cardinal Ascanio Sforza over the border into Tyrol, to throw themselves upon the Habsburg emper-or's dubious mercy.

Milan was now French, and my brother rode beside King Louis through the cheering crowds of Il Moro's conquered duchy.

Alfonso turned pale when he read the reports sent by Naples's am-bassadors. Representatives of nearby princelings rushed to do homage to Louis as their new overlord: "With a deplorable lack of dignity or foresight," Alfonso remarked, bunching up the dispatches and tossing them into the fire. "Can they not see what ill wind this brings? What is to stop Cesare now from deciding that, as he liked the apple, why not take the entire tree?"

"Papa promised us he will not touch Naples," I said from my chair, where I sat in an awkward splay-legged position, my stomach grown twice as large in the past month. I felt clumsy, heavy, and waterlogged; I was tired most of the time, preoccupied with my impending delivery. I wanted only for there to be peace, though I feared nothing could change Cesare's ambitions.

"Italy must never fall to one power," Alfonso expounded, causing me to cast an uneasy glance at our servants in the background. "It is craven, let alone unconscionable, to hand over city-states like prizes at a joust. Why will His Holiness not see that? At this rate, he will let your brother become a new emperor. Already he declares that since the over-lords of the Romagna refuse to pay their papal tithes, the city-states of Imola, Forlì, Faenza, Urbino, and your own former husband's Pesaro have forfeited their rights. Cesare marches there to deprive them of it."

"Yes," I muttered, despising this resurgence of tension in our marriage because of my family. "Yet perhaps he will not be so successful. Has not Il Moro's niece Countess Caterina Sforza, who rules over Imola and Forlì, replied that it will take more than a Spanish by-blow to dislodge her?"

"At least she shows the courage others lack." My husband paced the room. "The Romagna is the gateway to the Apennines and port of Ravenna. Does your father mean to carve out a kingdom for Cesare from St. Peter's territories?"

This time, I could not restrain myself. "If, as you say, the Romagna is part of the territories of St. Peter, then it lies under papal authority, though the lords there fail to recognize it as such. Surely in this case Cesare only goes to claim what is already ours?"

As soon as I spoke, I regretted it. My husband paused, staring at me as if I had uttered an obscenity. "*Ours?* The Borgia are not heirs to the keys of the kingdom. His Holiness may grace the see as our appointed vicar on earth, but when he dies, may it be many years hence, he cannot bequeath God's earthly possessions to his progeny."

I frowned, disliking the righteousness underscoring his statement, though of course he *was* right. The Holy See was not hereditary. Still, Alfonso seemed so determined to expect betrayal from my family at every turn, though Papa had taken pains to reassure him, that in the moment I had to accept that the damage done between my husband and my family might be irreparable. Despite his newly granted deed to Nepi, Alfonso would not be placated. Nor, apparently, had he found any comfort in the return of his sister, Sancia, who'd taken residence with Gioffre in the palazzo vacated by the fugitive Cardinal Sforza.

I said nothing more. On November 1, the worries over my marriage were drowned by pangs that had me gasping on my birthing stool. The household plunged into panic, my women rushing about as though we had not prepared for this very moment for months—and all their panic was for naught. After only a few hours of labor, I delivered a son.

Alfonso came to see me; as he lifted our squalling infant in his arms, tears filled his eyes. "He is beautiful. As beautiful as you are."

I sighed. While the labor had been brief, it had exhausted me and stirred unsettling recollections of another, far less heralded birth and a child whose absence I had begun to take for granted. Nearly a year had passed since I last visited my first son, and watching Alfonso, who appeared suffused with awe by our newborn child, I had to stop myself from finally telling him.

Alfonso said, "Shall we name him Rodrigo in honor of your father? Would you like that, *amore*?" He was trying to make amends for our recent argument, so overjoyed that he offered me this peace offering.

I nodded, whispering, "Yes," while I bit back my confession. It was not the time. Later, once we'd weathered these first months of having a babe of our own, I would tell him.

Papa was ecstatic. He had the child brought to him in the Vatican, where he walked the halls cradling his namesake, greeting envoys and bishops while baby Rodrigo burped up his midday meal. The christening he ordered was lavish, almost to the point of ludicrousness.

As a new mother, I had to wait forty days before I was blessed and released of the stain of childbirth, so I could not attend the ceremony in the Sistine. Alfonso told me of how Rodrigo, swathed in ermine, was borne by Captain Cervillon of the papal guard to the silver font, where my son remained unusually quiet until the baptismal water trickled over him. Then he let out a bellow, shattering the solemnity and sending Alfonso rushing toward him. But it was Papa, wearing nearly as much ermine and white silk as our child, who sailed forth to rescue his grandson, scooping him up in his arms. Immediately, Rodrigo quieted, as if he recognized the power of the man holding him.

Alfonso tried to sound amused—"Already he is more a Borgia than a son of mine"—but I heard the tightness in his voice, his unspoken regret that he'd named our child after my father. Again, I felt unease. Papa's possessiveness should have reassured Alfonso; he had given my father a grandson, and to a Borgia, family meant everything.

Though Alfonso did not believe it, I was certain we were now safe from any harm.

A WEEK LATER, Cesare slipped into Rome like a lone wolf.

BECAUSE I'D NOT yet been officially churched, my appearance at an intimate Vatican dinner held in Papa's apartments and attended by a select roster of guests was strictly private. We dined on roast pheasant, sugared hen, and smoked boar; halfway through the dessert course, the cardinals presented me with two chased silver dishes containing two hundred ducats, each coin ingeniously wrapped in colored foil to resemble a sweetmeat.

"We shall donate these in our son's name to the orphanage of the Convent of San Sisto," I declared.

At my side, Alfonso lifted his cup—"A toast to my wife!"— prompting the others to follow suit and the cardinals to glower, as they'd not offered their largesse for me to turn it over to charity but rather, as I surmised, to put me in their debt for future favors.

Goblets were clinking in the candlelight when my brother materialized in the doorway—clothed in black, his dark-coppery hair cascading to his shoulders, wearing a face mask that could not disguise his identity. Uneasy recognition rippled through the assembly, the men turning pale, the women frightened yet also seeming to expand like petals under a midnight sun.

Papa behaved as if Cesare's impromptu arrival were of no importance, ignoring my brother as he leaned by the sideboard, arms crossed at his chest. The servants tiptoed around him, clearing the platters and brushing the tablecloth of crumbs, while the guests hastily finished their desserts and scattered like deer that sense a predator in their midst.

I found myself turning to Cesare, taking in his lean form and insouciant stance, his covert smile as he watched the guests take their leave. He is satisfied, I thought. He has accomplished his every ambition, graduating from cardinal to Papa's adviser to conqueror of Milan in little more than the two years since Juan's death. Though he must have noticed me still seated there at the table, having learned by now that I'd given birth, he gave no indication of it.

Alfonso took me by the hand. As I kissed Papa's cheek, he murmured, "*Farfallina,* you look tired. Tomorrow I shall order the forty-day rule suspended so you can be churched."

I nodded. Still hand in hand with my husband, I stepped to the threshold, where I paused inches away from where my brother stood. He finally turned to me, his cat eyes gleaming within the mask. Dipping his head, he made as if to bow. I started to open my mouth, to welcome him back and offer congratulations on his marriage, his victory over Milan, and his impending success in the Romagna. But Alfonso's grip on me tightened, propelling me out the door.

"Not a word," he said in my ear. "You have not seen him. Not tonight."

"Not *seen* him? But he was just there!"

Even as I spoke, the door shut behind us. With a glare at Alfonso, I pulled my hand free, kicked at my hem, and strode down the corridor. "You might have allowed us a moment," I said as he came up beside me. "He is my brother. I deserve the chance to—"

"If he had wanted you to greet him," interrupted Alfonso, "if your father had wanted it, do you not think they would have asked us to stay?"

I scowled, trying to think of something to retort, but the somber look he gave me dampened my ire. It was true; Papa had not acknowledged Cesare's presence at all.

"They must have much to discuss," I heard myself say, seeking an excuse that sounded feeble even to my ears, "seeing as Cesare will soon lead their campaign into the Romagna."

"Yes," said Alfonso grimly. "They now have an entire world to partition between them."

PART V

1500–1501

Caesar or Nothing

*The pope intends to make the
duke of Valencia a great man, and king
of Italy, if he can.*

—JOHANN BURCHARD,
MASTER OF CEREMONIES AT
THE BORGIA PAPAL COURT

CHAPTER THIRTY-ONE

It began with an unexpected death.

A loyal servant, assaulted as he left a dinner with friends, left to bleed on filthy cobblestones, his throat cut. It brought back disturbing echoes of Juan, the ruthless expediency of it, which is probably why Alfonso did not tell me himself about the incident. But I heard it, anyway, through my women. Murilla brought the news with my morning figs and cheese. Leaning to me as I slid a jeweled knife under the wax of my correspondence, she whispered in my ear.

"Cervillon?" I repeated, stunned. "Captain Cervillon of the papal guard? Are you sure?"

Murilla assented, her diminutive dark-brown face full of sorrow. Behind her, framed by the open door, was Nicola, pale-faced, and my other women, who leaned toward one another in conspiratorial glee, as if they had heard an irresistible scandal.

My hand was trembling. I made myself set down the letter opener, winter's light reflecting dully upon its inlaid-pearl handle. "But he was fine at Rodrigo's Baptism. He has family, children. . . ." Even as I spoke, I recalled with a sickening start that Cervillon's family resided in Naples. He had gone there to visit them, taking advantage of his mission to persuade King Federico to come to terms with Papa, which would allow Alfonso to return to me.

"*Dio mio,* have mercy on his soul," I said, crossing myself. "He was a good man; he did not deserve such a terrible fate."

He was hastily entombed, I learned, in a church in the Borgo, close to where he'd been slain. No one was allowed to veil his corpse or examine the extent of his wounds, though witnesses reported that his masked assailant had come at him so fast, he never had the chance to pull his sword from its scabbard.

"They preferred to slaughter him, like a beast, rather than let him go free," said Alfonso that night in our rooms, when I told him that I knew. "He wasn't murdered because he had outlived his purpose but rather because he knew secrets that might undo them."

I bowed my head, unlacing my robe and slipping between cold sheets. A fire burned in the hearth. My brass braziers glowed with scented coals, imported Flemish tapestries hung on the walls, and Turkish rugs cushioned the tiles underfoot, and still my bedchamber felt like a mausoleum, so cold I could see my own breath.

Alfonso doused the candles, the hiss of dying flames giving way to silence. Moments later, he slid naked into bed beside me. He did not enfold me in his arms, as was his custom; instead, he lay rigid, staring at the tester above us.

"It was your brother's doing," he finally said. "Cesare ordered Cervillon's death before he departed for the Romagna, because the captain requested His Holiness's leave to return to Naples. He said he missed his family too much to be away from them any longer but refused to bring them here. His Holiness must have told Cesare, fearing what Cervillon might reveal."

I did not want to hear it; I did not want to know that Cesare was responsible for another brutal death. Still, I had been shaken by Cervillon's murder, so much that I now began to feel my own gnawing apprehension take hold, overcome by the memory of Cesare approaching me in the Vatican gardens, even as Michelotto stood over the bodies of Pantalisea and Perotto.

"Why would Papa or Cesare fear Cervillon?" I finally ventured. "What secrets do you think he could possibly have to merit . . . ?" My voice waned as I felt, rather than saw, Alfonso's gaze shift to me. A flare in the ebbing fire sent shadows leaping across the walls.

"You truly do not know?" he said. "Cervillon was your father's confidant; he knew intimate aspects of His Holiness's affairs. I believe he even knew who murdered Juan—but," he added as I let out a sharp gasp, "that is not why Cesare had him killed. Cervillon must not have had any proof or they would have eliminated him long before now. He died because of Cesare's plan. He knew what was coming and could not stomach it. If he'd returned to Naples, he would have warned my uncle, who in turn would have alerted the other city-states. They might cower behind their walls now, but we would have roused them from their stupor. Cervillon knew your brother aspires to far more than plunder of the Romagna."

"How much more . . . ?" I whispered, though I already knew. I could hear Cesare as if he lay between us, his lips at my ear: *The time has come for a new age—the age of Borgia. And I shall be its scourge.*

I shivered. Alfonso drew me to him. He exuded heat; as I set my cheek on him, his chest burned like a kiln. He seemed impervious to the chill that seeped all the way into my soul.

"He wants everything," Alfonso said. "All of Italy. He will have it, too, if he can. His Holiness cannot curb him. That visit of his, when I told you he was not there, was staged. He wanted everyone in the room to see him. He stayed only three days, closeted with His Holiness, long enough to obtain whatever he needed before returning to his troops. Now Cervillon is dead and the Romagna will fall to his sword. The virago of Forlí and Imola will lose her domains; it is only a matter of time before she surrenders or perishes in the rubble of her strongholds. The others—Faenza, Camerino, Urbino, and the rest—will throw themselves on his mercy. Thus shall he conquer, using their cowardice against them—or their blood, if they resist."

"What about their corruption?" I said, remembering how my father had railed against the lords of the Romagna and their murderous courts, recalling how my own former husband, Giovanni, had stood in the courtyard of Pesaro as his secretary's amputated hands twitched at his feet. "What about the violence they cause? Does it not merit them being brought to justice?"

"Cesare might impose justice now," he replied, "and may even believe in it, but what he truly craves is power. Have you not heard his motto? It says it all: 'Caesar or Nothing.' He styles himself like an emperor. Emperors need empires. He's only just begun to amass his."

I had not heard it. I closed my eyes then, trying to find reassurance in my husband's proximity, in the strong beat of his heart in my ears. "What shall we do?" I said at length. His arms tightened about me, reminding me that I must soon make my choice, the one he had warned me about. My family or him: It had come to that.

"We must survive," he said, "no matter the cost."

❦

THE YEAR 1500 arrived with ill portents. A comet streaked fire across the sky in Umbria, and a statue of the Virgin in Assisi wept blood. Everywhere, prophets, diviners, and backstreet witches searched for omens in wine dregs, predicting chaos to a gullible populace already unsettled by the fall of Milan, the war in the Romagna, and threat of a poor harvest after torrential rainstorms.

Nevertheless, the turn of the century was also a Jubilee Year for the papacy, in which thousands would flock to Rome to secure indulgences, witness the symbolic opening of holy doors in the basilicas, and venerate the sacred relics. Thus, the doomsayers' cries were quelled either by the crash of falling masonry—Papa had commanded beautification of the city—or by the silence of the dungeons into which they were thrown for sedition.

In January, word came of Caterina Sforza's capture. Rumor was she had suffered degradation at the hands of Cesare's troops, until he intervened and took her under his personal charge. As his prisoner, the countess was sent to Rome under guard to be lodged in confinement in the Castel Sant'Angelo. This victory, however, was muted by Il Moro's unexpected march on Milan with an army financed by the Hapsburgs. The same citizens who'd delighted to see the last of him turned out in droves to help him oust the French. The Sforza reclaimed their city, and Il Moro's subsequent challenge to his neighboring city-states to join forces with him against Borgia tyranny brought a sudden halt to Cesare's campaign.

Alfonso brought me the news, coming upon me as I sat rocking little Rodrigo in my arms.

"Lucrezia," he said, his voice grave, "we must prepare."

❦

WE GATHERED AT the Porta del Popolo on our dais, while February rain drifted upon the canopy shielding us and soaked the multitude who'd gathered with us to witness Cesare's return.

Tension suffused the sodden air. For days now the Vatican had been awash with accounts of my brother's triumph in the Romagna—some exaggerated, for he'd only taken a few territories, others more pragmatic, dwelling on the renewed coalition headed by Milan against us, but all overlaid by a sharp sense of anticipation. Cesare had accomplished far more in less time than Juan ever had before him; no one doubted now that he had earned his coveted title of gonfalonier.

Alfonso stood rigid beside me. He'd been honing his physical prowess every day, with archery or falconry in the mornings, sword training in the afternoons. I had grown so used to the metallic clash of blades in the palazzo courtyard that I barely lifted protest anymore, though I had to move Rodrigo and his attendants to a separate wing, where the sounds of my husband's exertions were muffled enough to not disturb our babe's rest.

He had grown his beard again, thick and luxuriant, like ripe wheat. I had not the heart to request that he shave it, though my own cheeks and throat were raw from its scratch on the rare occasions we made love. He was distracted these days, forever on alert; I knew his beard was how he masked himself, concealing his face and thoughts from prying eyes.

A murmur in the crowd shifted my attention to the scene before me. Tasseled carpets depicting our Borgia bull and spiked sun hung limp from the gate, the road running underneath it speckled with wilted petals. The crowd pressed en masse against the guarded cordons of the road as the procession suddenly came into view; the dreary rain and gray skies, the filth on the cobblestones, even Alfonso's brooding expression, faded to insignificance.

Cesare had always had a flair for the dramatic, but never more so than now. He was preceded by a train of pack mules, bearing possessions seized from the fallen fortresses in the Romagna, and by line after line of soldiers and mounted grooms, their livery emblazoned with his Valentinois coat of arms, a proud display that ensorcelled his audience. The hush from the crowd was so complete, I could clearly hear the soughing of caparisons and damp snapping of wet pennants—and everywhere I looked, I saw black.

All black. Everything black.

From harness to saddlecloth, cap to doublet and hose, Cesare had dressed his entourage in that color he had adopted as his badge—the hue of eternity and chameleon adaptability, which could meld with any tint yet retain a hue all its own. A river of night flowed past us, an enormous fluid darkness, flickering here and there with a glint of polished metal, the fiery spit of jewels, and the gold Order of St. Michael that hung in heavy links about Cesare's throat.

He rode alone at the end of the procession, austere in latticed velvet that adhered to a body so forged by battle, he himself resembled a sword—erect on his magnificent sable horse, his beauty both breathtaking and terrible. And as he rode past the dais and bowed his head to our father, who sat ensconced in furs on his throne, Cesare's gaze rose for a moment to meet mine—just a moment, so fleeting it was almost inconsequential.

But I saw what was smoldering there, in his hooded green eyes—I understood.

He was back. Nothing would ever be the same again.

CESARE DID NOT approach me in the cold winter days following his arrival. He accepted a Golden Rose in honor of his military achievements, the title of captain general and gonfalonier, as predicted. After that, he became a fixture at Papa's side, his manservant Michelotto never far behind. My babe Rodrigo was presented to him at one of the Carnival events, toted out to remind the assembly of the fertility of our Borgia line. As he gazed intently upon my son's blue-eyed visage, at his fine brownish hair that had already begun to turn fair, Cesare looked bemused, as if Rodrigo were an icon of uncertain provenance. Leaning over to kiss my son's cheek, he mumbled something I did not hear, then looked up at me.

"You do us proud, Lucia," he said. As he uttered these words, he ignored Alfonso, standing paces away with Sancia, who was dressed to the teeth in turquoise silk. Then he strode away, rousing again in me that insidious jolt of fear.

I found myself clutching my child to my chest.

"He is jealous," Sancia said. "He cannot abide that you bore my brother a son, an heir of the blood of Naples, whom His Holiness dotes on. To him, it's another obstacle, a menace to his position. He will not rest until—"

"Sancia," cut in Alfonso. "Enough. You frighten her."

"Good," Sancia retorted. "She should be frightened. We should all be frightened now that he has returned. He would see us to our graves."

Alfonso said quietly, "I have matters well in hand; I assure you, there's nothing he can do."

His conviction eased the erratic pounding of my heart; I returned my son to his nursemaid and we proceeded to the festivities. My smile was quick and laughter ready as I feigned amusement at the tumblers and other entertainments, even as I sensed Cesare watching me.

During the final feast before Lent, as I moved through hordes in search of Alfonso, whom I'd last seen near Papa, Cesare crept up behind me. I whirled about, the bejeweled mask I held to my face slipping. He too wore a mask; I had not recognized him in the crowd because he wore white, a color many had donned this night. Now that we were inches apart, I also recognized his garb. It was the unicorn disguise he'd worn at my wedding to Alfonso.

"Will you avoid me forever?" he said. "I see such caution in your eyes when you look at me. Do you find me so changed that you can no longer love me?"

Angrily, I tossed my head, repressing the urge to remind him that if he saw caution in me, he had only himself to blame. "What nonsense. You've not changed a bit. You might think it grand to skulk around the Vatican, scaring bishops and cardinals, but to me you are as obvious as ever. Pray, when does this charade end, so we can learn what you are really about?"

"Ah, Lucia. Such wit." He paused, plucking at the crisscrossed laces of his doublet. "I almost had him, you know. I was within a few leagues of his miserable fish town when I received word that Milan had fallen again to the Sforza. Had the news come a few days later . . ." He sighed.

It took me a moment to understand of whom he spoke. When I did, my voice hardened. "Are we not past all that? If I can forgive and forget, surely so can you."

"Forgive?" His smile was like a blade, cutting across his mouth. "I would bathe in his blood for you. Giovanni Sforza of Pesaro owes us a debt that I will see paid."

"Not 'us.'" I took a step closer, watching the impact it had on him, the slight dilation of his pupils behind the mask, the parting of his lips.

It relieved and perturbed me that I still held such sway over him. "I do not want any part of your revenge. I will not live the rest of my days thirsting for the demise of a man who has no meaning to me anymore."

His hand shot out so fast, his fingers were about my arm before I could react. "He disdained you," he said, every word enunciated with the fervor of condemnation. "No one—*no one*—harms my sister and gets away with it, not while I live." He paused, his grip tightening. *"Vae illi homini qui cupit,"* he whispered.

Beware the man who covets.

His words pierced me like shards. It was the same oblique message Papa had imparted on the day I saw him after Juan's death. As my breath stalled in my lungs, I remembered when Cesare and I rode together back to San Sisto and I asked him if he was responsible. He had denied it but he had lied. And I had let him deceive me, clinging to the illusion I'd always sought refuge in, where he was still my beloved brother—impetuous and ardent, often unscrupulous and disquieting, but also misunderstood in his struggles to prove his worth. Now, in this heart-shattering instant, as I gazed upon his face sliced in two by his mask, his fingers coiled about my arm like a serpent's tail, I recognized at last the stark, undeniable truth.

Papa had tried to tell me. The man who covets was Cesare; he had wanted everything Juan possessed. Our brother had indeed died by his hand. And our father knew it. He'd known it from the moment Juan's body was dragged from the Tiber. It was why he had canceled the investigation in the murder, to spare us all from confronting any evidence against Cesare that might arise.

Cesare must have seen my horror. He released me, retreating a few steps. That careless demeanor he cultivated as a façade returned to shape his face. "There it is again: that look. It seems we've only one more secret between us, beautiful Lucia."

His evoking of the child I had hidden away was deliberate, an intimacy he thought would keep us bound, but I no longer cared to acknowledge his wounds, soothe his injuries, or tend his neglect. I had been blinded by him only because I wanted to be. I let myself believe his lies because the alternative was too terrible to contemplate, when all along I'd sensed the demon inside him—the one he himself warned me about what now seemed a lifetime ago:

Hatred is my devil. As long as Juan lives, I'll never escape him. I am doomed to abide forever in his shadow, never becoming who I was meant to be.

He made a formal bow, an elegant movement that was as much a mockery as a display of his fearsome agility. "I bid you good night."

He was gone before I could blink, blending into a surge of chattering courtiers, an exhalation of white smoke. I did not hear Alfonso approach until his hand was on my shoulder, startling me. "What did he say to you?" he asked.

"Nothing," I whispered. I continued to stare at the empty space where my brother had stood, knowing I had lost him to the dark netherworld he'd chosen to inhabit, where nothing was sacrosanct and everything had a price.

Then I turned to Alfonso. "Take me home."

CHAPTER THIRTY-TWO

Hail and spitting rain pelted the streets, and summer lightning slashed the skies, white light illuminating my rooms with such blazing relief that my Rodrigo started to wail and I ordered all the shutters and draperies closed.

It was early afternoon, but the storm was relentless. Resigned to sitting all day near the braziers, I tried to concentrate on a book of Virgil's sonnets, though the intricate phrasings swam before my eyes. I felt the rise of a headache that made me want to go to my bedchamber and nap.

I was about to bid my women to accompany me, when loud voices echoed in the corridor. I rose, telling Murilla to go hush whoever was making such an infernal noise, lest they wake Rodrigo. She barely made it to the door before it burst open. Alfonso ran in, covered head to toe in a shroud of dust.

My women cried out. He resembled a purgatorial specter out of Dante, bits of plaster and grit clinging to him in crumbling patches, embedded in his unkempt hair, in his beard, and on his cheeks and hands, his wild eyes and teeth like gashes within the crusted pallor of his face. I took a faltering step toward him, thinking for a horrifying second he was injured somehow, attacked, but then his words leapt at me in urgent, near-unintelligible fragments:

"His Holiness . . . the audience-chamber roof . . . he is buried . . ."

Gathering fistfuls of my skirts, I fled the room with Alfonso at my heels, crying out my name, as I raced down the staircase and through the galleries into the passageway leading to the Sistine and the Vatican.

Minor courtiers, clerics, and underlings converged in a frantic wave toward my father's stateroom, where Papa had been receiving envoys. I had almost attended the event but decided against it because of

Rodrigo's fear of the storm, knowing only my presence could comfort him. But Alfonso had gone. Now, as I reached the bronze double doors that stood open to the expanse beyond, roiling with clouds of the same dust that coated my husband, I heard a bone-chilling scream. It took me a moment to realize that it had come from my lips.

Alfonso caught me by the waist as I started to plunge inside. Shadowy figures seemed to drift about the chamber like apparitions. "No," he gasped, pulling me back. "You must not! It is not safe. A beam crashed through the roof over his throne. There is rubble everywhere."

"*Dio mio,* no!" I was fighting to get away from him, to rush inside and help, but he refused to release me, hauling me aside against the far wall until I ceased thrashing. "You cannot do anything. Lucrezia, they are working to dig him out. You will make it worse if you go in and risk yourself. They have enough to contend with already."

"Dig him out?" I stared at him wildly, as if he spoke another language. "Is he still alive?"

He pulled me to him, whispering, "No one knows. One moment he was smiling, beckoning the ambassadors, and the next—it must have been lightning. The roof caved in so suddenly. They are doing all they can to rescue him."

I made myself breathe, drawing in shallow drafts of air that tasted of shattered plaster, of pulverized wood and paint from the roof's collapse. Time seemed to move in fits and starts. I saw men coming and going through the doors, all bathed in that hellish grit, their voices colliding, as cries from within echoed and faded into the toppling of broken stone.

Finally, after what seemed an eternity, I heard yelling, a heaving of rubble, and leaden silence. I turned in Alfonso's arms to the doorway, unaware that I too was now covered in a white film that I would spend days scrubbing from my pores.

"He is here!" someone shouted.

I blinked, looking uncomprehendingly at Alfonso. He stepped forward, uncertain. I clung to his hand. Then they came through the doors—a collection of exhausted grooms, cardinals, and envoys in tattered clothes—carrying between them a sagging makeshift stretcher fashioned from ragged crimson velvet that had once been the papal canopy.

"Papa!" I started toward it, dreading what I might find.

The men parted at my approach. I had to force myself to focus. He lay prone, shards and splinters stuck everywhere, a bloody wound on his forehead, other smaller injuries puncturing his large hands, which were clasped loosely—lifelessly, it appeared to me—across his chest. I detected no motion under his debris-littered robe, no sign of movement.

"He is dead," I whispered. I had started to cross myself instinctually, tears seeping from my eyes, when a hoarse voice said, "He is not dead. Never say that. Never, *ever,* say that."

I looked up in a daze. My brother stood with his black velvet coated in plaster. Dust drifted about him, a gravelly halo. He looked as if the roof had fallen upon him, as well.

He lurched to me, eyes like reddened slits in the grime of his face. "He is alive and he will live. God's hand is upon him. He would not allow His humble vicar to perish so ingloriously. It is treason to say it." He seized me by my shoulder, shaking me. "Treason!"

Alfonso loomed between us. "Unhand her." His voice was low, but the menace was apparent in every fiber of his body. "Now, my lord. You forget yourself in your anguish."

Cesare's fist clasped me harder; I sensed a recoiling around us, the abrupt rise of palpable fear, then Alfonso said in his impassive tone, "You do not want this. Not here. Not now. His Holiness has suffered a grave accident and we must behave accordingly, even though we may not like it."

A harsh sound—part mirth, part derision—tore from my brother's lips. He reeled around, barking orders at the men. They began to stagger away with my father supine between them, his feeble whisper calling out, "Cesare, *hijo mío.* Come here, my son. . . ."

As he stalked after them, Cesare did not look back.

"You must leave Rome as soon as possible!" Sancia banged her fist against the sideboard. It had been a fortnight since my father's injury— two weeks of unbearable waiting as he convalesced behind closed doors, attended by physicians, my every request to see him denied. Finally, word had arrived this morning. Papa was on his feet and wished us to join him tonight in the Vatican for dinner. I was astonished by his command but eager to see him; until then, Alfonso and I had planned to spend a quiet afternoon with our child. But then Sancia arrived in a whirlwind of accusations.

"Sister, you are overwrought." Alfonso looked up from the chair where he sat holding Rodrigo, who plucked at one of his doublet ribbons. It reminded me with a sharp pang of guilt of my other son, how he had done the same with my sleeve the last time I'd seen him. . . .

I pulled myself back to attention as Sancia exclaimed, "I may well be, but you, brother, are far too serene. Rome is no longer safe for you. Cesare is allied with France, but he has seen how fragile it all is, how fleeting. If His Holiness perished, where would he be? The bastard son of a dead pope who has earned the enmity of all Italy—he would not long survive. He will not abide being at Fortuna's mercy. He will do whatever he can to protect himself."

Alfonso met my wary look from across the room before he returned his gaze to Sancia. "He may protect himself, but that is no reason to think he plots against me—or no more reason than there's ever been. Cesare has learned that should His Holiness die unexpectedly, he stands to lose everything. He recognizes as much as I do the importance of maintaining balance in uncertain times. With Milan back in the hands of Il Moro, the French king who supported Cesare so assiduously must now find himself obliged to reconsider his obligations. Cesare cannot afford to alienate Naples. Therefore, he has no cause to move against me."

"No cause!" Sancia's shrill disbelief startled Rodrigo, who turned wide eyes to her. She spun to me. "Lucrezia, you know I speak the truth. Tell him that if he does not leave, we may as well throw open the palazzo gates and invite the wolf inside."

Alfonso was clucking at our son, a smile on his lips.

"Perhaps we should heed her," I ventured.

My husband lifted suddenly sharp eyes. "Why? Do you have any knowledge of a plot?"

I hesitated. Ever since his return, we'd lived under Cesare's menace. The accident that nearly killed Papa had heightened my brother's superstitious side; I'd heard he now consulted with astrologers and seers, as our mother did, remarking offhandedly that a prophet warned him that he was destined for an early grave. Yet besides his newfound affinity for the occult, I'd not seen or heard anything else to justify Sancia's worry.

"When it comes to Cesare," I said, "we should never underestimate. I have no knowledge of a plot," I added, raising my voice as Sancia let out an outraged gasp, "but that doesn't mean something isn't afoot. I never suspected that he—" I faltered, until Alfonso's gaze sharpened and I had no choice but to continue. "I never suspected he would murder my maid Pantalisea and Papa's servant Perotto," I said in a low voice.

"With a garrote," added Sancia, making me wince. "He strangled a defenseless woman in the Vatican garden while his manservant, Michelotto, the one with the dead eyes, killed the pope's attendant. He has no remorse. Murder comes as naturally to him as breathing."

A frown creased Alfonso's brow. My nails dug into my palms. I should tell him what else I knew, about Juan's death. I should tell him so he could be fully aware of the lengths to which Cesare was willing to go. The words choked me, however, as if saying them aloud would destroy whatever hope for reconciliation might yet exist between my husband and my family.

"Why would he kill your maid and—His Holiness's servant, was it?" Alfonso asked. "That seems rather garish, even for him. What possible threat could they have posed?"

"It was Perotto who posed the threat," I said quickly, preempting Sancia in my desperate attempt to avoid more questions, which would only lead Alfonso into the tangled web surrounding my stay in San Sisto. "He must have known something, as we think Cervillon did, about Papa and Cesare's secret dealings. Perotto served Papa in his apartments; I often saw him present during private conversations."

I kept my gaze level, my voice as assured as it could be under the circumstances. I did not want Alfonso to sense the panic rushing through me, the need to deflect before he adopted a direct approach I could not hope to evade.

He sat quiet, considering. Then he handed Rodrigo to me and unfurled his strong limbs from the chair. "Then it seems the time has come for me to have a word with him."

Fraught silence fell, broken by Sancia's horrified whisper, "Are you mad?" He ignored her, reaching for his cloak. "Alfonso, you must not do this. You must never see him alone! It is what he waits for—the opportunity, handed to him by you."

Alfonso flung his cloak over his shoulders and buckled on his wide belt with its poniard and sword. "I am fully armed. And wherever I go, my man Albanese goes with me." He chuckled. "Besides, I doubt Cesare would dare assault me in the middle of the Vatican when we're due to dine tonight with His Holiness. How would it look if I end up being the meal?"

Sancia posted herself at the door, barring his exit. "This is no laughing matter. If you must find out what he plots, if confronting him is the only way to convince you, then send Lucrezia to him instead. Let her discover the truth, if he is even capable of telling it."

Alfonso went still. When he finally spoke, his voice was terse. "I'll not send my wife again to conduct my business. Whatever Valentino has to say, he can do so to my face. But I plan to return here to dress for tonight. If I do not, then you will know I am dead."

"You must not—" cried Sancia, but Alfonso motioned her aside. She stepped away reluctantly. As he moved over the threshold, he turned to look at me. I had risen from my chair, our son in my arms. Despite the tumult, Rodrigo had fallen asleep; as I glanced down at him, sudden foreboding made me want to beg Alfonso to stay here with us.

"I would have a word with you alone," I said. Handing Rodrigo to Sancia, I went to my husband as Alfonso warned her, "Do not wake the baby with your dramatics."

Together, we moved through my antechamber, where my women sat, and into the corridor. His manservant, Albanese, lounged in the gallery, his hand poised on his sword hilt. The sight of him immediately reassured me; with a man like him to defend Alfonso, it was indeed improbable that anyone would dare attack him.

Alfonso said softly, "You mustn't let her frighten you. Sancia has always had a vivid imagination. She can spin a conspiracy out of idle rumor."

"She's concerned for your safety," I said, thinking of how my brother had let slip his role in Juan's death. "As am I. Promise me, you will not see him alone. He cannot be trusted."

"I have no doubt. But your brother is not a fool. He cannot afford to alienate me, not when everyone else might turn against him. Cesare has made too many enemies in too short a time; his conquests in the Romagna have woken others to his threat, as has his behavior since His Holiness's accident. He dwells on the dagger's edge. I am in no danger when he might have to beg me for Naples's support."

I searched his eyes. "Still, I'd rather you waited. Perhaps we should request Papa's leave instead to depart Rome. The terms you negotiated with him allow us that privilege."

"You would do that for me? Leave your family, your city?"

"You know I would. I would go anywhere with you." I meant it. If he had said the word in that moment, I would have ordered my women to start packing. There was nothing left for me here—nothing save my secret son, whom I now realized I must leave in Vannozza's care if I wanted to protect Alfonso and Rodrigo. If I dared try to take little Giovanni with me, my father would make sure none of us left. He would never allow us to raise his grandson by Juan in Naples.

Alfonso brought his lips to mine. "I love you, wife. I will not meet with him alone, so you needn't worry. I promise to return as soon as I can, so we may go together to the Vatican. Then we shall see about whether it is time for us to leave Rome, yes?"

As always, the teasing lilt in his voice made my knees weaken. He murmured, "Perhaps we can find a moment alone, too, before dinner, if you can persuade my sister to leave."

I arched a brow. "If you desire that, my lord, I suggest you trim your beard. I would rather not go to the Vatican wearing a veil."

He threw back his head, guffawing, and strode off with Albanese.

I returned to my rooms, my unease dissipating—until I stepped into my bedchamber and Sancia whirled to me, having settled Rodrigo in his crib.

"Would you let him walk into that devil's lair?" she demanded.

I marked the anxiety that had drained her complexion. "He promises to be safe. He said he will be back in a few hours to accompany us to dinner." I stepped to my son's cradle, reached down to adjust his blanket. "I don't believe Cesare will harm him," I added, without looking at her. "As Alfonso pointed out, he needs to know Naples is on his side."

"How can you say such a thing?" Her tone was subdued now, and more alarming because of it. "I once thought the same of him: I believed that while he might harm others, he'd never touch his own family." I heard her skirts rustle as she stepped to me. "But he does not care; he is not like us." Her voice caught, bringing my eyes up to hers. "When he promised me marriage, when he said he loved me, only to toss me aside like a candle-shop whore, I realized I would never know him, because no one can. He is a cipher; he may look and sound like us, but he can be whatever we want him to be, because he lacks all feeling. His power lies in his ability to deceive. Tell me you still trust him. Tell me you know he has not lied to you, as well."

Her words plunged me back to the feast before Lent, when I looked into Cesare's eyes and saw the darkness there, the insatiable need for dominion. He had an endless emptiness inside him that not even Juan's murder had sated. But what more could he possibly want that he had not already achieved? He was Papa's most trusted intimate, just as he'd always longed to be; was hailed as a conqueror, with the Romagna trembling in his wake. It seemed impossible that he would ever consider anything as heinous as depriving me of my husband or my son of his father.

"Yes," I finally said. "He has deceived me. But I've also known him all my life, and I must believe that I, at least, still mean something to him." I turned back to my son. "He knows that if he ever harms Alfonso, it would be the end of me," I whispered. "And the last thing that Cesare desires is my death."

She went silent, gnawing at her lip. I reached out, pressing her hand. "Now, I must rest a while before tonight. You should, too. We shall see each other later in the Vatican."

She lowered her eyes. I almost did not hear her murmur, "Are you so certain?"

I paused. In that instant, it occurred to me how much I had changed. Times past, I would have leapt to Cesare's defense, challenged anyone who dared question his devotion to me.

"I'm not certain of anything anymore, save Alfonso's love," I admitted quietly. "But should the need arise, I will speak to Papa. I will ask him to find a way to . . ." I paused, seeing her mouth tighten.

"There is no other way," she said. "If Alfonso is to remain alive, he must leave Rome."

I felt my shoulders sag. I could not deny the wisdom of her advice. Yet even as I decided that I must indeed act, I thought again of my other son, whom I must leave behind. If I went to Naples, what would become of him, an innocent, caught up in my family's machinations?

I sighed. "Very well. If it will ease your mind, I'll talk to Papa tonight."

She kissed my cheek, grasping my face between her hands. "I am so sorry to have caused you such upset. You are not like them; you may be a Borgia, but you have true goodness in your heart. It is why Alfonso loves you so. But his time is running out. You must act before it is too late. Promise me that you will, no matter what Alfonso says."

"I promise. You must promise me in return that you will not worry."

"I'll stop worrying when I see you both on the road to Naples," she replied, and she went to the door. "Rest now. I will return for you later."

"Not too early," I called out. The door clicked shut after her. I gazed upon Rodrigo. His eyes were closed, his arms flung over his head in the same way I'd seen Alfonso do in his own sleep.

Determination overcame me. For Rodrigo's sake, we must go. But before we did, there was one thing I must do. Throwing on my cloak, I called for Murilla to accompany me.

"HE IS QUITE well, as you can see," said Vannozza. "A strong and healthy boy."

We sat outside on her flagstone terrace under the trellised jasmine, its fragrance clinging to everything as I watched my two-year-old son run about, rattling his toys as he lifted and discarded them with impetuosity. His robust, taciturn nursemaid sat on a stool close by, intent on his every move. He barely paid me mind, enduring my kisses for a few moments before he tried to get away, his light-blue-green eyes, which reminded me with a cruel stab of his father's, darting to his nursemaid, whom he clearly preferred to me, a perfumed and cloying stranger.

My mother sipped from her goblet. "Children at his age will do as they please. He has quite a will, as you can see. Like a Borgia." Her smile turned icy as I shot a look at her. "I am raising him to survive in our world."

I clenched my teeth. It was not the time or place to confront her with the news that I'd decided to leave him in her care, if she, in turn, swore to me that she would write every week to keep me apprised of him. Nor could I tell her that once I settled in Naples, I would find the right moment to tell Alfonso. This decision lifted a weight from me that I no longer wished to carry; no matter his reaction, henceforth I wanted only the truth between my husband and me.

As if she could sense my thoughts, my mother added, "We are all very proud of our little Juan." She paused again, as if to anticipate my eruption at her deliberate use of my son's Spanish name. When I failed to speak, my hands clenching as I watched Juan squeal and chase after a butterfly fluttering overhead, she added, "Are you going to tell me why you are here?"

"To see my son, of course." I drew a steadying breath, to blunt the anger rising inside me. "Is the money I send for his upkeep sufficient?"

"More than enough. We do not need it. Your father sends a fortune every month for our expenses, and I have my own money. The child lacks for nothing." She set her goblet on the table between us. She looked older, the afternoon sun highlighting crevices about her mouth, deep pleating at her eyes, and thick gray in her hair. She did not employ any means to prolong the illusion of youth. She had become a matron who was every inch her age, and, to my surprise, I realized she did not mind. A lifetime of seduction and rivalry had left her vanquished yet triumphant. Here in her villa on the Esquiline, under a roof she paid for herself, her coffers filled with coin she earned through her own labors, she had become a free woman, beholden to no one.

"You have not come to see him in over a year," she said at length. "Yet now you arrive without prior word. Something must have happened to bring you here, with that dwarf of yours to boot. I hope she knows how to keep her mouth shut."

"Murilla can be trusted." I fixed my stare on her as my mother raised her hands in a mock-warding gesture, as if to remind me that I had thought the same of Pantalisea and look how she ended up. "The reason I'm here," I said, "is because I am concerned. After Papa's accident and everything else, I wanted to make sure he was well."

"And would this 'everything else' you refer to involve your brother?"

"Why would you say that?' I said, immediately suspicious. Cesare had always trusted Vannozza, regardless of whatever disparagement he'd uttered to me about her. Did she know something about his plans?

She shrugged. "No reason. No one tells me much these days, least of all Cesare, but I know he's had his struggles of late, what with your father nearly being killed and these impossible twists of fate in Milan. One minute Il Moro has fled the city, the next he is back with a Hapsburg army to rout the French, and then, only a few days ago, he was captured. Milan has fallen once more to Louis of France." She rolled her eyes. "Who can keep up?"

I heard a slow-building roar in my ears. I did not feel myself move, but suddenly I was on my feet, drawing my cloak from the chair and summoning Murilla. Then I felt a grip on my arm. Glancing down, I saw my mother's hand detaining me. The skin of her hand was astonishingly smooth, I thought absently, not like her face; only here could the vestige of past vanity be glimpsed.

"What is it?" she said. "You look as if you've just seen Lucifer himself."

"Milan. You said the French have captured it again. . . ."

She frowned. "Cesare told me in confidence, though I'm quite certain the news will spread within the week. It is hardly your concern. He only mentioned it because he has spies in Il Moro's court, so he hears everything first. He says this time Il Moro will spend the rest of his days in a French dungeon, which is what every Sforza deserves."

I pulled from her grip. "I have to go. I—I am already late."

THE SUN SLIPPED past the horizon, shedding its coralline skin, tinting the stones of the streets with crimson as I hastened to my palazzo. In St. Peter's Piazza, pilgrims prepared to bed down in corners and nooks under the colonnade, even spreading threadbare blankets on the steps to the Apostolic Palace, where stern guards watched from their posts. Usually, such disrespect for the Vatican's sanctity would never have been tolerated, but Papa had given special orders to allow anyone without other quarters to sleep there because of the jubilee, though their very presence attracted footpads and vermin.

Hurrying into Santa Maria in Portico, I told my guards to bolt our gates for the night and raced up the staircase to my rooms. I prayed Sancia had ignored my request to not arrive too early and I would find her here, waiting impatiently. As I went into my antechamber, Nicola broke free of my other women and whispered, "The signore is in your chamber. He has been here well over an hour. He had me take Rodrigo back to his rooms."

Alfonso! I'd forgotten that he said he would return to dress for tonight. Thrusting my mantle at Nicola, I moved into my bedchamber.

"I have urgent news," I said as I burst past the half-open door. "Milan has fallen."

He stood at the window overlooking the piazza. He had lit a few tapers, their warm light welcome as the room began to darken. For a long moment, he did not look at me, bringing me to an uncertain standstill.

"Alfonso? Did you hear me? I was just visiting my mother. She told me Milan fell to the French; King Louis holds Il Moro prisoner. Sancia was not exaggerating. My brother must indeed be plotting. He kept this news from us for a purpose."

"I knew already." His voice was low. "Cesare is not the only one with spies. Of course, he did not tell me, but neither did he endeavor to keep it from me. Every informant in Milan has been reporting it." As he turned about, I saw shadows on his face, hollowing his bearded cheeks and diminishing the luster of his eyes. He had trimmed his beard; it was cut close to his jaw.

"But you did not mention it earlier," I said, taking an uncertain step toward him. Something about his stance, an indefinable remoteness, stoked my anxiety. "Sancia was just saying how we could be in danger, and surely this is reason enough to—"

"Why did you not tell me?"

I froze in mid-step. "What?"

"You know what." His voice drove at me. "This child you bore, the son—why did you not tell me about him?"

My mouth opened but no sound came out, my throat locking on itself as he stared from across the space between us, which suddenly widened like an abyss.

"Is it true?" he asked.

My hand reached out, trembling. Tears scorched my eyes. The pain in his face was visceral, imploring; yet I could not say what he needed to hear until he lowered his head with a moan and sank his face in his hands.

"Yes. I have another son," I whispered. "God forgive me."

"God?" He wrenched his face up. "What about my forgiveness? You lied to me. You *betrayed* me."

I staggered forward, tripping over my hem. "I did not mean to. I was so ashamed, humiliated, and frightened—I did not know where to turn. They told me I must keep it secret, for the sake of the annulment from Giovanni Sforza and—"

"For *their* sake, more like it," snarled Alfonso. "For the family's sake. How they must have laughed at me: the Neapolitan fool, lured into the snare while you and Cesare reared a bastard, born of your foul love."

Horrified understanding flooded me. He had confronted Cesare—and my brother had told him a monstrous lie. "That is not true. Whatever he said to you, it is not true!"

"Oh?" He came within inches of me. His gaze was searing, his face scored by grief, as if he had aged years. "It never ends, does it? The lies upon lies, the deception and treachery—you Borgia revel in it. You are everything they say—monsters who can only love each other. I am well rid of it. I am well rid of you."

Striding past me, he threw the door wide open.

"Alfonso," I screamed. *"Alfonso, no!"*

I ran to him, but before I could grasp him, implore him to stay and listen, he said in a voice I had never heard before, so hard and steadfast it was as though he had turned to stone: "Do not touch me. Do not follow me. You will never utter another falsehood to me again."

He did not stop, did not turn back, as I crumpled to the floor.

MY WOMEN GATHERED me up and took me, weeping uncontrollably, to a chair. I perched on it as if it were made of thorns, longing to rip my nails across my face and make myself bleed.

After what seemed an eternity, I heard the distant toll of bells, announcing the hour of Compline, and remembered we were expected to dine with Papa in the Vatican. Rising to my feet, I said in a mere thread of a voice, "My gown and jewels—fetch them."

I stood cold as they layered me in emerald silk, the color my father loved best on me, and affixed the pearled sleeves and stomacher, the diadem about my brow, and earrings to my lobes. Only as they started to unclasp the crucifix at my throat to replace it with a lavish jewel did I resist them, pivoting instead to the glass to regard my reflection.

The face staring back at me was blotched, white as ash, tendrils of stray jasmine from my sojourn to my mother's house still caught in my hair.

"Let me apply some powder and rouge, my lady," ventured Nicola.

I waved her aside. "Let them see me as I am. Let them see their beloved Lucrezia."

Wrenching at my skirts, I had only just reached the door when the screaming began.

IT WAS SANCIA in the courtyard, wailing. As I rushed down the staircase, my heart hammering in my throat, I saw she was drenched in blood. With a cry, I rushed to her, calling to my women for help, when she gasped, "Alfonso! You must come at once."

HE HAD BEEN taken to an apartment in Papa's new tower, Sancia said; he, his manservant Albanese, and their squire were assaulted as they crossed St. Peter's Piazza, by men pretending to be pilgrims. Night had fallen and they were surrounded. They fought to defend themselves but there must have been too many, for the squire had died, while Albanese and my husband suffered grave injury. Separated from Alfonso, Albanese sought refuge in a nearby house. Alfonso dragged himself to the Apostolic Palace, his would-be killers at his heels. They would have finished him there, on the threshold of the papal residence, had the papal guard not emerged, alerted by sounds of confrontation.

"But why were they outside?" I asked, as we hurried through the Vatican.

"He was going to find you. He arrived in the *sala* for dinner and saw you were not there." She began to cry again. "He had words with Cesare; I could not hear everything they said, but Alfonso was furious. He threatened your brother for lying to him. Then he left. He must have been heading back to the palazzo."

A scream clawed at my throat as I said, "Did Cesare . . . follow him?"

"No, he went back into the *sala*." Sancia's voice was ragged. "His Holiness was there, too, and several cardinals. We heard the shouting through the windows moments later; His Holiness dispatched the guard, and they—they . . ." She pressed a hand to her mouth. "They dragged him inside. Oh, Lucrezia, he was bathed in blood. He cannot survive."

"Do not say that." I came to a halt, seizing her hands. "He is young, strong. He will not die. He cannot." I kept repeating these words in my head, a desperate litany as I hauled her through the torchlit passage into the Sistine, moving through the chapel to the Vatican corridors, barely registering the courtiers gathered in huddles to whisper.

I was breathless by the time we reached the new tower Papa had recently built, which he had not yet inaugurated, because of his accident. Shoving past horror-struck spectators crowding the doorway, I looked frantically for Alfonso.

There were men everywhere, members of Alfonso's household jabbing fingers at a group of sullen bravos surrounding Cesare, yelling, *"Assassini!"* as my brother looked on with a faint sneer. My father stood among his cardinals, gripping a gold-headed cane, his white cassock limp about his person, the toll of his convalescence showing in his haggard features. One of the cardinals leaned to him; he swiveled to where I stood. Sudden silence descended.

Streaked blood stained my father's robe. I forced my gaze past him, terror scrabbling in my stomach as I moved to the settle they had pulled from one of the adjoining *salas*. Papa murmured, "He is unconscious. He sustained several wounds, but our esteemed Dr. Torella assures me that, with proper care and rest, he will recover."

I barely heard his forlorn voice as I reached the settle, unable to make sense of anything at first as Torella shifted aside, wiping his hands on a soiled cloth, revealing an inert body sprawled there. Alfonso seemed unreal, a wax figurine like those the populace hoisted during Carnival, not my husband at all. Our family doctor had tried to clean him, to stanch the bleeding; his doublet lay in a sodden heap on the floor, along with other pieces of his attire: a rumpled velvet cap, one gauntlet, his belt with its empty scabbard and poniard sheath—all splashed with that same awful shade of red.

I heard nothing, saw nothing, but him, as I sank to my knees, taking hold of his limp hand. I fought back panic when I felt how cold he was. His eyes were shut, his skin so pale I could see veins under it. The severity of his wounds was beyond my comprehension, jagged punctures already salved with herbs by Torella—a deep gash across his shoulder, another on his head, and one that looked to have almost cut into the very bone of his thigh, the stanching cloth already saturated with fresh blood. As I looked upon him, terrified that Sancia had been right and no man could possibly survive this, I gleaned the slight rise and fall of his chest.

He was alive.

I started to cry. Pressing my lips to his hand, I whispered, "My love, I am here. I am with you." Sancia's blood-soaked skirts made a damp dragging sound on the floor as she came beside me; I felt her touch my shoulder. I looked up, found that Papa and the others in the room had gone still, some regarding me with pity, some looking anywhere but at me. I searched the averted faces for Cesare, knowing that if he were responsible, I would see it the moment I met his eyes.

As though he sensed my intent, he remained immobile, fenced by his bravos. I passed my gaze over them, failed to find his favorite, Michelotto, among them. Then I returned to Cesare. In that instant, it was as though the room emptied of its occupants, so that only he and I remained, alone and bound to this hour we had been fated to live since our births.

He returned my stare, his eyes almost unreadable.

Almost—but not quite.

"Leave us," I heard myself say. Agitated murmuring rose among the men; I heard Dr. Torella issue an urgent advisory to Papa, who leaned to me. "*Hija,* we cannot leave him alone. He needs curing; an experienced physician must keep watch over him. There will be fever. He must be moved to a more suitable chamber for his recovery."

"Leave us," I repeated, without taking my gaze from Cesare. Disgust curled his mouth. Turning on his heel, he flipped his wrist in disdain as he walked out, with his bravos close behind.

Sancia went rigid. "We will watch over him," I told Papa, turning back to Alfonso. I eased the matted hair from his brow. "Only we and Dr. Torella are to enter or leave this room. I want guards posted at the door at all times. See to it."

We did not rest. We did not sleep and we barely ate. Had it not been for the platters of bread, cheese, and meat and the flagons of water delivered twice a day at Papa's command, we would have become desert dwellers, parched and gaunt, as we took turns in our vigil over Alfonso. The world ceased to exist, every waking moment narrowed to this chamber in the private apartment of the tower where I'd had him moved.

He sank into delirium, thrashing so much on his bed that he ruptured his sutures. We had to hold him down as Torella sewed the wounds anew, dousing him with enough milk of the poppy to ensure we could roll him to one side and change his pus- and sweat-drenched bedding.

The fevers were terrifying, flaring up at night just as we collapsed onto our chairs in utter exhaustion and tried to fill our stomachs with whatever we could swallow. Sancia stayed by my side, lending herself entirely to the task, but when he began to moan and clench his sheets, perspiration sprouting from him like a humid mist that soaked his chemise, as he muttered unintelligible words and his flesh blazed and turned icy at the same time, she retreated to a corner, helpless, to whisper prayers. I clambered onto the bed and pulled him close, seeking to warm him and stave off the corruption Torella had warned would be his doom. The wounds must not corrupt; fever was a hallmark of this. If I could not thaw him, if his shudders turned to teeth-chattering shivers and he began to whimper, I barked at Sancia, "Quick, help me! We must strip him!" Divesting him of his chemise, ignoring the sight of his thinning, pallid frame, I bathed him in warm wine steeped with thyme and garlic, forcing drafts of willow, birch, and meadowsweet past his arid lips, whispering in his ear: "Stay with me, *amore*. Do not go."

When the fever finally broke, he lay inert, as though he were already dead. In desperation, I had little Rodrigo brought, cradling him as he giggled and burped, oblivious to his moribund father. I tickled his plump ribs and kicking feet, making him chortle, all the while watching Alfonso for a sign that he heard our child's laughter, that it would rouse him from death's insistent grip.

One night I fell apart like a child myself, arms wrapped tight about my midriff as if my guts might spill out, rocking back and forth on the stool by his bed and sobbing, begging him to wake. Sancia had staggered out moments before to relieve herself and to empty our overflowing privy pail, to see the sullied cloths we used to cleanse his wounds burned and fetch us clean garments. The chamber reeked of our confinement; it had been three weeks since the assault, and Torella had suggested moving him again so that the room could be aired. I flew at the doctor, screaming that moving Alfonso would be his end; he barely held on to life as it was. The doctor retreated with a resignation that rent me asunder. He had given up hope. He had done everything he could and Alfonso had not regained consciousness. Everyone believed it was already over.

It was then, as I wept alone at his bedside and felt my own being cave in, as the grief I had fought so hard against rose up to drown me, that I heard his voice. At first I thought I imagined it. I went still, tears sliding down my face as I blinked back the haze to stare at him, full of doubt.

His brow creased. I let out a gasp, leaning closer. "Alfonso?"

Slowly, he opened his eyes. For a long moment he regarded me, the intense amber of his gaze piercing me to my very soul. Then his fingers twitched, curling outward, and with a strangled sob, I reached for his hand.

"I . . . I love you," he whispered. "Do not . . . leave me. . . ."

"Never." I kissed his hand. He sighed, his eyes closing again. I froze, thinking it was the end, the final rally before—

I felt his hand tighten. His eyes opened again. He moved his lips. This time, he did not have enough strength to give his word voice. But I heard it nonetheless, like the howl of a wolf in my mind: "Cesare."

BY THE FOLLOWING week, he could sit up. Soon after, he was well enough to rise. Every day I helped him from the bed so he could limp across the room. He was weak, complaining his leg hurt "like a hundred devils." I knew the pain was almost unbearable, because he would clutch at me, digging his fingers into my arm, swaying as though he stood on shifting ground. But he gritted his teeth and forced himself to keep walking, until he crossed the short distance between his bed and the window on his own. I refused to abandon his side, sleeping on a trestle near his bed, bathing and changing in the anteroom, until one morning he successfully made his painstaking walk. A few moments after I had assisted him back into bed, sweat from his efforts beading his brow, Sancia arrived with his midday meal. As I went about arranging the piles of books Alfonso had insisted she fetch from the library to relieve his boredom, she began to speak to him in a low voice. He suddenly growled, "He said that?"

I paused, glancing at them. Sancia perched at Alfonso's side, a tureen of soup poised in her hands. "What is it?" I asked.

"Your father," replied Alfonso. He shifted, wincing. I rushed to him as he let out a sharp cry of pain. "Damn this leg!" Blood spotted the linen bandage under his smock.

"You overexert yourself." I pressed him against his pillows to check the bandage. "This linen needs changing again. Let me fetch a new binding—"

His hand caught my wrist. "You must hear this. Sancia, tell her."

His somber expression brought me to a halt. We had not spoken of what he uttered upon waking, though it had settled between us, a feral reality we would have to face. Nor had he mentioned the reason behind our estrangement on the night of the assault, though he now knew Cesare had misled him, seeking to drive us apart. I had told myself it would serve little purpose to give voice to the undercurrent surrounding us; the most important matter was for Alfonso to fully recover. Now fear roiled to the surface as I directed my gaze to Sancia.

She sat still, hesitant.

"Go on," said Alfonso. "She deserves to know."

I braced myself. Her reticence could only mean she had heard something horrible. "Our ambassador from Naples," she said, her voice flat, as if she had stripped it deliberately of any emotion. "He told me that he asked His Holiness if there was any truth to the rumor that Cesare had ordered this attack. His Holiness replied, as he has before, that he believes your brother innocent of wrongdoing, only this time he added that if Cesare was responsible, he must have had his reasons."

I could not speak, could not find enough air to draw into my lungs.

Then I heard myself whisper, "He must have misunderstood. Papa would never say such a thing. . . ." My denial faded into silence. I remembered how Papa had sent Giulia to entertain Juan and my husband, how he ordered the deaths of Pantalisea and Perotto. I had told myself that Giulia lied, that the deaths of the servants were necessary to protect me, but I could no longer deny the horrifying truth, no matter how much I wanted to; nor could I find refuge in memories of my childhood, when Papa had dominated my entire being. He had done terrible things in the name of power. He had plundered his way to the papal throne and sacrificed our well-being to his ambition.

Now he had given Cesare the freedom to do the same.

Alfonso turned thunderous. "I will not wait for them to strike again. I have been thinking over that night: I cannot say for certain who the culprits were. It was dark; they came at us from under cloaks that they had laid on the steps and pretended to sleep under like beggars. I could not recognize any faces, because they wore masks. But they must have had horses nearby, an escape route planned, for they fled as soon as the guards came. They were waiting for me; they knew my route. I confused them at first because, when I left Santa Maria, I took the passage through the Sistine. Otherwise, I'd never have reached the *sala* or had words with Cesare." He paused. "His Holiness will do nothing to save me. My life is still in mortal danger."

"Then we must strike first." Sancia turned to me. "Cesare deserves death for everything he has done and will yet do, if he is not stopped."

Beware the man who covets.

As if my brother had whispered in my ear, materialized out of the thudding fear in my heart, I heard his words—no, his *warning*—and understood. The one thing Cesare had coveted most in this world, more than power or respect, more than even Papa's adulation, was me. He sought to kill Alfonso for the same reason he had murdered Juan, because he could not bear for anyone else to have me.

I forced my voice up out of the coiled knot in my chest. "You and Sancia must stay here. You cannot venture outside for any reason. Let me speak to Papa. Let me gain his promise to ensure our safety. I am his daughter. He will not refuse me."

Alfonso shook his head. "If you do that, it will only forewarn them. They will double the guards at our door and then we'll truly be trapped." He struggled against his sheets, trying to rise. "I must be the one to go. Perhaps if His Holiness can be assured that I have no desire to stay in Rome or challenge Cesare, he will think twice about—"

I started to tell him it was no use. No matter what he promised, I was the one whom Cesare fought to keep, whom he feared to lose. He would strike again at Alfonso for taking me away. I was the only one he had ever loved. I had to be the one who put an end to his madness, but sudden voices outside the door cut short my protest.

The tureen dropped from Sancia's hands, clattering to the floor. I heard shouting, a staccato reply of barked orders. Before I could cross the chamber, Sancia thrust something into my hand. I did not have a chance to look at it, but as I closed my fingers about the gem-studded hilt, I knew it for her stiletto, which she had wielded against Giovanni Sforza. It felt like a child's toy as the door crashed open to reveal a figure looming on the threshold.

He inclined his head. "Madonna." His mouth twisted in a grimace, pulling at the ugly scar across his upper lip. "I trust you are well."

"What—what are you doing here?" I kept my back to the bed, where my husband struggled to rise as Sancia said urgently, "Alfonso, behind me. Stay behind me!"

"His Holiness requests your presence." Michelotto's eyes flickered. "He wonders how long you plan to remain in this chamber, when you have your duties and son to attend to."

"My son is safe," I said, "while my husband is not, as His Holiness well knows."

"Nevertheless, I am ordered to escort you to His Holiness and have this room searched. We have reason to suspect a plot against my lord."

Behind me, Alfonso cried, "The plot is against me, not him!" and I lifted my chin.

"Why was I not informed of this beforehand? You will leave at once until I can verify—"

"I am afraid you are the one who must leave, my lady," Michelotto interrupted. Stepping aside, he revealed a collection of men behind him. My heart started to pound. They were Cesare's bravos, the same ones I had seen after the attack on Alfonso. "We will attend to this matter," Michelotto said.

"No." The dagger felt cold in my palm. Glancing behind me, I saw that Alfonso had managed to rise from the bed, gripping the post while Sancia shielded him. "We stay here," I said, returning my stare to my brother's henchman. "Search this chamber if you like. We have nothing to hide."

Michelotto took a step forward—just one, but the effect it had on me was immediate, rousing the memory of how he had come to me in Pesaro to facilitate my spying on Giovanni, which had ended with the secretary's execution. With an inchoate roar, I flung myself at him, brandishing the dagger and slashing at his face. *"Get out now or I will kill you!"*

He spun away, blood spraying. The men behind him surged at us. I started to scream wildly as three of them neared me, until one knocked my hand gripping the dagger aside with a blow that shuddered up my arm into my neck, agonizing as liquid fire.

"No!" I shrieked. "NO!" Taking hold of me, they dragged me toward the door as I bellowed, kicking my legs against them, trying to free my hands to rake my nails across their cheeks. They hauled me into the passageway. Four others waiting there grabbed me. I could hear Sancia's terror, her anguished cries above the crash of furniture being overturned and Alfonso's outraged shouts. Two more men appeared, hauling Sancia between them. After they pushed her through the door to send her careening against me, they slammed the door shut. Alfonso still railed from within, "I demand to see His Holiness! *I demand justice!*"

The men holding me released their grip. I threw myself at the door, yanking at the latch, banging with my fists and crying out his name. Sancia fell to her knees with a heartrending wail.

To my overwhelming horror, Alfonso's cries were silenced.

"No," I whispered. "Sweet Jesus, no . . ."

The door opened. Michelotto emerged. He had blood on his face, pooling into his collar. I had cut him above his old scar; he would bear another one now as my brand, deeper than the first. Arching his brow at me, he swiped his sleeve across his wound.

I shoved past him, my entire body moving with disjointed awkwardness, my heels crunching on the fragments of a broken chair, across the splayed spines of books, the rumpled carpet, and overturned stools.

My eyes lifted. The tester curtains were draped halfway across the bed, unraveled from their knotted tassels. The sheets and coverlets hung over the side in crumpled folds, bunched, as if he had clawed at them in his final moments, trying desperately to clamber across the bed.

One of his arms dangled, its flesh bruised. He was facedown, shoulders and head submerged under a pillow that still bore the imprint of Michelotto's smothering hands.

My husband was dead.

I WALKED ALONE down the passageway, leaving Sancia to tend to the body, not saying a word as she stood stunned, bewildered, in the wreckage. Courtiers, secretaries, and other menials stopped to stare before scurrying from my path, denizens of a world I no longer recognized.

No one tried to stop me; no one spoke as I took the staircase to my father's apartments and stepped through his door. Only then, as his manservant swerved from where he busied himself at the sideboard, did I see in the youth's startled expression the image I must present: my gown torn at the shoulder from where the bravos had handled me, my own palm dripping scarlet beads from my futile exertions with Sancia's blade.

Papa sat in his upholstered chair behind his desk, two secretaries hovering nearby as he consulted stacks of official papers, his papal seal on the blotter at his side, his sharpened quills and ink in the rock-crystal holder shaped like a galleon.

I came to a halt. In the sunlight pouring through the window behind him, which overlooked the Vatican's private gardens, he appeared faceless.

"Why?" I whispered.

He froze, gazing at my disheveled gown spotted with the blood from my cut hand, my hair tangled about my face. Then he gestured and his staff fled the room.

He started to stand. "My child, I called for you over an hour ago and expected—"

I stepped to him. *"Why?"* Rage seared my voice. "Why did you let Cesare do this?"

His shoulders twitched, as if he were about to shrug. I could not believe what I was seeing, what I was hearing, as he affected a sorrowful tone, as though he were standing before the Curia delivering a eulogy.

"It could not be helped. Rome can be such a lawless place. Our beloved son-in-law was beset by thieves and wounded, his life despaired for. We did everything we could, but he ignored our physician's advice. His wounds reopened. Corruption set in." He sighed. "An accident, a tragedy: *That* is what we shall say."

Agony lanced my soul. I remembered how much I loved Papa, how I had anticipated his visits in my childhood, when he took me on his knee and filled me with tales of Spain, of crusader knights and lace palaces upon the hills. I saw him again triumphant at the Sistine window on the day he won the papacy, his laughter rumbling, his boundless enthusiasm and passion for life. I tried to recapture the memory of his love, to seal it within me and keep it from seeping out, so that I could have something to cling to as I drifted upon this churning black sea.

His Holiness will do nothing to save me.

It was like trying to embrace mist; it disappeared until I felt nothing but the emptiness of its departure. The trusting child I had been, the doting daughter and adoring sister, who had defended my family against all odds—they had killed her, too.

Laughter drifted from the gardens. One of the windowpanes was cracked open to admit a breeze. I moved to it, past my father, who sat motionless at his desk. Pausing with my bloodied hand on the sill, I saw two figures below—one lean in black damask, poised among the rose beds, as his companion twirled, bare shoulders swaying within her low-cut silk gown. She was the one laughing—a melodic, artificial display that betrayed her as a courtesan, trained to show delight at anything a customer quipped. As she danced under the window, she lifted painted eyes. She was beautiful, even from a distance, with olive skin and rouged lips, her hair a flowing mane that gleamed in the sun. A hint of surprise creased her face; I saw her turn, beckon Cesare.

He looked up. His imperturbable gaze met mine, held it for an endless moment. Then it passed through me, as if I were a ghost. Turning from the window, I said, "I wish to leave as soon as he is buried. I will take my son and go to my castle at Nepi—if it is still mine."

"Of course it's yours," Papa said, with audible offense. "I gave it to you. You may go there whenever you like."

"Then I have Your Holiness's permission?"

He grunted, lowering his chin. Taking it as assent, I moved past him once more.

He said softly, *"Farfallina,"* and I flinched. "You must understand. He plotted against us; he would have done the same to Cesare, given the chance. He was a traitor. Unworthy of you."

I regarded him, appalled by his self-delusion. Then I felt a smile break across my lips—bitter as the last dregs of love I had for him. "He was everything to me. Everything, and more. I will never cease to mourn him or forget what you have done."

Then I continued to walk to the door. His next words sank like talons into my back.

"You took Juan from me."

I froze. I had to force myself to look over my shoulder.

His eyes were like obsidian—cold as a serpent's after it has spat its venom. "You killed him. Juan had to die because of you; that is why Cesare murdered him. I knew it from the moment I learned about your bastard, though I did not want to believe it. I tried to deny it, tell myself it could not be. But there it was—my son's blood, spilled for you. An eye for an eye, remember? We each must surrender what we love for the good of the family. Consider this sacrifice yours."

A shudder went through me. Without a word, I turned from him.

"You will not make a scandal!" he called out after me. I heard his fist slam on the desk. "Do you hear me? You will mourn as a wife should; hide away for a time to grieve, but then you will return here, to us, where you belong. I'll not have it said you oppose us. Enough trouble you have caused already."

Though only a fragment of my pride remained, a hollow sliver that would bring no comfort, I refused to surrender it by replying.

That pride was all I had left of the girl I had been.

CHAPTER THIRTY-THREE

He was laid to rest in the chapel of Santa Maria della Febbre near the basilica, under a slab of stone, the funeral Mass and tapers mocking the very faith they purported to exalt.

Sancia came to say goodbye a few days later, finding me in my rooms, where my belongings were secured for my journey. My women retreated, leaving us alone.

"What will you do now?" I rose from my crouch by a chest, pushing damp hair from my brow. I had thrown armfuls of clothing into the *cassone;* I had no idea what I packed, if I would reach Nepi to find myself with a surfeit of furs and silks and no undergarments. I did not care. Already the palazzo felt like a tomb.

"I leave for Naples." Sorrow incised her face, bruising the beautiful pools of her eyes and slashing her cheeks. "They do not want me here, and I do not want to stay. Gioffre will come with me, or so they claim. We shall see when the time comes."

"He loves you," I said. "He is not like . . . them."

"I'm far more concerned for you. They will never let you go, no matter how far you run. Already there is talk of another marriage—"

I held up my hand. "It is not important. Come." I held out my arms; as we embraced, I whispered, "I love you as if you were my sister. Never doubt it. You are as much a part of his son as you are part of him. Should you ever find need of me, you must send word."

She clung to me before she drew back. Wiping tears from her cheeks, she started to turn away. Then she paused. From within her cloak she pulled out the stiletto, which I had dropped during our struggle to save Alfonso.

"This is yours." She set it on a nearby table. "Use it to avenge him."
Without another word, she left.

ESCORTED BY MY women and men-at-arms, my son bundled in fleece
and borne in a litter by his nursemaid, I rode from Santa Maria under
a remorseless sky wiped clean of clouds, its blue so vivid it was like the
hem of the Virgin's mantle.

I did not turn to look at my palazzo as I departed, riding past the
balcony of the Vatican with its scarlet tapestry, where my father had assembled with his cardinals to bid me farewell. I rode with my spine
erect and head uplifted, as though it were my triumphal exit, as if I were
still the beloved wife who knew where her place was.

Not a cheer came from the crowds gathered at the sides of the road.
Instead, the fickle populace of Rome, as apt to show their contempt by
tossing obscenities as to celebrate with flowers and song, regarded me
with pity, the men doffing their caps, the women lifting rosaries twined
in their fingers as they beheld my black veil and gown, upon which not
a single jewel showed. I still wore my gold wedding band under my
gauntlet; I could feel its chill, narrow width about my finger.

I wanted to believe I left nothing behind, that Rome, with its savage
entanglements and lethal secrets, held no more power over me.

But that would have been a deception, and I'd learned to never
again lie to myself.

GRIEF IS SELFISH. It enshrouds us, clutches us to its desiccated breast
like an anxious mother. It does not want us to leave, though we know
we must if we are to survive. Only madness lies ahead for those who
cannot escape it, for grief will consume those who have nothing else to
live for.

I had my child; in the isolation of Nepi, I devoted myself to him.
Every day I held him in my arms, singing silly refrains of the nursery,
tickling his feet, and basking in his gleeful laughter. Everything about
him reminded me of his father.

"You will know him," I promised, pressing my lips to his soft cheek.
"You will take pride in him, because I will tell you who he was—the

bravest, most noble man I have ever known, who loved you with all his heart."

I suffered every night as darkness encroached, after the servants cleared dinner from the table and then heaped kindling on the fire, to keep the cold at bay, before finally leaving me with the castle dogs at my feet. I fell into the past. I made myself remember, no matter how much it hurt; I wanted to feel every moment, from that day I first saw him on the road, when he accompanied his sister, his smile resplendent, daz-zling all who beheld him. I closed my eyes and felt our first tentative kiss in the library, the way he held himself back, as if I were a fragile gift he must not squander. I rejoiced at our wedding, laughing in our cham-ber as he peeled off my clothes and I cried out in ecstasy at his touch. They had seemed to go on forever, those days when we loved, yet when I stopped to relive them, I realized they had amounted to only two years.

A brief respite in the desolation that now stretched before me.

Yes, I suffered. Only God knows how much.

Yet I also waited, preparing for the one I knew must soon arrive.

HE CAME WITH the winds of autumn, breathing war across the plains, the thunder of his ten thousand soldiers scattering peasants from his path. He was returning to the Romagna, secure now in his might, armed with the papal title of gonfalonier and defender of the faith, along with enough cannon to destroy any resistance.

A messenger brought me advance word. By dusk, he was riding up to the castle with his select companions, through the raised portcullis into the courtyard.

I dressed in my widow's weeds and stood in the hall. His booted footsteps were soft as a cat's on the flagstones. He would see me alone at least, without the insulting company of his men.

"My lady sister." Cesare bowed, his figure limned by firelight. He wore black, as I did, but his was of exquisite cut, tiny silver points spar-kling on the lacings of his sleeves, his shapely legs caressed by leather hose. He did not attempt to embrace me as I extended my hand to him, with the polite indifference I might show to any uninvited guest.

"You must be hungry," I said. "Shall I have a meal prepared?"

His smile was taut, revealing a hint of teeth. "Later. Only wine now, if you would?"

I turned to the decanter on the sideboard, poured him a goblet. As he took it from me, his eyes flared slightly, as they had that day in the villa above Pesaro, when I gave him a draft. Unspoken suspicion shivered between us. Then he deliberately, without taking his eyes from me, raised the goblet to his lips. I almost laughed. Did he think me so clumsy as to employ poison?

I watched him divest himself of his cloak, draping it over a chair near the hearth. He paced to the fire, stood for a moment contemplating the flames. "I would not have you hate me," he said at length. "I realize I may hope in vain."

I did not reply. I saw no reason. He was not asking me a question.

He sighed. "Papa is concerned. He's written several times since you left, and not once have you answered." He glanced over his shoulder. "Do you hate him, as well?"

"What I feel doesn't make any difference," I said, gathering my strength. Despite his stated purpose, I knew why he had come, but the fury I anticipated failed to engulf me. Even that meager refuge of anger and thwarted guilt, of shame that I'd let it happen almost as much as he had planned it—because I had not recognized the threat he truly posed—had turned to cinders inside me.

He nodded, as if he accepted the inevitability of my statement. "I bring more of his letters," he said, motioning to his cloak. "We have proposals."

"Oh? So many that he felt compelled to send you to pander to me?" I preempted him. "You can spare us the inconvenience and tell His Holiness that I have no desire to wed again. Lest it has escaped his notice, both my husbands have been unlucky."

His arid chuckle raked up my spine. "Indeed. But you will find that, regardless, many are still eager to call themselves thus, including one you have met before."

I went still.

"Alfonso d'Este, Duke of Ferrara," he said. "Do you remember him?"

"I have never met . . ." I faltered as the memory surfaced: an evening in my new palazzo and a somber ducal son who'd presented me with a hooded falcon as a gift, his attentions provoking Giulia Farnese to unleash her hair before him like a sylph.

There can be no moon without the sun.

"I see you do," said Cesare. "He is a widower, his first wife having died in childbirth. His family is also one of the most influential in Italy, his own sister the esteemed Isabella, Marchioness of Mantua. Marriage to him will bring considerable rewards."

"To whom? Me or the family? Or are we still one and the same to you?"

He looked back to the fire. "We were once, not long ago."

"Not now." I had heard enough.

I had turned to exit the chamber when he said, "No one will force you. We simply ask that you take some time to consider it. You are only twenty, not so old that this tragedy will not wear thin after a while. And even if it should not, you still have your sons to care for."

Slowly, I turned back to him. "Is that a threat? Would you use my own children against me?"

"I never said that. They are our blood—or at least one of them is. The other one"—he grimaced—"concerns me less. But they still require some normality, if they are to avoid our—"

He did not have time to finish. My hand whipped out, cracking hard across his face. "Monster," I breathed. In my gown pocket, Sancia's dagger dug against my thigh. "Try to harm my sons in any way and, I swear on my soul, you will die for it. I will kill you myself."

He did not lift a hand to his cheek. "Mama warned us. She told you we would be each other's doom. I only seek to spare you such a fate, seeing as I failed to spare you anything else."

"You have spared me nothing. *You* did this to us—you, and no one else."

He bowed his head. "I cannot deny it. I know that I alone brought us to this place. I made us who we are." He lifted his face; his mouth curved in a chilling smile. "But you must allow that I, too, was once innocent. Papa made sure to excise it from me. He did what fathers have always done, seek his own immortality through his seed. He took on the burden of what we would become before we had the chance to discover it for ourselves. He shaped us with his illusions, his flaws, never once realizing that what he created was only a distorted reflection of his own self. He destroyed us. But your sons needn't suffer our sickness."

"*Your* sickness. Not mine." As I spun away once more, he grasped me. I smelled his rancid breath, saw the bloodshot threads in his eyes, and sensed under his camouflage of velvet and leather the toll of the incurable disease consuming him.

"I know I am dying," he said, adept as ever at reading my thoughts. "I have heard all the portents that I am not long for this earth. It is no fever I carry, but rather the mark of my death. Until I am gone, I must take what I can. By blade or treaty, scaffold or chain, they *will* bow to me. They will tremble at the name of Cesare Borgia, the forsaken son, who no one thought would be more than his father's shadow. There is no one to stop me now, nothing greater than the sword I wield. I will cut through it all. I will break and reshape Italy in my image. It will be my legacy."

He leaned to me suddenly, as if to kiss me. Then he paused. Laughter purred in his throat. "Is that Sancia's needle you hold to my gut?"

I pressed on the hilt. "You say there is nothing greater than your sword. What about me?"

He met my eyes. The arrogance in his expression faded. For a paralyzing moment, I saw the visage of the beloved sibling I had adored, the companion of my life, whose existence had been so entangled with mine, the very weft of my days felt incomplete without him.

"You cannot bring him back," he said. "Nothing you do can bring him back." He lifted his chin to expose his long throat. "I give myself in atonement, my blood for his. I once told you that to see you safe, I would die a thousand deaths. To avenge him, you need only one. You have earned this right. It is what we must do to prove our strength. Do it. Show the world what a Borgia you are."

Desire overcame me—hot and fierce, rampant as a bull loosed in the arena, charging with horns down, curved and pointed, and oh so sharp. I craved it: the thrust of my blade into him, the heat of his blood splashing my fingers. I wanted to watch the surprise of it, the shock, cloud over his eyes and shutter them forever.

"Do it, Lucia," he whispered, and I heard it then, what I had longed for without knowing it: his desperate plea, to be released from what he had become. Only through me could he ever find redemption. In taking away the husband I had loved, he'd chained himself to me until I freed him.

I flung the knife aside. "I am not one of you. I never will be again."

His entire body seemed to fall into itself then, a raw wreckage of bones. He stood without moving as I backed away, tears glazing his eyes as I widened the distance, making it impassable. I left him alone, a scourge that might wreak havoc on the land but never again within my heart.

When I woke the next morning, my brother was gone.

I DO NOT know what my future holds. As I seal my letter with my signet and prepare it for delivery to His Holiness in Rome, uncertainty overwhelms me. How will I fare, an exile from my own city, bound for a realm where the sins of my past may be hidden but never forgotten?

Gazing out the window into the distance, hearing my son rattling a toy on the carpet behind me, I conjure that duchy where I will assume my new incarnation as duchess of Ferrara, second wife of a stranger who once gave me a bird of prey and whose features I barely recall. This is my choice, if such it can be called. Better I accept this than wait for my father to decide for me. Ferrara lies many miles from Rome, though no distance would be great enough. But at least there I may start anew, esteemed as a noble wife, even if I can never escape my memories.

Will I find love or despair? Will my new husband give me haven or another purgatory to endure? Will I find redemption?

I cannot know the answers. Only by braving the unknown can I hope to find peace and forgive myself. My father once said, infamy is an accident of fate—but I know better. I know now that infamy is a poison that runs in our blood.

Yet every poison has an antidote.

And I am not a Borgia anymore.

AFTERWORD

In 1502, two years after the murder of her second husband, Lucrezia married Alfonso d'Este, Duke of Ferrara. The duke did not travel to Rome to fetch his bride. Instead, his brothers escorted her to her new home in Ferrara with all the pomp that Pope Alexander VI was capable of, even as Cesare sowed terror in his quest to subdue the Romagna.

In wedding Lucrezia, the proud d'Este clan secured alliance with the Borgias, which spared them Cesare's spleen, though Isabella d'Este, the twenty-eight-year-old marchioness of Mantua and Lucrezia's new sister-in-law, renowned as the arbiter of all things fashionable in her era, expressed outrage that someone of Lucrezia's repute and low birth was now part of her family. These two women were destined to be rivals as Lucrezia embarked on a tumultuous final chapter in her life. Gaining respect as duchess of Ferrara, where the distance from her family's machinations allowed her to display her accomplishments as a patroness of the arts, Lucrezia survived the fall of the Borgias, but her marriage remained one of political convenience. As fruitful as the union was, neither she nor her husband was faithful; Lucrezia had at least three extramarital affairs, including a relationship with Isabella d'Este's own husband, Francesco of Mantua. Surviving evidence of this affair includes passionate love letters that he and Lucrezia exchanged. It ended when Francesco contracted syphilis, a disease spreading throughout Europe, and from which Cesare Borgia also suffered.

Lucrezia died in Ferrara on June 24, 1519, at the age of thirty-nine, from complications after giving birth to a daughter, who died soon after. She was buried in the convent of Corpus Domini. Of her seven children sired by d'Este, she was survived by Ippolito II, Archbishop and later Cardinal of Milan (1509–1572); Leonora, who became a nun (1515–1575); and Francesco, Marquis of Massalombarda (1516–1578).

Cesare Borgia waged a dramatic campaign for power, becoming one of the most feared and brilliant strategists of his age, carving out a domain from the fractious papal states and earning the admiration of Machiavelli himself, whose treatise on Renaissance statesmanship, *The Prince,* is allegedly based on Cesare. Leonardo da Vinci was also employed by Cesare in 1502–03 as an architect and engineer, overseeing reinforcements and construction in Cesare's territories. Under Borgia patronage, da Vinci built the canal between Cesena and the port Cesenatico, facilitating the transport of goods and weaponry.

Rodrigo Borgia, known as Pope Alexander VI, died unexpectedly in 1503 of poison. Cesare narrowly escaped the same fate, having ingested the substance that killed his father during a feast. He was bedridden for weeks before he rallied; once he did, Rodrigo's successor, Pope Pius III, reconfirmed him as gonfalonier. But Pius died after a mere twenty-seven days on the papal throne, and the Borgias' lifelong foe, Giuliano della Rovere, secured the next conclave. Della Rovere had hoodwinked Cesare by offering support for his military ventures in the Romagna—which he promptly disregarded upon his election as Pope Julius II. Cesare was left to face both Pope Julius's indifference and the enmity of King Fernando of Spain, who'd never forgiven him for his French alliance. During a campaign in Naples, Fernando's captain general betrayed and imprisoned Cesare. His lands were seized by the Holy See. In 1504, he was transferred to Spain, first to the Castle of Chinchilla de Montearagón; he was later moved to the more formidable Castle of La Mota in Medina del Campo, a site readers will recognize from my first novel, *The Last Queen.* Following an extraordinary escape from La Mota, Cesare fled to the Navarrese territory of Pamplona, ruled by his father-in-law, King Juan II. The king was in dire need of an expert commander to thwart Castile's incursions, and as a condottiere for Navarre, Cesare captured several cities held by Fernando.

On March 11, 1507, enraged by the resistance of the fortress during his siege on the city of Viana, Cesare chased a parcel of knights only to find himself caught in an ambush. Abandoned by his men, he was killed by a spear thrust. His body was stripped, including the leather mask covering half of his face, disfigured by syphilitic sores. His naked corpse was left on the ground for hours.

At King Fernando's command, Cesare was interred in a mausoleum in the Church of Santa Maria in Viana under the epitaph: HERE LIES IN LITTLE EARTH ONE FEARED BY ALL, WHO HELD PEACE AND WAR IN HIS HAND. For centuries afterward, controversy raged over whether the Borgia son who had caused such mayhem and ill will deserved to rest in hallowed ground.

At Alfonso d'Este's insistence, Lucrezia had to relinquish Rodrigo, her son by Alfonso of Aragon. Raised by his maternal family, Rodrigo inherited his late father's titles but was held captive upon Pope Alexander's death. After frantic intercession by his mother, he was sent to Naples to reside with his aunt, Sancia, who died in 1506 at the age of twenty-eight. Rodrigo perished of a fever when he was twelve, preceding Lucrezia in death by seven years.

Gioffre Borgia remarried after Sancia's death, fighting against the second French invasion of Naples in 1504. He sired four children before his demise in 1518. His descendants ruled the city of Squillace until 1735.

Giovanni Borgia, known as the *Infans Romanus,* the Infant of Rome—a motto that demonstrates his obscure origin—came to adulthood under the care of various relatives, including Cesare and Vannozza dei Cattanei, before her death in 1518. Alexander VI had issued two separate bulls, one proclaiming the boy as his own by an unmarried woman, another as Cesare's by the same. Coincidentally, the first bull became public during Lucrezia's third marriage, further obscuring the parentage of this enigmatic child. Giovanni later went to Ferrara as a companion to Lucrezia, where he was styled her "half brother." After serving in France and the Curia, he died in 1548. By that time, he was of negligible importance, the Borgias having passed into lurid myth.

It was their myth that first captured my interest in this Spanish family, whose meteoric rise and fall in the Vatican has aroused so much speculation. Hundreds of years later, we remain enthralled by the Borgias, their larger-than-life passions and heinous deeds.

Lucrezia, in particular, has come to personify evil through her longestablished and erroneously attributed role as a malignant seductress.

Research reveals she was nothing like her legend. As most women of her status, she was a pawn in her family's ambitions, used to secure alliances, with no say in her fate. Nevertheless, she proved a survivor, steering a tenacious, often heartrending path through the chaos of her life, the only one of her siblings to display any depth of feeling beyond her own interests. I found no evidence that she poisoned or harmed anyone.

The loss of Alfonso of Aragon devastated her. She informed the ambassador of Ferrara during negotiations for her third marriage that "Rome had become a prison" for her. Regardless of her love for her father and Cesare, she had learned their true nature. Her only crime, if such, was to trust them for as long as she did. But she can hardly be faulted, considering she wasn't yet thirteen when she first wed and barely twenty when Alfonso was killed. She experienced more tragedy in her youth than many experience in a lifetime. For her, happiness would always be elusive.

The question of whether she committed incest remains as acrimonious and hotly debated today as it was during her lifetime. The rumor first surfaced as recounted in this novel, during Lucrezia's annulment from her first marriage. Giovanni Sforza made the accusation in a letter to Il Moro, writing that she was being taken from him because Alexander "wanted her for himself"—thus initiating an avalanche of innuendo that has haunted Lucrezia ever since. This novel presents one possible theory, but I must emphasize that it is fictional, as is my theory about Juan Borgia's murder. The frustrating truth is that we have no reliable documentation about what went on behind the Borgias' closed doors. As much as the family has been dramatized from every angle, we can never know the answers to the most controversial questions about them. Perhaps this very mystery can account for our enduring fascination.

That said, I've endeavored to stay true to established fact as much as possible, tricky as this can be when contending with disparate accounts. In some instances I compressed time to facilitate my story, as Renaissance Italy can be bewildering with its many twists and reversals. I also avoided tantalizing side plots that did not directly affect Lucrezia, such as the unsolved murders attributed to the Borgias of various relatives and perceived opponents.

. . .

MANY SOURCES ACCOMPANIED me while writing this novel. Although not intended as a full bibliography, I list below those I found most valuable in depicting Lucrezia's Vatican years:

Bellonci, Maria. *The Life and Times of Lucrezia Borgia*. New York: Harcourt Brace, 1953.

Bradford, Sarah. *Cesare Borgia: His Life and Times*. New York: Macmillan Publishing Co. Inc., 1976.

Bradford, Sarah. *Lucrezia Borgia: Life, Love, and Death in Renaissance Italy*. New York: The Penguin Group, 2004.

Burchard, Johann. *At the Court of the Borgia*. London: Folio Society, 1963.

Chamberlin, E. R. *The Fall of the House of Borgia*. New York: The Dial Press, 1974.

Erlanger, Rachel. *Lucrezia Borgia*. New York: Hawthorn Books, Inc., 1978.

Fusero, Clemente. *The Borgias*. New York: Praeger Publishers, 1972.

Hibbert, Christopher. *The Borgias and Their Enemies*. New York: Houghton Mifflin Harcourt Publishing, 2008.

Hollingsworth, Mary. *The Borgia Chronicles*. New York: Metro Books, 2011.

Partner, Peter. *Renaissance Rome*. Berkeley: University of California Press, 1976.

ACKNOWLEDGMENTS

In midst of writing this novel, my beloved twelve-year-old corgi, Paris, whom I adopted when she was six weeks old, fell ill with an esophageal disorder that took her life. She was with me for the first half of the book, always at my feet, and remained in spirit with me for the rest. I am grateful for her joyous presence in my life. She was my dog of the soul, whom I miss deeply.

I owe a debt of gratitude to several people who saw me through my grief and helped me find both the solace and time needed to complete this work.

First, I must thank my husband, who never stops believing in me and encourages me to persevere when I falter. He keeps me grounded in an existence that requires hours alone at the keyboard. I am also fortunate in my rescue cats, Boy and Mommy, both of whom give us the rare gift of unconditional love. I am a fortunate author indeed in my agent, Jennifer Weltz, who champions my work both here and abroad. She is always there to provide advice and see me off the ledge. Everyone on her team at the Jean V. Naggar Agency, Inc. (with a special shout-out to Laura Biagi and Tara Hart) ensures that the business of being a writer runs as smoothly as possible.

This is my fourth novel with my editor, Susanna Porter. Her concise editorial approach, keen observations as to how to deepen character or plot, along with her wit, enrich my work in unexpected ways. My assistant editor, Priyanka Krishnan, also contributed greatly to this book, with suggestions that helped me refine it. I am grateful to the publishing team at Ballantine, Random House, who work so hard to make books successful in this challenging marketplace.

Last, but never least, I must thank you, my reader. I very much appreciate your messages on social media, emails, and letters. Writers struggle in solitude to bring our stories to life. Without you, a book is just words. Your imagination gives the story life; for that, I am forever in your debt.

I hope to continue to be one of your storytellers for many years to come.

ANIMAL RESCUE REMAINS a vital part of my life. Every year, thousands of healthy, adoptable dogs and cats are euthanized in overcrowded shelters across our country. If you cannot adopt, please help support local rescues with donations of time, money, and articles needed to care for the many homeless animals they take in. Thank you!

About the Author

C. W. GORTNER's historical novels have garnered international praise and been translated into more than twenty languages. He divides his time between Northern California and Antigua, Guatemala. To find out more about his work and to schedule a book group chat, please visit www.cwgortner.com.

Facebook.com/CWGortner
@CWGortner

About the Type

This book was set in Garamond, a typeface originally designed by the Parisian type cutter Claude Garamond (c. 1500–61). This version of Garamond was modeled on a 1592 specimen sheet from the Egenolff-Berner foundry, which was produced from types assumed to have been brought to Frankfurt by the punch cutter Jacques Sabon (c. 1520–80).

Claude Garamond's distinguished romans and italics first appeared in *Opera Ciceronis* in 1543–44. The Garamond types are clear, open, and elegant.